Gettin' Lucky

How NOT to Spend Your Senior Year
BY CAMERON DOKEY

Royally Jacked
BY NIKI BURNHAM

Ripped at the Seams
BY NANCY KRULIK

Spin Control
BY NIKI BURNHAM

Cupidity
BY CAROLINE GOODE

South Beach Sizzle
BY SUZANNE WEYN AND DIANA GONZALEZ

She's Got the Beat
BY NANCY KRULIK

30 Guys in 30 Days
BY MICOL OSTOW

Animal Attraction
BY JAMIE PONTI

A Novel Idea
BY AIMEE FRIEDMAN

Scary Beautiful
BY NIKI BURNHAM

Getting to Third Date
BY KELLY McCLYMER

Dancing Queen
BY ERIN DOWNING

Major Crush
BY JENNIFER ECHOLS

Do-Over
BY NIKI BURNHAM

Love Undercover
BY JO EDWARDS

Prom Crashers
BY ERIN DOWNING

Gettin' Lucky

MICOL OSTOW

Simon Pulse
New York London Toronto Sydney

SIMON PULSE
An imprint of Simon & Schuster Children's Publishing Division
1230 Avenue of the Americas, New York, NY 10020
Copyright © 2007 by Micol Ostow
All rights reserved, including the right of reproduction in whole or in part in any form.
SIMON PULSE and colophon are registered trademarks of Simon & Schuster, Inc.
Designed by Ann Zeak
The text of this book was set in Garamond 3.
Manufactured in the United States of America
First Simon Pulse edition April 2007
10 9 8 7 6 5 4 3 2 1
Library of Congress Control Number 2006928446
ISBN-13: 978-1-4169-3536-0
ISBN-10: 1-4169-3536-3

For Noah, my technical consultant
and personal lucky charm

Acknowledgments

Big, huge, supergigantic thanks to Michelle Nagler, Sangeeta Mehta, Michael del Rosario, and Bethany Buck for keeping me in the S&S catalog; to Jodi Reamer for what will hopefully be the first of many successful collaborations (and for being only slightly more mature than I am); to everyone who read *30 Guys in 30 Days* and wrote to tell me that they liked it; to Lisa Clancy for always having her finger on the pulse (pun intended); to my friends, whose romantic adventures continue to amuse and inspire me; to the Harlans for the leg up on my field research and the myriad intercontinental writing studios; and, as always, to my family.

Prologue

Here's the thing: I've always had sort of a funny, love-hate relationship with luck.

There are a million and one old sayings, a million and two superstitions, all having to do with "getting lucky," and the truth is, I subscribe to each and every one of them.

I wish on dandelion seeds, eyelashes, and falling stars. I'd sooner throw myself in front of a bus than walk underneath a ladder. I won't get within ten feet of a black cat.

I have the complete annotated *Idiot's Guide to Feng Shui*, and my bedroom is in perfect karmic balance. (There was a brief stint where my wastebasket was accidentally shoved into the "friends and family" corner of the room, but—luckily—I caught it in time and sorted it all out before any real damage was done.)

I'm a Libra, "an honest friend with an artistic nature," and an eternal optimist. I do everything a human being possibly can—short of invoking the dark powers (what goes around, comes around, after all)—to make sure the wind is blowing my way.

Unfortunately, I tend to have mixed results.

This "courting good luck" stuff started after a particularly bad blow, dealt to me back when I was thirteen: My mother packed up and left my father and me. No note, no explanation, no tearful farewell. No farewell at all, for that matter. Just last year, we got our very first communication from her—a terse postcard announcing a change of address, a relocation to Tucson . . . Tucson!—with nary a phone number in sight. I'd love to go visit her—the desert climate is *very* good for my hair—but it seems that a happy reunion just isn't in the cards for us. Just my luck.

So, in summation: Mom leaving? Not so lucky.

Getting along super well with my father, to the extent that my friends want to barf when I go on about how he "gives me my independence" and whatever? Super lucky.

Being forced by my father, at the height of adolescent awkwardness (thirteen was *so* not my best year, but you wouldn't know 'cause I've burned the pictures), to relocate to a new town, new school, new life (he needed a fresh start)? Horrifyingly less than lucky.

As if living in Las Vegas wouldn't have been weird under the most ideal of circumstances.

Oh, yeah—did I forget to mention? I live in Vegas.

Don't worry. It's not all outtakes from a certain reality TV series that shot one season here at a local casino. Or if it is, I don't get to see any of that, unfortunately. I live just off of the Strip, on the semi-suburban outskirts of town. Lots of split-levels and whatnot. It's really pretty normal. So don't go thinking I scored big just by living in Sin City or anything.

Although, that's not to say that I haven't gotten lucky in certain very specific, very proto-adolescent ways. Did you ever see that movie, about that girl who was sort of clueless? She moved to a new town in sunny California and was instantly adopted by the most popular girl in school. I mean, sure, she was considered a "project" and promptly made over, but even still, she was primed for a much more palatable social fate than anything she would have come up with on her own. Or so I assume. I mean, it's a feel-good flick and all. I mention this 'cause in the movie of my life, I'm sort of that girl.

When I got to Las Vegas, I didn't know a soul. For reasons as yet unknown to me, I was immediately welcomed into the fold of Alana Mark and her Cult of Popularity. Now, to the best of my knowledge, Alana and I were complete and total polar opposites, but I'm no fool. I am fully familiar with the fates, and when Alana Mark sidled up and offered to share her Bonne Belle Lip Smackers with me, I knew enough to smile and lacquer up. Being friends with Alana afforded me all sorts of A-list access: to parties, to gossip sessions, and perhaps most importantly, to boys.

Of course, even in my wildest incarnation as a teen queen, I was still a one-guy kind of chick. I was lucky enough to snag Jesse Dain, a hardcore jock. (Seriously, he represents the pinnacle of the varsity holy triumvirate: baseball, basketball, and football. You might think one boy wouldn't have enough stamina to start in all three sports. You might think that, but you'd be wrong.) Jesse didn't seem to mind that, for me, a workout is walking from the den to the kitchen during a commercial break from *America's Next Top Model*. (I am *addicted* to reality shows. It's like a disease or something.) Jesse didn't seem to mind anything about me, period. We'd been going out since second semester sophomore year, which meant that our one-year anniversary was just around the corner. I had all sorts of plans for fun ways to make the evening special. (Not like *that*. Well . . . maybe a *little* bit like that. But just a little.) We'd been separated over winter break—including New Year's Eve. The fates *must* have been laughing at me, though I couldn't for the life of me figure out what I'd done to deserve such cruel treatment.

So by the time winter break of my junior year was over, I was raring to get back to school. I mean, not so much for the school part, obviously, even though I usually get decent grades. No, the thing was that I was *dying* to see Jesse. And Alana, too. Which was pretty ironic, given what ended up happening.

My luck was about to change, big-time.

One

**TOP FIVE EXOTIC, COOL LOCATIONS
TO SPEND NEW YEAR'S EVE**
*(in no particular order)

1. A private capsule on the London Eye.
2. The top of the Eiffel Tower (clichéd, especially ever since a *certain* movie star went and ruined it for the rest of us, but still).
3. Backstage at a Killers show with the cast of *The O.C.*
4. A chalet tucked into the highest corners of the Swiss Alps.
5. Zip-lining along the Costa Rican jungle canopy.

(For all of the above scenarios, one should assume a romantic interest in tow.)

Note that nowhere on this list is Spring Brook, New Jersey. This is because Spring Brook, New Jersey, is not an especially cool place to spend New Year's Eve. Particularly if it is the home of one's grandparents, median age seventy-two. Double-particularly if one's boyfriend is spending the holiday in Aspen, with his hotshot ski-patrolling friends.

Not that I'm bitter or anything.

See, Dad's always felt guilty about dragging me across the country and away from his parents, who seem to be under the belief that the sun rises and sets with yours truly (which, under normal, non-kiss-centric holidays, is just fine by me). After Mom left, he needed a change of pace, and since he's a restaurant manager, Vegas seemed like a safe bet (ho ho, no pun intended). But he tries to get back to see his folks whenever he can. There was no way that he was getting out of work over Christmas and New Year's, which are big-money holidays at any restaurant, and of course, especially in Vegas. The solution? Easy—he sent me.

Normally I wouldn't mind. My grandparents are totally sweet, and I actually really like spending time with them. But it's definitely an unwritten rule in the teenage handbook that not getting kissed at midnight on New Year's Eve is like a karmic slap in the face. Or, if it's not, it should be. It's in *my* handbook, anyway. I mean, the midnight kiss is the launchpad of a happy and prosperous twelve months, and smooching my grandfather on the cheek rather than my superhot boyfriend on the smacker just seemed like I was *asking* for trouble, karmically speaking.

But I digress. I made the best of it, laughing along gamely to Ryan Seacrest and sipping at sparkling apple cider. Jesse texted me at exactly midnight, which I thought was extremely romantic, even if it wasn't quite the same thing as real-time kissage. We did the best we could.

Now, though, I could hardly wait to see him. So much so that I'd traded in my direct flight from Newark International for a rockin' three-hour layover in Houston, Texas, just so I could make it home a full twenty-four hours earlier than expected.

It was all part of my grand plan.

Jesse had been home, back in Vegas, for

a full two days while I withered away in Central Jersey on a steady diet of PBS, classical music, and Kashi, the three absolutes of my grandparents' household. Jesse expected me to get in tomorrow, the day before school started.

But I was coming in *today*.

I was coming in today, and I was going to see Jesse. I'd worked it all out with my father, who was cool with me switching flights as long as I covered the change fee with my allowance (he is incredibly hardcore about "financial responsibility"). Never mind that I'd spent a glassy-eyed three hours wandering the Houston duty-free and robotically stuffing my face with sour gummy bears. Never mind that my face had a fine sheen of airplane scum settling across its surface. Never mind that my hair—washed and styled so impeccably first thing this morning, back in Spring Brook—had wilted worse than the cheeseburgers that I found at the airport food court. In my mind's eye, I somehow still managed to look like a supermodel. (My mind's eye is really forgiving.) And I was so going to surprise Jesse.

Thankfully, all of my flights were on

time and I made my connection and didn't lose my luggage or any of those annoying things that can happen when you travel. The oily skin and weird, limp hair was sort of the worst of it. My father was waiting at the airport when I got off the plane—he'd made up a sign for me in bright green Sharpie with my name on it, CASSANDRA ELISE PARKER, playing at being a fancy driver or something—and was in on all of my machinations.

He hugged me and grabbed my suitcase away from me, saying, "You look thin, Cass. Did you eat in New Jersey?"

Do you see why I adore my father?

I nodded. "I did, actually. A lot." Kind of too much, actually. Pigging out on Kashi is not recommended.

He smiled. "Grandma and Grandpa are pretty serious about their three squares," he agreed.

"Right?" I said, laughing.

He led me out to the parking lot, where we spent about twenty minutes trying to figure out where he had parked. One thing about my father: When he's at the restaurant, working, he is very much in the zone and focused. He takes his job seriously, which is probably why he's very good at it. The owner of the restaurant keeps asking Dad to take over a few other places that he owns, but Dad's not interested, even though I think it would mean a lot more money. He'd rather save up until he can buy his own place, free and clear. Like I said, he is very big into fiscal responsibility. Probably because the first year that we lived in Vegas, he wasn't so, um . . . fiscally responsible. Mind you, it's all been worked out by now—it's been three years—but he definitely learned his lesson the hard way. And is determined not to let me make the same mistakes that he made.

But, anyway. What I'm saying is, at the restaurant, he's on. He's a stickler for details. But in the rest of his life? Not so much. Like, I'll tell him what to pick up at the grocery store, and he'll forget. So I'll write a list. But then he'll leave the list at home. Frankly, I'm lucky that he remembered his car keys. I'm lucky he remembered my *flight*.

Yes, I'm exaggerating. But no, not by that much.

Well, after wandering in circles for a while, I started asking him pointed questions about details, and other cars, and signs, and whatnot, and eventually we had made our way to his car. It's a Prius, a hybrid, which I support. Which is good, because I don't think I'll be getting my own car until I can afford to buy it myself. But Dad, who, as I've said before, is incredibly cool, is very generous about letting me borrow his when possible.

So on the drive back home he wanted to know about Grandma and Grandpa. Really, there wasn't that much to tell. They're kind of old, but are very smart and very feisty, and we spent most evenings eating reduced-sodium dinners and watching documentaries.

"It was fun," I said, mostly meaning it. You know, not "Aspen-with-your-boyfriend" fun, but fun.

"But you can't wait to see Jesse," Dad said, filling in the blanks.

I nodded. "That's why I'm here," I said, even though he already knew that.

"Well"—he checked his watch—"we should be home in fifteen minutes. If you can get to Jesse by four, do you think you can be done surprising him, and back home, by six? I know it doesn't give you a lot of time, but I have to be at the restaurant for the dinner rush."

How could I say no? Dad wasn't even implying anything gross by his use of the word "surprising." At least, I hope he wasn't. And, anyway, we could always use Jesse's car if we wanted to go out later on.

"Of course," I said, sighing with satisfaction. I leaned back in my seat and went into a slow, trancelike state of Zen. I watched the scenery change through the blur of my window, from airport-related industrial waste to rocky, red-tinged mountains. Soon the glitter of the Strip would be upon us, and I would be home. My dog, a mangy and borderline insane Boston terrier named Maxine, would be waiting for me.

And so would Jesse.

Jesse only lives about five minutes from me, mainly because all of us who don't live in the city proper (which is most of us) live in the same three-mile radius of surrounding suburbs. And, while living just outside of Vegas, aka Sin City, might seem really edgy and exotic, it sort of only affects us in really peripheral ways. Sure, there are the occasional out-there dates where we go off to pose with Indiana Jones and Britney Spears at the wax museum, or gondola rides at the Venetian. And yes, if we go out to celebrate at a fancy dinner, there is an 80 percent chance that we'll catch a glimpse of a certain blond celebutante with a reputation for dancing on tables. Kids here learn to play online poker long before they've even been given their first PlayStation (you don't even have to bet money, thank goodness). But really, it's not so scandalous. Mostly we all live very regular lives.

Jesse's house, for instance, is a completely normal, completely modest split-level, trimmed in aluminum siding and boasting an ironically misleading BEWARE OF DOG sign on the front square of lawn. Jesse's mother has a froufy little white dog that would inspire terror in no one. But I suppose the sign is just for effect. Not that Maxine is all that hardcore, but I really can't get down with dogs small enough to fit in a pocketbook. Don't tell Jesse's mom, though. For now, at least, she likes me.

I pulled up smoothly, humming to the radio, parked, and killed the ignition. Jesse's car, a Civic adorned with stickers from all of his various athletic affiliations, sat in the driveway, so at least I knew he was home. This was good. My surprise really would have had much less of an impact if he'd been out, obviously.

I tapped my lucky rabbit foot that Dad had kindly allowed me to hang from the rearview mirror and briefly crossed my fingers. Even though Jesse and I had been together for about a year now, I still got a little bit fluttery when I hadn't seen him in a while. And I think the element of surprise was upping my nerves, too. I jumped out of the car and made my way up the front walk, taking a moment to smooth my hair down. It was looking slightly perkier now that I was back in the desert climes of Vegas. New Jersey humidity and I do *not* get along.

I rang the doorbell and tried to look nonchalant as I waited for someone to answer the door. In my mind, Jesse pulled the door open, erupted into a thousand-watt grin at the sight of me, and swooped me up into his arms, finally dipping me gracefully into a flawless Hollywood kiss.

In point of fact, what actually happened was that Jesse's younger brother, Paul, opened the door, and scowled at me.

Paul was twelve, which put him at prime sulking age.

"Hi!" I said brightly, trying to ignore the fact that he didn't seem to care one way or another about my arrival. "I came home early!"

He managed an all-but-imperceptible nod. "Okay. Jesse's upstairs. Our mom's not home," he added as an afterthought, smirking. He really was rushing into the adolescence thing full-force.

Despite the fact that I wanted to go charging up the stairs at top speed, I forced myself to walk like a normal, non-crazy, non-boyfriend-starved person. When I got to Jesse's bedroom door, I paused and took a deep breath. My heart was going crazy. Which later on I would look back on as some sort of omen or whatever, but really was probably much more straightforward and meaningless. I mean, how could I have known?

Music blared out of Jesse's room—Kelly Clarkson, which would ensure no small amount of teasing once our reunion kissing was out of the way. I giggled, rapped hard on the door, and called out.

"Surprise!" I shouted, gleeful.

I grabbed at his doorknob.

I turned it.

I pushed.

And gasped.

Jesse did not seem to have heard me knock at his door or call out to him. He did not notice that his bedroom door had opened and that I was now standing in his doorway. He was completely oblivious to my presence, for better or for worse.

For better, because I'd like to think that if he'd known that I was standing there, he might have ceased and desisted all suspicious activity.

For worse, because said suspicious activity seemed to involve swallowing my best friend's face whole.

The blood drained from my face and I felt faint. There, right before my plane-puffy and red-rimmed eyes, were Jesse and Alana. Kissing. And possibly doing some other stuff that was maybe a little more PG-13. His hand was buried in her straight-ironed, low-lighted, meticulously layered hair. Her premium-denim-clad legs were splayed across his legs. Kelly Clarkson sounded incredibly chipper about this whole state of affairs.

I, however, wanted to die.

"What the . . . ?" I started, grabbing against the frame of the doorway to keep myself steady.

Fortunately, just then Kelly stopped wailing, and Jesse and Alana were finally aware of my presence. They had the good grace, at least, to spring apart to opposite sides of the bed guiltily, Alana furtively straightening out the hem of her tank top.

A power guitar chord cut through the tension, and I nearly jumped out of my skin. Sheepishly, Jesse grabbed at a remote and shut the stereo down. Now you could hear a pin drop again. That, or the tiny tearing sound of my heart as it made its way through the meat grinder that was my best friend and boyfriend's betrayal.

Ouch.

The awkwardness threatened to suffocate us. Finally, Jesse cleared his throat, breaking the silence. He ran his fingers through his unruly brown hair.

"Cass," he started, looking equal parts embarrassed, ashamed, and confused. "You're home early."

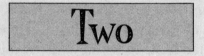

Two

"Omigosh. I like your skirt."

Those were the first words that Alana Mark ever said to me.

It was the second day of seventh grade. The second day of school was bursting with all of the terror and unfamiliarity of the first day of school, while being simultaneously devoid of the false hope that I'd be inexplicably catapulted into sudden popularity and spared the humiliation of sneaking away to a stairwell to gobble down my lunch, alone. (Hey—a girl can dream, can't she?) Since that magical experience had certainly not taken place on the first day, after all.

So you can sort of see how I was feeling, around the time that Alana Mark first approached me. I was brand-spanking-new, both to the school and also to Vegas, and while no one had pelted me with mashed potatoes in the cafeteria, or pantsed me during PE, I was feeling more than a little bit terrified and out of place. And hoping fervently that Alana saw none of this anxiety on my face.

She slid into the desk next to me, second row, third from the left, in intro to world civ. Her long, tanned legs peeked out from under the desk, revealing bright wedge flip-flops that I coveted instantly.

I'd noticed her yesterday, of course, though yesterday she'd sat behind me. She floated into the classroom with the exact opposite body language that I had been sporting all morning. Where I was shy and tense, she was all oiled limbs and effortless confidence. She had hair the color of Lindsay Lohan's (back when it was first red, that is, and then later on, when it was red again). She was impossible to miss. It was clear to the casual observer that she was someone Very Important at Lincoln Memorial Middle School. Yesterday she'd been flanked by a B-level hanger-on, a washed-out blonde (Sun-In, I'd guessed) who was clearly the junior high equivalent of Cacee Cobb. Today she was alone.

"Thanks," I said, glancing down to remind myself of what I was wearing. It was a denim skirt, elevated beyond the level of basic by a cute gingham ruffle along the hem. "I like your . . ." I scrambled to take her in without appearing to be some kind of psychotic stalker. She was sitting; I couldn't see all that much of her. ". . . nails," I finished, somewhat lamely. They were pink and glittery. It was the best I could do on such short notice.

"Thanks," she said, smiling brightly. She wiggled her fingers under my nose, then frowned adorably. Most everything about her was quite adorable. It was almost annoying. "They're already chipping."

I rolled my eyes. "Ugh," I said, as though we were coconspirators in the war against beauty. Which I was starting to hope we would be. A girl could do worse than to be aligned with Alana Mark. I could see that already.

"Omigosh. I forgot to cover my book," Alana went on, her eyes skating over my own. I'd forgone the standard brown bag in favor of clear contact paper over my magazine section of choice: the horoscopes. At the time, I'd thought they were cool. Now I felt like a big-time dork for being so incredibly on top of such drippy endeavors as covering one's books. Darn my father and his whole responsibility trip. Like I had absolutely nothing better to do than to skip home with my textbooks after the first day of school.

Well, I didn't, but Alana didn't have to know that.

I smiled and shrugged, like I just couldn't help being a total geek. "I'm new," I said, like maybe that excused my sudden lapse in cool factor.

"Yeah, I thought so," Alana said. "I saw you yesterday."

Which kind of made sense, since she'd had to walk past me to get to her seat. This meant I'd been noticeable in either a good way or a bad way. I hoped good. She wouldn't have been voluntarily talking to me if it'd been bad, right?

Right?

This transferring-suddenly-during-the-crucial-apex-of-puberty wasn't doing a whole lot for my self-esteem.

"I mean, this place isn't *that* big," she

continued, throwing me a teeny tiny line. "And I've been going here forever." Her expression got serious for a minute. "Katy had to switch. To the other world civ class. I think it's"—she lowered her voice— "*remedial*."

I nodded and tried to look appropriately concerned for Katy's academic progress. Mostly I was just thrilled that Alana seemed to be confiding in me.

Alana drummed her nails against the surface of her desk, then sighed. "So I guess it's a bummer that she covered her book already, right?"

At that, I couldn't help but giggle. "Right," I said. Katy and I had that in common, then. Though I hoped I wouldn't get shunted off to remedial history. I'd always been a pretty solid-B student.

"So," Alana said, slightly more urgently this time, "can I borrow a pen?"

"Of course!" I replied, wondering if I actually had an extra pen available to give her. I needn't have worried. My father had loaded me up with more school supplies than a Staples. I was prepared for any writing-related contingency. I fished out an extra-fine in purple ink, and that was that. Purple, as it turned out, was Alana's favorite color. And *I* was Alana's new favorite, non-remedial seatmate.

Alana Mark and I were officially friends.

I wasted no time in investigating Alana's astrological sign. I was thrilled to learn that she was a Gemini, a fellow air sign. That meant we were both creative types, though she was—and this was not a surprise to me—somewhat more inclined to enjoy a good gossip session. She introduced me to Katy, who was exceptionally sweet, and not all that slow at all, outside of world civ, and the rest of her cohorts, a group of girls and guys almost as notable as Alana herself. As previously mentioned, Alana loaned me her lip balm, and I kept her in lavender ink for the duration of the year. Socially speaking, I was made. And I couldn't have been happier.

In the meantime, my father and I were getting accustomed to the Vegas lifestyle. He worked long hours at the restaurant, which didn't so much bother me, since I had cable, the Internet and, thanks to Dad, an endless supply of gourmet leftovers in the fridge. Besides, he liked to say that he was never more than a phone call away, a theory that had held up under a Maxine-related crisis or two. (That dog will eat *anything* she gets her nose into, no joke.)

What I didn't realize at the time was that, while the restaurant's kitchen would close at eleven, when my father stayed on, it wasn't to help out with late-night room service orders, like he said. Or, maybe it was, but that was sort of a side point. Mainly he hung out in the hotel's casino.

Mainly he hung out at the blackjack table.

Now, I've played electronic blackjack myself (I mean, not only do I have high-speed wireless, but I live in *Las Vegas*, come on), so I can kind of get the allure. It's a very fast-paced game and it's very simple. If you can add or subtract, you can play. So I don't blame my father for getting sucked in. And when he came to me, completely chagrined, and explained to me that he had perhaps developed the slightest little gambling habit and *perhaps* had run us into an *eensy* bit of debt, I tried to understand that, as well.

I must admit that I was a little bit disappointed. But I was beyond the age of thinking that my parents were infallible (given as how my mother had essentially abandoned us just a few months prior—that was rather fallible behavior, I had to admit).

Anyway, the good news was that my father had caught himself before an eensy habit became a super-giganto-humongous habit. He joined a gambling support group (there are *tons* of those around here). He paid off his debts and went to his group meetings every day for a year. He told me that he has never again sat down at a blackjack table—he's never again so much as glanced at a slot machine sideways. He pulled extra shifts at the restaurant and was even promoted in the process. That was three years ago, and by now he's even paid down a good chunk of the mortgage on our house. He doesn't usually involve me in the nitty-gritty of our financials, but I know enough to know that we are completely in the clear.

The other thing that I know? That my father, a devout believer in the culinary landscape of Vegas, basically frowns on the whole "let it ride" culture of this town. Not that I can blame him.

Moving to Vegas, making friends with Alana, Dad's brush with Gamblers Anonymous—these were the defining incidents of my tweendom. You could have seen the glass as half-empty: Mom leaving, moving, Dad sucking it big-time at the blackjack table. But to me, the world was a can of fizzy, flavorful, non-diet cola, and it was utterly and absolutely half-full. Mom leaving meant that Dad and I were closer. Dad's gambling taught him so much of that famous "fiscal responsibility" that these days we had an inground swimming pool. And moving meant that I now had the chance to be a part of the social inner circle at school. To me, things were looking up.

And I know Oprah and whoever are always talking about the "power of positive thinking" and blah, blah, and sometimes it can sound a little bit woo-woo. But the thing is that I think they're onto something. I mean, I myself must be living proof of this. 'Cause there I was, chirping away about silver linings and etc., and along came Jesse. And if *that* doesn't count as some really sweet karma, then I don't know what does.

"Nice kicks."

Those were the first words that Jesse Dain ever spoke to me.

It was first-semester sophomore year and we'd just trounced the Midvale Tigers in the third home football game of the season. I was hanging around outside of the locker room, waiting for Alana to finish changing. (Of course Alana was a cheerleader. Did you really have to ask?) I'd been staring at the tiled walls of the hallway, sort of zoning out with that post-adrenal coma thing that happens once something very tense and very action-packed has ended. When I heard Jesse speak, I snapped back to the real world and hoped like hell I hadn't been squinting or rubbing my nose or making that weird spaced-out face that I make when I think I'm by myself. That would have been embarrassing.

I must have been okay, because Jesse smiled, and I melted.

I glanced down at my feet to see what shoes I was wearing. They were old-school Vans in a pale pink. Not my most innovative fashion statement, but I would take the compliments where I could get them.

"I've got the same ones," Jesse continued, nodding approvingly.

"Yeah?" I teased. "You wear a lot of pink?"

I couldn't believe I was teasing him. It just showed how much I'd changed since that first day of school so many years before. I was comfortable (or, okay, semi-comfortable, but still—that's something) teasing Jesse Dain.

Of course I knew who Jesse was. Like Alana, he was an A-lister, and like Alana, he was hard to miss. He was tall, stocky, but extremely fit, and his bright blue eyes had the easy familiarity of a pre-breakdown Tom Cruise. He was usually surrounded by a gaggle of beefy friends and/or a collection of doting females, many of whom were in Alana's—and, by default, my own—extended circle. I knew he was cute, and I knew he was good. Good at sports, that is. Alana and her cheer-freak friends devoted at least half their time on the field spelling his name. So those were two cool things to know about Jesse. And the third cool thing was that, shockingly, he suddenly seemed interested in me.

"He thinks you're cute," Alana had told me just the week before, during a free period that we'd spent at the mall. We were lucky to have such prime shopping in such close proximity to the high school. "He's been asking me all about you." She slurped on a diet soda for good measure.

"Shut up," I said, smiling. This was good news. Jesse and I had biology together, and my pulse quickened every time he walked into the classroom.

I figured if Jesse Dain was truly interested in me, I'd know soon enough.

And soon enough, it seemed, had finally come. After weeks of what I couldn't be sure were stolen glances in class, he was standing in front of me. He was talking to me!

"Mine are green," he was saying. I'd been so stuck in a wash of reverie that I almost forgot what we were talking about.

Whoops.

"Green is good," I said. "You know . . . the color . . . I like green."

Jesse laughed. God, he had an adorable laugh. And perfect teeth. His parents must have been big into orthodonture.

"So," he said, interrupting my little fan club meeting of one, "are you going to the game on Sunday?"

"Not sure," I admitted. "I told Alana I would, but I have homework to do."

"You should come," Jesse insisted.

"A five-hundred-word essay on the

suffragettes will not write itself," I protested. It was all for show. I knew full well that I'd definitely be at the game. According to my horoscope, it was a good week to take a risk. Blowing off my report to flirt with a hot jock was probably as good a risk as any.

"We'll get something to eat afterward," he said, completely brushing past my sudden academic fervor. "And *then* you can work on your report. I'll get you home early." He winked. "Everyone's happy."

It was a sound enough plan, and, anyway, he didn't leave me much room to disagree.

Later on, as I thought back to that moment, it occurred to me that Jesse had never actually asked me out. Rather, he made a plan and then assumed (correctly, as it turned out) that I would go along with it. That was the way that the Jesse Dains of the world operated. He was a Leo, of course. Totally wrong for me. But my horoscope had told me to take a risk, and this risk, this Leo . . . was *sooo* cute. Obviously, when two astrological influences are acting in direct opposition to each other, you've gotta go with the one that says "Date the hottie," right? Even if he is a fire sign.

★

For a while, I had a pretty nice life in Vegas. Or, you know, one that most teens seem to want, at least according to the last *Ten Things I Hate About Teen Makeovers* movie that I saw. I was the romantic lead of my own movie, sort of a hybrid of Reese Witherspoon and Cameron Diaz. And I don't think that would have happened if I hadn't come to Vegas. So, you know, I had lot to thank Alana for. Alana and Jesse both. I owed them.

Well, wait. Okay, scratch that.

I *used* to owe them. Once upon a time.

Now? Not so much.

Something had to give, though. And soon. I mean, karma's a boomerang.

Right?

Three

You know what's crappy? Losing your best friend.

You know what else is crappy? Losing your boyfriend.

You know what's the complete and total *über*-suck?

Losing them both. At the same time. To each other.

In the days following my immediate discovery of brat-face Alana and scuzzball Jesse attempting to suck each other's face off, I found myself careening crazily from mood to mood. It was like the powers that be had a big fuzzy dartboard, and each ring represented a different state of mind. Whichever point they hit, there went my emotional state.

Fwoom—furious.

Fwoom—lonely.

Fwoom—sad.

Fwoom—incredulous.

Fwoom—self-righteous.

And then another five minutes would pass, and I'd go through the whole bipolar merry-go-round all over again.

I did have the occasional "I Will Survive" sort of triumphant outburst, wherein I envisioned myself meeting someone twelve times cuter than Jesse, replacing Alana as head cheerleader, and spontaneously going up at least a cup size, chestwise, but those scenarios were fairly unlikely, and, therefore, the moods were inevitably short-lived.

My father was working a lot that weekend, which, while it didn't help with my loneliness, was kind of okay by me since I had a hard time talking about what had happened without freaking out and bursting into hysterics. I'd told him that Jesse and I broke up, and somehow, in the telling, I'd gotten the point across that the problems in our relationship weren't entirely unrelated to Alana. And I'm sure he noticed a drastic increase in my moping. So I think he managed to connect the dots. He was good—brought home Ben & Jerry's and didn't complain when I downloaded excessive movies on demand. Which was exactly the sort of unobtrusive support that I really needed.

And, anyway, Maxine was the only one who really understood me. For real. She could tell what kind of mood I was in, even as my emotional state fluctuated by the minute, and she was happy to accommodate. Ice cream and chick flick meant melancholy, in which case she was perfectly willing to curl up next to me on the couch. And if, after a particularly slothlike couch-potato marathon, I started to itch for a little air or activity, she'd leap up excitedly as I laced up my sneakers, raring to go. We lived a shortish drive from Red Rock Canyon, which, though touristy, was a great place to hike. At least I knew I wouldn't run into anyone from school there. I could chill out on a ledge for a while, pat Max, and be alone with my thoughts. And there was no one around to chastise me if my thoughts were, shall we say, vaguely slightly cranky.

Of course, I couldn't escape from Alana and Jesse completely. School was still there, after all. The Great and Terrible Face-Sucking Betrayal, as I had come to fondly call it, had taken place on a Thursday. I'd had the weekend to immediately box up anything that had any and all connotations to either Alana or Jesse. Which meant that I'd spent most of Sunday staring straight ahead at my nearly bare bedroom. But you've gotta get rid of that stuff. Bad vibes and all. Empty at least implied the potential for a fresh start.

Alana had called me three times on Thursday, five times on Friday, four times on Saturday, and then two on Sunday. Obviously I didn't bother to pick up my cell. There was nothing, I reasoned, that she could say that would make it okay for her to be hooking up with my boyfriend. Nothing. I didn't want to know that it had been a one-time thing—that they'd been willing to completely betray me for a fling—and I *certainly* didn't want to know that it *wasn't* a one-time thing. I was screwed either way.

So you can see the difficulty of the position I was in.

Jesse's pattern was more consistent than Alana's. He stopped by on Thursday, though

Dad wasn't home and I didn't come to the door. He called me on Friday, but I didn't answer, and I didn't call back. On Saturday, he texted me a tentative "U THERE?"; on Sunday, he saw me online and IM'd "hey."

I immediately deleted him from my buddy list.

He was tenacious, but his efforts were dwindling. At this rate, he'd probably be reduced to a smoke signal in a week or so.

That was, if I got lucky.

I woke up Monday morning with a terrible knot in my stomach. At first I couldn't identify it; I'd been dreaming that I had just beaten Kristin Cavallari out for the affections of the most eligible Prince of Malibu. The worst part about that dream was waking up from it—there was no reason that I could easily identify to explain my growing sense of dread.

And then I remembered: school.

As in, today I had to go.

Today I had to go back to school and face Jesse and Alana. Or ignore them, as it were. Whichever proved easier (duh).

Alana and Jesse were my *real* friends—or, had been, that was. So facing them would be about as pleasant as tap-dancing on broken glass. But it wasn't just them. There were the Katys and the Margies and the Mikes and the Brandons—all of the hangers-on, my fellow second-tiers. They would all know what had happened. Or, if they didn't know already, they'd find out.

I knew what they would think, too—either they wouldn't care (being one of the luckier girls in the junior class can inspire a certain degree of jealousy), or they'd think I deserved it (for the same reason). Worst-case scenario, they'd . . . ugh, it was too horrible to even contemplate . . . they'd *empathize*. And then they'd feel sorry for me. And that was just more than I could bear.

Getting dressed nearly required a therapist's consult. I wanted to look good, rather than lovelorn, which required some effort. But I couldn't put in too much effort—too much effort was dangerous, like I was trying too hard *not* to be the pathetic jilted girlfriend. In the end I settled on a denim skirt and cute, fluttery top. No one can ever accuse you of being overdressed in a denim skirt. But it did fit me in just the right places. I'd found it at an outlet, the last one on the rack, smushed all the way to one side off the hanger, nearly invisible to the naked eye. It was my size, and it was marked down to thirteen dollars. Thirteen dollars! I mean, how lucky can you get?

I figured I could use a little extra luck for today.

I'm sure that *every* single student I passed in the hallway didn't *actually* stop in his or her tracks, look me up and down, and turn to his or her friend to whisper. I'm sure that *everyone* I saw wasn't necessarily speculating as to what I had done to inspire such disloyalty from my best friend and my boyfriend respectively. I'm sure *no one* was wondering if I was, like, *the world's worst kisser*, or hygienically *challenged*, or whatever. I mean, I'm 100 *percent positive* that people had other things to think about than yours truly.

Maybe they were just checking out my skirt.

It's a really cute skirt.

I didn't have any morning classes with Jesse or Alana, so avoiding them was just a matter of keeping my head trained aggressively to the floor as I made my way down the hallways (and crossing my fingers that I didn't bump into anything, which would render me literally and figuratively lamer than ever). I remember at the start of the semester thinking what a bummer it was that I didn't get to catch up with either of them until lunch. Now the thought of lunch suffused me with terror. I couldn't eat in the bathroom again, like I had that first day of junior high. That was . . . lame. *Beyond* lame.

I ended up grabbing a granola bar from the vending machine and smuggling it into the library. Not the heartiest meal, but considering I'd spent the weekend consuming my own body weight in chocolate and ice cream, a light lunch wasn't going to kill me.

Maybe I'd waste away from heartbreak, like that chick from that reality show who always wears those big sunglasses. She broke off her engagement twice. But I'm pretty sure her fiancé—*ex*-fiancé—never cheated on her.

I had big sunglasses.

I wondered if I could wear my sunglasses in class.

My mood swings had come back to me in a flash during English; we'd been reading sonnets (the Elizabethan era is *so boring*), and it suddenly occurred to me that one of the things I'd purged yesterday had been a box of cards Jesse had given me for various occasions: birthdays, anniversaries, the time I tripped and sprained my ankle. For one horrifying moment I seriously thought I was going to lose it all over the fourth row. I'd managed to keep it together, but suddenly cultivating a rock-star, sunglasses-indoors sort of persona seemed like it could be a strategic move.

I spent my lunch period hunched over a computer terminal, surreptitiously scarfing down my contraband snack. I checked my horoscope: *A change will befall you and your patience will be tested.*

Gee, ya think?

Even though Midvale is a public school, it's what they call a "magnet" school, which means that the board and a bunch of concerned parents lobbied for some extra funding from the state. Apparently, it wasn't too hard to convince the state that we were in dire need of their financial support, seeing as how we all live on the brink of Vegas and hedonism and won't someone please think of the children, blah, blah, blah. All it really ended up meaning was that we have a some-what developed arts program, and so in addition to your basic reading, writing, and 'rithmatic, we each have to take one random artsy course a semester. Alana and I had cho-sen the Modern American Film. I was way into the early works of Gus Van Sant. Alana, I think, just hoped to catch some Matthew McConaughey action for school credit. I won't go so far as to say that the class was crazy-hard or anything like that, but it turned out to be a little more challenging than just watching movies.

I had film class right after lunch.

Luckily, seats weren't assigned. I perched myself in the second row, far corner—close enough to the front that it wouldn't look like I was hiding, but close enough to the front that I wouldn't have to spend the entire class not-looking at Alana either.

The 3.2 minutes before she made it to class were probably the longest of my life. Would she try to talk to me? Would she apol-ogize again? Would she pretend that nothing had ever happened? That she had never MADE OUT WITH MY BOYFRIEND?

Ex-boyfriend, I reminded myself.

Exactly four seconds before the bell rang, Alana made her entrance. She was flanked by Katy (there was no such thing as remedial arts class) and had the good sense to look somewhat abashed as she swished past my desk. She glanced at me briefly, her blue eyes regretful. A lump rose in my throat briefly—she looked positively distraught—but I quickly tamped it back down.

Katy offered a "Hey, Cass" that sounded fairly sincere. I replied with a vague nod of my own. Katy hadn't done anything to me, after all. Other than consorting with the enemy, that was.

The bell rang, and our teacher, Mr. Albon, took his usual seat behind his desk. I liked Mr. Albon. He was grown-up cute in that non-gross way, and he talked to us like we weren't morons. He also knew a *lot* about movies.

"Welcome back," he said, smiling at us wryly. "I'm sure you're thrilled to be here."

Some of us groaned appreciatively at him. Others of us stared intently at our desks and imagined—silently, of course—our ex–best friends shaved bald.

It made the time pass quickly.

Albon was just warming to a discussion about documentaries, which, *yawn*. When I was little I hadn't even liked those segments on *Mister Rogers* or *Sesame Street* where they head off to the candy factory to show you how chewing gum is being made. While I am quite interested in *eating* a delicious Hershey's Kiss, or smacking on a piece of Juicy Fruit, I am less than intrigued by its origins. What can I say? Nonfiction bores me.

Suddenly Albon was talking about homework. Homework, on our first day back. It's like the *entire* cosmos was aligned against me. I wanted to scream.

". . . So I'd like you to read chapter three in your textbooks, and tonight, write up a two-to-three-page summary of a worthwhile documentary that you've seen recently."

Oh, no. What were the odds he'd let me report on *Mister Rogers*?

A hand shot up to my right.

"Yes, Kelly?" Albon asked.

"Can we do our project on reality TV?"

Kelly Connor was a tiny, skinny girl with super-pale skin and hair so black that I was sure she dyed it. She wore copious amounts of black eyeliner, which on anyone else might have looked skanky but on her somehow worked. It made her eyes, which were a shocking shade of sea-glass blue, seem all the more intense. Kelly was an artsy type, a total film snob. She ran a website called YOU ARE HERE, which mostly featured her own first-person rants on pop culture, school politics, and life in general. Kelly was kind of a fringe-y type—she definitely wasn't interested in the cheerleaders and jocks (which was to say, my crowd), but every kid at Midvale knew about her website. It was funny and well written.

Kelly took this class very seriously, and as a general rule, Alana, Katy, and I avoided her for just that reason. But I was interested in what she had to say. If I could parlay my love of a certain show about C-list celebrities forced to live together into an A, that'd be pretty sweet.

Mr. Albon looked taken aback by the question. He ran his fingers through his receding hairline. "Huh," he said finally. "You know, there's a question of authenticity."

Kelly nodded. "That was going to be the focus of my paper," she replied, sounding almost smug.

"Of course it was," Albon said. His eyebrows twitched, and he seemed to come to a decision about Kelly's project. "Then you're good. I'm interested to see what you come up with."

The bell rang. I gathered up my books quickly. I was half-tempted to thank Kelly for establishing a decidedly non-academic precedent for our homework, but ultimately thought it best to beat a hasty retreat. The last thing I needed was an awkward, forced confrontation with Alana.

Four

Something had to give.

I couldn't keep spending my lunch hours in the library. For one thing, it was boring and a little bit lonely. For another, the librarian had caught me yesterday, hunched over a keyboard and sucking down a low-fat yogurt, and read me the riot act. Food is strictly *verboten* in the library, and bringing it within ten feet of a computer is considered an act of aggression. Upon being discovered, I immediately became appropriately apologetic, swearing to Mrs. Melkin that it would *never*, ever happen again.

There was also the small but nonetheless unignorable fact that I was slowly but surely becoming a major buzzkill. The sad truth was that most of my friends had been extensions of either Alana or Jesse. They were all perfectly—if somewhat guiltily—friendly to me when they passed me in the halls at school or whatever, but the last thing I wanted to do was hang with them on the weekends or talk to them on the phone at night. I had a feeling they preferred it that way, anyway. They spent most of their weekends with Alana and Jesse, after all.

I needed a plan.

I checked every possible online astrology scope, to no avail. Saturn was in retrograde, which meant that my love relationships and my friendships were going to be compromised for the next few weeks. Beautiful. Numerology and the Chinese zodiac were no better. Any way that I looked at it, it seemed, I was completely and totally out of luck.

If I wanted things to turn around, I was going to have to be a little bit more proactive.

The sign in the window of Madame Lunichya's storefront read OPEN, but taking in the faint glow of light from within and the dusty cobwebs that swung from the doorway, I had my doubts.

Still, I was at a loss. And desperate times called for desperate measures.

I pushed against the door.

It opened with a creak.

I went in.

It appeared that Madame Lunichya was not a fan of the bright lighting. Once inside, it took my eyes a moment to adjust to the dark. I stood in the foyer blinking rapidly, wondering if she was going to come out, see me making faces, and think that there was something wrong with me. The alternative being, of course, that she *wouldn't* come out, and I'd spend the whole evening blinking around half-blind in the semidarkness. Either way, I was starting to feel pretty foolish. If Miss Havisham had been a budget psychic, her office might have looked a lot like this one.

"Hello," a voice said dramatically.

I leaped at least five feet into the air, startled. So much for maintaining my last shred of dignity.

"Hi," I began uncertainly. "Your sign said you were open." I slid my hands into the back pockets of my jeans, feeling completely awkward.

"I am," the voice said.

It was really starting to freak me out that I couldn't see whom the voice belonged to. I mean, I had to assume that it was Madame Lunichya. But why didn't she either turn on some lights, or come around to face me? This had to be some sort of bad business.

"You have come for a reading?" the vaguely accented voice continued.

"Yes," I said, grabbing at the printout I'd made of her address and turning around to show it to her.

By the time I'd turned around, though, the voice—and the body to whom it belonged—had somehow managed to disappear again. I heard a rustling in the corner, then the *click* of a light switch being tripped, and then she was there, in front of me, in broad daylight.

Even without the mood lighting, Madame Lunichya was a little bit creepy. More than a little bit. She was short and stood sort of hunched over. It was hard to tell exactly how old she was, because her hair was dark and thick, but her skin was leathery and deeply wrinkled. She had wrapped a bright scarf around her forehead and wore a long, flowing dress. Half a dozen silver bangles decorated one arm. Her fingernails were polished to bright red razors.

Points to her. If she was a faker, she'd gotten the costume dead-on.

"I, uh, saw you advertised on the Internet," I stammered, still holding out my crumpled piece of paper. "I made a reservation."

"I know," Madame Lunichya said shortly.

Of course she knew. She was psychic.

"Right," I said, feeling infinitesimally small and wondering if this had all been a terrible idea. I hoped not.

"You want to know what the future holds?" Madame Lunichya asked, leaning closer to me.

I backed up slightly. She was invading my personal space. I managed a nod. Of course I wanted to know what the future held. I mean, why else would I be visiting a psychic?

"Come," she said, the bracelets on her arm clattering together as she beckoned. "This way."

She led me through a beaded curtain that looked like a castaway from the set of *That 70s Show* and into a room that was, if possible, even dimmer than the foyer had been. This was beyond atmospheric; it was the set of a B horror movie. It was also cramped and musty-smelling. She sat me down at a round table covered in a woven black tablecloth.

"Do you get a lot of people here on their way to the Strip, like, wanting to know their fortunes?" I asked.

Lunichya raised one eyebrow at me as though I were insane. "The gamblers do not leave the tables to come here."

I shook my head. It was true: Out on the casino floors, clocks and windows were abolished. The house wanted to keep people glued to their seats, and for the most part, the house succeeded at this. I couldn't imagine that someone on a losing streak would disengage from a table long enough to make his or her way out here, to Lunichya's outpost. Generally people who've been losing just get increasingly more desperate and impulsive, anyway. Or so my father's told me.

"So," Lunichya said, interrupting my thoughts. "You want we should read the cards? Tea leaves? Crystal ball?"

The options were dizzying. My own area

of expertise ended with numerology. "Um, I have no idea," I confessed. "What do most people get?"

"Is no one way," Lunichya said. She sat across from me at the table and scrunched up her face in concentration, tapping her fingers against the tabletop as she took in my face. "I think, for you . . . we read the palm."

"Cool," I said.

She reached out and grabbed at my right hand. "Ah," she began thoughtfully, "you have the cone-shaped hand."

I did? I squinted at my hand and decided I'd have to take her word for it. It looked pretty basic and hand-shaped to me.

"This is a sign of a creative personality. You are inventive and philosophical," she explained.

Philosophical, sure. Especially when it came to matters of the heart.

Inventive, I wasn't sure about, though. I once tried to rig our coffee machine to go off when we turned on the kitchen lights, but it didn't work, and eventually Dad just ended up buying one of those Mr. Coffees that comes with a timer. She turned my hand over so that my palm was facing up. She ran her fingers across each of the creases in my skin, looking incredibly thoughtful all the while. I had to resist the urge to giggle—she was tickling me. But she seemed deadly serious, so laughing was probably the wrong tactic to take.

"You have a healthy life line. Live long," she said.

"Nice," I replied, feeling a somewhat misplaced sense of pride at this news.

"And here"—she pointed to help me see—"your head line and your life line are separated. You have healthy sense of adventure."

True again. After all, I'd taken the whole move to Vegas in stride, where I think there were probably a lot of kids who would have totally freaked.

"Oh," she said, frowning.

"What is it?" I leaned forward in my seat, feeling nervous.

"The love line."

Ah, yes. The love line.

"Is long and curved," she said, lightly tracing it. "This says you are pleasant and easy to be around."

"I like to think so," I agreed.

"*But*," she continued somewhat ominously, "it also means you tend to give your heart away easily. No matter what the cost."

I thought about meeting Jesse back in sophomore year. It was true, it hadn't taken much for him to win me over. In retrospect, I had to wonder whether I would have even fallen for him if I hadn't first learned that he was interested in me.

Whatever the catalyst for our love had been, it sure had cost me.

My eyes welled up, and I willed the tears not to come. Crying in front of Madame Lunichya would just be too humiliating. I sniffled loudly.

I wasn't fooling her. She put my palm down and patted me on the head. The gesture was clumsy and awkward, but I appreciated it nonetheless.

"You have been hurt," she observed.

Seriously, this woman was *amazing*.

I nodded quietly. "And I'm not sure what to do in order to get over it."

"You need . . . something new," Lunichya proclaimed after a beat. "Something different. How do they say, 'to shake things up'?"

"Shake things up?" I parroted. Okay, fine, so my profile said that I was "adventurous." Much as I liked the sound of "adventurous," "to shake things up" seemed like maybe not the best idea. The last time I'd been "shook up" had been three years ago, when my father hauled me three thousand miles across the country. I liked my life safe and predictable—everyone neatly compartmentalized.

Of course, the truth was that since my ex-boyfriend and ex–best friend had gotten together, all of my neat compartments had been blown wide open. And so Madame Lunichya was probably onto something. I had two choices: I could either wallow in the debris of my formerly tidy lifestyle, or I could move on.

I preferred the thought of a good, solid wallow. Self-pity could be fun. At the very least, it was a handy excuse to consume inappropriate quantities of gummy candy. Moving on, conversely, was terrifying.

Which was probably exactly why I needed to do it. Face my fears and all that.

"Something new," I echoed, turning the idea over in my brain.

It was worth a try. I just had to find it—my something new to try, that was. And I had to start as soon as possible.

I stood up hastily, nearly taking the table with me. "Thank you," I gushed. "You've been terrific. Really helpful." I pumped her hand up and down enthusiastically.

She withdrew slightly, clearly sort of grossed out by my exuberance. "You forget," she said darkly.

"What's that?" I asked brightly.

"For the palm reading. You forgot. To cross my palm with silver." She coughed meaningfully.

Right. Payment.

I forked over my fifteen bucks, and we were done.

I was that much closer to shaking things up and, with any luck, turning my life around.

Or so I hoped.

School had become more of a hindrance than anything else. I've always read about women who throw themselves into their work to get their mind off of a problem (Danielle Steel novels are, like, *brimming* with these sorts of heroines), but that's never quite done the trick for me. It didn't help that in this case my work—

school—was where Jesse and Alana were. They were difficult to avoid.

Once upon a time, school had been a social outlet. I'd drive in early and spend the moments before first period milling around my locker with Jesse, Alana, and our friends. These days I was in and out as quickly and painlessly as possible. I did my work, but the rest of the time I had my head buried in a magazine, or I was zoned out to my iPod. It was kind of pathetic, actually.

Madame Lunichya had been compelling, but she had sort of raised more questions than she had answered. After all, she didn't really tell me anything that I didn't already know. I'd been hoping that she could give me a sort of "heads up" about my future. But instead, she seemed big on the idea that I was going to have to engineer my own fate. Which I had no idea how to do.

Annoying.

". . . So I would argue that even if a reality television show purports to document footage of 'real life' events, in fact it is ultimately the product of the director's vision as much as any fictitious work would be . . ."

Yikes, I'd almost dozed off during Kelly Connor's report. How embarrassing.

Apparently Albon had liked hers enough to have her read it aloud to the class. I sort of admired her, but also felt bad. It could be so embarrassing to stand up in front of the class—the last thing I wanted to do was doze off.

It wasn't that she was boring me—I really liked that she'd gotten the teacher to approve a topic that was sort of outside of what you'd normally think of. And Kelly herself was a very compelling presence. She was all quiet, coiled intensity, and you could tell that she actually believed the stuff that she was going on about. But I'd stammered my way through my own presentation (having Alana in the front row was a huge mind-freak) and had spent the rest of the period recovering.

"Thank you, Kelly," Mr. Albon said, smiling as though he actually was impressed by her report. Pretty amazing—Albon wasn't easily impressed.

The bell rang abruptly, sparing the last two students from having to present today. Lucky stiffs. All at once, everyone began gathering up their books and stuff and filing out.

I took my time, keeping my eye on

Alana and Katy the whole while. The last thing I needed was to end up strolling down the hall shoulder-to-shoulder with the two of them.

"I have a problem."

The pronouncement came out of thin air, causing me to jump a few inches into the air. I landed and tried to regain my composure. "Yes?"

It was Kelly, her burning blue eyes fixed on me curiously.

"I'm Kelly," she said, holding out one slim hand for me to shake.

I took her hand, wondering briefly who-all in high school introduces themselves with a handshake. But, whatever, she was being friendly enough, if a little bit weird. "I know," I said, smiling. "I'm Cassandra. Cass." This was a silly formality, this introduction thing. We'd been in school together since ninth grade. Even if we hung out in different crowds, we knew each other. But whatever.

"I know," Kelly replied. "Okay." She folded her arms across her chest and looked very serious for a moment. "Have you seen my website?"

"Of course," I said, smiling, even

though it had a been a while since I'd logged on. "Everyone's seen your website."

"Yeah," she agreed, completely deadpan. She was so crazy-focused, I thought she might actually be able to shoot lasers out of her eyes. That's how bright they were. "Well, over Christmas break, I went back and took a look at the hits I've been getting. That one week alone, I had three times as many visitors as I had in any one week of the past semester."

"Wow," I said, wondering why she was telling me this.

"People are into it," she said, essentially stating the obvious. "They're getting more into it."

"That doesn't sound like much of a problem," I pointed out.

She laughed. "Yeah. The *problem* is that I want to make sure that they *stay* interested. My website is going to be used for a portfolio so that I can get into design school next year. It's important for me to keep the hits coming."

It made sense—and made me mildly panicked about the complete lack of college planning that I'd done so far.

"I want to start a daily horoscope column," she continued, as if in response to my unasked question. "Everyone loves horoscopes."

"You think?" I asked, surprised. I'd always thought it was a weird thing about me, my own obsession with superstitious stuff. Alana had humored me, but humoring was all that it seemed to be.

She shook her head at me like she was very sad for me. "There's a reason that there's a horoscope column in every major newspaper and magazine, right?"

"Right." She had a point.

"Anyway, I suck at that sort of stuff. I'm a Scorpio—that's as far as my knowledge of the subject extends."

This was interesting news. A Scorpio and a Libra could hang, that was for sure. *If* that was what she was getting at, after all. I still wasn't too sure where this was going.

"Scorpios are cool," I blabbed, sort of without thinking. "Very creative and intense." Which described Kelly to a T, as near as I could tell.

Who on earth would think that horoscopes weren't valid? Madness. Sheer madness.

"Right," Kelly said. "So the thing is, I

know we don't really know each other all that well or anything, but I was hoping that you'd maybe be into handling the horoscope stuff for the site."

"Oh, uh. Me?"

I'd never really done much writing, after all, beyond the occasional journal entry. And even those were . . . sporadic, at best. "What makes you think I'd be good at that?"

She raised an eyebrow at me. "You're kidding, right?" She pointed at the stack of books on my desk. Lying on top of the books were clippings from at least three different magazines—daily, weekly, and monthly horoscopes. Then she nodded toward the tiny four-leaf clover charm that hung off the zipper of my backpack.

"Call me crazy," she continued dryly, "but I have a feeling you'd be perfect for the gig."

I blushed. Obviously, being asked to do the job was sort of a backhanded compliment. It seemed like she maybe thought that I was insane. "Thanks," I began slowly, "but I—"

"I thought you might have some free time these days too," she interjected. Her voice was soft but meaningful.

I got her drift. If she had ears and went to school at Midvale (which, check and check), then she had heard about Jesse and Alana. The most recent news was that they were, for sure, dating. Ugh. It was like a fist to my stomach every time I thought about it, so I tried not to think about it too much.

I really didn't know Kelly at all. And I'd never given any thought to writing my own column. Astrology was something that I took seriously—who was I to speculate about other people's fortunes? I wasn't feeling especially attuned to the forces of karma these days, and didn't relish the thought of steering half of my class off onto the wrong course.

Then again, Madame Lunichya had instructed me to make my own fate, right? To shake things up? That meant trying something new. And I had a feeling that eating lunch in the library, while unusual for me, did not count as new. Especially since I'd been all but politely banned.

Working with Kelly would be a new experience. It was a scary thought, but also kind of cool.

What did I have to lose? Maxine sure wouldn't mind seeing less of me. I had a feeling that even she was getting a little sick of watching me mope.

And, anyway, I'd already paid for the palm reading. It was time to put my mouth where my money was.

I looked at Kelly, smiled, and took a deep breath.

"Sure," I said. "I'll do it."

Five

You're always the positive one, Libra, the person who steps in to help others even when you've already got tons to do. This week, it's okay to give some advice, but you don't have to take responsibility for everything other people are saying and doing!

I took it as a good omen that my own horoscope was clearly encouraging me to get involved with Kelly's website. It wasn't a ton of work, after all. Basically it involved going home and cross-referencing all of my favorite zodiac websites.

I made up a chart that listed all twelve of the zodiac signs, then went through each horoscope from each of my most trustworthy sources, both online (www.zodiaczone.com) and in actual, real-live book form (*Who Do the Stars Think You Are?*). I pulled what I thought were the most significant points from each horoscope, then created a composite horoscope for each sign. The composites were what I e-mailed to Kelly in a Word document.

I'd started as soon as I got home from school and walked Maxine, around 4 p.m. I may or may not have taken twenty minutes to scarf down half a pint of Chubby Hubby. By the time I had finished and e-mailed my work to Kelly, I was surprised to find that it was after midnight. Never mind that I'd have to somehow get my homework done during study hall tomorrow; I guessed that this was what all those romance-novel heroines meant when they talked about "getting lost in your work."

It was kind of a cool feeling.

I turned my feature in to Kelly on Tuesday morning. Two days later, I heard murmurs from kids who'd read their horoscopes up on the site. Kelly sure didn't waste any time.

I didn't even realize that I had been

nervous until I overheard one girl in the hall debating a point from her horoscope to a friend; she was all, "I mean, I think she actually, like, knew *me*, and *my situation*. It was amazing."

I did not, in fact, know that girl or her situation—couldn't even have told you her name. But man, was it ever a cool feeling to think that people were reading my stuff. And liking it.

Kelly cornered me just outside of Albon's class. "Congratulations," she said. "You're a hit."

"Thanks," I replied, blushing modestly. "You think people are into it?"

"You know they are," she said, calling me on the whole fake-shy thing. "It's all anyone's talking about today."

I took a moment to look directly into her eyes and decided that anyone as focused as Kelly—not to mention anyone who'd wear a T-shirt that said I HATE WHAT YOU'RE WEARING—was probably pretty sincere.

"Yeah," I agreed, grinning, "it sounds like people are into it." False modesty was a waste of time, anyway.

"So," she continued, still looking at me with the voodoo eyes, "will you do another?

I mean, will you do one for me every week?"

I blinked. Writing the feature for Kelly had been fun, sure. But to write one every week sounded strangely like . . . responsibility. "Um, I mean—every week?"

She ran her fingers through her hair, pushing her bangs out of her eyes. I noticed that her fingernails were a glittery baby blue. Alana and I had always been diehard devotees of the classic French manicure. "Look," she began, "I tallied the hits on the site. The thing is that I got thirty more than usual—and that was just last night. I'm sure it was because of the horoscopes. People love that crap." Her eyes widened as she caught my expression. "That's not what I meant," she said, smiling sheepishly.

"*I* love 'that crap,'" I reminded her.

"I know." She nodded, biting her lip. "And it shows. You did a great job." She paused. "Why don't you keep doing a great job. Please?"

Her eyes twinkled, and I had to laugh.

"Fine," I said, watching out of the corner of my eye as Alana and Katy shoved past us and into the classroom. "I'll do it. But we should get inside. We're going to be late for class."

I was wary of chatting with Kelly for too long, of her suddenly realizing the truth of why I was so a-okay fine with spending my nights tapping away at my computer. I mean, she knew about me and Jesse. And Alana and Jesse. And me and Alana. The whole freaking school knew, after all. But I didn't need for Kelly to know that ever since the breakup, my most meaningful conversations had taken place with my dog. That would just be too pathetic.

A boy sidled up to Kelly and nudged her. "The second bell rang. You're going to be late."

I knew the boy. He was in our film class, which—duh, explained why he was encouraging Kelly to get inside. His name was Elliot Something, and the only person I ever saw him talking to was Kelly.

Kelly rolled her eyes good-naturedly. "Chill *out*," she said, sighing dramatically. "Missing the first three seconds of class would hardly be the end of the world."

"No, we should . . . ," I said, trailing off nervously. I wasn't eager to get sent to detention for being late. Though detention was served at lunchtime. It would give me a good excuse for not hanging around the cafeteria. "Anyway, I'll do it," I promised. "I can get the horoscopes to you on Mondays."

"Sweet," she said, winking at me. To Elliot, she said, "Cass is going to take over the whole star-sign crap on my website."

"Cool," Elliot said, barely meeting my eye. "People are really into that." He nodded in my general direction, then led Kelly into the classroom without further comment.

After a moment, I followed them.

I worked on the horoscopes all weekend long. In fact, I was working on them at times when I should have been working on homework, but whatever. I figured there was always extra credit.

Kelly liked my second "feature," as she called it, and invited me to the library during our study hall to work on her website. She showed me the counter that indicated how many hits the site had gotten. She was right—it was through the roof since we'd posted horoscopes. Mostly I was just impressed by how many people visited the site at all. Kelly asked me what I did on weekends, and I had to admit that lately, I'd been alternating between hikes with

Maxine, working on the horoscopes, and Lifetime movie marathons. Which made Kelly laugh, but I *think* it was more with me than at me. At least, I hope it was.

"You should work on the horoscopes this weekend," Kelly said, pulling her hair into a ponytail and peering at the computer screen.

"I will," I said, nodding.

"But you should also come to my place on Saturday night. It's poker night."

I don't know why I was so surprised. I'd heard about some of these games before; Jesse and Alana both were big into them. I had always demurred, my father's experiences on my mind.

It wasn't all that odd that Kelly had her own game. But it was a little bit weird that she was inviting *me* to join in. Or, if not weird, it was unexpected. In three years of high school we'd never been more than casual acquaintances. But maybe some kids were just friendly that way. Or maybe she thought I was *really* pathetic.

I decided she was just friendly.

"I don't know," I said tentatively. "I don't really gamble."

Kelly laughed. "It's not such high

stakes. Five dollars to get in. You must know how to play, right? I mean, I don't think there is anyone in Vegas who doesn't know how to play poker."

"I know how to play," I said quickly. "I just . . . like my money when it's my own." I didn't have all that much, after all—just cash from the odd babysitting job here and there.

"I hear you," Kelly replied. "And, you know, no pressure. But it *could* be more fun than talking to your dog. Maybe you could just play a hand and see how it goes."

The offer was both tempting and terrifying. I really wouldn't know anyone on more than a casual "hey" kind of basis. But then, given that I hardly said more than that to my so-called friends these days, what did I have to lose, really?

Other than five bucks, of course.

I guessed that I could spare five bucks.

"One hand would work," I said. "But I should warn you, I'm not that good at the game."

Kelly smiled. "Don't worry. You'll get good. Quickly. Practice makes perfect, blah blah."

"Are you, like, down a player?"

I had to ask. Not that it was beyond the realm of possibility that Kelly would *want* to hang out with me. But it wasn't necessarily the first thought I would have had.

"As a matter of fact, we are, this week," Kelly explained. "Becs has pinkeye and she's under quarantine." She shuddered. "Gross. But I would have asked you, anyway. I've been dying to have you over to my house."

At my puzzled look, she giggled. It was a strange sound coming out of Kelly, who looked like a bonafide non-giggler. "It's my room. It needs serious feng shui. That strikes me as the kind of thing you'd be good at."

I rolled my eyes, but I had to laugh. *Of course* it was the kind of thing I was good at.

I supposed I didn't mind being so predictable. Not if it meant that I had a chance to start over with some new friends.

When you thought about it, it might be kind of lucky, really.

I wasn't sure how to dress for poker night. On the one hand, it was being held in Kelly's den, but on the other, it was a coed affair. Just because I was still in the process of mourning my failed relationship didn't mean that I wasn't interested in attracting the opposite sex. Everyone wants to be cute, right? I finally settled on a lightweight sweater, jeans, and my favorite pink sneakers. I decided it didn't matter that they were almost identical to the ones I'd been wearing when I first met Jesse. Jesse wasn't here right now, was he?

As I ran a brush through my hair, my father popped his head into my bedroom. "Did you walk and feed Maxine?" he asked.

I nodded and stepped back from the mirror, smacking my lips together to better distribute my lip gloss. "Yup. An hour ago. You're welcome."

"Thanks, babe," he said automatically. "You'll be ready to leave in five?"

"I'm ready now," I said. I was dropping him off at the restaurant on my way to Kelly's.

"Great. What have you got on for tonight?" he asked. "Hot date?"

His face blazed crimson the moment the words were out of his mouth. I could tell he felt twelve different types of sorry that a comment he'd intended so casually had been so loaded.

"Uh, no, actually," I stammered. As a

matter of fact, my own hot date was probably on his way out with my ex–best friend right about now. "I'm just going over to my friend Kelly's house."

He furrowed his brow. "I don't think I've ever heard you mention Kelly before." He was clearly relieved to be off of the topic of my nonexistent dating life and on to the issue of my imaginary friends.

"No, she's in my film class," I said. "We sort of just started hanging out. Anyway, it's not just me going over there tonight. . . ."

I trailed off. My father would *so* not approve of me attending a poker night, that much I knew. I hated to lie to him, but I hated the thought of sitting home for yet another weekend, moping, even more. I decided that a concentrated stretching of the truth was in order. "It's a game night," I finally managed. There. It was ambiguous enough not to be a lie.

Unlike Alana and my other former friends, Kelly actually lived right on the Strip proper. In a casino, in point of fact. Her mother was a showgirl, and her father was someone very, very important at the casino. I didn't know exactly what his job was, but he was the guy you didn't want to have to meet after a particularly lucky streak at the tables.

Each of the casinos on the Strip is built to a different theme, and each one takes its theme and really runs with it, 150 percent. So you've got Treasure Island, with a waterfall and a pirate motif; or the Luxor, which is actually built in the shape of a pyramid; and even the Paris, with a scale-model Eiffel Tower. Kelly lived in the Venetian, which I particularly love because of how it has an actual canal running through it. People elope to Vegas and get married alongside the canal, believe it or not. Crazy.

I deferred valet parking and found my way through the lot with the rest of the plebes, taking the elevator up to a special floor marked GUEST SUITES. Kelly had given me a key code for the elevator. It was all very exciting. I only had a key to my own house, none of this cloak-dagger business.

The elevator doors slid open directly into Kelly's apartment. The first thing I noticed as she opened the door was a crazy panoramic view of the Strip.

"Hi," I said, stepping through her doorway and into the apartment. "And wow." I gestured toward the neon sign from the Mirage. It was twinkling, fading in and out.

"Yeah, it's like, a *mirage*, get it?" Kelly asked, rolling her eyes. She snorted. "Now you see it, now you don't. This place is ridiculous." I assumed she meant the psychedelic skyline, but she just as easily could have meant Vegas, I suppose.

"Ridiculous, yes. But it's an awesome backdrop to a poker game," I acknowledged.

Kelly led me farther inside and into the enormous sunken living room. She'd set up a card table in the far corner, and on the opposite side of the room, on the coffee table, she'd laid out an impressive array of eats: chips, pretzels, chocolate, and every possible soft drink you could imagine. "Help yourself," she said. "Do you know everybody?"

I squinted at the four people who were already settled at the table. "By sight, yes, but I think that might be it," I admitted guiltily. Had my Alana-Jesse bubble really been so hermetically sealed?

"No worries," Kelly said, pulling me forward. "Guys—this is Cass, she's in film class with me, and she's been doing the horoscopes for my site. So if you've had any big brushes with fate this week—for better or for worse—you can blame her."

One girl, a redhead with supermodel proportions, hooted at me and clapped loudly. "Hi, Cass!" she screeched good-naturedly.

"That's Andy. Don't mind her; she doesn't have an inside voice," Kelly explained. "And that's James—"

"Jim," the boy interjected.

"He's been trying to build up a following of people calling him Jim, but it won't take," Kelly continued. "And that's Marcus, and you know Elliot from film class."

I *did* know Elliot from film class, I remembered. He was the one who had come up to us in the hall the other day, the one who always sat near Kelly and never said a word.

"We saved you a seat," Marcus said, tapping the folding chair between him and Elliot. He smiled lecherously.

"Don't be gross," Kelly chided him. She turned to me. "He's a weirdo, but harmless. And that really is your seat. That way, it's boy-girl-boy-girl."

"You're our substitute Becs," Andy shouted, still in her outside voice. Maybe it really *was* the only one that she had?

I poured myself a diet soda and settled into my place at the table. I looked around at this group of people—classmates of mine, but somehow, almost total strangers—and managed a weak but uncertain smile.

And then I got my butt kicked. Bigtime. Poker is a deceptively simple game. Really, the objective (meaning, more than *winning*) is to have the best hand at the table. Whether you can use community cards (as opposed to just the ones you're dealt) depends on the type of poker you're playing, but either way, it all comes down to either actually having the best hand . . . or tricking everyone else at the table into *thinking* you have the best hand. This little act of dishonesty is considered completely kosher in poker, and, in fact, if you're any good at bluffing, your peers will probably respect you just that much more. Technically, you don't even have to know the best hands to win. You just need to have the best poker face.

I knew what the best hands were. I just didn't seem to have them. *Ever.*

The game was simple and straightforward: Texas Hold 'Em. Kelly started out as dealer, and we all had a turn at big blind and little blind. True to Kelly's promise, the maximum bet in any round was five dollars. I still managed to lose thirty over the course of the night. And even when I had a decent hand, someone else's hand was better.

I just chalked it up to the luck of the draw.

Six

On Sunday, I went to the movies. I know some people think it's sad or lame to go to the movies by yourself, but I actually really like it. I always have. The thing is that I just really love movies—and sometimes some stranger choices like slashers or indie flicks. I mean, I wasn't especially academic about my appreciation, the way that Kelly was, but I was definitely a couch potato at heart. And if I waited around for other people to come with me to movies, I'd be waiting a long time. Especially since Jesse really only watched action-type stuff, and Alana was strictly romantic comedy.

Anyway, the Screening Room, which was a special revival house near where I lived, was showing a Hitchcock double feature: *The 39 Steps* and *The Lady Vanishes*. They weren't my top two choices, as far as the Hitchcock canon goes, but it was still a worthwhile way to spend a Sunday afternoon. So I went, stopping to get a kick, as I always do, out of the velvet curtain and the old-school ushers and all the other little touches that make the Screening Room special.

Neither of them are particularly long movies, but by the time *The Lady Vanishes* had ended, I was feeling like I was coming out of a coma and not just two back-to-back movies. My eyes were bleary, and it took me a few minutes to adjust to the natural light of the outside world. Once I could see again, I realized that I had traces of popcorn crumbled across the front of my jeans. Awesome. Maybe that was why Jesse had cheated on me—maybe he was more interested in a girl who could maintain basic personal hygiene?

It was a solid theory.

I was in the process of dusting myself off when I felt myself collide with another object. Specifically, a person-shaped object. I realized my mistake as soon as I heard my victim shout, "Ow!"

I looked up, mortified, to find that I

recognized my drive-by. He looked slightly less relaxed now, by the light of day, than he had looked at Kelly's apartment the night before, but there was no mistaking that it was Elliot. The disheveled, dirty blond hair gave him away.

"Sorry!" I stammered, feeling incredibly socially awkward. "I wasn't looking where I was going. Are you okay?"

Elliot blinked at me sort of blankly. "I'm okay," he said slowly.

He was looking at me so strangely that I assumed either he didn't remember me or that I had more popcorn stuck to other, more ridiculous parts of my body. "Cass," I reminded him.

He blushed. "I know who you are. I just . . . I guess I sort of spaced out there, for a minute. I was . . . thinking. Sorry for walking right into you."

"No, hey, me too," I said. "I was in a post-Hitchcock coma. Which is actually the best kind of coma to be in, I think. If you have to be in a coma."

Seriously? What the heck was I talking about?

"You went to the movies?" Elliot asked.

I nodded and pointed first at the

Screening Room, and then toward the grease stains settling into the front of my jeans. "He went to so much trouble making those movies so precise and atmospheric, it seems like the least I can do is to see it on the big screen."

Elliot looked slightly confused, but he smiled. "You're probably right. I don't see too many movies, myself."

I gestured toward the huge plastic bag he was carrying. It was from the local bookstore and was so full that it had segmented off into strained right angles where the books were threatening to burst through the plastic. "You're into the printed word?" I ventured.

"Yeah," he agreed. "But, you know, movies are good too."

"Whatever," I said, shrugging. "After last night's performance, I should be watching *Rounders* or something, not Hitchcock. Then maybe I could pick up some pointers."

Elliot looked totally baffled, the poor thing.

"Matt Damon. No-limits Texas Hold 'Em?"

"I don't see too many movies," he repeated, deadpan.

I sighed. "I suppose it doesn't matter," I

said. "I mean, all the movie tutorials in the world aren't going to make me a better poker player."

"You just need to practice," Elliot offered kindly.

"Forget that. It's all about luck," I argued. "I mean, it just comes down to the hand that you're dealt."

Elliot shook his head, looking totally appalled. "Luck is just a tiny percentage of the game," he said. "The trick is to play as if you know exactly what hand your opponent is playing, to eliminate luck completely."

I rolled my eyes at him. "Now you're just talking crazy."

Two days later, Andy passed me in the hallway and hip-checked me playfully on her way to class. "Cass!" she shrieked. "Becs's pinkeye cleared up, but now she has to babysit her younger brother on Saturday nights. You in for another round of poker?"

The words were out of my mouth before I even realized what I was saying. The answer was yes, of course.

A few days later, I tracked Elliot down in the school library. He was the only person who spent as many lunch hours there as I did. He was usually hunched over a crazy-thick book with teeny-tiny print and, near as I could tell, he adhered rigidly to the "no food or drink" rule. Maybe he was a big rules-follower. It made sense.

No wonder he was so good at card games.

"You're into math and science, right?" I asked him, coming up behind him and sending his book several feet into the air.

When he had regained his composure, he nodded. "Yeah. I mean, I'm in the honors classes." You could tell he was a little bit embarrassed by that piece of information. Little did he know he had just the sort of expertise that I was looking for. He swallowed. "Why?"

"Well, I'm thinking you probably know how to play percentages, right?"

"Like, what, for tipping? Like in restaurants?" His eyes had taken on a deer-in-headlights expression. "I think they make little cards you can use for that. Or you can use your cell phone calculator."

I clapped him on the back conspiratorially. "Not like in restaurants," I explained. "Like in poker."

I convinced Elliot to meet me for a little poker tutorial. It was kind of funny how much convincing he needed. I mean, he wasn't exactly a social butterfly—that much, I got—but it kind of surprised me, the amount of cajoling that I had to do.

In a way, it was refreshing—after all those years of being sidekick to Alana Mark and girlfriend to Jesse Dain, I had to admit I'd grown somewhat accustomed to getting what I wanted, when I wanted, at least as far as the high school social scene was concerned. But I also had a knack for reading people. Maybe it had to do with being kind of tuned in to vibrations and auras. I knew to appeal to Elliot's love of all things orderly; I begged him to go through the logistics of poker with me. Step by well-calculated step.

He didn't live on the Strip, but he did live across town. And apparently he didn't have a car. It must be said, public transportation kind of sucks in Vegas. We agreed to meet that weekend, on Saturday, which I assumed would be cool with my dad. Usually he wouldn't have needed his car until the early evening.

Of course, just this once, his hotel had to be catering a private party. The only solution was for Dad and me to pick up Elliot and bring him to the hotel; we'd get to hang and conduct our little card shark lesson poolside (hey—there are some definitive perks to being a teen in this bizarro-world town), and later I'd drive Elliot home.

"Hi!" my father boomed cheerfully as Elliot slid into the back seat of the car. "Don Parker. Nice to meet you."

"Elliot Forest," Elliot replied. He clutched a camo-green messenger bag to his lap and looked generally terrified. I stifled a giggle; he seemed so small and ill at ease, you'd think we were kidnapping him. He was the exact opposite of Jesse's smooth confidence.

"So what are you guys studying?" Dad continued, jovial as ever.

Right, *studying*. I'd almost forgotten the tiny white lie I'd offered my father as to why I was spending the afternoon with Elliot. I felt kind of lousy, fibbing to my dad and all, but he seemed so thrilled that I was finally getting the heck out of the house that I'd decided it was all for the greater good. I'd told him that Elliot was helping me prep for a test. Seeing Elliot now—wire-rim glasses perched at the tip of his nose and over-stuffed bag threatening to spill out all over the seat next to him—I was relieved to know that he was at least playing the part.

Too bad I hadn't let him in on my little deception.

"Uh, Elliot and I are in film class together," I jumped in, craning toward the backseat to shoot Elliot a meaningful look. It was the truth, after all—it was just fairly unrelated to our planned afternoon activities.

Elliot looked a little bit puzzled, but was cool enough not to say anything.

"So, Elliot, have you been reading the horoscopes on Kelly's website?" I asked, eager to change to the subject. To my father, I added, "Elliot is good friends with Kelly Connor."

"The girl who runs the website," my father mused. "Got it." He's an attentive guy, my dad.

Elliot shrugged and blushed slightly. "Um, I'm not actually all that big on, you know, zodiac and stuff."

I gasped dramatically, slapping the back of my palm to my forehead. "Heresy!" I shrieked. "Say it isn't so!"

He didn't reply, so I calmed myself, worried that I was frightening him with my spaz-out. "What's your sign?" I asked, when my heart rate had returned to normal again.

Elliot shrugged again. Forget about his air supply; if he wasn't careful, his shoulders were going to swallow up the rest of his torso. "Aries."

"Ahh," I murmured.

No wonder we'd never really been friendly—I mean, aside from the whole "hanging-in-different-groups" thing. Aries and Libra are the worst possible match—totally 180 degrees on the zodiac wheel. He was precise, where I was artistic. He was dedicated, where I was . . . all over the place. He was peanut butter, where I was . . . jelly?

Okay, so astrology wasn't, like, an *exact* science, but it had served me well in life thus far.

"This is . . . nice," Elliot ventured, sounding as though he really thought anything but.

We were out by the pool of my father's hotel, having parted ways with him upon arrival. I'd say that Dad was cool and didn't mind giving me my space, but this went beyond space—I'd venture that my father was seriously psyched to find me spending the afternoon with, in his parlance, "a young man."

Little did he know that this young man could never be a contender.

I mean, really—an *Aries?*

And then there was that whole socially-awkward, school-nerd aspect of Elliot. Adorable though he was, that simply could not be ignored. Besides—I was still nursing a broken heart.

"Well, I mean, I like hanging out here," I said, taking a long sip of my Diet Coke.

We were perched at two adjacent lounge chairs tilted toward each other, a small glass-top table between us. We'd each ordered sodas and were splitting an order of French fries. To the casual observer, the only indication of any illicit activity was the deck of cards set just next to the plate of fries.

"We can move, you know . . . out of the sun," I offered weakly, not really meaning it. February in Vegas is downright balmy—perfect weather for working on your tan. Moving out of the sun? Madness.

"I'm fine," Elliot insisted, squinting

from behind his glasses. I'd been some-what horrified to discover that his every-day reading glasses were actually made of that chemically treated glass that tints in sunlight. Instant sunglasses. Cool. Not. Elliot was just lucky that his nerdiness was so acute as to actually be somewhat endearing.

"I used SPF 45," he went on, "so I should be good for another"—he glanced at his watch—"three hours and twenty min-utes." He had one of those crazy plastic diver's watches that calculated the time in, like, six different zones and had a stopwatch that ran down to the millisecond. It was at least three times the size of his wrist.

"But who's counting?" I teased. Poor Elliot. At least geek chic is coming back in.

"All right," I said, pushing my soda aside and drawing myself up in my seat. "If we've only got three hours and twenty min-utes, we'd better make them count."

"I can always reapply the sunscreen," he pointed out reasonably.

I groaned. "Not the point." I pushed the deck of cards across the table toward him. "Come on. Make me a ringer."

He looked at me doubtfully.

"A competitor?"

He raised a skeptical eyebrow.

"A player?"

"That I can probably do."

Two hours and sixteen minutes later (not that anyone was counting, of course) and my head was swimming.

Ace high, active player, early position, flop, forced bet, full house . . .

Living in Vegas, I'd heard all of these terms before, of course. Like I said, my ex-boyfriend was a huge card player. So even if I'd always abstained, I knew the terms, their meanings, and I knew the basic rules of poker. But I'd always assumed that one's success mostly depended on—yes, you guessed it—luck.

"It's got nothing to do with luck," Elliot corrected me, his hazel-brown eyes flashing intensely even through the tint of his now-darkened glasses.

"Why, because you can bluff?" I asked, slurping away at my third soda. It was hot out, and the fries had pretty much sucked any moisture out of me. I didn't want to dehydrate. Elliot didn't seem like the kind of guy who'd be able to take that in stride.

"Well, pretty much, yeah," he said. "The thing is that it's not just what you've got in your hand, but also what your opponent has in his."

"Which, unless you're Rain Man, there's no way of knowing," I grumbled. It was a good movie—very popular among the Vegas population.

"Yes and no," Elliot said. "No, you never will know exactly what cards your opponent's holding. But you've got to make your best guess based on the cards *you're* holding. Just eliminate any variable that you can, and then work backward from there. What would he or she need to beat you, and what's the likelihood that he or she has it? You're playing for percentages, not luck."

I was a terrible math student. This did not bode well.

"So when do I bluff?" I asked. I was as horrible at bluffing as I was at algebra. Which wasn't surprising, given how unconvincing I was at telling even the simplest little white lie to my father.

"When you're pretty sure that their hand sucks at least as much as yours does," Elliot said.

He made it sound so simple. And I

guess, in his mathematically minded brain, it was. You either had the cards, or you *acted* as if you had the cards. You either knew what your opponent had, or you *acted as if* you knew.

I didn't need poker lessons, I needed acting lessons.

Unfortunately, Elliot wasn't offering those.

Seven

The following Monday morning, I was surprised to find myself actually a little bit okay with waking up and heading to school. I mean, I wasn't, like, doing cartwheels over it or anything, but the grouchiness that seemed to settle over me when the subject of Jesse, Alana, or anything related to them came up had abated somewhat. Which, I figured, was something.

I'd spent Sunday afternoon playing poker online—I found a site where you didn't have to use real money—and though I hadn't exactly cleaned house, I'd won a few hands. Which was way better than I'd done at Kelly's apartment on poker night.

So I was feeling pretty good about

myself as I pulled up into the school parking lot. I had film class first period and was psyched to tell Elliot about my wins. I knew he'd appreciate any improvements I'd made, seeing as how I'd kept him a poolside prisoner for an entire afternoon. Kelly would be into it too, I was sure, since any improvements I made on my own game would up the potential competition of her poker night.

I walked brightly toward the front entrance to the school. I even hummed a little bit under my breath, much to my own embarrassment. But whatever, I was in a good mood and I deserved to dork out on my own if I was so inclined. I slung my tote bag over my shoulder and hoisted the huge double doors open. It was an effort, but that wasn't what pulled all of the breath out of my lungs like a sucker punch to the solar plexus.

As the doors parted, I saw Jesse standing behind them.

He must have been coming from the office. Maybe he was getting permission to leave early, maybe he'd needed something from the principal's secretary. It could have been anything, really. Once upon a time I would have known his schedule by heart, of course, but not anymore.

He looked cute. I hated to admit it to myself, but he did. He must've gotten a haircut over the weekend; I could tell from the rigid lines of his sideburns. Jesse always hated the way he looked immediately after a haircut, but something about the goofiness of it, that week before it had really grown in a bit, was super appealing to me.

He saw me at the exact moment that I saw him. There was no chance to dime-turn out of there, feigning oblivion. I recoiled, which must've confirmed for him that I was, in fact, aware of his presence.

His eyebrows shot up—twin question marks.

He opened his mouth as though he was about to say something.

I couldn't imagine what he would say. A weak apology would only add insult to injury. A deep, sincere apology would probably mess with my head. And a non-apology might just about tear me up.

Right, then. Nothing good could come of an encounter.

I channeled whatever minute reserves of

energy remained coiled deep within. It was much, much easier said than done.

Jesse's eyes widened. Maybe this was difficult for him, too.

Good.

I sputtered out a weak little cough and tore down the hallway, stumbling slightly as I speed-walked off.

Awesome, Cass, I thought, hiccupping as I ran. *You are so cool.*

I pushed the voice in my head out as best I could. I was late enough for first period as it was.

Or so I told myself.

I made it to first period just as the late bell rang, sliding into my seat as I attempted to shrug off the asthmatic hiccups that had seized me as I—*let's be honest now, Cass*—fled the sight of my ex-boyfriend. Also, my ankle hurt from when I had tripped. I rubbed it absently, feeling big-time sorry for myself.

"What's up?" Kelly whispered urgently. I tried to shrug it off, but by this point, she knew me better than that. *"What?"* she insisted, this time reaching over her desktop to poke me with her mechanical pencil. I noticed that her hair was done up in two elaborate braids down her back, Pippi Longstocking style. On anyone else, this hairstyle might have looked seriously insane, but Kelly, as usual, managed to walk that fine line between cute and mildly threatening.

"Ow." I rubbed my elbow where she had poked it and glared at her. "I didn't need that. Jesse encounter," I offered by way of short-handing the situation. Though the sharp pain in my elbow had, in fact, distracted me from the dull throbbing of my ankle.

"Oooh." She sucked her breath in appreciatively. "Rough. In that case, I apologize for my violent outburst."

"Apology accepted," I said primly, sitting back in my seat.

Albon came in a few minutes later, and class progressed without much fanfare. I took the opportunity to sink into a little mind-movie of my own. Suddenly I was that chick from that eighties movie, the one who borrows her mother's white leather outfit for the rockin' house party but spills some crazy drink on it. Obviously she can't afford to have it cleaned or replace it, so she lets the dorkiest guy in school pay her to pretend like he's her boyfriend. Shockingly, he turns out to be pretty cool, and after much mayhem, they end up together.

In my version, I was the popular cheerleader chick. I mean, for *real*, the popular cheerleader chick. Not just some random stray that Alana had adopted and launched to wild high school celebrity. That left Jesse to be the social outcast. A stretch, sure, but hey—it was my mid-morning fantasy.

And since it was *my* fantasy, Jesse's social fate was all mine to manipulate to my heart's content. Who cared if I ruined my mom's best outfit that I *totally* stole without permission? Who cared if I couldn't afford to have it fixed? Not I, that was for sure. Mom and I ('cause in this little alternate reality, my mom was still around, and she was the cool type of mom who has absolutely no qualms about sharing her slammin' wardrobe with her favorite—and only—daughter) had closets full of amazing outfits. She wouldn't even notice that this one was gone. So I had no need for Jesse's money, or Jesse's desperate grab at A-list status. Ours was not exactly a cutesy little love story.

Rather, it was a vision of revenge: pure, sweet, and unfettered.

I reveled in it. At least until Albon roused me with a brisk slap of his palm to his desk.

"For your next project," he announced, "you will be required to work in groups."

Who in the what now? We'd had a huge test on "the birth of the Hollywood block-buster" just before winter break. To be dropping another major assignment on us now? During the bleakest, boringest months of winter? So what if we didn't have snow in Vegas; that was just cruel and unusual.

Albon smirked as the usual rash of hushed protests broke out among my fellow classmates. "As we've discussed, the production team and crew is one of the most integral aspects of making a successful movie. It may seem obvious, but trouble on the set can sink even the most promising films."

Huh? What was he getting at? His ramblings, though accurate enough, were really only relevant if we were going to be making a movie.

"Over winter break you were expected to read chapter six in your anthology:

'Getting Technical.' You should be familiar with the basics of camera work and film technique."

Very sneaky, Albon. A quick glance around the classroom revealed exactly how many students had done the reading. Thankfully, I was one of them. My odd obsession with movies and pop culture had finally come in handy.

"There will be four to a group," he continued. "All self-selected. But choose wisely. The fate of your film may depend on it."

We were making a movie? How cool! All at once, my enthusiasm for the project overrode my panic at the thought of working in groups. I hadn't been in a position to group off since Alana and I were still friends. Of course, Katy and Alana immediately scootched their desks together territorially, scoping out the rest of our classmates for potential cling-ons. I saw Katy shoot a wistful glance in my direction, but I immediately swiveled in my seat so that I was out of her line of vision. Ugh. I *so* didn't need her pity.

A hand clamped down on mine. "You can be my little Spielberg junior."

It was Kelly, who was now in the process

of sidling her entire desk closer to mine in a manner that paralleled Katy and Alana. I felt a pang of—what? Nostalgia? Relief? Excitement? Who knew. I couldn't quite identify it, but I decided to go with it.

"We need two more," I stated.

Kelly rolled her eyes. "*Clearly*, Elliot is in our group." She signaled to him like an air-traffic controller bringing in a 747. Even with his myopia, Elliot couldn't miss Kelly's spastic gesticulations. He wandered over toward us, ever-present messenger bag at his side. I giggled when I noticed that, despite his precise scientific calculations on Saturday, his nose had turned a healthy shade of pink.

"I should warn you, I really don't know too much about movies," he said, pushing his glasses back up his sunburned nose.

"Well, that's okay," I said cheerfully, pleased with my new group. "I do."

"We've got to find one more helpless victim," Kelly pointed out.

Elliot shook his head. "It won't work. There are an odd number of kids in this class."

We looked around the room. Sure enough, it seemed as though everyone else had already paired off into their happy little quartets.

Kelly shrugged. "I guess we're on our own." She wrinkled her nose. "Bummer. I think that means we're each going to have to do one-fourth more work."

"Or one of us could just do double," Elliot pointed out.

"Either way," I chimed in, abstaining from offering a quick little equation of my own.

"You don't mind?" Kelly asked me, surprised. "Seriously, it could take us a lot longer to finish our movie with only three people."

I shook my head. "We'll get it done." According to Albon, a local electronics outlet had offered to loan us the cameras and stuff, yet another perk to being a magnet school. And I was pretty sure it wouldn't take us too long to master iMovie.

"You sound pretty confident," she observed.

"Well, you know," I replied, extremely matter-of-fact, "three has always been my lucky number."

This was true, based on the fact that my grandparents had married on March 3.

Threes had been a theme at their wedding, which I thought was sort of adorable. It was kind of a nice way to counter the old jinx of bad things happening in threes.

Elliot sighed. "That's not the most scientific way to go about these things, you know," he said.

"No," I agreed. "It's not."

Fortunately, that seemed to be a sufficient explanation for Elliot. For now, at least.

Friday night was poker night. As usual, Dad had no qualms whatsoever about letting me go to Kelly's. I was starting to feel more than a little bit guilty about deceiving him, sure—he was such a great, understanding dad—but at the same time, I was feeling cheerier lately than I'd been feeling in weeks. I rationalized the dishonesty to myself by clinging to the idea that it was for the greater good. My theory seemed all the more plausible when I found a penny faceup in the parking lot of the Venetian. I mean, that's always a good sign. I'm a huge believer in the lucky penny.

"I brought the guacamole," I said, holding a huge Tupperware container out as

Kelly pulled her front door open. It was my specialty, one of my only culinary talents.

"Great," she said, eyeing the monstrous batch. "That'll come in handy if there's, like, a flood or whatever and we're forced to hole up underground for a week or so."

"Oh, it'll never keep that long," I teased, waving my hand in her face.

I was the last to arrive, and I couldn't help but note that I felt much more comfortable walking into the living room, where everyone was gathered, than I had at my first poker game. I guess it helped to have spent time outside of school with Elliot—I was starting to slide him firmly into the "friend" category. He offered me a shy wave as I placed the guac on the coffee table and broke out a bag of chips to go with.

"Homemade?" James asked, looking dubious.

"It's the only thing I know how to make—other than microwave popcorn, and even that's touch and go—but trust me, I make it well," I assured him.

"She's not lying," Andy shrieked enthusiastically, shoveling the dip into her mouth slightly maniacally.

"Can I get you something to drink? A

Diet Coke?" Kelly offered, dropping a can neatly next to me on the table before I could even answer her.

"Have you been practicing?" Marcus asked me, manhandling the deck of cards as his lips curled into a smarmy smile. I couldn't quite pinpoint it, but for some reason, there was always something smarmy about Marcus. He was even less appealing to me with Dorito-breath, a condition with which he was currently afflicted.

I glanced at Elliot, who briefly made eye contact but quickly looked away from me. "Yup," I said. "A little bit."

"Awesome," Kelly said, settling into her seat and sliding the dealer button in front of her. "Then I guess we can get started." Marcus dutifully slid the deck over to her.

It was like the World Series of Poker. Or, at least, in my mind it was. It was a good hour before anyone folded for real. James moved all-in on a semi-bluff straight draw with an ace and a ten after a king-queen-queen flop. Marcus called quickly with an ace and a king, and took the pot with a pair of kings when two blanks fell on the turn and the river. James was a decent sport about it, though. Probably because at that point he was only down thirty bucks. This was my kind of crowd—they knew how to cut their losses.

A short time later, Andy was low on chips and moved all-in with a suited ace and a seven. Marcus was holding an ace and a king and was only too thrilled to call. Marcus may have been a good poker player, but he was kind of a slimeball, I was starting to realize. And the Dorito-breath was in full force. The flop came ace-king-nine, Marcus's two-pair held up, and Andy went out. She was slightly less gracious about it than James had been, but we managed to placate her with a healthy dose of guacamole.

Kelly hoped to get head-up against Marcus—I think mainly because his cackling was starting to seriously creep her out—but drew to a disadvantage when her turn at being dealer was over. After that, her confidence was shot. She was out of the game, but offered to deal for the rest of us.

Suddenly, our game had been reduced by half. And I was one of the three left standing (or, um, sitting). I couldn't believe it. I looked around the table. Elliot's face was impassive. Marcus looked extremely pleased with himself. The moment was tense.

Kelly slapped two cards down in front of each of us. Marcus slid his lucky charm—a silver chip he'd gotten as part of a custom set—and looked at his hand. He chuckled to himself.

Subtle. Not.

Elliot lifted the corners of his cards tentatively. His face was a blank, completely inscrutable. I couldn't help but admire his poker face.

My cards were crap.

We each tossed a few chips into the pot. I couldn't get a read on anyone else's hand. I mean, Marcus was pretty much *always* grinning like a big weirdo.

The flop was useless to me.

Marcus raised, guffawing to himself.

Elliot raised, impassive as ever.

I paused. Tapped my fingers on the table. Took a sip of soda.

And folded.

"Yes!" Marcus cried, slamming his fist down on the table.

I glared at him. "Hey, it's an improvement over last week," I said, crossing my arms defensively over my chest.

"That's why he's being such a jerk," Kelly said, shooting daggers of her own out of her eyes. "Because you're finally a threat to him."

"Oh, hey, come on, now," Marcus protested. "Let's not get carried away here." He chuckled. "A threat."

"Maybe I'm not a contender just yet—," I started.

"But she's sure holding her own as a player," Elliot chimed in. "I mean, she kicked *your* butt for a few rounds of betting, right?"

At this, Marcus only grunted.

I laughed, and Elliot winked at me. Which made me laugh even harder. It was a nice feeling, laughing so much, I was afraid I might pee in my pants (I didn't). I mean, it had been a while since I'd laughed like that.

It was only later that I realized how completely atypical Elliot's behavior—the winking, the joking, the speaking up in a group setting—really was. From the little that I knew of him, he was more of a shrinking violet than a snapdragon.

Maybe he was changing. Maybe we all were.

Knock on wood, that was.

"Venus is in retrograde?"

Kelly squinted over my shoulder as I tapped away at her computer. I'd stuck around after the game ended to help her clean up, and then we'd decided to update the website. Now that the horoscopes were up, I was into keeping them current. I mean, as someone who took those things pretty seriously, I wanted my readers to be able to trust the information I was giving them.

"Yup, it's retro-licious," I said. "Bad news. It's pulling backward. Everyone's love lives are going to get all wonky. 'Cause, you know—Venus, with the . . . love . . ."

Kelly nodded skeptically. "I can't believe how much you buy into this stuff."

"Not just me," I reminded her. "You're the one who said that your site had, like, a million extra hits since you posted the horoscopes."

"Fair enough," Kelly agreed. "I have to give the public what they want." She rolled her eyes.

"Come on," I prodded her. "Obviously I'm reading this stuff the best way that I know how. I mean, clearly I would rather that Venus keep its retrograde off of my own love life. I've had more than enough love retrograde for one semester."

"Seriously," Kelly said. She paused for a beat, then added, "Ugh."

"I second that," I said.

For a moment the mood threatened to darken, which so wasn't my intention. "Uh-uh," I said, shaking my head. "No moping." Tonight I'd had almost-pee-in-your-pants laughter, after all. That was momentous. No way was I going to get all serious and depressy again. "We have to do something— something other than feeling sorry for me," I announced. "This is Vegas. There must be something going on somewhere."

A sly smile crept across Kelly's lips. "I have a thought," she said slowly.

Thirty minutes and a judicious application of DuWop Original Lip Venom later, and we were ready to put Kelly's plan into action. Or, at least, Kelly was. I had my doubts.

"This is never going to work," I whispered to her through clenched teeth.

"It will if you just act cool," she said, poking me in the ribs. "Quit freaking out."

"It is very difficult to act cool when one's

lips are on fire," I pointed out. The Lip Venom was making my mouth sting.

"Beauty is pain," Kelly said. "And you look hot."

When I'd suggested that we do something fun, Kelly had lit right up. Turned out that she was as much of a pop-culture fanatic as I was—not too surprising, given that she was in the film elective with me.

I should have asked. If I had asked outright what other sort of hobbies she had, I would have figured out a lot sooner what a slave she was to celebrity gossip. "I have a total tabloid fetish," she confessed to me. I mean, Kelly was, like, my long-lost BFF, or something.

Anyway, Kelly had read the latest *In Touch* (I was still making my way through *Star*—I was sorta behind this week) and knew that a certain young celebutante prone to man-stealing, table-dancing, and occasional fits of guest DJ-ing was in town tonight. She was staying at the Wynn, in one of their swankiest VIP suites. And, if history served, she was *definitely* going to hit the clubs tonight.

Kelly was dying to get a picture of Celeb for her website. Hence the Lip

Venom—which was seriously making my lips twitch—and our outfits: super-skinny jeans, sparkly halters, sky-high peep-toe shoes, and makeup to rival a Vegas drag show. We were standing on line, waiting to get into Tao. Celeb *loved* Tao.

So, it seemed, did about thirty thousand other hopeful would-be clubbers.

"I still can't believe you just had these clothes in your closet," I mumbled. To say that they were not Kelly's usual style was a vast understatement.

"It's like a costume," Kelly said, shrugging. She pointed at my feet. "I still can't believe you're managing to walk in those."

Kelly's feet were a size bigger than mine; I'd stuffed the heels of the shoes with toilet paper.

"Yeah, well, where there's a will, there's a way," I noted.

"You look fabulous," Kelly assured me. "I guess blondes really do have more fun. Now, concentrate on looking older," she instructed.

"My boobs are hanging out on display for half the city. I'm not sure what else I can do that would compete with that," I replied. If I didn't look older, at least I looked sluttier. Which at least gave me that much more in common with Celeb. I shook my head. "Aren't you worried that your parents are going to kill you when they find out?"

"Why would you assume that they'll find out?" Kelly asked, genuinely baffled. "They both work late on Fridays. We'll be back home before they're even off."

I nodded. My own father was working late as well, and had been so psyched for me when I asked to stay over at Kelly's that I was actually a little bit embarrassed.

The bouncer at the head of the line beckoned toward us. Kelly grabbed my wrist but wisely refrained from shrieking triumphantly.

"Just you two?" he asked once we were standing in front of him. Kelly nodded as I stood very straight and concentrated on looking as much older as I possibly could.

The bouncer gave us another suspicious once-over but must have decided that he liked what he saw. My slutty outfit was working for me, that was for sure. "A'right," he said finally, looking extremely serious. "You're in." He stamped both of our hands and hustled us inside to the protests of a group of less fortunate guys standing behind us.

Inside, the club was a dark sea of writhing bodies. The air was humid, and trance music pounded. "Soothing," I said to Kelly jokingly.

She peered at me. "What?" she asked, tugging at her ear.

I shook my head. It wasn't worth it.

This place hadn't changed since the last time I'd been here. In July, Alana's father had booked a VIP booth for a bunch of us for Alana's sixteenth birthday. We'd had to wear humiliating bracelets that declared our under-agedness to the world, but otherwise, it had been an awesome night. We drank sparkling cider, danced, and in general acted incredibly fabulous. I'd spent the night with Alana on one side of me and Jesse on the other.

Ugh.

Kelly caught sight of my expression and shook her finger in my face disapprovingly. "We agreed not to be serious!" she said, struggling to be heard over the music.

"You're right," I said. I shook it off. "So what's our game plan?"

Kelly put her mouth right up to my ear. "I think the quickest way to get kicked out would be if we were to try to get served drinks. So I say we skip that."

I nodded. "Sound thinking." Getting kicked out would be a waste of some hard-core primping.

"There are only a few places she'd be. One: the VIP section. Which we can't get into, but we can still stalk."

"Check. Stalking. No prob. I have no shame."

"We should also case out the bar. If she's not actually dancing on top of it, there's a decent chance she'll at least be draped over it."

"She does love her Tab energy," I agreed.

"And if all else fails," Kelly finished, "we'll just have to stake her out at the ladies' room."

I raised my eyebrows. "You've given this some thought."

Kelly winked. "I'm no amateur."

True to its name, the VIP section was not open to the huddled plebeian masses. An enormous football player of a security guard waved Kelly and me away before we could even get within spitting distance.

"Ridiculous," Kelly said, wrinkling her nose distastefully. "Like anyone in there would even care. I mean, we're not autograph hounds or anything."

"Um, no, just two girls looking for a photo op so we can slap a picture of a famous person online," I replied, gently pointing out the slight flaw in Kelly's logic.

"Whose side are you on?" she grumbled.

"Yours, babe," I said, pointing at my extremely overexposed chest. "I don't dress like this for just anyone."

We wandered over to the bar, but even in the crush of over-excited high rollers, we could tell that Celeb was nowhere in sight. There was a conspicuous lack of blond roots and anorexic hangers-on.

I worried about getting any closer to the bar. I turned to Kelly. "Bathroom?"

She shrugged. "Yeah, I guess."

The line to the ladies' room rivaled the line we'd had to wait on to get into the club. Everyone on it looked various degrees annoyed, impatient, uncomfortable, or chemically altered.

Suddenly, Kelly grabbed at my elbow.

"Ow!" I whirled around to look at her. Her death grip was cutting off my circulation. "Yes?"

She leaned her head to mine. "It's *her*," she whispered through clenched teeth.

"Where?" I whipped my head to the right and to the left, craning my neck for a view.

"Be cool," Kelly commanded, now actually digging her nails into the flesh of my forearm. "Eleven o'clock."

"Eleven o'clock, what? Kelly, it's twelve fifteen."

"No," Kelly hissed, finally, blessedly, letting go of my hand to tilt my head over to her right. "Eleven o'clock."

"Oh. Right." Of course. Eleven o'clock. There she was—dead center, completely obvious to anyone who was slightly less clueless than me. She was in full-party mode: the blond hair cascaded down her back in heat-treated ringlets, the silver minidress shimmered with her body's slightest move. The logoed handbag screamed, "Notice me!"

How could we not?

Kelly reached into her purse and slyly slid out her phone, flipping it open and switching on the camera mode. We crept forward silently, stealthily. It was all very James Bond-meets-Liz Smith. I was totally proud of us.

"Say 'cheesy,'" Kelly singsonged. She darted forward so that she was standing just in front of Celeb.

She clicked her phone.

The flash exploded.

Celeb screamed.

"Uh, now might be a good time to go," Kelly suggested. She grabbed at me again—this time, I was grateful—and we fled the scene. In the distance, Celeb was shrieking about lawsuits and paparazzi, and we *so* didn't need to get caught up in that.

We made it to the elevator and collapsed into it, laughing.

"I can't believe we found her!" I gasped. "I can't believe you got the picture."

"Yeah," Kelly agreed, giggling maniacally. "I guess sometimes you just get lucky."

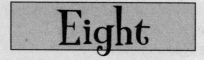

Eight

"You two are shameless."

Elliot slurped down on his soda and shook his head disapprovingly at Kelly and me from his perch across the table from us. "Pathetic," he added, emphatic.

"Because we're fame-stalkers?" Kelly asked, incredulous. She toyed with her French fries. "Please. If chasing after celebrities is wrong, I don't wanna be right." She flashed a giant grin at Elliot and chomped down on a fry for emphasis.

"It's a total invasion of privacy," he said.

"Yeah . . . ," I agreed, "but it was fun."

After our little A-list stakeout, Kelly and I had gone back to her apartment. We changed into comfy clothes and gorged on chocolate chocolate chip ice cream while we uploaded the photo on the website. It was awesome; Celeb in all her borderline-hysterical, red-eyed frenzy. I was proud of us.

We'd had an impromptu sleepover and slept in the next morning. When we did finally rouse ourselves, we'd decided a late brunch was in order. The Venetian did a great buffet, Kelly promised me. We called Elliot to invite him to join. "Otherwise, he'll never leave the house, and that's just too sad," Kelly explained. "Weekends are his time for"——she lowered her voice dramatically——"*studying*."

I shuddered. "We must save him from himself."

As it turned out, Elliot hadn't so much thought that he needed saving, but we were able to persuade him to meet us through a creative interpretation of the truth.

"So, you guys wanted to talk about the film project?" Elliot asked now, pushing his soda aside and revisiting the BLT that was languishing on his plate.

Ah, yes. The film project; aka our decoy for getting Elliot out on a Saturday after-noon.

"Here's the deal," Kelly hedged.

"Yes?" Elliot asked suspiciously.

"We were thinking that rather than, you know, getting to work on the nitty-gritty of the project, that we'd, um . . . spend today doing some research."

"Define 'research,'" Elliot demanded. You could tell he was kind of onto us at this point.

"There's a Tarantino festival on at the Screening Room, starting at three," I chimed in brightly.

Elliot sighed. "That's really not the same thing as working on our project."

"Elliot," I said, my voice deepening with passion, "Tarantino changed the face of modern filmmaking. It's *imperative* that we familiarize ourselves with his technique." Kelly and I had rehearsed this argument.

He looked at me plaintively. "Is there any chance that either of you will leave me alone unless I give in?"

Kelly shook her head. "Unlikely."

"Fine," he said resignedly. "But two movies is my limit. After that, my knees start to hurt. I hate those movie theater seats."

Of course, the best of the movies were going to be screened later that night, during prime moviegoing hours. But I decided to let it go. I mean, Elliot had dragged himself away from his precious schoolwork to spend the afternoon with us. These were my new buds, and we were hanging on a Sunday afternoon. Good times.

I knew better than to press my luck.

"So, okay—I guess my question is, why *vampires*?" Elliot blinked as his eyes adjusted to the daylight again.

"Silly Elliot," I said, patting him on the shoulder affectionately. "I think that if you really give it some thought, you'll find that the question is, why *not* vampires?"

He crinkled his forehead in thought. "Nope," he said, after a beat. "No idea."

"Because they're *cool*," Kelly said. "I mean, come on—*The Lost Boys*? *Blade*? *Buffy the Vampire Slayer*?"

"Forget about that," I interjected. "More important than the vampires is George Clooney."

Kelly grew silent at this, lost, I had to presume, in agreement.

"All in all," she said finally, "a fine way to spend an afternoon. I do enjoy *From Dusk Till Dawn*."

"Though not having *anything* to do with our project," Elliot interjected, practical as ever.

"It was team-bonding time," I corrected him, smiling widely. "You'll see, now—when the pressure's really on us, we'll work like a well-oiled machine."

He looked doubtful. "I suppose."

I ruffled his hair playfully. "Trust me. I have a way with these sort of things. It's like a sixth sense."

"I don't believe in that stuff," Elliot insisted.

I dug my four-leaf clover key chain out of my bag and waved it at him. "Don't worry," I assured him. "I believe enough for the both of us."

"You're in a good mood these days," Dad commented.

"You're not wrong," I agreed.

It was no wonder that he'd taken note of my newly lightened attitude; I was actually humming to myself as I set the kitchen table for us for dinner. Dad was making tacos, which would perk me up any day, but as it was, I'd been extra cheery since getting home from the movies with Kelly and Elliot.

"I was pretty worried about you for a little while there," he said, kind of glancing at me out of the corner of his eye, as if testing to see how frank we were going to be with each other.

"Well, so was I," I said. I took a deep breath. I appreciated his concern, of course, but I really didn't think it was necessary to jeopardize my good mood with a big, sappy heart-to-heart. "But, you know, life goes on."

"Anything in particular spark this new and improved outlook?" Dad asked, taking his cue from me to treat the subject somewhat lightly.

I thought for a moment. "New friends."

Dad peered at me. "Friends of the male persuasion?"

"Please," I said, snorting to myself. "I made some new friends in film class. Kelly Connor and Elliot Forest. You met Elliot, remember? We're working together on a class project."

"Elliot. Your new friend of the male persuasion," Dad observed wryly.

"No. I mean, *yes*, he's a boy, but no, he's not a boy like that," I protested. The thought of getting romantic with Elliot actually made me laugh out loud, which immediately made me feel bad. "I mean, I guess he's, like, cute, or whatever," I said hastily, feeling bad for talking any sort of trash about someone as shyly sweet as Elliot—"you know, in that sort of brainy, quiet, unkempt way—"

"Ah," Dad cut in, realization dawning.

"But, you know, we're just so different."

"Because you're, what? A huge airhead?"

I blushed. "No, I mean—okay, well, he's an Aries. We are total opposites on the zodiac wheel. We have *nothing* in common."

"Hmmm," Dad said, but refrained from offering anything else.

"I don't like that noise," I said.

"No noise," Dad countered. "I am refraining from passing any judgment."

"Yes, I know," I said. "That's the noise that you make when you are refraining from passing judgment. So, please. Judge away."

Dad shrugged, pouring another healthy dollop of olive oil into the hissing skillet and stepping backward as the oil splashed back up onto him. "It's just that I would hate to see you pass up something great all because of this predilection that you have toward superstition."

I rolled my eyes. "Dad, come on. There's

a reason that people adhere to superstitions. I'm sorry, but it's true. Jesse and I were totally mismatched, according to our signs, but I ignored it and I went for him, anyway. Look where that got me. I'm just not going to make the same mistake again. It's too risky."

Dad must have noticed the slight hitch in my voice, because his expression softened and he backed off. "I hear you, Cass," he said. "I just want you to give people a chance."

"I do," I said. It was true. Elliot was a great guy, and a fun new friend to have. Even if half the time he seemed completely terrified by how outgoing I was. But friendship was where it started and ended.

I considered myself lucky to have become closer to Kelly and Elliot. They came into my life at a time when I needed new friends. I didn't take that for granted. And I wasn't going to jeopardize it, either.

No way.

Poker night. This time, James dealt.

Straight flush. I tossed my bet into the pot.

Kelly bet.

Marcus bet.

Elliot bet.

Andy folded.

More cards. No use to me. I raised.

Kelly raised.

Marcus raised.

Elliot folded.

I called.

Kelly had nothing, not even two pair. I laughed at her and she shook her head, munching contentedly on a potato chip. "Whatever," she said. "It's only one hand."

Marcus chuckled. "You should start taking these things more seriously," he admonished, totally seeping his smarm in Kelly's face. He flipped his cards down. "Seriously."

Full house.

"It's good advice, Marcus," I said. I looked him straight in the eye and laid my cards down onto the table. "Really good advice."

James hooted and scooped up the pot, pushing it across the table toward me.

Kelly laughed so hard, I thought soda would shoot out her nose. "Awesome, Cass," she said, literally slapping her hand against her leg. "Completely awesome."

Elliot and I stayed behind to help Kelly clean. Elliot, however, mainly spent the time marveling over my transformation. "You're . . . a ringer." he said, eyes wide.

"Okay, except that would imply that I'm cheating," I protested. "I just, you know, took your advice. I've been, like, practicing and stuff."

"Um, yeah, you have," Kelly said. "I mean, you don't make that kind of turn-around without practice."

"It started with some lessons from Elliot," I said modestly. "And, I mean, you know, I got dealt good cards."

"Oh, hey now," Elliot interjected. "What have we learned about blaming luck?"

"Right, right," I said, nodding. "No luck. Luck is not a factor." I swallowed a sip of soda, then tossed my empty can into the plastic bag of recyclables that I was gathering together. "You realize that's, like, heresy, to me," I reminded him. "I'm just not wired to think that way."

"Yeah, you've mentioned that," he said. "But considering how much your playing has improved, you should consider converting."

"I'm a little uncomfortable with the use of religion as metaphor," Kelly said, joking, "but then again, Cass's turnaround is clearly nothing short of divine intervention." She placed the roll of paper towels in her hand down on the living room coffee table. "Cass," she began.

"You've got serious face," I said, instantly nervous.

"Sort of," Kelly admitted. "It's kind of a 'good news–bad news' sort of situation."

"Good news first, please," I said, worried.

"We've built somewhat of a reputation," Kelly said.

"Um, like what sort of a reputation?" I asked. "Is this because I wore that shirt when we went out the other night?"

"No, you freak," she assured me. "Nothing to do with that. What I mean is that we have a reputation for good poker playing. Like, as in, everyone now knows that you're really good at it. I was blogging about it online."

"Definitely a good thing. I want to be a legend in my own time," I said. This was cool. Maybe I could be, like, a hustler. Like Tom Cruise in *The Color of Money*.

"So, the thing is, see, that now there are people who, like, want to join our game," Kelly said.

"Ohmigod," I squeaked, realizing. "It's

like I'm famous! I'm like Lauren Graham on *Celebrity Poker Showdown*—except with blond hair. And maybe taller. And, you know, blue eyes." I took a deep breath. "Not the point, I know. But—awesome!" Like, how flattering?

"I thought so too," Kelly said carefully. "I'm glad that you agree."

"Wait a minute," I said, the realization finally dawning with all the subtlety of a block of cement. "The bad news, please? Who, exactly, is so crazy-eager to play against me?"

Kelly winced, but didn't say anything.

I whirled to face Elliot. "You," I said, pointing at him. "You must know."

Elliot shifted uncomfortably. "Sort of."

And then it hit me.

"It's Jesse, isn't it?" I asked, trying to keep my face from crumbling. "Jesse wants in on our game."

"Not just him, Cass," Kelly said, her eyes widening with sympathy. "I mean, he's got a whole band of poker buddies too. They travel together."

"Right. So, like, Jesse, and, um, Jake, and that other guy from the football team?" I asked, my voice raising into a slightly hysterical pitch. "Am I leaving anyone out?"

"Well, we've got a ten-person cap on our games," Elliot reminded me. "So there were four open slots."

"Jesse, Jake, and Dennis. You're leaving one person out," I said, my voice dangerously low. There could only be one other person Jesse would want to bring in to our game. It would be like a Midvale High Grudge Match.

Kelly sighed and put her hands on her hips. We both said her name in unison:

"Alana."

To say that I was uninterested in playing poker with Alana and Jesse was an understatement of epic proportions. In point of fact, I was able to quickly compose a short list of slightly more desirable pastimes than card-playing with my ex-best friend and ex-boyfriend:

1. Develop life-threatening illness, i.e., flesh-eating bacteria or mysterious, non-specific bird flu.
2. Stick sewing needles directly into my eyeballs.

3. Tap-dance naked at the next Midvale pep rally.
4. Shave my head and dye remaining stubble electric blue.
5. Endure Brazilian bikini wax.

I explained as much, and, um, rather impassionedly so, to Elliot and Kelly. They were understanding, but perhaps less so than I might have hoped. That is to say, they weren't going to let me off the hook.

"Look, Cass," Kelly said, leveling with me, "I know Jesse's a jerk. I mean, *I* knew that he was a jerk before anything even happened with him and Alana. But he's a notoriously good poker player. It'll be a good game."

"I hear you," I replied, nodding with slow deliberation. "And yet, I don't think you're getting me. Like, I might *literally die* if I have to play against him and Alana. From seething rage. People can die from that, you know. Anger. Or worse, I'll kill them both. Throttle them or smash their heads together."

Elliot made a sour face.

"I'm sorry," I said, glancing at him. "I'm sure that someday in the not-too-distant future, I'll totally forgive them, but for now,

I'm sort of more in a head-smashing kind of place."

"Right. Head-smashing," he replied, as if making a mental note. He took a step backward away from me for good measure.

"I think you're looking at this completely the wrong way," Kelly cut in. "I mean, Jesse's good, but so are you these days. I mean, you're getting better all the time. Going up against him could be good for your ego."

"Yeah," Elliot chimed in. "I mean, you might actually *win*."

"Thanks for the vote of confidence," I quipped dryly.

"No, I mean it," Elliot insisted. "You're a good player. And we can definitely practice some more. As much as you want, so you feel ready to take him."

"Definitely," Kelly added. "I've never been that into doing my homework, anyway."

I had to admit, my interest level was slowly rising. The idea of kicking Jesse's butt was pretty appealing. "So you're saying that this could be like a revenge thing?" I asked, warming to the thought.

"That's *exactly* what I'm saying," Kelly said, breaking into a crafty grin.

"I see," I said, drumming my fingernails on the coffee table as I sailed off in concentration. "I see."

"So will you do it? Please?" Kelly begged, her voice rising to a squeak. "Pretty please with an extra scoop of chocolate chocolate chip ice cream?"

"And a cherry on top," I countered.

She nodded emphatically. "Absolutely. As many cherries as you want." She clapped her hands together in excitement. Her enthusiasm was wreaking havoc on her carefully cultivated cynicism, I noted.

"No promises," I said, waving my hand at her. "Not yet."

"But you'll think about it?" she asked, her eyes twinkling.

"I'll think about it," I vowed. "There's something I need to check first."

It's your week, Libra—if you haven't noticed, things are starting to go your way. Venus is still in retrograde, which means you'll want to avoid making any big decisions in love-land, but Saturn's aura is burning bright: Creative energy is yours to tap! Fun and games are more fun, now. You're on a roll!

I called Kelly from home after I'd had a chance to check my horoscope online. The stars wouldn't steer me wrong, I knew.

She picked up on the first ring. "What's the verdict?" she asked breathlessly.

"I'm in," I said.

Kelly's response was a shriek so loud that I had to hold the phone at arm's length. Maxine, who was curled up at the foot of my bed, peered at me curiously and made a whimpering sound.

I crossed my fingers that I wouldn't regret my decision.

Nine

The game was called for Friday night. I kept my head down in school that afternoon—I had to save up all of my energy if I was going to go up against Alana and Jesse that evening. Walking from class to class, it felt somehow as though everyone I passed was whispering and casting sidelong glances toward me. I told myself I was imagining things, but I wasn't sure that was the truth.

We were playing at Kelly's; of the core six of us, her place was best suited for a poker party. According to Kelly, Jesse had lobbied for holding the card game at his parents' place, but thank god, she held firm. I *definitely* wasn't ready to return to the scene of the backstabbing. Frankly, I hadn't even been able to listen to Kelly Clarkson without gagging ever since walking in on Jesse and Alana. Visiting his house could cause full-on GI failure.

Kelly asked me to come over early; I think she knew I needed the moral support. Either that, or she was afraid I might chicken out. Which, come to think of it, I almost did.

In the end, though, I decided to put faith in my horoscope—after all, it had never let me down before—and do as Kelly said: that is, to see this as an opportunity to regain some dignity. Never mind that Jesse had heard I was improving. I knew that he mainly wanted in on our game because Marcus and Kelly were known pros; Jesse was insanely competitive. Anyway, with any luck, my newly honed prowess would catch him off guard.

I made the guac while Kelly quizzed me on the best poker hands. She needn't have bothered; that was amateur stuff.

"You're ready," she pronounced, setting out an ice bucket and a bunch of bottles of soda.

"I hope so," I replied. Unfortunately, I wasn't so sure.

The doorbell rang, and I nearly jumped out of my skin. "Maybe I'm not as ready as I thought," I said sheepishly.

Kelly patted me on the shoulder as she strode past me to answer the doorbell. "Relax," she said, smiling. "It's just Elliot. He promised to meet us before everyone else got here so that we could be your moral support."

"Aww," I said. My voice was mock-saccharine, but I was actually touched, big-time.

"The cavalry's here!" Kelly sang, leading Elliot into the living room.

He offered me a sheepish wave. "Hey, Cass. Ready for your debut?"

"Oh, sure," I said, trying to sound at least ten times breezier than I felt. "I'm feeling lucky tonight."

He frowned. "Cassandra," he said, "you know—"

"That luck has nothing to do with it, blah, blah, blah," I said. I winked to show I was teasing. "I know it, I've heard it, I own it," I continued. "And I'm not going to forget everything that you've taught me. But somewhere back there, in the farthest corners of my mind, I'm still hoping to get lucky tonight."

"That's what I like to hear!" Kelly squealed.

Which was just when the doorbell rang again.

All of the visualization and positive-thinking techniques in the world couldn't have prepared me for the full-body shock that I experienced when the doorbell rang for the second time. I shivered briefly, as though I were actually, physically ill.

You're being stupid, I told myself. *It might not even be Jesse at the door.*

It *could* just be Alana.

The doorbell rang again, this time in a succession of short, staccato beats. Whoever it was, was getting impatient.

"Kelly, are you going to—" Elliot wandered out into the hallway. He stopped short when he saw me. "You don't look so good."

I bit my lip. "I don't feel so good."

"Maybe this was a bad idea," Elliot said, his brow furrowing in concern.

"You're telling me this *now*?" I asked, my voice creeping to an alarming octave. He and Kelly had been the ones who were so sure we should embark on this little battle of the network stars.

"Everybody, calm down," Kelly said, padding into the hall and waving her hands at us in a gesture that I'm sure was intended to be soothing. She turned to me. "You go splash some water on your face. And you"— now she pointed directly at Elliot, who flushed with embarrassment at being called out—"go . . . refill the ice bucket!"

"It's full—," Elliot protested.

But Kelly wasn't daunted. She dashed off to get the door.

I followed Kelly's advice and made my way to the front bathroom. Her mother had done the room up in mirrored paneling and lavender, which did nothing to offset my raging nerves. I could see my sheet-white face from almost every angle, made—if it were even possible—pastier by the glow of the tinted wallpaper.

Get a grip, I told myself, breathing heavily. *Get it together.*

I splashed some water across my face and spritzed myself with a little atomizer that I found by the side of the sink. Only after I sprayed it into my hair did I realize it was actually a room deodorizer. Whatever. At least now I was free of the lingering smells of must and pet odor. I was all that much more prepared to wipe the floor with my ex-boyfriend now that I smelled like a freshly waxed kitchen floor.

Okay, I was dousing myself in cleaning projects. It was safe to say that I had officially hit rock bottom.

Hiding in the bathroom is doing nothing for your self-image, Cass, I thought, urging myself out of my hiding place. I took a deep breath, smoothed out my hair, and followed my friends into the living room.

Traitor. Brutus. Backstabbing freak.

I couldn't believe my eyes. Not only was Alana here, and looking incredibly self-satisfied, but she was wearing a beaded halter top that I had given her for her last birthday.

Oh, low blow.

Was she trying to throw me off my game?

Shake it off, Cass. Use your anger.

It was like the force. If I could tap into it, my righteous indignation could make me stronger.

I hated that freaking halter.

"Nice halter," I managed to choke out, waving a limp hello to my former friend.

She smirked, looking equal parts sheepish and entitled. "Hey, Cass."

"Hi, Cass."

It was Jesse.

It was Jesse, and I was Jell-o.

"Hi," I squeaked. The word caught in my throat and came out like it had several syllables. I could smell the room spray wafting off of me as my body heat soared.

Dennis and Jake stood behind the happy couple, looking mildly disinterested in the *O.C.*-style drama unfolding before them. I waved halfheartedly in their direction.

I forced my lips to turn upward in what I hoped was a fair attempt at a smile. "So, do you guys, uh, wanna play some cards?"

It was going to be a long night.

Dennis was the dealer. Something about how it was a courtesy to let the guest act as house. Whatever, I could barely cough out a sentence without managing to sound severely brain damaged, so it wasn't like I was in the best position to put up a fight. I sat across the table from Alana and Jesse, flanked on either side by Kelly and Elliot. I'm not gonna lie; it was nice to know that my buds had my back. My stomach had started churning from the moment the front door first rang, and it wasn't looking like it was going to calm down anytime soon.

I don't know what I thought I'd feel upon seeing Jesse for real, face-to-face, in a scene I couldn't flee from. Hurt, sure, with maybe a little bit of embarrassment. And, hey—why not throw a little anger in there, too, while you're at it? All seemed like perfectly respectable reactions.

But what I hadn't counted on was feeling them all so acutely, and *all at the same time*. My brain was so fuzzy, I thought it was going to catch fire. I could barely focus on my cards. Which didn't matter, because they sucked, anyway. On our first hand, I folded after the first round of betting. Jesse and Alana exchanged a glance. I think they thought I didn't notice them, but I totally did. I'm sure they were wondering why they'd heard so much about my so-called poker skills. I mean, I was even second-guessing myself. My cheeks were buzzing, and my molars were humming. I was completely self-conscious. I was starting to seriously wonder if I was having an out-of-body experience. Except if that was the case, I figured I'd be a lot less itchy.

After my third fold of the night, Kelly dragged me into the kitchen under the pretense of getting everyone some more soda.

"*What* is going on with you out there?" she hissed. "This is worse than the first time you played with us."

"Thanks," I sniffed.

"Sorry," she said, sounding slightly softer. "But it's true. I thought you'd be so into stomping all over Jesse and Alana. But this is just . . . painful to watch."

"It's kind of painful to *feel*, Kelly!" I reminded her, willing my voice not to crack. I rolled my eyes and jerked my head in the direction of the living room. "Do you not notice how they are, like, totally and completely a couple? They don't seem even remotely embarrassed at how badly they screwed me over."

"It's been a little while, Cass," Kelly reminded me. "As horrible as it sounds, maybe they've moved on."

I shuddered, then straightened myself back up again. "I mean, at least they don't have to look so *happy* about taking my money. Please."

"At least you don't have to *let* them," Kelly said, whispering fiercely. "Listen—you are a good poker player. As good as anyone out there." She wrinkled her nose, disagreeing with herself. "Except for Marcus."

I narrowed my eyes. "Your point being?"

"You're letting them spank you."

"And, thank you for the imagery." I sighed.

She shoved against me, one part playful, one part concerned. "Wouldn't you rather it be the other way around?"

Kelly was right. There was no point in going down without a fight. I knew what I had to do. What I needed to do. *Wanted* to do.

I didn't want to spank Alana and Jesse.

I wanted to kick their asses, big-time.

"We're back," Kelly said, settling into her folding chair.

I slammed a two-liter bottle of Coke onto the table with enough force to rattle everyone's drinks. Elliot glanced up at me, startled. I smiled sweetly at him, then sat down at the table. This time, I was careful to meet every single player's eyes.

"Deal me in."

It was time to turn the game around, and I was going to be the one to do it.

I rapped my knuckles lightly against the underside of the table, just to be safe. It was a flimsy IKEA sort of wood, but it was wood, nonetheless. It would have to do.

Dennis cracked his knuckles and shrugged. He slapped two cards down on the table toward me.

I lifted the corners of my cards, just enough so I could see my hand.

Crap.

Dennis fiddled with a cigarette lighter. It was a silver Zippo, very retro. He was using it the way that some players use chips or other lucky markers. They set it on top of their cards between bets, in part to tell the dealer that they're sticking, but mostly for luck. A not-so-small part of me was itching to bust out a marker of my own, but I knew Elliot, my sensei and dungeon master in all things poker, would not approve. After all, I was supposed to play as if I didn't consider superstition to be a science unto itself. Which—ugh.

"No smoking," Kelly said shortly.

Dennis raised an eyebrow. "I wasn't."

"Um, are we playing, or what?" Alana looked up from her cards, trying in vain to mask the half-smile that had crept across her face. She was not, shall we say, a master bluffer.

The community cards were no good for me. This was awful. I fidgeted in my seat. I could hear Elliot's voice in my head, like that horrible voice-over at the beginning of very sappy romantic comedies or that television show with all the hot doctors. *No luck involved,* voice-Elliot said. *Act as if you know exactly what hand your opponents are holding.*

That was the thing. Worst-case scenario, they still had better hands then I did.

I was screwed.

"I fold," I said, my eyebrows pushing together in frustration. If I kept losing, eventually I was going to look like Sasquatch: nothing but a huge frown and a big old unibrow. Sexy. Not.

Jesse cackled and called. And gleefully scooped up everyone's chips. Alana's eyes widened—he had totally invaded her space to grab at her stash—but she didn't say anything. That half-smile apparently hadn't been worth as much as she'd thought. She chewed at her lip furiously.

I sighed, squinted, and sat up straighter in my seat. "Another hand?" Jesse looked surprised, but I pressed on. "Come on, people, um, are we playing, or what?"

Or what, as it turned out.

I mean, not that we didn't play. We played exactly five more hands. And then I had to call it a night. Not because I didn't want to keep going, but rather because by that point I was completely tapped out. I had no more cash, and no one was interested in playing for my tortoiseshell hair clip. Short of playing strip poker—which was *so* not happening—I was out of options.

Jesse was the big winner of the night. Which wasn't a surprise to anyone who'd, like, had eyes in their head during the game. He won almost every hand. I knew he was a decent player, but nothing like this. Even Marcus was stunned.

"Good game," he said, shaking Jesse's hand grudgingly at the end of the evening.

Jesse nodded. "You too." Whatever, he could afford to be magnanimous after he'd walked off with all of our cash. If I was going to keep playing poker, I was going to have to find a new babysitting gig or something, and soon. Maybe Maxine would pay me to walk her?

Yeah, not so much.

I busied myself clearing up. This was officially the second time I'd been humiliated by the joint efforts of Jesse and Alana. That was two times more than the approved humiliation level recommended by doctors and teen-magazine advice columnists. I was just stuffing some trash into the garbage bag when a voice came out of nowhere, breathing all sorts of hot air on the back of my neck.

"Good game, Cass."

I stepped backward and directly into Jesse. Super awkward—perfect.

"You think?" I stammered. "I mean, I guess it must have been, for you."

He actually laughed, a short, easy chuckle that, to me, demonstrated just exactly how over me he really was. *Ha-ha-ha, isn't it amusing how badly I beat your butt?* "Nah, you were good," he insisted.

"But you were better."

"I didn't know you played poker."

"I didn't," I said. "I learned."

"Oh, yeah?"

"Well," I reminded him, "I've had some free time lately."

He had the manners to look a drop embarrassed by this, his cheek flushing slightly. "Right," he said. I held my breath for a moment, wondering if he would somehow say something that would some-how, suddenly, make sense of all of his skankiness. He looked like he might be considering that.

Instead, though, he nodded his head shortly, like he'd just remembered something. Maybe the fact that Alana was waiting for him out in the front hall. "Good game," he said, and strode back out of the room.

"Yeah," I agreed, to no one in particular.

It took about thirteen minutes for me to stop trembling after he'd gone.

Ten

I woke up the next morning with a deep sense that something was Not Right.

Which was weird, considering that it was February 22, or: 2/22, which to me was incredibly lucky. I love stuff like that—repeating numbers and unintended patterns and whatever. To me it always seems like proof that Fate is somewhere out there, and—with any luck—working for me. But this morning there was a suspicion gnawing at the back of my mind. I dug up my lucky earrings—a pair of sapphire studs that Dad had given me for my last birthday (he knows I also love birthstone jewelry)—in a vague effort to ward off the unsettled feeling in my stomach.

Unfortunately, the sapphires totally fell down on the job. Something was definitely up.

"Something is definitely up."

Elliot rubbed his eyes and looked up at me, the glow of the computer screen illuminating his eyes and making him look slightly alien and a little bit creepy. "How do you mean?" he asked, sounding doubtful.

I'd chased him down in the library during a free period; I could tell he was torn between wanting to talk to me and wanting desperately to turn back to whatever extra-credit project he was currently geeking out on.

"I can feel it in my bones," I said, borrowing a favorite expression from my grandmother. She was very big on feeling things in her bones. Her bones knew all sorts of stuff—when it was going to rain, when my father was calling with bad news, when a Social Security check was going to be coming in the mail. . . . Those were good, helpful bones.

I figured some of it had to be genetic.

My bones had been nagging at me all day. It didn't help that when I got to my locker before first period, I found that my lucky horseshoe sticker had somehow lost its stick. All that was left was some tacky glue residue mucking up the inside of my locker door.

Elliot looked unimpressed at this amazing feat of physiology. He squinted at me. "And your bones are saying . . . what, exactly?"

I took a deep breath. "I think Jesse cheated last night."

There, that was it. Now it was out and in the open. I mean, I realized how it sounded, and I didn't want to be pegged as some kind of sore loser, but really, there was no other explanation available.

Elliot sighed and turned away from the computer. I'd definitely gotten his attention. Unfortunately, he seemed sort of weary. "What makes you think he cheated?"

"Other than the fact that he won, like, almost every single hand?"

"You said yourself he was an experienced player."

"So is Marcus," I pointed out. "For that matter, so are you. I mean, it'd be one thing if he had just wiped the floor with me. But he wiped the floor with *all* of us. Even his friends."

"True," Elliot conceded reluctantly. "But Cass, do you have any idea how hard it is to actually cheat at poker? Basically, you're either playing with a bogus deck or you can see everyone else's hand. And he was using Kelly's deck, so we know that's not the issue."

"Well . . . ," I hedged.

"You think he could see our hands?" Elliot asked, his voice rising skeptically. "Come on, we're better than that. Give yourself a little bit of credit."

"I don't care," I said stubbornly, aware on some level that I sounded like a bratty three-year-old. "He's not good enough to beat every single one of us at every single hand. Even those guys on TV aren't *that* good."

"He didn't win every single hand," Elliot countered.

I took a deep breath, forcing myself to be calm. Or, at least, calm-*er*. "He lost twice, Elliot. *Twice*. All evening. It's weird. I mean, I've known him for a while. He used to brag to me whenever he'd won at anything. I'd remember if he were so completely and totally super-fantastic at poker."

"You did say he was good," Elliot replied.

"*Good* is different from *completely* and *totally super-fantastic*," I insisted. "This is in a different category."

Elliot ran his fingers through his hair, making it stand up in a million different directions. He was so frazzled, it was cute. But that had nothing to do with anything. "I have something to say," he began. "I don't think you're going to like it."

"You're going to say I'm being this way because it pissed me off to see Jesse and Alana together last night," I guessed.

"Sort of," Elliot said sheepishly. "Except I might have said 'upset you.'"

"Yeah, fine, sure—you knew it bugged me to have to spend the evening with them. But my bones are telling me that there's something up with Jesse's game, and my bones don't lie. Don't you think it's weird how, out of the blue, he was just *dying* to play with us? You guys have been playing cards for a while now and he's never wanted in on your game before."

"I figured it just had to do with you, Cass—that he wanted to play against you since he heard that you'd gotten good." Elliot looked at me like he wasn't sure how I was going to take this last comment.

I snorted. "Yeah, I'm sure that's it. He just couldn't wait to test my skills."

"Cheating is hard to do," Elliot said again, in case I had forgotten that piece of information in the last three seconds since we'd been talking. "Why would Jesse do something like that?"

"You mean, why would someone as classy and upstanding as Jesse screw over his ex-girlfriend, his current girlfriend, and a table full of close friends and semi-acquaintances? Gosh, I don't know. I mean, I would never expect that sort of behavior from the little Boy Scout who, you know, *cheated on his girlfriend of two years with her best friend*."

Elliot coughed loudly. "Ah, um . . ." He faltered.

I put my hand on his shoulder to stop him before he spontaneously self-destructed. He was so mortified, I had to feel bad for him. "Dude, I'm just saying. I'm not buying that Jesse just spent all night getting ultra-lucky. A very wise person once told me that you've got to play poker as if there were no such thing as luck." I flashed my most winning grin at Elliot, hoping that he would be persuaded. It was a grin that had landed me a two-dollar raise in my allowance, HBO on Demand, and my name added to my father's emergency credit card. For the moment, though, Elliot seemed to be fairly impervious to its strengths. I held my breath.

"You may have a point," Elliot said finally. He took off his glasses, laid them on the table next to him, and looked at me. The green in his eyes glinted with intensity. "So what now?"

"Here's the thing." I smiled. "I have a plan."

Elliot and I found Jesse in the gym, shooting hoops with Dennis and Jake. Those guys were like Siamese triplets. It was unclear to me whether this free period was self-appointed or not. Not that it mattered to me, anyway.

We walked into the room just as Jesse sank a three pointer. Shocker: The ball swished cleanly through the net. It was like the rim didn't even exist.

"Nice," I said admiringly, coming up behind him.

He turned, clearly surprised to see me. "Thanks," he said, somewhat taken aback. "Uh, what's up?"

"Good game the other night," I said casually, like he hadn't marched into my new friend's house with my ex–best friend on his arm and proceeded to totally ream me. No, nothing like that.

"Yeah?" he said dubiously. "'Cause I was thinking maybe you weren't too into it."

"Hey, I mean, fair is fair," I said, resisting an almost visceral urge to choke on the words. "I guess you're just that good."

I was treading into dangerous territory. There was a chance that Jesse would see through my blatant attempts to appeal to his supersize ego.

He grinned, flashing his baby blues at me. "It's cool of you to be able to admit that."

My nostrils flared, but I felt Elliot's hand on my elbow and I took a deep breath. "I try."

Elliot stepped forward. "Anyway," he said, clearing his throat nervously, "we were wondering if you guys would want to play again."

Jesse glanced at Jake and Dennis, who both shrugged noncommittally. It wasn't the rave response that we'd hoped for, but it would do. "Sure. Though I'm not sure I understand why you guys are so eager to give your money away."

Elliot's eyes flashed, and I could see him bite his tongue. That was good. Pissing Jesse off really wasn't going to solve anything. At least—not yet.

"We're playing Friday," I told Jesse.

"We'll be there," he promised.

"This is never going to work," Kelly complained to me. Her hair was pulled into two separate pigtails that pointed downward, adding to her dejected appearance, and she was dressed in head-to-toe black. The overall effect was quite dramatic.

"Are you kidding? It's brilliant, however the whole thing plays out."

Operation Revenge was tonight, and I was ready. In fact, I was in such high spirits that I was sporting my favorite pink silver glitter Stila eye pencil—the one that had gone into permanent hibernation in the wake of my devastating breakup with Jesse. It was called Spaghetti Strap, and it made an awesome complement to what I thought of as my lucky T—rather, a bright pink tank top with flashy rhinestone studs along the straps. Visually, Kelly and I were on opposite ends of the spectrum, and it looked like we might be fairly yin and yang emotionally as well.

I grabbed her by the shoulders. "Kelly, this is a win-win situation," I explained.

She smirked. "Unless, of course, Jesse makes off with all of our money again."

I sighed wearily and turned my head to where Elliot was sitting cross-legged on Kelly's bed. "Elliot. Explain, please, our mission?"

"It *is* kind of well thought out," Elliot began reluctantly. "My plan: We tape the poker game like it's a reality show. No one will protest if we tell them it's for our project for film class."

"Then we can study the footage later, after the game is over," I jumped in eagerly.

"Oh, you mean *after* we've had our butts kicked by Jesse?" Kelly asked sulkily.

"Yes, there is a small monetary investment required," I admitted, "but you don't have to go in on every hand. I mean, no one's going to fault you for cutting your losses."

"They'll just never play with me again."

"But you just said you didn't even *want* to play tonight!" I cried, exasperated. I understood Kelly's hesitation—after all, I'd lost plenty of cash myself at that last game—but, seriously, this was going to be good.

Kelly nodded. "Exactly," she said.

Now she was talking like a Wes Anderson movie. There was no figuring her out, so I decided instead to plow ahead with my brilliant scheme. "So we study the footage and—*voilà!*—if Jesse has been scamming us, we've got him cornered. We expose him for the cheating, sneaky fraud that he is."

"And if he isn't cheating, but he's just really that good?" Kelly asked archly.

"Then I'm a little embarrassed," I admitted, "but we go ahead and edit the footage into a *High School World Series of Poker* vérité sort of thing. We can be the Michael Moores of Midvale. Either way, we ace the project. Teenagers playing cards?" I shivered. "Ooh, edgy."

"That's a low blow, appealing to my sense of 'edge,'" Kelly growled. She looked at Elliot. "And you approve of this little revenge plot she's got cooked up?"

Elliot bit his lip. "It does seem like Jesse's been on a hot streak lately. Who knows? And what have we got to lose?"

Kelly opened her mouth to reply, but, believe it or not, Elliot jumped in first. "Don't answer that," he said. She shut her mouth dutifully and glared at him.

"Awesome!" I chirped, clapping my hands together enthusiastically. "Who's got the tripod?"

Kelly raised her hand, still with the eyes of death.

"Cool," I said, grabbing her hand and dragging her toward the living room. "Let's go set up."

When the doorbell rang this time, I was ready for it.

"I've got it!" I trilled, practically skipping toward the front hall. Elliot looked at me like I had seven heads, and Kelly was still sulking somewhere in the kitchen, but I wasn't going to let their doubts dampen my enthusiasm.

"Welcome!" I announced brightly as I pulled the door open. My face fell when I realized who it was. "Oh," I said, turning and leading the way back into the apartment. "Hi."

"Gee, it's great to see you, too," Marcus said, deadpan. He, Andy, and James had come together, and they followed me toward the living room.

"Give her a break," Andy shrieked, play-slapping at Marcus's arm. "She's gotta be nervous about playing against Jesse again."

"Yeah, I mean, *I'm* nervous about playing against Jesse again," James chimed in.

"Relax, guys," I told them. "It'll be fine. No one could get that lucky twice in a row."

"Oh, we try to play as if there were no such thing as luck," Andy rushed to explain.

I waved her off. "I know, I know, I've been filled in. What I'm saying is that there's a chance we could turn things around tonight."

"Well, it's always nice to keep hope alive," Marcus said sarcastically.

"Sit, get yourself some chips—the guacamole is homemade," I said. The doorbell chimed again, causing James to visibly flinch. I, however, jumped right up into the air with excitement.

"I'll get that!" I insisted, and dashed off again.

"Okay, so," I began, "we just want to let everyone know that we'd like to tape the game tonight."

I wasn't sure whether I expected people to be cool with the idea, or to think it was insanely weird, so I decided to overcompensate by grinning like a maniac and sending my voice into a pitch that only dogs could hear.

I was met with seven blank stares. Kelly and Elliot were in on the scheme, of course. Marcus, James, Jake, Dennis, Andy, and Jesse seemed confused. Alana, on the other hand, was patting her head like she wished maybe she'd done something different with her hair today. She did love the spotlight, Alana.

"What for?" Jake asked, seeming completely perplexed.

"It's for our film class," Kelly said, jumping in quickly. Smart—everyone in school knew that she was way into movies, so the whole thing would sound much more believable coming from her.

Besides, we *were* doing it for our film class. Sort of.

"Have you started your project yet, Alana?" Kelly asked pointedly.

Alana coughed delicately and tossed her curtain of hair over one shoulder. "Um, no, not yet. We're still sort of . . . thinking through some concepts."

Oh, I am so sure.

Alana was not exactly known for thinking through concepts to their fullest. Historically, I'd always been sort of the "ideas girl" in our friendship. If I had to bet (which, no thanks—there'd be enough of that shortly), I'd say she was waiting for Katy to come up with some kind of epiphany. I'd also say she was in for kind of a long wait.

But I digress.

"Well," Kelly continued, straining to match my bizarrely enthusiastic tone, "*our* concept was to do, like, a cross between, you know, *Laguna Beach* meets *Celebrity Poker Showdown*." "Peppy" didn't hang that convincingly on Kelly—it came off more like "hyper-medicated"—but, points to the girl: She really was giving it her all.

I glanced at Jesse, apprehensive. He appeared to be mulling the whole thing over. He was squinting, which usually meant he was concentrating hard. If we let him go on for too much longer, he was going to wind up cross-eyed.

Alana sidled up to Jesse and nudged him suggestively. "What's the big deal?" She pouted. "You look hot tonight.

I took that to mean, in Alana-speak, "*I look hot tonight.*" I resisted the urge to barf. At least her charm, repulsive as it was to me, generally worked on members of the male persuasion.

"What the hell?" he said finally. "Could be cool." Either I was wrong about his scam, or he was more driven by ego than I'd ever even realized.

Once Jesse the high school demigod had spoken, everyone else began to shift in their seats and murmur variations on their agreements. I smiled with satisfaction. "My sentiments exactly."

Yeah, my ex-boyfriend was not camerashy *at all*.

I mean, I'd kind of always known that Jesse was sort of vain—he was one of the few boys I knew who kept a small mirror on the inside of his locker door. And checked it regularly between classes. And felt totally free to re-apply product as his hair texture evolved throughout the day. But now that there was a camera fixed on him, his obsession with himself shot up to a shocking new level.

"Should I deal you in, baby?" he asked Kelly, winking at her and laughing.

I had to give Kelly credit for not collapsing in hysterics right then and there. She wasn't exactly the "baby" type. I knew she was concentrating her every last ounce of strength so as not to leap out of her chair and toss the bowl of tortilla chips upside down over Jesse's head.

"Sure, yeah," she said, smiling at him flirtatiously. Poor sucker, he had no idea she was joking. "I'm feeling lucky tonight."

Jesse chuckled at that. "Cass is feeling pretty lucky too," he said.

I blinked when I heard my name being called. "Hmm?" I asked, munching down on a chip.

"I said, you're feeling lucky," Jesse repeated. He pointed at my chest.

I crossed my arms over my boobs self-consciously. They weren't exactly tiny, and it tended to weird me out when people just pointed at them outright. "Um, what?"

"Your lucky tank top," he said.

Oh, right. That. I used to wear it whenever I had a test. Jesse would know that. Seeing as how he was my boyfriend for two years, until I caught him sucking my former best friend's face off.

I was surprised that he remembered. Surprised, and a little bit touched. But mostly grossed out. Jesse sucked. It wasn't too hard to keep that in mind these days. Particularly given that he and his friends were now pretty much staring at my chest. I rolled my eyes and shook it off. "Well, we all have our little rituals," I said, pointing at his lighter. As usual, it sat on the table next to him. It never moved position, even when he was dealing. Talk about a security blanket. And he didn't even smoke, the freak.

"Touché," Jesse said, winking at me. He really was getting a little too free with the winking tonight. Someone needed to tell him that it was sort of repulsive.

Jesse slapped two cards down on the table in front of Kelly, who managed to turn up the corners of the cards without revealing even the slightest hint of emotion. I was in awe of her poker face, for real. He dealt for the rest of the group, who reacted to their cards with varying levels of impassivity. Elliot, of course, was cool and calm as always. I decided he might be my poker hero.

I hoped I was managing to keep it

together, but on the inside, my heart was beating so intensely that I was pretty sure everyone could see it through the tank top. Lucky, my ass. I could have used a lucky ski parka or something. Either the telltale heart or my sweaty forehead was going to give me away, and soon.

My cards were crap, but I didn't care. I was way into exposing Jesse. There was no doubt in my mind that he was cheating. It just seemed so much like something he would do. Mind you, I may have been just a touch biased, but Jesse did not strike me as the most trustworthy person. At least, not these days, anyway.

By the third hand in, Jesse was up twenty dollars. It could have been good playing. It could have been good cards. It could have been both. But I doubted it.

Kelly was awesome. Every hand, she'd get up and reposition the tripod. Dad had lent me his digital video cam for the night. (I'd told him I was working on my film class project, which—hey—wasn't a lie.)

It was funny to see how people reacted when they knew they were being filmed. Elliot basically shrank back into his seat in concentration. Which, like, for him, was totally normal behavior. Dennis's features were frozen into this crazy Cro-Magnon expression that I'm guessing he thought was sexy. Alana ran to the bathroom every twelve seconds or so to reapply a healthy dose of Lancôme Juicy Tubes: Desert. Seriously, her lips were so glossy they looked like they were going to slide right off. I would have given her the heads up if it weren't for the economy-size grudge I was still holding.

I couldn't believe I'd ever thought that Jesse looked like the guy from *Smallville*. (Clark Kent, not Lex Luther. Though the guy who plays Lex Luther is *really* drool-worthy too. I'm just saying.) The longer we played, the more his eyes were flashing and the brighter his grin got. He teeth were totally threatening to devour his face. And Alana had taken on the slack-jawed gaze of a drugged religious fanatic.

It was astonishing. Once upon a time, I was close to both of those people. And if you'd told me then that, sometime soon, they'd both betray me and I'd find myself befriending an intense but cool Goth-chick and her quiet, sweet, slightly geeky techno-nerd friend, I would have told you you were sipping some very toxic Kool-Aid. But, nonetheless, here we were.

Jesse cackled and scooped up a pile of poker chips.

"*Man!*" Marcus exclaimed, slapping the flat of his palm against the table.

Jesse leered and leaned forward, managing to get in all of our faces at once. I was psyched; this had to make for good footage. "Another hand?" he asked, practically drooling on the cards. He palmed his lucky lighter and caressed it in a manner that made me feel actually sort of dirty.

I forced down the bile that threatened to spew from my throat and smiled like a morning news anchor. I was down fifteen dollars and had almost depleted this month's allowance. This was the beginning of the end, for me.

I looked at Jesse, forcing myself to gaze directly into the hypnotic, *Magnolia*-Svengali light. I was impervious. I was all-knowing. And I was *so* going to catch him in the act.

"Totally," I said. "Deal me in."

Eleven

"I think the thing to do is to just, um, freeze-frame right there . . . no—rewind . . ."

"Cass, please. It's late. We're tired, and the frame, she has been frozen for fully twenty-seven minutes. There's nothing on this tape."

Kelly had been a trouper for the first hour or so of our post-poker video rehash. Obviously she had a Mac, so it took no time for us to upload the evening's footage onto her hard drive. She was fully familiar with iMovie, as was I, and Elliot . . . well, Elliot plus computers kind of always equaled no problem. But as Kelly so delicately pointed out, we'd been going over the footage for, um, a while now, and though I was carefully scanning for any unsavory activity, so far, I had come up with a big, fat zero.

Still—I held out hope.

"Look, I'm sorry," I said, leaning forward toward the monitor and holding my finger down on the mouse so that the video was stuck in an endless loop of fast-forward/rewind. "I know everyone at school thinks that Jesse is like some kind of omnipotent being. I mean, I thought it myself for a while. But even I know that no one could possibly be *that* lucky. He and Dennis totally cleaned house in the last two poker games. That's ridiculous."

"I agree," Kelly said. "Maybe he's a wizard. Maybe it's voodoo. Maybe we're all just figments of his twisted imagination." She arched an eyebrow at me dryly.

Elliot shook his head. I could tell the whole conversation was killing him; it was bad enough that we were speculating about luck, but to drag magic into the discussion was just plain heresy.

"He must be unmasked," I insisted, frowning. "If for no reason other than the fact that he was acting like such a jackass tonight. I mean, really—the way he was making out with that cigarette lighter? Boy doesn't even smoke . . . ."

I stopped.

And looked up.

I was having a "eureka" moment.

"Cass?" Elliot said, sounding concerned. "Are you okay?"

I cocked my head to one side, lost in concentration. Then I leaned forward again, poised to rewind the video.

"Ugh." Kelly sighed. "You are only torturing yourself. Yes, I get that he is, like, your arch nemesis, and I get that what he did with Alana is totally repulsive, but Cass—let it go."

"Shh!" I said, waving at her frantically. I beckoned the two of them toward a tiny spot on the screen. "Look."

They grudgingly obliged me, each leaning over one shoulder. Kelly smelled liked that shampoo from the semi-pornographic commercial. Elliot smelled like Ban. I knew it was Ban because my dad uses it, too. For a moment I kind of wished Elliot smelled like something other than my father.

"What are we looking at?" Kelly asked,

sounding bored and impatient, and taking me out of my little olfactory reverie.

"You tell me," I said. "I pose this question: Why would my ex-boyfriend, an insanely fit, compulsively competitive athlete-type, be grabbing at a cigarette lighter so intently? Considering, you know, that he hasn't taken a puff off a cigarette since his twelfth birthday, when a friend nicked a pack from his mom's dresser and dared Jesse to try one."

Kelly shrugged. "You said it yourself. Everyone has their little lucky totems. You're wearing that tank top. And the eyeliner to match."

"The eyeliner's not lucky, just cute," I corrected her. "And, anyway, you're missing the point."

"That's because it's one fifteen in the morning," Kelly said, yawning. "Seriously, I need my beauty slee—"

"Hold on," Elliot cut in, sounding excited. "Freeze-frame right there." He reached over my shoulder and did it for me. Now it felt like we were engaged in some kind of alternate, vaguely flirty version of the game Twister. "Do you see it?"

"See me losing my entire babysitting

fund in one night? Yes, I see it. In fact, I lived it. So maybe I don't need to be *re*-living it," Kelly suggested, half-joking but half really not.

"Look closer, Kells," Elliot said, using a nickname I didn't even know existed. Kelly didn't strike me as a "Kells" kind of girl, but she let it go, so what the heck did I know, anyway? "Look at the lighter."

Suddenly Kelly shifted herself closer to me. Now I could smell the orange Tic Tacs on her breath. "Oh, man," she murmured. "What an ass."

"I will resist the urge to offer a hearty 'I told you so,'" I said smugly.

Elliot thrust his index finger toward a point on the screen. "The lighter. It's working like a mirror for him. The way he's got it poised just in front of the deck when he deals—"

"He can see what cards he's passing to all of us," I said. My heart quickened. *What a* total *ass*. I mean, I'd completely known he was cheating, but somehow, the proof still grossed me out, big-time.

Kelly grabbed the mouse out of my hand and scanned the tape forward a few minutes. "There—now he's sending some kind of signal to Dennis. No wonder the two of them have been raking it in."

Sure enough, when you looked carefully, you could see Jesse ever-so-casually splay out one, two, or three fingers on his free hand. There also seemed to be a complicated system of knuckle raps and finger taps that to the casual observer would appear to be nothing more than a tiny physical tic. They obviously didn't think we'd ever play the tape back and study it so intently. But, yeah, Dennis was completely reacting based on the hand signals Jesse was feeding him. And they're staring off into the distance "nonchalantly," as though nothing were amiss at all.

"Elliot, you always said that it was almost impossible to cheat at poker," I remembered.

"It is," he agreed. "This is one of the only ways to do it. And, man—he's doing it well."

"He's very good at cheating," I observed.

"Ugh," Kelly said, making a face. "What a sleaze. Just a cheater, through and through."

"Worse that that," I continued. "Keep in

mind whom he's cheating *on*. It's his girl-friend, and one of his best friends. Barf. That guy has, like, no soul whatsoever."

I guessed that I should have felt relieved or validated or something. I mean, it was kind of gratifying to know that my suspicions had been proven correct. But I felt oddly deflated instead. I'd spent two years with Jesse. I didn't exactly want to know that he'd been a total heel the entire time. It hardly spoke to my own better judgment.

"I feel like . . . I feel like I should tell Alana," I said, surprised to hear the words coming out of my mouth. "I mean, he's scamming her. She kind of deserves to know."

Kelly stared at me like I was an alien. "Um, hello? Are we talking about the same Alana here? Alana Mark, the girl who *claimed* to be your best friend and then ran off with your boyfriend?"

"That's the one," I agreed glumly.

"And you think she deserves *your* consideration?" Kelly was totally incredulous. Which, come to think of it, I didn't exactly blame her.

"I . . . I don't know," I said, feeling extremely confused. On the one hand, I despised Alana these days. That was for sure. But on the other hand, somehow, knowing that Jesse was screwing her over kind of made me feel bad for her. On a totally other hand, did any of this erase the fact that she completely stomped all over my feelings? No way. But still . . .

There were way too many hands here to consider.

"My head hurts," I said, grumpy. "Ugh." I pushed my chair back from the computer and stood up. "I think I need to sleep on this." I turned to Elliot. "Do you want a ride home?"

"You're not staying over?" Kelly asked, surprised. It had sort of become a ritual—the staying over, and the hitting of the buffet in the morning for brunch. This friendship was wreaking serious havoc on my eating habits.

I shook my head, trying to work some of the kinks out of my neck in the process. I hadn't realized how tense I'd been all night, but now, my shoulders had crept somewhere up toward the vicinity of my ears. Awesome. "I think I need to be in my own bed. Besides, Maxine is starting to develop abandonment issues." It was true. The last couple of days I'd come home from school to find her water dish overturned in the middle of the kitchen, which I figured was some sort of not-so-subtle message about her feelings on my increased absences.

"Yeah, that'd be great," Elliot said, pushing his glassed back up from the tip of his nose and shouldering his ever-present messenger bag. I had no idea what he carried in that thing—other than crazy-thick books about stuff like science. Could've been top-secret government secrets, could've been back issues of *Us Weekly*. The likelihood was that it was neither. But I was way too tired, and too bummed out, to give the matter too much thought this evening.

Yeah, I'd sleep on it. Things always looked better in the morning, after all. Or so I hoped.

As we left the apartment, I crossed my fingers behind my back, just to be safe.

The car ride was deathly quiet. My mind was a minefield of emotions. I was still sort of shaken up just at the mere fact of having spent an evening with Alana and Jesse—no matter how much bravado I piled on, the truth was that it rattled me, big-time, to see them together. Then there was the whole fuel-to-the-fire thing: Jesse was just a cheat, through and through. Add to that some bizarre and unexpected lingering loyalty toward Alana and I was one very mixed-up chick. Elliot hadn't said a word since we'd buckled up either, but I was too distracted to really ask him about it.

I clicked my blinker on and made a left turn down off of the Strip and onto the main road that took us to the burbs. Cabs whizzed by on either side of us. Vegas doesn't know from late, of course. People here behave like it is 10 p.m. on a Saturday night pretty much any old time of the week. For some reason the whole thing struck me as extra-super-surreal this evening. Maybe because I was having such an extra-super-surreal night to begin with.

The silence was beginning to verge on awkward. I clicked on the radio, and suddenly the car was suffused with a crazy thumping bass line, The Pussycat Dolls or that track from Madonna's latest personal reinvention. Not an improvement over the silence. I quickly clicked it off.

I cleared my throat nervously. Elliot rubbed his nose. I wondered why we were suddenly acting like such spazzes around each other. It's not like he'd discovered that *his* ex was some sort of pathological cheater.

Not that I even knew who any of Elliot's exes were. I mean, now that I thought about it, I knew absolutely *nothing* about Elliot's romantic life. That was sort of weird. Usually, when you first become friends with a guy, your immediate thought is whether or not he has a girlfriend—i.e., how platonic your relationship with him will be. The issue had never come up with Elliot. I guess because I'd been in such hardcore rebound-mode when we'd met that I just wasn't thinking of *anyone* that way. And then, we were just sort of . . . in the friend zone.

It's not like Elliot wasn't attractive, though he wasn't exactly my usual type. He was Jesse's polar opposite, which had its pros and cons. Where Jesse was buff and athletic, Elliot was wiry and quiet. But, like, he totally had a cute face, and those hazel eyes were completely intense. I guess, when I really stopped to think about it, I'd always sort of assumed that if Elliot was going to end up with anyone, it'd be Kelly. They were such good friends, it seemed like the next logical step.

Why was I even thinking about this, now?

Oh, right—because the alternative was listening to a manufactured pop group "sing" to electronic beats. Not that I'm opposed to pop music, but it was just kind of setting the wrong vibe. I wasn't feeling very "pop-y" tonight.

I turned left onto Elliot's street, tapping my fingernails on the steering wheel. I pulled into his driveway and set the car in park, fidgeting a little bit. What was my damage? I turned to him.

"Sorry if I've been kind of a drag tonight," I said. "Even if I suspected that Jesse was cheating all along, it still sort of took me by surprise." I shook my head. "I wasn't expecting to feel this freaked out about it."

Elliot nodded slowly. "I think it's only natural," he said quietly. "But the thing is"—he looked thoughtful—"that I really don't want you to feel bad."

I rolled my eyes. "Easier said than done."

Elliot smiled. "I know, but I mean . . ." He sounded like he was struggling with the words a little bit, which was kind of cute.

"That, like, *specifically*, I don't want *you* to feel bad."

Hmm. Now he was just speaking in tongues. I tilted my head toward him. "Huh?"

"I just—" Now Elliot was squirming. What was going on? "BecauseIreallycare-aboutyou."

The words tumbled out of his mouth so quickly that it took me a beat to process them. Elliot cared about me?

Just as I realized what he was getting at, I felt his fingers on my forearm. I looked up, startled. He was gazing at me quite intently.

The thoughts rushed through my mind like one of those electronic billboard banners you see outside of a casino, the one that announces all of the upcoming shows and stuff. *Oh, God—Elliot likes me. I mean,* likes *me, likes me. Like, maybe wants to make out with me. Which—what? Where? When? How?*

And then, before I could take my little mind-trip any further, Elliot had fully leaned across the front seat and planted one on me.

Yeah, we were kissing. We were *kissing*!

It was awesome. Like, really awesome.

I had totally lucked out.

★

Kissing Elliot was amazing but also really bizarre. He was nothing like Jesse— much softer, less confident, more gentle. It was nice, but it was also definitely different. And unexpected. And different. And did I mention unexpected?

When we finally came up for air, I noticed that Elliot was flushed. "I'm sorry, Cass," he stammered. "I, uh, don't know what came over me. It's just—I'd been thinking for a while . . ."

He *had*? For a *while*?

Elliot was a friend, a poker tutor, and a classmate. And—oh, God—we had a project due.

All at once, the ramifications of kissing Elliot hit me full-on. Like, if there were serious feelings involved, and we were kissing, but we weren't going to be boyfriend-girlfriend, things could get majorly awkward. I had just gotten to know him and Kelly. I wasn't emotionally stable enough to make a whole new set of friends for the second time in one school year. And an Aries and a Libra? Could. Just. Not. Happen.

Like, how much of a while? And how had I missed it so completely?

"Don't apologize," I interrupted. "It was nice."

"Yeah?" he said, his eyes sparkling hopefully.

"Yeah . . . ," I began carefully.

"But."

"Yeah . . . but." How to say this? There was no way to deliver the news that wouldn't sound at least semi-awful. "I'm kind of a mess right now. I mean, I love being friends with you, but I just don't know if I'm ready to date." An Aries. It was the truth.

For a split second, all of Elliot's features crumbled, almost like his face was going to melt right off. He looked totally devastated. But he gathered himself together gamely.

"I get it," he said, obviously struggling mightily to sound upbeat. "Honestly." He fiddled with the zipper on his messenger bag. "I like being friends with you, too." He kind of made a face like he couldn't believe what he had just said.

"Good," I replied. "So that's what we'll—"

I stopped. He was already out of the car and halfway up his front walk, messenger bag slapping against his leg as he walked. His eyes were cast downward.

I rolled down the passenger-side window and opened my mouth to call out to him. But what would I say?

I rolled the window back up.

I watched Elliot go into his house, then I kicked the car back into reverse. I hit the radio and drove off to the sounds of America's Top Forty.

Somehow, it seemed appropriate. I mean, whatever.

As it turned out, I was apparently the only member of our little clique who hadn't known about Elliot's feelings for me. Kelly was stunned when I confessed as much to her.

"How could you have missed it?" she asked. I had cornered her in school Monday morning just next to her locker. She pulled out a notebook and slammed the door shut. We made our way down the hall toward Albon's class. I was terrified at the prospect of having to face Elliot today. Sunday had passed with me in a continuous confused state of silence, staring blankly at his handle on IM but not daring to contact him. I mean, what was there even to say?

"You're kidding, right? I mean, were

there, like, signs that I was supposed to pick up on?"

Kelly fixed her peepers on me. It was quite intimidating, as they were heavily rimmed in what may or may not have been grease paint. "Okay, Exhibit A: He tutored you in poker."

"Because I begged him to," I said.

"That's not why he did it," she replied. "But whatever. Exhibit B: He was all about trying to calm you down last week, when you were freaking out about playing poker with Alana and Jesse."

"Because he's human, and I was, like, having a comprehensive nervous breakdown. I mean, that's just, um, *manners*."

Kelly gave me a "whatever" kind of look and continued. "And finally, there's the way that he gets all sorts of quiet and awkward when you're around."

My eyes bugged out of my skull, and I stopped in my tracks. "You can't be serious," I protested.

"I swear. On Fellini."

Okay, she *was* serious.

"But Kelly," I pointed out, "Elliot is *always* quiet and awkward. That's just, like, his personality."

She shook her head. "It's different, the way he is with you."

I sighed. "Honestly? I never really thought about it. I mean, he's an Aries—it would never work with us."

"Horrors!" Kelly said, clapping one hand to her cheek in exaggeration. "Well, *clearly*, your love can never be."

I hip-checked her playfully. "I know you don't buy that stuff, but it's real to me. And, anyway, I always assumed that eventually *you* and Elliot would get together."

Now it was Kelly's turn to come to a screeching halt. "Are you out of your mind?" she demanded.

"Why is it so crazy?" I asked. "Obviously you guys are totally good friends."

"Exactly," Kelly said. "I've known Elliot since we were five years old. We were in kindergarten class together. He still remembers how I accidentally peed in my pants on the first day. You do not date the guy who has seen you pee in your pants. Ask him about it—he'll give you all the gory details."

"Um, no, thanks," I said, shuddering.

"Exactly," Kelly said. "When someone has seen you wet yourself by the finger-painting corner, it sort of takes the mystery out of it all."

"I hear you," I said. "Thankfully, I don't have any personal experience with the subject."

"Moving on," Kelly said. "So, you're not into him, then?"

"It's not that I'm not into him," I said slowly. "More like, I'd never thought about it before."

"And now that you're thinking about it?"

"Well, for starters, I'm obviously still on the rebound, big-time, from Jesse."

"Obviously."

"And then there's the fact that we're *so* not a match."

Kelly rolled her eyes with exasperation. "I can't believe you're going to blow off a great guy over something as silly as his astrological sign."

"I know you can't," I said, patting her arm fondly.

Kelly assured me that in a few weeks, things would go back to normal between Elliot and me. I knew that his grades mattered too much for him to let this little situation ruin our class project. We had some great footage that was going to make for a kick-ass film subject. We were going to take down one of Midvale High's über-heroes—and we were going to do it for credit.

Awesome.

I wasn't going to let something like a wayward kiss between cosmically mis-matched friends get in the way of that kind of karmic payback. Nuh-uh. And I knew that ultimately, Elliot wouldn't either.

I guess I felt like I hadn't fulfilled my quota of awkward moments for the week, because on Wednesday, I waited for Alana outside of her English class. She looked surprised to see me. Or rather, she looked surprised to see me *at first*. Her expression quickly mor-phed from bemused curiosity to mild annoyance.

She ran her fingers through her hair, per-haps forgetting my status as ex–best friend and, therefore, impervious to the magical powers of enchantment possessed by her fol-licles. I noticed that she was wearing a long-sleeved T-shirt from Fred Segal that we'd bought during a long weekend in Los Angeles with her parents a few years back. That had been a really fun trip. Alana and I thought we saw Drew Barrymore in the parking lot of Barneys, but on closer inspection we realized the girl in question was actually about a foot taller than Drew. But it had been the closest we'd come to a celeb-sighting, so we'd made a pact to tell people that it had totally been Drew, and we'd talked to her for seventeen whole minutes.

Alana really needed to get some new clothes. Her wardrobe was inducing post-traumatic stress flashbacks for me.

"Hi," I began tentatively. "I, uh, need to talk to you."

She narrowed her green eyes suspiciously. Now she looked like a creepy refugee from a horror movie. "Yeah?"

"Yeah." I swallowed and decided to go for broke. "It's about Jesse. He's, um, been cheating—"

"Not on me," she said, cutting me off. "Trust me."

Okay, ouch. But now that'd I'd started down this road, I wasn't sure if or how I should back off. "I wouldn't know about that. But that's not what I'm talking about."

"Oh?" she smirked. *Flip* went the hair again.

"It's the poker game."

"The one you lost? Badly?"

I nodded. "Alana, I know we're not friends these days"—*and frankly, that's totally your fault, you big ho*—"and maybe you have no reason to believe me, but you're gonna have to just trust me: Jesse's been cheating. He's been spotting cards. With a mirror. I mean, a lighter. Dennis is in on it. That's why the two of them keep raking it in."

I could tell from the glimmer in her eyes that there was at least a small part of her that saw how this could be true. But she was incredibly, understandably reluctant to let me know that.

"Why would I make something like this up?" I pressed.

"Because Jesse dumped you for me and then kicked your ass at poker and took all of your money?" she suggested.

Oh, right. That.

"Yeah, okay, but if you want to look at it that way—you dumped me for Jesse too. So I don't really have any motivation for helping you out."

"No, you really don't," Alana agreed. "So why are you?"

"I don't know," I admitted, realizing how totally deranged I sounded. "I mean, I'm still furious about you and Jesse hooking up."

For a moment, she softened. "I am sorry."

I waved my hand dismissively. That was just too much for me to deal with right now. "Whatever. I can't even get into that. I mean, I totally can't even go there."

"Okay," she said, nodding contritely. "I get that."

"But we were friends for a long time, and that doesn't just go away," I said. "And I guess it was one thing when Jesse was fooling around behind my back—I mean, that was awful enough. But now, I realize he's just, like, all in all, a scummy guy. And I felt like maybe you should know that." I took a deep breath and stepped backward a bit, giving her some space to process the information. I had no idea how she was going to take it. Her head could start spinning around any minute.

She tilted her head to one side, as though she was weighing the possibility that I could be telling the truth. Suddenly the head-spinning scenario seemed that much more likely. "I'm just supposed to take your word for it?" she asked finally.

"Nuh-uh," I said, shaking my head no. "I actually have proof."

Twelve

"That bastard!" Alana pushed away from the computer and stared at me, mouth agape.

I nodded tersely. "That was pretty much our feeling," I said matter-of-factly, jerking my head in Kelly's direction to indicate our solidarity on the matter.

"He's—I mean, that's just—and all this time—," she sputtered, her hair swinging wildly as she grew more and more frantic.

"All this time," Kelly repeated.

"What a total jerk!" Alana said finally, crossing her arms over her chest to signify that she had reached her ultimate breaking point.

"I know," I agreed. "I sort of couldn't believe it."

After I'd blown the whistle on Jesse to Alana, she'd wanted to see the proof with her own eyes. Not that I blamed her. If I hadn't seen Alana and Jesse getting down with my own two eyes, I don't think I ever would have bought it. I mean, some thoughts are just too, too outrageous. So, anyway, we met up with Kelly after school and went back to her place to watch the video. After that, Alana had no choice but to believe us.

"Um, okay," Kelly said, breaking into my little reverie, "here's a question that might be sort of touchy: Remind me again *why*, exactly, you're having such a hard time believing this about Jesse? I mean, this is a guy who cheated on his girlfriend of two years with her best friend."

At that, Alana and I both flushed guiltily and looked down at the floor.

I decided to tackle this one first. "I know he's slime," I began tentatively, "but you know, I wouldn't have been with him for so long if I'd thought he didn't have any redeeming qualities at all. I can despise him forever, but a small part of me needs for the relationship to be, you know, validated on some level, at least. Like, there has to be something about him that was worth my time."

"Yeah, and"—Alana paused to clear her throat self-consciously and I leaned in closer, incredibly interested in whatever she was going to say—"I mean, I thought he really cared about me. I would never have gone behind Cass's back, you know, like, if I thought it was just some random hookup." She looked at me intently. "We were going to tell you—at least, I was. Jesse and I talked about it. I promise, hurting you was the last thing that I wanted."

Yay?

No, to be honest, I did see her point. Not that it made me feel any better about what they'd done, but at least it made a tiny, minuscule, microscopic iota of sense.

"Um, I'm glad to hear that," I said gruffly.

She offered me a small, searching smile.

As reunions went, this one was hardly heartfelt. I mean, no one was leaping up to, like, "hug it out" or anything. But it was a step.

"Ahem," Kelly said, sitting up very straight in her special, spine-aligning chair. Kelly was extremely dedicated to things like posture, which I assumed had to do with how many hours a day she spent hunched over her computer. Alana and I both looked up at her questioningly.

"This is all very sweet and beautiful," she said, "and I'm glad you two are finally airing out, you know, your issues. But there's a larger problem here, which is that *your* ex-boyfriend"—she shot me a look—"and *your* current boyfriend"—she glanced accusingly at Alana—"is a total ass."

"And?" I said. After all, I had done my job—despite all of my little misgivings, I'd ultimately sucked it up and decided to be the mature one, and to talk to Alana about Jesse's poker scam.

Kelly shook her head in disbelief. "*And* . . . I think something needs to be done."

"Huh." I bit my lip. "I suppose you're right. But what?"

Alana, who'd been sitting pensively at my side at Kelly's desk, looked up. Her eyes sparkled with a devilish glint that I knew all too well. This was a glint that had gotten me into much, much, trouble. And I suspected it was about to get me into trouble yet again.

She raised her index finger as though she were raising her hand in class.

"I know we're not BFF again, Cass," she began. "We're probably not even 'F.' But I have an idea."

From: Kconn1@cynet.com
To: [Midvale HS, ALL]
CC:Amark@cynet.com,
Cparker7@cynet.com
Subject: WATCH YOUR BACK

Hey all you party people—check it out:
www.kconn/YOUAREHERE/cheater.avi.
   *Pay extra-special attention to the
dealer, his lighter, and his buddy sitting
right at his eleven o'clock.
   You can thank me later.
XX,
Your friends over HERE

"Awesome undercover skills, Kelly!"

"Yeah, really nice one!"

"What an ass."

"That jerk owes me fifty bucks from our last game . . ."

The e-mail blast to, um, our entire high

school was actually Alana's idea, as was the choice to post the incriminating video on Kelly's website. But I had to say, it was an amazing idea—devious in the extreme. People knew Alana and I were in on it somehow—clearly we were involved, what with being individually cc'd on the e-mail blast— but it was Kelly who was getting all the credit. Not that she minded in the least. She was proud of knocking Jesse down a few pegs.

For my part, I was sort of stunned at how quickly our classmates pounced on the trickle of blood in the water. I guess kids did set aside a sort of special reserve of disdain for the so-called "in crowd" and weren't all that disappointed to see a sports god felled. I personally couldn't blame them. Anyway, Jesse was a total persona non grata around the campus in the wake of this massive reveal. And I was kind of into it.

So we were suddenly the B-list celebrities of Midvale, what with people calling out to us and cheering when we passed them in the hall. It was almost like the end of just about any John Hughes film, for real. And I had a feeling our film class project had just taken a turn for the more complex. Which wasn't a bad thing.

Of course, that all depended on Elliot and me actually saying three words to each other. Ever since our smoochage, we'd mostly avoided each other around school. It wasn't all that difficult, though it did make me pretty self-conscious. I would come to film class early and bury myself somewhere toward the back—or else Elliot would. And now that I was one-third of Midvale's answer to Bunim-Murray, I was usually engaged in whatever conversation at the beginning or the end of class. The project wasn't due until mid-March. I had a few more weeks to decide how to deal with the sitch. Mostly I just kept asking myself, *What would Rory Gilmore do?* (And yes, I recognize that Rory Gilmore doesn't actually exist. But anyway, moving on . . .)

Today, for instance, I had somehow ended up sitting directly behind Elliot. Which was cool, because it meant I got to avoid that awkward-eye-contact and stuff. But it was also rather distracting, as I learned as the minutes of class ticked by.

Albon was giving a lecture on "ethics in television." Like, whether or not it's cool that we get to watch college kids having sex on camera on shows like *The Real World*.

Yawn. I wished he would come right out and say it: He'd seen Kelly's video, and he thought we were gross for taping Jesse and Dennis—even if they were the ones who were cheating in the first place. But instead, he was talking in circles and fostering "a healthy debate." Which was, it must be said, extremely boring.

I'd taken to tracing small circles on the page of my notebook. When I ran out of space for the circles, I began to loop long, winding lines around the dots.

It was abstract. I was into it.

I was also, truth be told, rather into the scruff of hair that crept down Elliot's neck and curled over the edge of his collar. He was wearing a striped rugby shirt that on anyone else might have looked inexcusably preppy but on Elliot was adorable in the most Seth Cohen sense of the term.

I shook my head. The boredom had gotten to me. No way was I fixating on Elliot's neck.

But, still . . . we hadn't really spoken—no more than an awkward "hi" in the halls, that is—in more than a week. Which, once upon a time, would have been normal for us. But these days, I had to admit, I really missed him. I missed him and his utter and complete disdain for my flaky, New Age "let's leave it in the hands of fate" attitude.

I had to deal with this. I needed to be friends with adorable Elliot and his adorable Seth Cohen neck-scruff.

The bell rang, and for a moment it seemed like I'd have my chance. Elliot stood and began stuffing his notebook into his messenger bag. He must have sensed me staring at him because he finally happened to glance up. His eyes widened questioningly.

I opened my mouth, having no idea what I was going to say.

"Hey."

I looked up, startled. It was Alana. We were allies now that we'd collaborated in screwing Jesse over, but that didn't mean we were, like, blood sisters or anything. It had only been a few days since our grand revenge. I didn't know how things between us were going to play out. And I had no idea what she wanted from me right now.

But talk about your timing.

"Uh, what's up?" I stammered.

"Can we . . . talk?" she asked me, sounding extremely uncertain.

It was a total trip to hear Alana sound so insecure. Even with everything that had gone down between us, it kind of broke my heart a little bit. But—I still needed to talk to Elliot.

"I . . . have a class . . . ," Elliot mumbled, his face sweaty and red.

Okay, so, um, maybe later, then?

I turned back to Alana. "I have . . . I mean . . ."

"Right," she said, getting it immediately.

Right. "I'll see you later," I said, and ran off, not knowing if I meant it or not.

Wednesday night was chili night at Chez Parker. You might think that we Vegasites wouldn't eat chili, what with how it's hot and heavy and we live in, like, the desert. It would make sense, I guess. But chili is one of the few things that I know how to make from scratch, and I make it well. Wednesday is Dad's night off from the restaurant, so I told him I'd take care of dinner. It seemed like the thing to do.

There are two good things about chili: It's very easy to make well, and you end up with a ton left over that you can freeze.

However, while you make it in one big pot, cleanup is not one of the better things about chili for dinner. There's a lot of scrubbing, and one has to be extremely vigilant about errant flecks of tomato—particularly if one is washing dishes in a pastel Juicy tank top. Which, as it happened, I was.

Dad had offered to do the dishes, like he always does when I take care of the cooking, but he looked so tired—like, seriously, I thought he'd go facedown into his chili bowl at any minute—that I had to take pity on him. Cut to me at the kitchen sink getting all sorts of sudsy while I try to be the dutiful daughter. Highly glamorous. Not. Maxine sat just at my feet, staring at me like my canine stalker. She didn't seem to understand that once the dinner dishes had made it from the table to the sink, there wasn't much chance she was making off with too many scraps. What can I say? My dog is not exactly a brain trust.

Given as how I was in a particularly domestic frame of mind (seriously—like, Rachael Ray, eat your heart out), you can imagine how totally unprepared I was for

211

my father to return to the kitchen only to tell me that "you have a visitor."

I shut off the faucet and stepped back from the sink. What had once been an extremely cute tank top was now splotchy and waterlogged. My hair, which I'd piled up into a crazy ponytail-bun-hybrid for dish duty, was fast unraveling down my back. I was wearing rubber gloves.

Suffice it to say, I was not expecting company.

I peeled the gloves off my hand. They were sticky with moisture. "A visitor?"

"A gentleman caller," Dad clarified.

I raised my eyebrow. Curiouser and curiouser, seeing as I how I knew so few gentlemen. And those few that I did know were unlikely to be calling on me.

It was only when I got into the hallway in all my maid-to-order splendor that I realized that a certain, tiny part of me had been hoping my house guest was Elliot. Which probably meant something. Something that I wasn't necessarily equipped to think about right exactly now.

It didn't matter, anyway, because it wasn't Elliot. And hence my disappointment. The person standing in my living room was, like, the exact polar opposite of Elliot.

Instead, it was Jesse.

And he looked pretty upset.

"What a . . . pleasant surprise?"

No way was Dad going to let me have Jesse in my room alone—I mean, he's laid back, but he's not, you know, insane—so instead we went out onto the patio. The screen door was totally not soundproof, but it did give the charming illusion of privacy. Which, this being Jesse, I wasn't even sure that I wanted.

"Yeah, sorry about that," Jesse said. "I guess I should have called first."

"I can't promise I would have picked up," I shot back. What could I say? I had a couple of months' worth of backed-up hurt, anger, and humiliation brewing inside of me. I'd managed to keep it at bay by avoiding Jesse all this time, but seeing as how he was standing right in front of me, that option seemed to be off the table. For the time being, at least. Hence the hostility.

"You know, I'm the one who should be mad," he said.

I snorted. "Really? Please, do tell."

"You completely shot me down—in front of, like, the whole school!"

"Well, then, maybe you shouldn't have been scamming, like, the whole school," I countered. "I mean, don't tell me you didn't have this coming to you."

"I don't think anyone is ever going to play poker with me again," he said, sounding woeful.

"Jesse," I replied, "I don't think anyone's ever going to play *anything* with you again."

He paused for a moment, tossing that idea around in his brain. Jesse wasn't used to being shut out, certainly not when it came to the social scene. I imagined this was a pretty difficult process for him.

But, I mean, too freaking bad, right?

"You're probably the wrong person to come to for sympathy," he said ruefully.

"Probably," I agreed. "But there must be some unsuspecting female out there who hasn't gotten word of your rep yet. So, you know—fingers crossed." I smiled.

He winced. "Alana broke up with me."

Somehow I was not exactly shocked by this crazy and unexpected turn of events. "Now," I began, "when you say 'broke up' with you, do you mean, like, in the proper sense of the term? Like she actually called you up and told you she didn't want to be with you anymore? Or was it more, like, you just came home one day and found her straddling one of your basketball buddies? I mean, I'm just curious."

He turned bright red, which I must say, I enjoyed immensely. "No, I mean, she broke up with me. Like, she told me in person. Not over the phone."

"How lucky for you." I smirked. "I guess Alana can be very considerate—when she wants to."

He sighed and looked at me helplessly. "What do you want from me?"

"Nothing anymore, Jesse." As I said the words, I realized it was true. I was angry and frustrated, sure—but I was also sort of over him. Now that I knew the real Jesse, I knew that he was a jerk and a cheater, through and through. And I had no interest in having him in my life.

Jesse and Alana had both taken me under their respective wings when I first got to Vegas, and I'm not going to lie—at the time, I'd felt incredibly lucky. I'd managed to avoid a lot of pain and awkward social navigation at a very, uh, formative age. But they'd both let me down, big-time. And in the time since I'd lost them as friends, I'd gained something else. *New* friends, of course, in the case of Kelly and— God, I hoped, still, please—Elliot. But also an awareness that what I'd thought of as luck was sometimes just . . . well, *me*. Taking care of myself.

Sometimes luck had nothing to do with it. Sometimes I just knew what to do.

Go figure.

"You're the one who just showed up on my doorstep," I reminded him. "I mean, what is it that you want from me?"

He stepped forward and lowered his gaze. Jeez, I'd forgotten about those eyelashes. He could be, like, an eyelash model, or something. They were that long.

Shake it off, Cass. They're just eyelashes.

Cheating *eyelashes*.

"To be honest, Cass, I've been thinking about us a lot lately—I mean, even when I was with Alana."

Oh, barf.

"And I miss you."

Double barf.

"I guess I was wondering what you might think about us . . . giving it another shot?"

Oh. My. God.

He fixed me with the level-three high-beams version of his soulful, steel-blue Tom Welling gaze. Suddenly, the thought of barfing was the furthest idea from my mind.

Mainly because I was going to pee in my pants laughing.

I absolutely lost it. I mean, the last thing I expected from Jesse was that he would want to get back together with me. Please! He cheated on me—with my best friend! And then he cheated me out of money!

Seriously, I was going to pee in my pants.

"Uh, it's not that funny, Cass," he said, sounding testy.

I couldn't see his face because I was literally doubled over, and my eyes were actually tearing, I was laughing so hard. But I could guess what I looked like. I had a feeling he wasn't, um, laughing with me.

"Yes—it—is!" I gasped.

And then I keeled over and cracked up some more.

At some point in the midst of my incapacitating hysteria, Jesse must have just given up. I wouldn't know, because, as I say, I was pretty much hanging upside down. But I did hear the screen door slide open, and then slide shut again. The next thing I knew, it was just Max and me out on the patio, her licking at my face confusedly, not knowing at all what was going on but appreciating my amusement much more than Jesse had.

And, I must say, that was perfectly fine by me.

Thirteen

I couldn't avoid Alana forever. Or maybe I just wasn't trying hard enough. My encounter with Jesse had softened me up. A bit.

On Thursday, she cornered me in the library. Very stealthily.

"So," she began, collapsing against a shelf and sliding down until she was sitting on the cold, tiled floor of the library. We were tucked away within the stacks for privacy. It was SOP for personal conversations.

I crouched down next to her. "Yeah?" I still had my suspicions, after all. She was still the same chick who was getting all PG-13 (and possibly some R action, too) with *my* boyfriend while I was away in the land of the blue-plate specials.

"Well"—she fixed those hypnotic emerald eyes on me and I had to force myself to concentrate, to remember that she'd used her powers of persuasion for evil, rather than good, when she'd gotten all gropey with *my* boyfriend—"it's just that you never let me apologize."

My eyebrows flew up. "Apologize?" Was she serious? "Alana—you were making out with my boyfriend. Over Christmas. While I was away visiting my grandparents. I mean, what are you going to say? 'I'm sorry I tripped and accidentally stuck my tongue down Jesse's throat'?"

She smiled weakly. "That would at least be a start."

I shook my head. "No way."

"I don't know," she said. "I mean, I thought all that time at Kelly's house—you know, I thought that was a start. Toward a reconciliation." She sighed. "I meant what I said, you know. Whether it was wrong or right—"

"It was wrong—," I interjected. "Completely."

"Whether it was wrong or right," she repeated, "I did have feelings for Jesse. I'd had feelings for him for a long time. I didn't tell you about them, for obvious reasons. I mean, I was hoping they'd just go away on their own. But they didn't. And then he—"

"*Please.* Spare me the details," I begged her. "I had an eyeful, remember? Trust me, it was plenty."

"That was not the way that I wanted you to find out," she insisted.

"Really? How thoughtful of you," I snapped. I couldn't help it. So she had planned to break it to me gently, the fact that she was messing around with my boyfriend? I mean, it was amazing that Angelina Jolie hadn't tracked her down and, like, knighted her or whatever it is that Angelina Jolie does when she's into someone. Alana could be, like, a junior UN Goodwill Ambassador. Or something.

"I just wanted you to know that our friendship meant a lot to me. And I wouldn't have deliberately done anything to ruin it," she said.

I rolled my eyes.

"I liked him. Cass, I thought I *loved* him, or I would *never* have hooked up with him.

Cross my heart and hope to die. I mean, I swear on . . . I swear on my Japanese straightening treatment."

I swallowed. That was some serious swearing, there. Alana's hair was practically a presence of its own at Midvale. It had its own fan club and everything. Seriously. Just Google it.

"You're not saying anything," she observed. "Say something?"

I took a deep breath and looked at her. "I hear what you're saying," I began, cautious. "And I appreciate it."

"But?" her eyes looked round and full of doubt.

"But . . . you have no idea what it felt like to walk into that room, thinking I was going to surprise my boyfriend, and—hello!—instead, finding a welcome home surprise for me."

"It hurt," she ventured.

"Like lemon juice poured over a thousand tiny, salt-filled paper cuts," I confirmed.

She shivered at the imagery.

"Even more than finding out that Ryan was leaving Reese. That's how much it hurt," I went on. "I'm glad you apologized. And I'm grateful to hear your side of the story, really I am. And now that we know that Jesse is just a huge sleazebag, I'm glad that we exposed him for the gross fraud that he is."

"Me too," she said, beaming brightly at the thought.

"But that doesn't really change anything between us," I said softly. "I still need . . . time. It can't be like it was, okay? Not for a while. Maybe not ever."

I glanced at her to see how she was taking the news. Her eyes were shiny and rimmed with red, which I knew was a harbinger of tears, but to her credit, she was putting up a good front and keeping the waterworks at bay. I could tell that she was hearing me. And, to be honest, it made me feel a little bit nice to know that she was being sincere. Does that make me a horrible person?

"I get it," she said, sounding unhappy. "I wish things were different, but I understand."

"I wish things were different too," I said. For, like, a thousand reasons.

"I, um, also wanted to tell you that I broke up with Jesse," she said finally, her voice very small.

"Good call," I said, really meaning it. Alana was gorgeous, funny, and incredibly popular. And, as her former BFF, I was glad to see that she had retained some good judgment. I patted her on the back reassuringly. "You'll replace him in a day."

"I have a date with Clay Ellwood on Friday," she admitted tearfully.

At that, I had to laugh. "Of course you do. Have fun."

"I'll try," she said wistfully. She stood up, brushed off the seat of her jeans, and gathered her books for next period. "Thanks for agreeing to talk to me, Cassie," she said.

I felt a pang in my gut. Alana was the only person who called me Cassie, and I hadn't heard that nickname since . . . well, since early January. Normally it drove me crazy. Now it was upsetting me for totally different reasons.

Jeez, sometimes breaking up with a friend is, like, ten times more painful than breaking up with a boyfriend. I do not understand how Lindsay Lohan can be so capricious about it. "Anytime," I said sincerely.

"And . . ." She paused. "If you ever want

to hang out, or . . . whatever . . . just let me know."

"I will," I promised her.

I meant it too. I just didn't know if or when that time would ever come.

Fourteen

"Raise."

"Raise."

"Fold."

"Crap—I'm out."

"—"

"—"

"Uh, Cass?"

"Huh—what?"

I snapped up and blinked, taking in my five poker buds sitting around our table, eagerly awaiting my turn. I wanted to fake it, to pretend like I'd been paying extra-special attention all along.

Unfortunately, I had no idea what was going on.

I'd spent the first half hour of our

evening aggressively setting out munchies and making sure the iPod playlist was ambient without being overwhelming. Then I shuffled and reshuffled the deck, despite the fact that Andy was only going to do the same once she arrived and took her seat as dealer. I racked up the chips. I counted my money. I recounted my money.

Anything to avoid having to look Elliot in the eye.

In the past week I'd been forced to seriously reevalute my feelings for Elliot. First there was my sudden and all-consuming obsession with the back of his neck. Then there was my disappointment at the fact that it was Jesse, and not him, who had shown up as my surprise gentleman caller at the house.

And then there was That Kiss.

Try though I might, I could not wipe the memory of that kiss from my mind. It had been, no joke, electric—maybe even more so because I hadn't seen it coming, but it had somehow been emotional in a way that Jesse's never were.

I kind of wanted to kiss him again. No, that's a lie. I *really* wanted to kiss him again.

But that would be wrong, I knew. For starters—and I don't care if you think I'm crazy—he is, as discussed, an Aries. My sixth-grade best friend was an Aries, and shortly after exchanging a blood oath of friendship, we had a falling out over a pair turquoise-sequined barrettes. She sucked, okay? Aries sucked, as a match for me.

So you could see where I had my misgivings.

Then there was the fact that even our kiss seemed to have set something off-balance between Elliot, Kelly, and me. What if we started kissing regularly (mmm, there I was, distracted again), and all of a sudden the three of us couldn't hang out anymore?

No way. Not an option.

Which meant that as far as Elliot and his kisses were concerned, I was out of luck.

"Um, Cass?"

"Yeah?"

"What's your story?"

Right. The game. Whoops.

"I, uh . . ." I ran my fingers through my hair and tried to concentrate. I had a decent hand, actually—four of a kind—but the community cards were swimming, and I couldn't make heads or tails of the table. I barely dared look up and across the table at Elliot, but when I did, he was hunched down over the table, furiously fixated on his cards and defiantly resisting eye contact.

"Uh, you know? I fold," I said finally, shaking my head as though that would clear out the mental cobwebs. "Actually, I kind of have, like, a stomachache. Maybe the avocados were bad this time."

Kelly looked at me like I had suddenly started speaking Japanese.

"I think—I think I'm gonna go—," I said, pushing back from the table and grabbing my coat off the living room sofa.

Kelly opened her mouth to protest, but thought better of it when she noted the look in my eye. On my way out I heard Marcus whoop with delight—I'm sure he had turned over my cards and realized how lucky he'd gotten when I folded.

On the drive home I willed myself to get it together. I couldn't, though—there *had* to be some way in which Elliot and I were compatible. Maybe I needed to explore numerology, or the Chinese zodiac? Maybe we were both lions, or rabbits, or, um, "springs" or "cools." Maybe our doppelgängers had been hot and heavy in some alternate universe, or in a past life.

But I didn't live in an alternate universe.

I lived in this one. And in this one, Elliot Forest and I were destined, it would seem, to be just friends.

I was in a complete daze as I unlocked the front door to the house and let myself in. But what I found once I'd entered woke me up pretty quickly.

It seemed that Dad was home, back from his lunch shift early. And he was looking pretty angry.

I came upon him as I made my way into the kitchen. That was my first stop whenever I got home—it was where Maxine usually hung out. Tonight, however, instead of her wagging tail and lolling tongue, I found Dad sitting at our kitchen table, a big old comic book thundercloud dangling over his head.

"Hello, Cassandra," he said quietly. "I'm glad you're home."

This could not be good. Nothing that began with the use of my full name ever ended well.

"Hey," I said as brightly as I could muster. "What's up?"

"That's a good question," he said slowly. "If, for example, I was to ask you what was up, what would you say?"

"Not . . . much?" I ventured, confused.

"Well, what about these new friends of yours? What do you do when you hang out with them?"

Uh-oh.

"Nothing?" It was a question. A question that basically acknowledged the fact that I was *seriously* busted.

"So you're telling me that when you get together with your friends, for hours at a time, on a weekend night, you do nothing at all? You just—what, cease to exist?"

Jeez, Dad could be pretty sarcastic when he was trying to make a point.

"Um . . . well, sometimes . . . we play cards," I offered vaguely.

He nodded. This was obviously the answer that he'd been waiting for. "'Cards.' I see. And by 'cards,' you mean poker, right?"

I sighed deeply. "Yes, poker."

Now it was Dad's turn to sigh, as he ran his fingers through his thinning hair. I knew he had to be pretty furious with me, since he's usually very careful not to exacerbate his male-pattern baldness. "I saw the website. With the footage. I just wanted to see those astrology columns you've been telling me about. Imagine my surprise. I can't believe you've been running a weekly game. Cass, we've talked about this."

"Yes."

"You know how I feel about gambling."

"Yes."

"Look at me when we're speaking."

I obliged, grudgingly.

"Cass, I know that lots of kids play poker these days."

Gee, you think?

"And I know that you're a responsible girl—"

"I am—," I insisted.

"*And* that we live in Vegas, where gambling is as much a part of life as, oh, I don't know, breathing."

"Yes."

"But you know my history with gambling. It's dangerous, Cass, and it can become an addiction. And I don't want you getting caught up in any of that—at all. No matter how harmless a simple game of poker may seem to you."

I nodded solemnly.

"I like to think that we have a good relationship, that we're very open and honest with each other."

"We are," I agreed.

"I don't think I'm excessively strict."

"You're not." I meant what I was saying.

"So I would think that you would at least have the respect to adhere to the few rules that I do put out there."

I was silent. There was nothing left to say. I'd blown it, of course. I'd totally violated Dad's trust, and I just had to pray that I hadn't damaged it forever.

"You're grounded."

"Okay." That much I expected.

"For one week."

"Huh?"

A week? A week was nothing. I could spend a week locked in my room having DVD marathons of WB teen programming of the nineties. Hardly was that a punishment.

I looked at Dad. His eyes were twinkling, and I could tell he was struggling not to let the corners of his mouth twitch into a grin.

"You're going easy on me?"

That did it. Dad finally had to chuckle. "Don't get me wrong, Cass—I'd better never catch you gambling again. But I love the horoscopes—and I love the fact that you didn't let Jesse get the best of you."

"Yeah, me too." I had to smile.

"I don't like that your friends gamble, but I'm glad to see that you've made some new friends. You've been much happier lately than you were when you and Jesse first broke up. That much is obvious. I was pretty worried about you for a while, there."

"Yeah, me too."

He stood up and gave me one last glare—this one devoid of much bite. Then he reached out and hugged me. It felt nice. Lying to him all this time had actually been pretty hard on me; in a way, I was glad to have everything out in the open. And the punishment was both totally deserved and totally tolerable.

"So, I guess I should go sequester myself in my room, huh?" I asked.

Dad winked at me. "First feed the dog."

That, I could handle.

The very pretty coed who had abandoned her dreams of going to Stanford just so she could follow her high school crush to New York had just found said crush making out with her first official college girlfriend. Naturally, she was devastated.

I could *totally* relate.

I was knee-deep in raw cookie dough and Diet Coke and teetered in that awkward space between a sugar rush and a sugar crash. It was Saturday afternoon and I had been watching television for about five hours. I was actually sort of starting to gross myself out. Even Maxine had given up on me, wandering off to the kitchen in the hopes that between-meal food might magically appear in her bowl. I had twenty-four more hours to go of my grounding, and at this rate, they'd have to forklift me out of the house when the punishment was officially over.

The doorbell rang, and Maxine went ballistic. She hated when delivery guys or whatever showed up. I loved how she totally thought she was intimidating despite weighing, like, thirty pounds.

I answered the door absently, my mind still half-focused on the drama unfolding on the flat screen in the den, and contemplating the next course in my junk-food feast. What I found when I opened the door, however, cleared my head of all of those trivial matters.

"I, uh, heard you were under house arrest."

I dropped my cookie dough spoon on

the ground. Maxine immediately grabbed it between her teeth and dashed off to relish her new toy.

"Hi," I said, sort of meaning, *wow*.

Believe it or not, it was a gentleman caller—this time, a *real* gentleman. My eyes almost bugged out at the site of Elliot in my doorway. He was as scrawny and wide-eyed as ever, which made him down-right adorable.

I'd been building toward trying to talk to him—like, for real, talk to him—all week in school. But I'd always chickened out at the last minute. I'm sure Kelly could see through all of my spasmodic behavior, but she was either far too polite or way too disgusted to call me on it.

Elliot looked confused. "Can I, uh, come in?"

I realized I'd been staring at him silently for a beat or two too long. "Of course!" I said, now overcompensating with an enthu-siasm that smacked of mild psychosis. I stepped aside to let him in.

"My father's not home, so we can't go into my room," I explained, leading him into the den. I wasn't looking to violate any more house rules in the foreseeable future.

With Elliot over, the television suddenly seemed about six times too loud. I turned it to mute and sat down awkwardly on the couch.

"What's up?" I started.

"I . . . well . . . we never really talked after the other day."

"True," I said. Suddenly my mouth was very dry.

"I know you talked about wanting to stay friends. Because . . . well, I'm not totally sure that I get that. But I think it has something to do with us not being compatible."

"Astrologically compatible," I confirmed. "Aries, Libra. Bad news."

"Right." He dove into the ever-present messenger bag and fished out a piece of paper. He proceeded to unfold the paper and smooth it out over his leg. He cleared his throat nervously. "This was something I found," he explained. "And I guess that's why I'm here. I thought you might like to hear it: *'You are a sympathetic person who feels deeply for others. You are very sensitive and understanding when it comes to your friends, and you show them lots of understanding and compassion.'*"

He paused and looked at me expectantly.

"That's the description of a Pisces," I said suspiciously. "What are you reading that to me?"

"Because my birthday is March twentieth," he explained, which makes me—"

"On the cusp! You're on the cusp!" I stood up so quickly, I knocked my half-eaten tube of cookie dough on the floor. Maxine, never one to miss an opportunity, dashed in, grabbed it, and took off. I watched her go.

"Do you need to . . . ," Elliot asked, waving in the direction of the dog.

"Eventually," I said. I was way too riveted by what he had to say.

"So the thing is that I think a Pisces and a Libra are—"

"A lot more compatible than an Aries and a Libra," I finished for him, warming to the thought.

"And, you know, supposedly Pisces are really introspective and creative, and really into movies and things like that. Which, you know, is not exactly my forte. So was thinking you could maybe . . . help me?"

"I could," I said, shyly. "I can't play poker anymore, anyway." I blushed.

"Then we'll have to find something else

to do," Elliot said. By this point, we were both standing, and he slowly moved closer to me until the space between us was little more than a centimeter or two. He reached out and took my hands in his. "If you really are worried about ruining the friendship, I understand. But I kind of hate that idea."

I shrugged. "Nah. We weren't such good friends, anyway."

He kissed me. And it was just like I remembered in the car, except better. Better because I'd had some time to figure out what I wanted, and I knew that what I wanted was Elliot. And he wanted me, too.

I mean, how lucky could a girl get?

I pulled back suddenly.

"Something wrong?" Elliot asked, sounding nervous.

"Just that I *really* don't think my father would approve of this," I said. "I'd say we could take a ride or something, but you know—still grounded."

"Right." He nodded, looking thoughtful. "Well, in that case, we'll have to come up with a Plan B."

I was all for a Plan B.

Elliot disappeared back into his messenger bag. When he emerged, he was holding a hefty DVD boxed set. He held it out to me: *The Essential Hitchcock*. I beamed and jumped up and down with glee. I kissed him again—house rules and grounding and parental authority aside. And let me tell you—it was worth it. I even got to touch the neck scruff, at long last. Also worth the risk—and the surprised look that Elliot gave me just before he burst out laughing.

"Hitchcock's my favorite," I told him, giggling a little bit myself.

He gave me an affectionate "duh" look. "Well, in that case"—he winked at me—"it looks like we're in luck."

About the Author

Micol Ostow most heartily does not endorse gambling. At least, not on a writer's salary. She lives and works in New York City, where she is perpetually short on cash but long on cheese, chocolate, and coffee. She relies on a tiny, noisy French bulldog named Bridget Jones to keep her (semi)sane. Visit Micol at www.micolostow.com.

LOL at this sneak peek of

The Boys Next Door
By Jennifer Echols

A new Romantic Comedy from Simon Pulse

★

Suddenly things looked way, way up. My eyes found Sean in the darkness, next to the stairs, with his back to me. He stood a few inches taller than his friends who'd just graduated too, who surrounded him. Sean was always surrounded.

As I crossed the room to him, folks kept stepping in my way, wanting to say hey and have conversations with me, of all things. The one time I *wasn't* interested in being well liked.

By the time I finally reached him, my heart pounded. But it was now or never. I made myself grin at Sean's friends as I slid my hand across his T-shirt, feeling his hard stomach underneath the cotton. I almost flinched at how good and how intimate it felt, but through the marvel of my willpower, I did not flinch. I lay my head playfully against his chest, as I'd seen girls do when they claimed to be just friends with a guy but everyone whispered something more was going on.

I half-expected him to shout, "Get off me!" and shove me away. Not because Sean would ever do that to a girl—he had more charming ways of extricating himself from cretins—but because my life generally had been a long series of mortifications, and Sean shouting in alarm at my embrace would fit right in. The other half of me expected him to chuckle gently, but not make a move of his own quite yet. It might take him a while to get used to the new me.

He didn't chuckle. He didn't shove me away. He did *exactly* what he was supposed to. Even better. He slipped his arm around my waist and drew me closer against his warm body. I felt him nodding at something one of the other guys said about baseball, but he didn't say a word to me or anyone. As if a greeting like this from me were the most natural thing in the world. He smelled even better than usual, too—just a hint of cologne. A woody scent with undertones of musk and gunpowder.

I snuggled against him, nose close to his warm, scented chest, and enjoyed a few more seconds of this tingling paradise. What heaven, if my whole summer could be like this—

His low voice vibrating through my body, he asked his friends, "Have you been watching the Braves? Tim Hudson or what?"

Oh God, I was hugging *Adam*!

Hey, the scene fit right into my life after all!

I jerked away from him. Almost instantly I realized I should not jerk away, because the situation would be slightly less mortifying if I pretended I'd known it was Adam all along.

The damage was done. Worse, I didn't have a chance to burst out the front door and run, not walk, *run* all the way home, dash upstairs to the computer in my room, and book a one-way ticket to Antarctica to join the commune there for teenagers too socially challenged to join the chess club. He caught my elbow. "Later," he called over his shoulder to the guys, and he pulled me into a corner. He bent down to whisper in my ear, "You're blushing."

I opened my lips. I didn't seem to be taking in enough oxygen through my nose. "I'm sunburned," I breathed.

Adam was smiling, enjoying my discomfort too much for my taste. "You thought I was Sean."

Get smitten with these sweet & sassy British treats:

Gucci Girls
by Jasmine Oliver

Three friends tackle the high-stakes world of fashion school.

10 Ways to Cope with Boys
by Caroline Plaisted

What every girl *really* needs to know.

Ella Mental
by Amber Deckers

If only every girl had a "Good Sense" guide!

WANTED

Single Teen Reader in search of a FUN romantic comedy read!

How NOT to Spend Your Senior Year
CAMERON DOKEY

Royally Jacked
NIKI BURNHAM

Ripped at the Seams
NANCY KRULIK

Cupidity
CAROLINE GOODE

Spin Control
NIKI BURNHAM

South Beach Sizzle
SUZANNE WEYN &
DIANA GONZALEZ

She's Got the Beat
NANCY KRULIK

30 Guys in 30 Days
MICOL OSTOW

Animal Attraction
JAMIE PONTI

A Novel Idea
AIMEE FRIEDMAN

Scary Beautiful
NIKI BURNHAM

Getting to Third Date
KELLY McCLYMER

Dancing Queen
ERIN DOWNING

Major Crush
JENNIFER ECHOLS

Do-Over
NIKI BURNHAM

Love Undercover
JO EDWARDS

Prom Crashers
ERIN DOWNING

Gettin' Lucky
MICOL OSTOW

Available from Simon Pulse 💕 **Published by Simon & Schuster**

"Why don't you just say in the first place that you are meeting me?"

"I like watching them fluster."

Kedah would like to see Felicia fluster, just a little, yet she was always so measured and poised and gave away so little of herself.

He would like to know more.

The thought surprised him. Kedah did not fraternize with his staff, yet over the past few weeks he had found himself wondering more and more about Felicia and what went on in her head.

It was a pretty head—one that was usually framed with shoulder-length hair but today it was worn up. It was too severe on her. Or was it that she'd lost a little weight? He could see that she'd put on some makeup in an attempt to hide the smudges under her eyes.

Gorgeous eyes, Kedah thought.

They regularly changed shade—today they were an inviting sea green but he would not be diving in.

One Night With Consequences

When one night...leads to pregnancy!

When succumbing to a night of unbridled desire it's impossible to think past the morning after!

But with the sheets barely settled, that little blue line appears on the pregnancy test and it doesn't take long to realize that one night of white-hot passion has turned into a lifetime of consequences!

Only one question remains:

How do you tell a man you've just met that you're about to share more than just his bed?

Find out in:

An Heir Fit for a King by Abby Green

Larenzo's Christmas Baby by Kate Hewitt

An Illicit Night with the Greek by Susanna Carr

A Vow to Secure His Legacy by Annie West

Bound to the Tuscan Billionaire
by Susan Stephens

The Shock Cassano Baby by Andie Brock

The Greek's Nine-Month Redemption
by Maisey Yates

An Heir to Make a Marriage by Abby Green

Crowned for the Prince's Heir by Sharon Kendrick

Look for more **One Night With Consequences**
coming soon!

Carol Marinelli

—

THE SHEIKH'S BABY SCANDAL

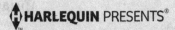

HARLEQUIN PRESENTS®

Recycling programs
for this product may
not exist in your area.

ISBN-13: 978-0-373-13942-2

The Sheikh's Baby Scandal

First North American publication 2016

Copyright © 2016 by Carol Marinelli

Printed in U.S.A.

www.Harlequin.com

Carol Marinelli recently filled in a form asking for her job title. Thrilled to be able to put down her answer, she put "writer." Then it asked what Carol did for relaxation and she put down the truth— "writing." The third question asked for her hobbies. Well, not wanting to look obsessed, she crossed her fingers and answered "swimming"—but given that the chlorine in the pool does terrible things to her highlights, I'm sure you can guess the real answer!

Visit the Author Profile page at Harlequin.com for more titles.

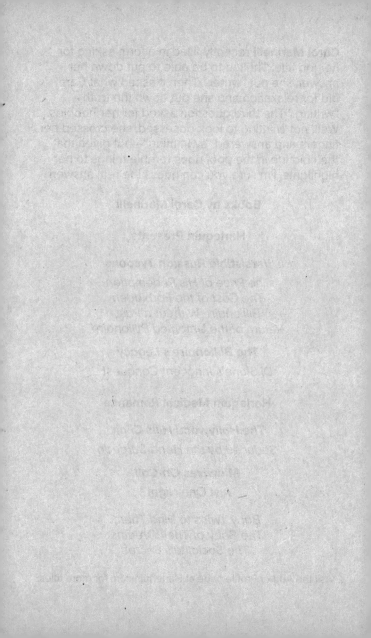

PROLOGUE

'KEDAH, WHERE ARE YOU? That's enough, now!'

The royal nanny was getting exasperated as she again called out to her small charge, but Kedah had no intention of being found—he was having far too much fun!

Kedah could see the nanny's feet go past as he hid behind the large statue that she had checked just a few seconds ago. He could run like greased lightning, and he smothered his laughter as she now moved towards the grand staircase.

'Kedah!' The nanny was sounding very cross. As well she might—Kedah was a handful.

The people of Zazinia adored him, though, and they would all be lined up outside the palace hoping to get a glimpse of him. Usually there was just a small crowd when the royal plane landed but, thanks to the cheeky young Prince, the numbers had grown of late.

Never had there been more interest in a young royal. Kedah's chocolate-brown eyes were flecked with gold and his winning smile had drawn rapt attention from the moment the first photographer had captured it. In their eyes he could do no wrong—in fact, Kedah's boisterous boyish ways only served to endear him further to the public. He was as beautiful as he was wild, they often said, and it would seem that he could not stand still.

He tried to!

For the people of Zazinia, a dreary parade was made so much more entertaining when they watched little Kedah's attempts to obey the stern commands that were delivered out of the side of his father's mouth.

Just a few weeks ago there had been a procession, and Kedah had had to remain still for the best part of an hour. But he had quickly grown bored.

'Control him!' Omar, the Crown Prince had said to Rina, his wife, for the King had started to get cross.

It was so hard to control him, though.

When his mother had warned him to stand still, Kedah had merely smiled up at her and then held out his arms to be lifted. Rina had tried to ignore him—but, really, who could resist? In the end she had complied. Kedah had chatted away to her, despite being gently hushed. She had smiled affectionately and put her hand up to his little fat cheek, looked him in the eye. She'd told him to behave for just a few more moments, and that then it would be time to return to the palace.

The King's silent disapproval had been felt all around. He did not approve of his son's young wife, and certainly he felt that children should be seen and not heard. Omar had been tense, Rina had done her best to appease all, and yet Kedah had chosen to be impervious to the strained atmosphere and turned his attention to the crowd.

They had all been staring at him, so he'd smiled and waved to them. It had been such a break from the usually austere and remote royal shows that the gathered crowd had melted *en masse* and, quite simply, adored him. Kedah was funny—and terribly cheeky. He had so much energy to burn that he was the work of five children, and the royal nanny struggled with this particular charge!

'Kedah!' she called out now, to thin air. 'I need to get you bathed and dressed so that you can go and greet your father and the King.'

He crouched lower behind the statue and did

not respond. He was not particularly looking forward to the senior royals' return. They had been gone for a few days and the palace felt so much more relaxed without them. His mother seemed to laugh more, and even the staff were happier without the King around.

Neither did Kedah want to change out of his play clothes just so he could watch a plane land and his grumpy father and grandfather get out. And so, as the nanny sped down stairs in search of him, Kedah ran from behind the statue and tried to plan his next move.

Usually he would hide in the library, but on this day he ran somewhere he should not. Jaddi, his grandfather, had his own wing, and there were no guards there today—which meant that he was free to explore. But his eager footsteps came to a halt midway there. Even though his grandfather was away, Jaddi was intimidating enough that Kedah chose not to continue. And so, at the last moment, he changed his mind and turned and ran to the Crown Prince's wing, where his parents resided.

There were no guards there either.

To the left there were offices that ran the length of the corridor, and to the right was the entrance to his parents' private residence.

Kedah rarely entered it. His parents generally came and visited him in the nursery or the playroom.

Knowing that he would be told off if he disturbed his mother from her nap, for a second he considered the balcony—but then chose to run to the offices instead. He had long ago kicked off his sandals, so his bare feet made barely a sound.

Even though he was in a rush to find a hiding place, Kedah stopped for a moment and looked up at the portraits, as he always did when he was here.

They fascinated him.

He looked along the row of Crown Princes gone by. All were imposing-looking men, dressed in warrior robes with their hands on the hilt of their swords. All stared down at him with cool grey eyes and grim expressions.

He looked at a younger version of his grandfather, the King, and then he looked at his father.

They looked so stern.

One day, his mother had told him, *his* portrait would hang there, for he was born to be King. 'And you will be such a *good* king, Kedah. I know that you shall listen to your people.'

He had heard the brittle edge to his mother's voice as she'd gazed up at the portraits. 'Why don't they smile?' Kedah had asked.

'Because being Crown Prince is a serious thing.'

'I don't want it, then!' Kedah had laughed.

Now he looked away from the portraits and ran to a meeting room that had several desks. He went to hide under one, sure that he would not be found there.

Or perhaps he would, for there were noises coming from behind a large wooden door and he recognised his mother's voice as she called out. He knew that that was his father's private office, and wondered why she would be in there.

And then he heard a low cry.

It sounded as if his mother was hurt, and Kedah's expression changed from happy to a look of concern as he heard muffled sobs and moans.

His father had told him to take care of his mother while he was away. Even at this tender age, Kedah knew that people worried about her, for Rina could be unpredictable at times.

He came out from under the desk and stood wondering what he should do. He knew that the door handles were too high for him. For a moment he considered running to alert the royal nanny that his mother sounded distressed, but then he changed his mind. Often his mother wept, and it did not seem to endear her to the staff nor to the rest of the royal family.

And so, instead of getting help, Kedah selected a chair and started to drag it across the room. The chair was made of the same wood as the heavy door, and it felt like ages until he had got it close enough to climb upon it and attempt to turn the handle on the office door.

'Ummu…?' Kedah called out to his mother as he climbed onto the chair and turned the heavy handle. 'Ummu?' he said again as the door swung open.

But then he frowned, because his mother seemed to be sitting on the desk and yet she was being held in Abdal's arms.

'Intadihr!'

His mother shouted that Kedah was to stay where he was, and she and Abdal moved out of his line of sight. Kedah did as he was told. He was not sure what was happening, but a moment or so later Abdal walked past on his way out.

Kedah had never really liked him. Abdal was always cross whenever Kedah came to the offices and pleaded with his mother to take him for a walk. It was as if he didn't want the young Prince around.

Kedah stared at Abdal's departing back as

the man walked quickly along the corridor and then, still standing on the chair, he turned and looked to his mother. Rina was flustered, and she smoothed down her robe as she walked towards him.

Kedah did not hold his arms out to be lifted. 'Why was Abdal here?' he asked. 'Where are the guards?'

There were no flies on Kedah—not even at that young age.

'It's okay,' Rina said as she lifted him, unyielding, from the chair. 'Mummy was upset and didn't want anyone to see. I was crying.'

'Why?' Kedah asked as he took in his mother's features. Her face was all red and, yes, he *had* heard her sob. 'Why are you always sad?'

'Because I miss my homeland sometimes, Kedah. Abdal is also from there. He is here to ease the transition and to help our two countries unite. Abdal understands how difficult it can be to get the King to agree to any changes. We were trying to come up with a way that will please all the people.'

Kedah just stared back at his mother as she hurriedly spoke on.

'Your father would be very upset if he knew that I had been crying while he was away. He is tired of arguing with the King and he has enough on his plate, so it is better not to tell him. It is better that you don't tell anyone what you just saw.'

Kedah stared into her eyes more deeply and tried to read her. His mother did not look sad. If anything, she looked scared, and that had his heart tightening in a fear for her that he didn't understand.

'I don't want you to be unhappy.'

'Then I shan't be,' Rina said, and brought a hand up to Kedah's face and cupped his taut cheek. 'After all, I have so much to give thanks for—I have a beautiful son and a wonderful home…'

'So don't you cry again,' Kedah said, and those gorgeous chocolate-brown eyes of his narrowed. He removed his mother's hand from his cheek and looked right into his mother's eyes. For one so very young, he spoke with command. *'Ever!'*

'Kedah, there you are…'

They both turned to the sound of the royal nanny's voice, and he did not understand why the nanny stammered and blushed as she apologised to Her Royal Highness for losing sight of her young charge.

'I've been looking for him all over the palace.'

'It's fine,' Rina said, handing Kedah over. 'We'll say no more about it.'

A little while later his father and the King returned, and life went as before.

Kedah continued to be boisterous, and yet from that day there was a defiant edge to his antics. From then on those brown eyes narrowed if anyone got too close. He kept his own counsel and he trusted no one.

A few years later his brother was born and that signalled happier times, for Mohammed was a model child.

Weary of the wilder young Prince, the King insisted he be schooled overseas, and little Kedah attended a boarding school in London. He somehow knew that he held a secret that, if ever revealed, might well destroy not only the people he loved but the kingdom his family ruled.

And as he matured Kedah knew how dire the consequences would be for his mother. If her infidelity was exposed she would be shamed, and the King would have no choice but to divorce her and separate her from her sons.

But secrets had ways of seeping out through even the most heavily guarded walls. Servants gossiped amongst themselves as children played at their feet, and royal nannies eventually married and indulged in pillow talk of their own. Rumours spread wide when they were carried on desert winds—and returned multiplied, of course.

And as Kedah grew, and returned to Zazinia during term breaks, the portraits fascinated him for a different reason.

Perhaps what was being said was true and he was *not* his father's son. After all, he looked nothing like any of them.

But his doubts were not because of the rumours that refused to fade with the passage of time—Kedah knew what he had seen.

CHAPTER ONE

YOU NEED FELICIA HAMILTON.

Crown Prince Sheikh Kedah of Zazinia had always made sure that he needed no one.

He was reliant only on himself.

That late afternoon he sat in his London office and rolled a rare spherical diamond between the pads of his index finger and thumb as he read a newspaper article on his computer. When there was a knock on the door and he called for Anu to come in he saw that she looked rather tense. He wondered if she had read the article too.

What was being discussed in it would distress her, he knew. She had been a loyal member of his team for a number of years and was also from his homeland. She would understand how damning this article was.

'Ms Hamilton is here for her interview,' Anu said, and her lips pursed a little.

'Send her in, then.'

'She asked for a few moments to freshen up.'

Oh, Anu tried, but she could not hold her protests in. All the staff who came into contact with Kedah had a preliminary interview with Anu first. Yesterday she had met with Felicia, and found the young woman did not tick any of the usual boxes that might get her through to a second round interview. She lacked hospitality experience—though she made up for it in attitude—and that would *never* do when working for Kedah. He was not exactly known for consulting with his staff. He had a packed schedule and he expected his team to work quietly and seamlessly in the background—which was something Anu could not see happening with Miss Hamilton.

Anu had reported this to him yesterday, and yet Kedah had told her to call Felicia back and invite her to come in this afternoon.

'Kedah, I really don't think that she is suitable to work as your PA.'

'Anu, I understand that you have concerns, and they have been noted. Can you please alert me when Miss Hamilton decides that she is ready?'

As the door closed behind Anu, Kedah replaced the diamond in the inside pocket of his jacket and returned to the news article that he had been reading.

It was in English. No one from his homeland would dare to publish such a piece. Not yet.

Heir (not so) Apparent!

Beneath the daring title there was a picture of Kedah, wearing a suit and tie and a rich, arrogant smile. It spoke of the recent death of Kedah's grandfather and how, now that Omar was King, certain difficult topics needed to be raised. It briefly discussed Kedah's British education and subsequent jet-set lifestyle and playboy reputation. It mentioned how, at thirty, he still showed no sign of settling down.

The article also spoke about his younger brother Mohammed and his wife Kumu and their two sons. Unlike Kedah, Mohammed had been schooled in Zazinia, and there was a considerable faction in the country who considered that, for stability, Mohammed would make a more suitable Crown Prince and subsequent King. The article stated that some of the elders were now calling for the Accession Council to meet and for a final decision to be made.

At the end of the piece there was a photo of

Mohammed and Omar, but most damning of all was the caption below: *Like Father, Like Son.*

Apart from the years that separated them, Mohammed and Omar were identical—not just in looks but in their staid, old-fashioned ways.

The only change that Omar had made while Crown Prince had been an update to the education system. Over the years Kedah had made no progress with his father either. Kedah was a highly skilled architect, yet every design he'd submitted had been rejected and every suggestion he'd made either immediately turned down or later overruled.

He had hoped, now that his grandfather was dead, that things might change, but his latest proposal for a stunning waterfront hotel and shopping complex had been rejected too.

His father had pointed out that the new building would look onto the private royal beach.

'There are ways around that,' Kedah had insisted. 'If you would just let me—'

'The decision is final, Kedah,' the King had interrupted. 'I have discussed it at length with the elders...'

'And you have discussed it at length with Mohammed,' Kedah had said. 'I hear that he was *very* vocal in his criticism of my plans.'

'I listen to all sides.'

'Well, you should listen to me first,' Kedah had said. 'Mohammed is *not* the Crown Prince.'

'Mohammed is the one who is here.'

'I have told you—I will not live in Zazinia if I am to be ineffectual.'

Kedah turned off his computer so he did not have to see the offensive article.

Earlier today, when it had first appeared, he had called Vadia, his assistant in Zazinia, and had been assured that it would be pulled down from the internet. There was no denying, though, that things were coming to a head. Even before their grandfather's death Mohammed had decided that *he* would make a better Crown Prince and future King. Many of the elders thought the same, and—as the article had stated—there was a strong push for a meeting of the Accession Council to discuss the future of the royal family formally.

His father would have the final say, but rather than declaring outright that he would prefer his younger son to be King one day, Omar seemed to be pushing Kedah into stepping aside.

Kedah refused to.

Instead he was busy making plans.

He had many rich and influential friends, and he knew a lot of bad boys too. Matteo Di

Sione was both. He had a reputation that rivalled even Kedah's.

They had met up in New York a couple of weeks ago—and not by chance. Kedah hadn't told Matteo the issue, just that he was expecting turbulent times ahead and needed someone tough who could handle things. Matteo had made some discreet enquiries on his friend's behalf and had come back to Kedah with his findings.

You need Felicia Hamilton.

Kedah glanced at the time. Usually a potential employee who arrived late for an interview and then asked for time to freshen up wouldn't even make it through the door of his office.

What the *hell* was she doing? he wondered.

She was reading.

Felicia hadn't actually *intended* to keep Sheikh Kedah waiting for quite so long. The West End was gridlocked—thanks to a red carpet awards show taking place tonight, the taxi driver had told her. So Felicia, sitting in the back and doing some final research on Kedah on her way to the interview, had decided to walk the last couple of blocks. But then a very interesting article had turned up on her tablet and, after arriving at his impressive office, she'd wanted a few more moments to go through it.

Now perhaps she understood why she had been called back after that disastrous interview yesterday. Anu had spoken to her as if Felicia wanted to *work* for Kedah—a real job, so to speak—and after an awkward twenty minutes, during which it had become increasingly clear that Felicia was not the type Sheikh Kedah employed, the two women had parted ways.

Still, her phone had rung this morning and Felicia had smiled to herself when she had been invited to return and meet with the man himself. Of course Kedah didn't want a PA—it was her troubleshooting skills he required.

Now she knew why!

It would seem that Crown Prince Sheikh Kedah of Zazinia was fighting for the throne— and Felicia was now sure he wanted to commence the clean-up of his reputation.

From what she knew of him, it would take more than industrial strength bleach!

If there was a scale for playboys, then Kedah was at the extreme top. In fact his partying ways were legendary.

How the mighty fell!

Today this oh, so arrogant man would reveal his troubles to Felicia. Of course she would look suitably unshocked as he did so, and assure him that whatever trouble he was in she could sort it.

Felicia was *very* good at her job because she had been doing it all her life.

She had been taught to smile for the cameras alongside Susannah, her long-suffering mother, long before she could even walk. She had on many occasions sat in the family lounge with spin doctors and PR people as they had debated how her father's multiple affairs and the trashy headlines and exposés should best be dealt with.

There had even been times when they had come to her school. Felicia could remember sitting in the headmaster's office with her parents, being reminded that cameras would be on them when they left. She had been told what to do as they walked, as a family, to the waiting car.

'Remember to smile, Felicia.'

'Susannah, hold his hand as you walk to the car and don't forget to laugh when he whispers to you.'

And her mother had done as she was told. Susannah had done everything that had been asked of her. But in the end it had all been to no avail. When Felicia was fourteen her father had decided to update to a younger model and had walked out on them.

A legal wrangle had ensued.

The lovely private boarding school that had been such a haven for her had disappeared when the school fees hadn't been paid, and with it had gone Felicia's friends and her beloved pony.

Susannah had fallen apart, and it had been up to her daughter to be strong. They had rented a small house while waiting for the money to be sorted out and Felicia had enrolled in the local school—but she hadn't fit in. Her dreams of being a vet had long gone by then, and she'd left school at sixteen. She had taken an office job to help with the rent.

Those days were gone now.

Felicia was highly sought-after, and her troubleshooting talents were coveted by the rich and famous. Her mother lived in a house that Felicia had bought and paid for, and Felicia owned her own flat.

Some questioned how she could defend these men—but, really, Felicia was just doing what she'd been taught.

The only difference was that now she was paid.

And paid handsomely.

She ran a comb through her dark blonde hair, touched up her lip gloss and added a slick of mascara to bring out the green of her eyes. As she headed out Anu told her to take a seat. Guessing the newspaper article would soon be taken down, she took a few quick screenshots on her phone as Sheikh Kedah now kept *her* waiting.

Oh, well! She had done the same to him.

Working with this type of man, Felicia had found that it was terribly important to establish early on that *his* ego had to be put aside and that from this point on *she* ran the show. It was even more vital to establish that they weren't suddenly best friends and, given the reputations of the men she dealt with, to make it clear they would never be lovers.

Felicia would be very nice at first, of course, while he told her what was going on, but then her smile would fade and she'd tell him what had to be done if he wanted to come out of this intact.

The truth was that Felicia despised these men.

She just knew, from wretched experience, how to deal with them.

'You might want to put your phone away,' Anu suggested.

Felicia was about to decline politely when a rich, deep and heavily accented voice spoke for her.

'I'm sure Ms Hamilton is just keeping up to date with the news.'

She looked up.

She had prepared thoroughly for this moment—determined not to let such a superfluous thing as his stunning looks sideswipe her. She had examined many photos to render herself immune to him. Only no photograph could fully capture the beauty of Sheikh Kedah in the flesh.

He was wearing an exquisitely cut dark suit and tie, but they were mere details for she had little interest in his attire. And it was not the caramel of his skin against his white shirt or his thick glossy black hair that forced her to try to remember to breathe. Nor was it cheekbones that looked as if Michelangelo himself had spent a couple of days sculpting them to perfection. Even sulky full lips that did not smile hardly mattered, for Felicia was caught in the trap of his eyes.

They were thickly lashed and a rich shade of chocolate-brown with golden flecks and—unlike most of her clients—he met her gaze steadily.

Oh, she was *extremely* good at her job. For, despite the jolt to her senses, Felicia did not let her reaction reveal itself to him and instead stood up, utterly composed.

'Come through,' he said.

And she smiled.

Widely.

She had a smile that took men's breath away. It was a smile so seemingly open that hardened reporters would thrust their microphones a little closer and their lenses would zoom in, so certain were they that it would waver.

It never did.

And long ago she had trained herself not to blush.

'I'm sorry I'm late,' Felicia said as she walked towards him. 'The traffic was terrible.'

He almost forgave her, for in turn Felicia was not what Kedah had been expecting. He had thought, given she had been invited for a formal second interview, that she would be in a suit, but Felicia looked rather more like a lady who lunched and was wearing a pretty off-white dress.

It was fitted enough that it showed her slender frame and pert bust, while short enough to reveal her toned legs. She was wearing high-heeled strappy sandals and looked nothing like the hard-nosed woman he had been prepared for. In fact she was as delicate-looking as she was pretty. She was so soft and smiling that Kedah was quite sure Matteo had got it all wrong.

Felicia Hamilton was the very *last* person he needed. Moreover, she was exactly the soft and submissive type he desired!

Naturally he had looked her up and had seen a picture of her in a boxy suit with her hair worn up. She had been coming out of court, with a terribly famous and thoroughly disgraced sportsman by her side. She had spoken for him and her voice had been crisp and to the point.

Today Kedah had expected brittle, and yet there was a softness to her that confused him. Her hair was long and layered and framed a heart-shaped face, and her fragrance was light and floral, meeting his nostrils as he held the door open for her and she passed him.

'Please…' Kedah gestured. 'Take a seat.'

Felicia did so, placing her bag by her side and crossing her legs at the ankles. Though he seemed utterly composed, Felicia was prepared for anything. Often the door had barely closed before her future client broke down. *'For God's sake, Felicia, you have to help me!'* they all too often begged. *'You have to stop this from getting out!'*

Yes—*client.*

Oh, she might call them her boss when she was in front of the camera lens but, as Kedah would soon find out, it was Felicia who was in charge.

Yet instead of begging for her help Kedah calmly offered refreshments.

'No, thank you.'

'You're sure?' he checked.

'Quite sure. I had a late lunch.'

And his troubles would be a very sweet dessert!

He walked around the desk and took his place and Felicia ran a tongue over her glossed lips as she waited for him to reveal the salacious truth.

'You come highly recommended.'

'Thank you.'

'Ms Hamilton?' he checked. 'Or can I call you Felicia?'

'Felicia's fine,' she offered. 'How would you like me to address *you*?'

'Kedah.'

She nodded.

They went through the formalities. He told

her he was an esteemed architect, which of course she already knew.

'I used to sell them off, but now once I design a hotel I tend to hold on to it,' Kedah explained needlessly.

She just wished he'd get to the point.

'So I have a fleet of hotels across the world, which in turn means I have a lot of staff...'

Felicia nodded and wished they could lose the charade and get to the good bit.

'Do you have much experience in the hospitality industry?' he asked.

Felicia frowned. She'd expected a confessional—to sit, seemingly non-judgmental, as he poured out his past—yet he seemed to be actually interviewing her.

'Not really. Though of course I've stayed in an awful lot of hotels!'

Oh, she had. And if Kedah was going on word of mouth then he'd know that she worked for just a few weeks a year.

He didn't even deign to smile at her small joke.

'As I hope Anu explained, the role would involve extensive travel. If you work for me the hours will be very long. Sometimes there are eighteen-hour days. If we are away you would also work weekends. Do you have other commitments?'

'My current employer is my only commitment,' Felicia answered. It was the truth—whatever his crisis, it would have her full attention.

'Good.' Kedah nodded. 'How soon would you be able to start?'

'As soon as the contract is signed.' Felicia smiled. 'I trust Anu gave you my terms?'

'Indeed she did.'

Felicia Hamilton commanded quite a fee.

'What about your personal life?' he asked.

'That's not your concern,' Felicia answered.

'Be sure to keep it that way,' Kedah said. 'I don't want to hear that your boyfriend is upset because you missed his birthday, or that your mother-in-law has surgery next week and you need some time off. Care factor? Zero.'

Felicia's response was to laugh, and for once it was genuine. Honesty had been somewhat lacking in her life, and she would far prefer the truth than a dressed-up lie.

And now she waited—*how* she waited—for that cool facade to crack and for Kedah to admit that he had royally stuffed up and needed his past to disappear. But instead he spoke of hotels and designs, and she stifled a yawn as he told her about Hussain, a graphic designer he regularly used.

'He's excellent. He actually studied with my father many years ago. We have worked on many designs together—mainly in the UAE.'

Felicia stifled another yawn.

'Why don't I show you some examples of my work—as well as a few of the hotels we shall be visiting in the coming weeks?' Kedah said, and then dimmed the lights.

Felicia wondered for a brief second if refreshments might be in order after all. Was she about to get a private screening of the trouble Sheikh Kedah was in? A steamy sex tape? The Crown Prince bound and gagged in a seedy encounter, perhaps?

Kedah watched that tongue pop out and moisten those lovely lips as she sat straight in the chair, giving him her full attention.

Then he smiled unseen as her shoulders slumped and she sat through the forty-minute presentation that took her through some of his luxury hotels. She fought to keep her eyes from crossing as she watched it.

What the hell...?

'Do you have any questions?' Kedah invited as he flicked on the lights.

No! She just wanted him to cut to the chase and reveal the truth. 'Not at this stage,' she said.

'There must be things that you want to ask me?' he invited. 'Surely you have come prepared? You will have looked me up?'

'Of course I have.'

'What do you think your role might entail?' he asked as he went through her file.

Maybe he was shy, Felicia thought. Though that made no sense. He looked far from shy. But perhaps he needed a little help revealing his dark truths, so she decided to broach things gently. 'I would guess, from my research, that I'll be running a dating agency with only one man on the books,' Felicia said, and watched him closely for a reaction.

Kedah merely looked up from the papers and stared back at her as she continued.

'Though of course rather more discreetly than my predecessors.'

'Discreetly?' Kedah frowned.

'You tend to hit the glossies rather a lot.'

'That's hardly my staff's fault.'

'Well, they should monitor what's said. If a woman's upset…'

'As far as my sex life goes, you would just have to deal with the bookings and the brochure, Felicia…'

'Brochure?

He didn't enlighten her. 'What I am saying is that you do *not* police comments or apologise on my behalf. I am quite grateful for "the glossies", as you call them, for if women expect anything more from me than a night in bed, possibly two, then that is their own foolish mistake. They cannot say they haven't been duly warned.'

No, not shy, Felicia decided as he continued to speak.

'But I do expect discretion from all who work for me. Naturally you will have to sign a confidentiality agreement.'

'I told Anu yesterday that I shan't.'

Kedah, who had gone back to going through the papers, glanced up.

'Nobody would employ a PA without one.'

'If you look through my references you'll see that they do.' She gave him a smile, as if she was asking if he took sugar with his coffee—one lump or two? 'You either trust me or you don't.'

'I don't,' he responded. 'Though please don't take it personally. I don't trust anyone.'

'Good, because neither do I.'

Kedah was fast realising there was nothing apart from her appearance that was delicate.

She was actually rather fascinating, and any doubts he might have had about her being up to the job were starting to fade.

He had no intention of telling her his situation just yet, of course, but he had decided that he wanted her onside. 'We can't go any further without you signing one.'

'Well, we can't go any further, then,' she said, and reached for her bag.

He didn't halt her.

'Thank you for wasting my time,' she added, and gave him another flash of that stunning smile.

Kedah noted that it didn't quite reach her eyes. They were a dazzling emerald-green— a shade that was one of a forest reflected on a lake…emerald, yet glacial.

He watched, quietly amused, as she began to flounce off.

'Sit down, Felicia.'

There was such command to his tone that it stopped her.

His voice wasn't remotely raised. If anything his words were delivered with an almost bored calm. But he might as well have reached for a lasso, for it was as if something had just wrapped around her. Oh, Felicia *heard* his words—yet she *felt* them at the base of her spine, and it tingled as he continued speaking.

'I haven't finished with you yet.'

CHAPTER TWO

IF EVER A voice belonged in the bedroom, it was Kedah's.

Not just a bedroom.

A boardroom would do nicely too.

For the second time in an hour Felicia was transported to that headmaster's office—but it was a far nicer version this time!

He was utterly potent. She almost wanted to keep walking towards the door, just for the giddy pleasure of finding out that she had a scruff to her neck as he hauled her back.

What she could not know was that the very controlled Sheikh Kedah was actually thinking along the same lines.

Felicia was absolutely his type.

He stared at the back of her head and then took in her rigid shoulders, let his dark eyes run the length of her spine. Her face was heart-shaped, and so too were her buttocks, and his eyes rested there for a moment too long.

Then he forced them away.

Kedah did not need the complication of a fake PA who turned him on.

He liked softness on his pillow and sweet, batting eyes, and he didn't care if his women lied as they simpered.

It was, after all, just a game.

And then he thought of the games he might play with Felicia.

He wanted to haul her to his knee and give her the job description as he ravished that mouth.

Know my hotels inside out, meet my staff, handle the press, and keep my world floating as I fight for my title. Now, let's go to bed.

Of course he did not say that.

This was business, and Kedah was determined it would remain so.

'Take a seat,' he said.

Felicia breathed out through her nostrils as he mentally undressed her. She felt as if he had even seen what colour knickers she had on. Flesh-coloured, actually. Not because she was boring, she wanted to hasten to add, but because of the white dress.

Oh, help!

And though common sense told her to leave now, to get out while she still could and most definitely should, neither had Felicia finished with *him*.

She wanted to know why he'd brought her here. She was positive that he didn't really want her working as his PA. So she turned around.

'Why are you so against signing a confidentiality agreement?' he asked, in such a measured tone that Felicia wondered if she'd misread the crackling tension.

'They're pointless.' She fought for professionalism and cleared her throat as the interview resumed. 'If, as you've stated, you trust no one, then a confidentiality agreement, no matter how watertight, cannot protect you.'

'It offers some level of security.'

'Well, it doesn't for me,' Felicia responded. 'What if something is leaked and you assume that *I* was the source?'

He didn't answer.

'I'm pretty unshockable, but what if you do something abhorrent?' she challenged. 'Am I supposed to turn a blind eye just because I've signed up for silence?'

'I'm bad,' Kedah said. 'Not evil.'

That made her smile, and this time it reached those stunning cold eyes.

'Sit down,' he said again. 'We can discuss it at the end of your trial.'

'There's nothing further to discuss on that subject—and also I don't do trials.' Felicia did sit down again, though. 'A one-year contract is the minimum I'll sign.'

'I might not need you for a year.'

That was the first real hint that there *was* more going on here. Maybe he felt awkward about telling her about his past—but that made no sense. There was nothing chaste about that blistering gaze. Perhaps there was something big about to come out? A huge scandal about to hit?

Felicia was tired of playing games. She wanted to know what she was getting into before she signed.

'Kedah, I'm not a defence lawyer.'

He simply stared back at her as she spoke, and she thought that never before had she had a client so able to meet her gaze.

'You *can* tell me whatever it is that's going on.'

Still he said nothing.

'I'm quite sure I already know.'

'Do tell,' he offered.

'I think you need me to restore your reputation,' she told him. 'And I can. Let me get to work, and in a matter of weeks I'll have you looking like an altar boy,'

'I hope not.'

'So do I…'

She faltered. Her voice had dropped to a smoky level that had no place at work—actually no place in her *life* till this point. Felicia dated, but she preferred the safe comfort of feeling lukewarm to this feeling of being speared on the end of a fondue stick and dipped at his whim.

She cleared her throat. 'Well, an altar boy might be pushing things, but if there's anything you're worried about…'

'Worrying is a pointless pursuit—and, as I thought I'd made clear, I'm fine with my reputation,' Kedah answered smoothly, and although his expression did not display even a trace of amusement Felicia felt as if he was laughing at her. 'In fact I've loved every minute that I've spent earning it.'

Kedah was entranced, for Felicia hadn't so much as blinked, nor had she blushed, and he decided then that she was hired.

'Okay, no confidentiality agreement. But mess with me, Felicia, and I will deal with you *outside* of the law.'

Now she blushed—but at a point far lower on her body than her face. She was about to make some glib comment about being tipped over his knee but rather rapidly changed her mind.

'Six months,' Kedah said.

'A year,' she refuted. 'And when I'm no longer needed you pay out the rest of my contract and I'll be on my way.'

'Is that what generally happens?' For a moment he let his guard drop—just a little. He was curious about her job. Fascinated, in fact. 'You do a few weeks' work for a year's pay?'

She nodded and Kedah—albeit briefly— forgot his own dark troubles. He wanted to know more, but Felicia shook her head when he asked.

'I don't discuss my previous clients, and of course I'll provide you with that same courtesy.' Her voice sounded a little frantic now. 'Now you need to tell me what's going on if I'm to do my job.'

'Felicia,' he offered, in a rather bored drawl, 'I didn't hire you to tidy up my reputation. This leopard shan't be changing his spots. I want a PA and I hear that you're amongst the best. Do you want the role or not?'

Her smile slipped and those once glacial eyes clouded in confusion.

He pushed forward the contract.

'We need to discuss terms and conditions,' Kedah explained, and then went through them.

Basically, for the next year she was his.

Well, not *his*!

Just at his beck and call. Even if he was in Zazinia without her she would be working here.

There would be no reprieve.

Felicia wondered if now was the time to state, as she usually did, that she never slept with clients.

She looked at his long slender fingers as they turned the page and moved on to remuneration.

'Regarding your salary…' he said.

'Kedah.'

She watched as with a stroke of his pen he doubled it.

'I expect devotion.'

Now! she thought. He had given the perfect opening, Felicia knew. Right now she should smile and nod as she warned him that there were certain things out of bounds.

And there were.

Of course there were.

But actually to state that nothing could possibly happen might make her a liar. Even if *he* didn't, Felicia trusted her own word, so she refrained from her usual terse speech.

He crossed out the confidentiality clause, and initialled it, and then it was time for them both to countersign.

Felicia read through the contract again, and noted that her starting date was today.

Now.

'Kedah…' Felicia felt it only fair to warn him. 'I don't think I'll make a very good PA.'

'On the contrary,' he said. 'I think you'll be excellent.'

There was more to this.

Quite simply, there had to be.

And Felicia wanted to know what it was.

With a hand that somehow remained steady she used her own pen to sign her name and initial in all the right places and that was it—she was tied to him for a year.

Unfortunately not literally.

'Why are you laughing?' he asked, when she suddenly did.

'Just something I said in my head.' Felicia replied, and tried to right herself.

She looked out of the window to a bosky summer evening and knew the rush Kedah gave her was a giddy one. She wanted to go home now, to collect her thoughts.

'I'm looking forward to working with you, Kedah,' Felicia said, and held out her hand to shake his.

'Good,' he said, but did not shake her hand.

It became suddenly clear she was not dismissed.

'Anu will show you to your office. I believe my assistant in Zazinia will be free to speak with you in an hour.'

'I thought…' she started. But, as she was about to find out, the interview was over, the negotiations were done, and Kedah had nothing more to discuss.

'That will be all for now.'

It would seem that at five p.m. on a Friday her work day had just begun.

The gorgeous office would tomorrow have Felicia's name on its door, Anu told her, and there was an award-winning chef a phone call away who would prepare whatever she chose for supper.

And so she got busy.

It was late in Zazinia but Vadia, Kedah's assistant there, looked fresh and crisp on the video link.

'The offending article has been taken down,' she informed Felicia. 'If you could let Kedah know that?'

So she didn't use his title when she spoke of him either, Felicia thought as Vadia continued.

'I am trying to schedule the finishing touches on his official portrait. The artist is due to go overseas for surgery in a couple of months' time, so if you could tell Kedah that it is becoming rather pressing?'

'I shall.'

Then she went through his upcoming agenda, and it was so full that Felicia wondered how on earth he'd had the time to earn his reputation.

'I shall speak with you again tomorrow.' Vadia smiled.

Tomorrow was Saturday. Not that a little thing like the weekend seemed to matter in Kedah's world.

'If you can just push Kedah for an answer regarding the artist? Also remind him that the next time he's home we will be arranging the date for his bridal selection.'

As easily as that Vadia slipped it in. In fact she spoke as if she was trying to pin him down for a dental appointment.

'Bridal selection?' Felicia checked.

'Kedah knows.' Vadia smiled again. 'Just inform him that his father, the King, wants a date.'

As Vadia disappeared from the screen Felicia

sat for a moment, trying to assimilate all she had found out today. While Kedah might insist that his reputation wasn't an issue, it might prove to be one for any future bride.

Especially if said reputation continued unchecked.

Was that why she was here? Felicia pondered. Was he soon to marry and she was to take charge of his social life here in England? *No way.*

Felicia was used to putting out fires—not sitting back and watching them be lit.

Anu was the gatekeeper to Kedah's office, and as Felicia walked over to ask her something she saw that she was happily taking her supper break and eating a fragrant meal as she watched the awards show live on the computer.

'Oh, she won!' Anu smiled and put down her cutlery, and clapped as Felicia came to her side and watched a pretty young actress take her place on the stage. 'She's such a lovely person,' Anu said. 'Just genuinely nice!'

Please! Felicia thought, about to point out to Anu that actresses *acted*, and that was what Miss Pretty was doing right now as she thanked everyone—absolutely everyone…not just God, but her neighbour's blind cat too—in her little breathless voice.

'She's just acting…' Felicia started, and was about to say what a load of whitewash it all was when Kedah stalked out of his office. 'I was about to come in and speak with you,' Felicia said. 'Vadia needs some dates—'

'Not now,' he interrupted. 'Felicia, can you find out what after-party Beth will be attending and get me on the list? And could you also call The Ritz and have them prepare my suite?'

'Beth?' Felicia frowned.

'The actress who just won that award,' Kedah said.

'Do you know her?' she asked, but he had already disappeared.

'Not yet.' Anu smirked as she answered for him.

And the oddest thing of it all was that Anu didn't seem bothered one bit. Anu—who had looked as if she was chewing lemons all through Felicia's interview—didn't seem to mind in the least about Kedah's wild ways.

The staff at The Ritz were also clearly more than used to him. His suite was already prepared, Felicia found out when she called. And the organisers of the after-party would be delighted to add him to the list. In fact they asked if they could send a car.

'I'm not sure,' Felicia said. 'Can I call you back?'

'Just check with him,' Anu suggested, and gestured to his door for Felicia to go in. 'Though I doubt he'll want one.'

Felicia knocked and entered and there Kedah was—all showered and cologned, as sexy as sin, as he pulled on a fresh shirt and she got her first glimpse of a heavenly brown and broad chest. Michelangelo had clearly been at that, she thought, as she tried and failed not to notice the fan of silky straight black hair. Straight? Yes, straight, Felicia realised as she glanced down to where his trousers sat low on his hips.

'The party is all ready for you,' Felicia said, managing not to clear her throat. 'They offered to send a car.'

'Tell them no. I prefer to use my own transport.'

'Sure.'

His shirt was now done up, and he frowned as he pulled out a tie and saw that Felicia remained. 'Can you call down for my driver?'

'Of course,' Felicia said. 'But can we quickly discuss a couple of things? Vadia needs a date for your portrait to be finished and also to arrange your bridal selection.' She watched for his reaction, for Kedah to falter and possibly tell her the real reason she was here, but instead he finished knotting his tie and pulled on his jacket.

'We can go through all that another time. I'll see you tomorrow.'

He had that hunter's look in his eye, and Felicia guessed there was no point talking business now.

Nor brides.

'Hey, Kedah!' she called as he went to walk off.

'What?' His reply was impatient—there was an after-party for him to get to after all.

'I don't think Beth *is* actually that nice,' she said, and on his way out he halted. In a matter of fact voice, she explained better. 'Usually I warn my clients if I think they're courting trouble…'

Now she had his attention, and she watched as he turned around and walked over to where she stood. She'd expected a question, for him to ask for a little more of what she knew about the woman, but he came right over and faced her, stepped into her personal space.

Too close?

He was a decent distance away, and there was nothing intimidating about his stance, yet her body was on high alert and his fragrance was heavy on her senses. Without saying so, he demanded that her eyes meet his.

'I'm not your *client*, Felicia,' he said, in a voice that held warning. 'I'm your boss. Got it?'

And she stood there, prickling and indignant, as he put her very firmly in her place.

'I was just trying to—'

'I don't need warnings,' he said. 'And, between you and me, I've already guessed that Beth is not *nice*. My intention tonight is to prove it.'

Then he smiled.

Oh, it was a real smile.

Her first!

It stretched his lips and it warmed her inside. It was like ten coffees on waking and it was the moment Felicia discovered the skin behind her knees—because it felt as if he were stroking her there with his long slender fingers, even though his hands were held at his side.

'Goodnight, Felicia. It was a pleasure to meet you and I'm looking forward to *working* with you.'

She heard the emphasis on the word working and let out a slightly shrill laugh. 'Fair enough.'

She put her hands up as if in defence. 'You don't need another mother...'

'I certainly don't.'

'But know this,' Felicia said, and delivered a warning of her own. 'I shan't be arranging hotels and after-parties once you've chosen your wife.'

He stared at her for the longest time, even opened his mouth to speak, but then he changed his mind.

Kedah did not have to explain himself—and certainly not to a member of staff.

Which Felicia *was*, he reminded himself.

And a member of staff she would remain, for there were plenty of actresses and supermodels to be had.

'Be here at seven-thirty tomorrow and don't be late.'

He stalked out of the office. There was no slamming of the door—he didn't even bother to close it—but she was as rattled as if he'd banged it shut.

Oh, she would *not* fall for him.

Yes, if there was a scale for playboys then Kedah would be at the extreme end. The problem was Felicia could easily see why.

It was impossible not to want him.

It was the first time she'd realised she must heed her mother's advice.

'Never fall for a bastard. Especially not one who can make you smile.'

And Kedah did.

Oh, he most certainly did.

CHAPTER THREE

FELICIA BRISKLY MADE her way along Dubai's The Walk, towards the restaurant she had booked for their lunchtime meeting. There was no time to linger, or to take in the delicious view. Kedah's multiple assistants were kept far too busy for that.

At the age of twenty-six, Felicia Hamilton had a job.

A *real* one.

Instead of her regular four weeks or so of work for a full year's pay, and a long pause between jobs, Felicia now found herself working the most ridiculous hours as she travelled the globe with Kedah. Oh, their mode of transport was luxurious—Kedah had his own private jet—but even a mile up in the air there was little downtime. Kedah considered his jet another office, and it was the same at his luxurious hotels.

She'd never have agreed to a year of this had she known.

Except not only had she agreed to it—Felicia herself had been the one to insist on it. He had told her exactly what to expect at the interview. He'd even offered her a trial period, which she'd declined!

Oh, what a fool. Had she taken the trial then she would have been finishing up by now!

Or would she...?

Even after close to eight weeks spent working hard for him Felicia still didn't believe that Kedah just wanted her as a PA.

She wasn't even very good at it.

Felicia was the one who generally gave orders. Now each day she stared down the barrel of her to-do list, as did his other assistants. One PA would never be enough for him.

There had to be another reason she was here.

Felicia was trying hard to work it out, but really there was little time for daydreaming. Her schedule was relentless.

She was up at six each day, and it was often close to midnight before she crashed—just as Kedah hit the town with his sweet and oh, so pleasing date of choice for the night.

Felicia honestly didn't know how he did it.

Since meeting him she was on her second lot of concealer, to hide the shadows under her eyes.

There had been a tiny reprieve last night. Kedah had asked her to book theatre tickets for himself and his latest bimbo—which she had done. But while his absence had given Felicia an early night, she had spent it sulking.

This morning Kedah had been off looking at potential hotel sites, and she had sat in bed on the phone, liaising with his flight crew for their trip to Zazinia tomorrow.

Now she was meeting him for lunch, to go through the agenda for his trip home. There the artist would be able to work on his portrait, and there his father would discuss a wedding with his son.

That *had* to be the issue, Felicia decided. She was quite sure that Kedah had no desire to marry.

The restaurant she had chosen was dark and cool, and uninviting enough to keep the less than extremely well-heeled away.

'I have a booking,' she said. 'Felicia Hamilton.'

'Of course.'

When she had booked the restaurant Felicia had told them she was meeting an important guest and would like their very best table. She hadn't told them just how important her guest was, though.

It was a little game she played, and she smiled as she was led through the stunning restaurant to a gorgeous low table.

Indeed, it *was* beautiful.

There were plump cushions on the floor and the table was dressed with pale orchids. As she lowered herself onto a cushion she could hear the couple behind her laughing and chatting as she set up her work station.

She took a drink of iced water as she waited for Kedah to arrive, and again tried to fathom what trouble his wedding could pose.

There might be a baby Kedah? Felicia pondered. A pregnant ex, perhaps?

But, no, she was quite sure that Kedah would handle that in his own matter-of-fact way.

What about a pregnant prostitute?

That would surely rock the palace and destroy any chance for Kedah to remain as Crown Prince. Though she couldn't really imagine Kedah having to *pay* for sex—or even caring what others thought if he chose to do so.

Felicia took another long sip of iced water. She tended to do that when she thought of Kedah in that way—and she thought of Kedah in that way an awful lot…

Despite her very strict 'Never mix business with pleasure' motto, Felicia occasionally indulged in a little flirt with him—or rather, a very intense flirt. And there were odd moments when she felt as if her clothes had just fallen off. He made her feel naked with his eyes, although he was always terribly polite.

Felicia knew she'd have trouble saying no if he so much as crooked a finger in her direction. He hadn't, though—which was just as well, because he'd be in for a rude shock. There was no way Felicia would turn into one of those simpering *Your pleasure is all mine, Kedah* women he had a very frequent yen for.

Sweet.

That was the type of women he chose—or rather that was how they appeared until they were dumped. Then it was Felicia who dealt with their angry, tearful outbursts.

She had almost been able to picture Beth, the actress, kicking her neighbour's blind cat when she'd told her that Kedah would not be taking her calls anymore.

'Have you thought about a gift?' Felicia had asked her, while trying to keep a straight face.

Yes, she had found out on her third day of working for Kedah that his aggrieved exes were sent a brochure from which to choose a gift.

No diamonds or pearls from Kedah—jewellery was too personal, of course. But a luxury holiday brochure was theirs to peruse. After all, what better than a week in the South of France or a trip to Mustique to help soothe that wounded heart? The only downside was that Sheikh Kedah would not be there.

He had already moved on to the next.

Beth had chosen to take her broken heart for a little cruise around the Caribbean. Felicia might have told her she'd have stood far more chance of a repeat night with Kedah if she'd told Felicia to pass on to him precisely what he could do with his brochure.

No one ever did.

But, while Kedah seemed at ease with his wretched reputation, there *had* to be more to why he wanted her nearby than to introduce her to the managers of all his hotels around the globe.

Why did Felicia need to know that the Dubai hotel manager was an anxious sort but a wonderful leader? Why had he taken great pains to have her meet his accounts managers and his team of lawyers?

It just didn't make sense.

She looked up because, from the rustling and whispers amongst the patrons, it would seem that someone stunning had just arrived—and of course there he was.

She had recovered from the faint-inducing sight of Kedah in a suit, but here in Dubai he wore traditional attire and each day was a delicious surprise to the senses. On this fine day the angels had chosen for him a robe in cool, completely non-virginal white, and such was his beauty and presence that he turned every head as he made his way over.

His *keffiyeh* was of white-on-white jacquard, with knotted edges, and was seemingly casually tied. He was unshaven, but very neatly so. His lips were thick and sexy, the cupid's bow at the top so perfect one might be forgiven for thinking it tattooed. But this was all natural. Felicia had inspected that mouth closely enough to be very sure of that.

He looked royal and haughty and utterly beautiful, from his expensive cool head right down to his sexy leather-clad feet. Then his eyes lit on her, and the beautiful mouth relaxed into a warm smile—one that didn't just light up his features, but his whole being.

Auras were supposed to be indistinguishable, even non-existent, yet Kedah wore his golden glow like a heavy fur coat.

He was a wolf in prince's clothing. Felicia knew that.

Such delectable clothing, though!

And *such* a stunning man…

Of course it wasn't only the women who noted his suave arrival—inevitably the head waiter came dashing over, clearly troubled at the inadequate seating arrangements for such an esteemed guest.

'You didn't say that you were dining with Sheikh Kedah,' he admonished her.

'I *did* say I was meeting an important guest,' Felicia said sweetly.

'Then please accept our sincere apologies. We have given you the wrong table—it is our mistake. Allow me…' He was gathering up her phone, her tablet, the whole mini-office that she set up whenever she met with Kedah.

'Of course.'

Felicia smiled to herself as she was bundled over to a stunning table—one where there was no chance of hearing their neighbours' conversation. The only sound was the gentle cascade of a fountain, the view of the marina was idyllic, and here the floor was entirely theirs.

'You played your game again,' he commented as they sat down opposite the other.

'I did.' Felicia nodded, and then met and held his gaze.

His eyes were thickly lashed, and he had a way of looking at her that honestly felt as if she were the only person present on the planet. He gave his absolute full attention in a way that was unlike anybody Felicia had ever known.

'Why don't you just say in the first place that you are meeting me?' he asked, because this happened rather a lot when Felicia booked their meetings.

'Because I like watching them fluster when you arrive.'

Kedah would like to see Felicia fluster—and yet she was always measured and poised and gave away so little of herself.

He would like to know more.

The thought continually surprised him. Kedah did not get involved with staff, yet over the past few weeks he had found himself wondering more and more about Felicia and what went on in her head.

It was a pretty head—one that was usually framed with shoulder-length hair. But today her hair was worn up. It was too severe on her, Kedah thought. Or was it that she'd lost a little weight? And he could see that she'd put on some make-up in an attempt to hide the smudges under her eyes.

Gorgeous eyes, Kedah thought. They regularly changed shade. Today they were an inviting sea-green, but he would not be diving in.

He did not want to muddy things—he needed her on board and, given that his relationships ran to days rather than weeks, he did not want to risk losing her over something as basic and readily available as sex.

Yet all too often they tipped into flirting. Kedah usually didn't bother—there was little need for it when you were as good-looking and as powerful as he. Yet he enjoyed their conversations that turned a seductive corner on occasion. Though Felicia had promised him discretion, there were times when he wanted her naked in bed beside him. He wanted to laugh as she told him tales about her former bosses.

Or 'clients', as Felicia referred to them.

That irked him.

He had seen her list of references, and some of the names there had had his jaw gritting. And, yes—he'd wondered all too often how close Felicia might have been to them. That was another thing that irritated him, but it would hardly be fair to question her about it.

He remembered now that he was cross with her for last night.

'Felicia, when I ask you to make a theatre booking for my date and myself, please do better in future.'

She knew he was referring to the previous night. At five, he had suddenly decided he wanted two of the hottest tickets in town.

'I got you the best available seats,' Felicia said. 'And I had to call in a favour to secure them.'

'Again…' he sighed '…you declined to say for whom you were booking.'

'You told me at my interview that you expect discretion.'

'I *expect* the best seats,' Kedah said. 'Had they not recognised me, I'd have been stuck behind a pillar. When you ring to make any booking in future, you are to tell them that it is for me.'

'That will ruin my game.'

'Tough,' he said. 'Right, let's go through my schedule. I want you to arrange some time for me to go to the States in a couple of weeks.'

And as she stared at him a thought suddenly occurred to her. Maybe he was already married—maybe that was the scandal that was about to hit.

'Do you go to America a lot?' she asked.

He nodded.

'Where?'

'All over. Though mainly New York. My friend Matteo lives there.'

'The one with the motor racing team?'

Kedah nodded.

Wild Matteo, who was known for his penchant for gambling and high-octane living.

'Have you ever been to Vegas?' she asked him.

'Felicia…' Kedah sighed again. 'Where is this leading?'

'I just wondered if you'd been to Vegas with Matteo…' She gave him a smile. 'And perhaps done something there that you might regret?'

'I don't waste time with regrets,' he said. 'And I don't like wasting time—which we are. Let's go through tomorrow's agenda.'

They were saved from that, though, as the waiter somewhat nervously approached with mint tea. As Kedah looked up she felt the shifting of his attention. He was polite and engaged with the waiter, and as they spoke in Arabic she watched as he put the young man at ease.

He was arrogant, and yet he was kind.

Arrogant in that he expected the best and most often got it.

But then he could also be very kind.

'What would you like to eat?' Kedah asked Felicia.

'Fruit,' Felicia said. 'Something light.'

'Sounds good.'

He ordered, and when they were alone again he asked her how she was finding the hotel. Given he had not just designed the hotel but owned it, Felicia knew this was no idle enquiry.

'It's amazing,' she told him. 'Though I'd love to have some time to actually enjoy the facilities.'

Instead rather a lot of her time had been spent driving around to meet with the staff at his other acquisitions, or standing in the blistering sun scouring potential sites for Kedah to build on.

'I think I've found the site for its brother,' Kedah told her.

'Do buildings have a gender?'

'Mine do.'

'From conception?' Felicia asked. 'Do you decide before you start the design that this one is going to be a boy?'

He smiled, and for Felicia the rays were as golden as the sun outside as he pondered her question.

'I guess I do,' he said. 'I want to go and have another look at the site after lunch, and then meet with a surveyor. You'll need sensible shoes.'

Joy!

Their lunch was served—citrus fruit and

dragon fruits and sweet plump figs, as well as a light lemongrass mousse that just melted on her tongue. As they ate he asked her more questions about the hotel and she answered honestly.

Most of the time he liked it that she did—he was terribly used to his staff pandering to him. Her opinion was always refreshing, as well as at times rather blunt.

Kedah was, of course, up in the royal suite at the hotel, where every detail was taken care of and his every whim predicted. He wanted to know what it was like for a Western businesswoman traveller, so she was slumming it on the luxurious twenty-fourth floor with her own lap pool and butler.

'It's gorgeous.'

'Tell me what I don't know.'

Felicia thought hard. It really was difficult to be critical about somewhere so divine, but she pondered his question for a moment and was finally able to find a tiny fault. 'I think the service is a bit inconsistent.'

He watched as she bit on a piece of dragon fruit and waited for her to elaborate.

She soon obliged.

'Like, last night there weren't any chocolates on my pillow.'

'Poor Felicia.'

'I'm just saying,' she told him. 'You come to expect these things. Now, if I'd *never* had chocolate on my pillow I wouldn't have missed it, but I really sulked last night when they forgot...'

Or had she sulked because Kedah had gone off, out to the theatre? She wasn't sure, but certainly chocolate would have helped if that had been the case.

'First world problem.' She smiled.

'Noted,' Kedah said. 'If you came back to Dubai would you choose to stay there again?'

He was rather taken aback when she immediately shook her head.

'I don't think so.'

'Why?'

'I like trying new things.'

'If you're satisfied there should be no need or inclination to try anything else. I want to know why you wouldn't return.'

'Well, it's stunning, but...' She let out a breath and then decided she should perhaps check before being completely frank. 'Kedah, do you *really* want me to criticise one of your babies?'

I dare you to, his eyes told her. 'Go on,' he said politely.

'Well, as nice as it all is, I find it to be a bit impersonal,' Felicia responded, and she watched his tongue roll into his cheek. 'You *did* ask.'

'I did.'

'It just needs those extra touches,' Felicia offered.

'Such as…?'

'I don't know.' She shrugged. 'Maybe coloured towels, or something. I'm sick of white.'

She was—for she looked at his robe and she wanted it gone. She looked down to her hands and wanted them to be suddenly wrapped in his.

And *that* was the trouble with Kedah.

Not the terribly long hours, nor the jet lag, and it wasn't even the endless little black book she ran for him.

It was *this*.

These moments sitting with him.

These moments when flirting was a thought away…when she felt every conversation would be better executed in bed.

'You can do better than that,' he said.

Felicia had to drag her mind back to their conversation, actually force herself to remember they were discussing his hotel and not lean across the table and tell him that, yes, she *could* do far, far better.

'I don't have much experience in hospitality, remember?' she snapped wondering for possibly the millionth time what the hell he had hired her for.

Kedah could be boring!

Truly.

It was a terrible thing to admit but, just as when he had dimmed the lights and, instead of thrilling her, had proceeded to numb her brain with his hotel presentation, now—when they were in sumptuous surroundings and there was all this energy present—they sat discussing, of all things, towels.

He was driving her to distraction.

'The décor is black and brown in my American chain of hotels,' Kedah mused. 'The towels there are too.'

'Yum…' Felicia snarked.

'It actually works very well.'

'Why am I here, Kedah?' She was exhausted with not knowing. 'Why are we sitting here discussing bloody *towels*…?'

'Décor is important.'

'Then hire someone who cares!' she snapped. 'And tell me why I'm here.'

'You'll know when you need to.'

'Are you married?' The question tumbled out. 'Was there a drunken mistake that turned into a Mrs Kedah that I'm going to have to explain away?'

'Is that why you were asking about Vegas?'

He put his head back and laughed and she wanted her mouth on his throat.

'Felicia, I'm not married.'

'Is there a baby…?'

'You have too much imagination.'

'Er… Kedah, I don't think you and your lady-friends are merely holding hands. Accidents happen.'

'Not to me,' he said. 'I make sure of that.'

He honestly admired Felicia, because even as they discussed his strict use of birth control she didn't blush.

'However,' he mused, 'it wouldn't be a problem.'

'Your father would *welcome* the news?' Felicia asked, in a somewhat sarcastic tone, but it didn't faze him.

'It would be dealt with. I wouldn't be the first Crown Prince in our history to have a child out of wedlock. But Vadia would deal with that sort of thing—not you. Enough now,' he said, and went back to his schedule. 'We'll meet in the foyer at five tomorrow morning and get to Zazinia around midday,' he said. 'My time will be taken up with family stuff. There won't be much for you to do.'

'So why can't I just fly home?'

She was itching to get home—for a night in her flat without the alarm set for the crack of dawn the next morning. For a full twenty-four hours away from the burn of his eyes.

'Because…'

He couldn't answer straight away. Usually he *didn't* bring his London PA home with him. Occasionally he brought Anu, because she was from Zazinia, but there was absolutely no reason for bringing Felicia other than that he wanted her there.

'It's cheaper to have you there with me than to fly you home separately.'

'Oh, please!' She smiled sweetly.

'The Crown Prince's wing is being refurbished. I might need you…'

'To haul stone from the quarries?' she teased.

'To take some photos and jot down my suggestions.' He was stern. 'If it's not too much trouble?' She really was a terrible PA. 'As I said, I'll be busy with formal stuff. My portrait needs to be completed. Then there will be a dinner with my family.'

'That will be nice.'

Kedah gave her nothing—not a roll of the

eyes, not even a small smile at her slightly sarcastic comment—but she knew there was trouble between the brothers.

'And then there's the matter of your wedding.'

'Yes.'

'And will you?' Felicia asked. 'Be taking a bride?'

'I might.' Kedah nodded.

He was tired of his father using his marital status as an excuse for things not to move along. Perhaps he would call his father's bluff and tell him to get things underway.

When he had said that he might be considering marriage, for the first time Felicia's expression faltered. She fought quickly to right it, but Felicia knew she'd been seen and so moved to cover it.

'I loathe weddings. I hope I shan't have to arrange that?'

'Don't worry.' He shook his head. 'The palace will take care of all that. You'll just be arranging a few final wild nights for me, leading up to it.'

'Look out, London.' Felicia rolled her eyes.

'Look out, world,' he corrected, for if he were to marry then he intended to use his last weeks of freedom unwisely. Except he hadn't been.

Lately he hadn't. Last night it hadn't just been the seating arrangements that had got on his nerves.

It had been the company.

He had wanted Felicia beside him, and that might have been the reason he had dropped his date back to her hotel early.

'Then again,' Kedah said, 'if I am to choose a bride in a matter of weeks, perhaps it *is* time for me to be more discreet.'

She did not meet his gaze. Perhaps she had missed the opening, he thought, for she was signalling the waiter and asking for more water.

That was bold for here in Dubai. Usually only a male would signal the waiter, but then that was Felicia: bold.

Tough.

She was possibly the one woman who would *not* go losing her head if they were to sleep together.

'Felicia…' he said, and then, for once unsure how to broach things, he asked another question. 'Are you enjoying your work?'

'Not really,' she admitted. 'It's nothing like I expected. I thought I'd be putting out fires after big Kedah-created scandals.'

'How did you get into all that?'

She hesitated. Usually there was no way that Felicia would discuss her personal life, and yet if she wanted to know more about him maybe it was time to reveal something of herself. And he *was* good company.

Terribly so.

She might not be thrilled by her job description, but there was no doubt that she enjoyed being with him.

It was when she wasn't that her issues arose.

And so she found herself telling him a little. 'My father had a prominent job, but as far back as I can remember he got embroiled in scandal. Affairs, prostitutes...' Felicia coldly stated the facts. 'My mother and I were regularly schooled in what to say and what not to say. How to react...how to smile. Now I get paid to tell others the same.'

'Did your mother leave him in the end?' Kedah asked.

'No, after all he'd put her through it was my father who ended the marriage,' Felicia said. 'All the times she'd stood by him counted for nothing in the end. He planned how to leave her and did all he could to protect himself and his new girlfriend. The family home went—as did my boarding school. And I found out that my friends weren't really my friends. By the time he had dragged out the court proceedings I was well out of school. I left at sixteen and got a job in an office to support my mother.'

'Yet *you* are the PA everyone wants. Why?'

'My first boss. I never even saw him much, apart from setting up a meeting room. Anyway, scandal hit—as it often does—and the PR people he had working for him were seriously clueless. I knocked on his door and told him I could sort it for him.'

'How old were you?'

'I'd have been about nineteen,' Felicia said.

'He believed you?'

'He had no choice. He was up to his neck in scandal. I spoke to the press. I laughed at their inferences. I dealt with it just as I'd been taught to while I was growing up.'

'How is your mother now?'

Felicia didn't answer. She just gave a small shrug.

He sensed that she was finished talking about it. The subject moved back to work and there it remained, even after their meal had concluded.

Yet Kedah was curious.

'You'll need sensible shoes,' he reminded her as they walked to his car.

'Then you need to buy me some.'

She attempted humour, but she was still all churned up from thinking about her mother.

A little while later they stood on a man-made island and Kedah told her his vision for the hotel he was thinking of building there.

'What do you think?' he asked.

Usually he cared for no one else's opinion, yet he was starting to covet hers.

'It sounds a lot like the other one.'

It was possibly the most offensive thing she could have said, and yet her honesty made him smile.

'That's why I call them brothers.'

'Can't they just be siblings?' Felicia asked. 'Could this one not be a girl?'

He thought for a moment and, as terrible an assistant as she was, Felicia gave him pause.

Perhaps he *could* consider a gentler version of the other hotel. The Dubai skyline was ultra-modern, and there were some stunning architectural feats. From tall rigid towers to soft golden buildings in feminine curves. Perhaps it was time to try something different.

'See over there…?' He pointed. 'That was my first design. Well, along with Hussain.'

'Now, that's *definitely* a he!' Felicia said, because it was a huge phallic tower, rising into the sky.

'You're getting the idea.' Kedah smiled. 'It was my first serious project. Well, my second. I had designed a building for my home, but it was vetoed.'

'Is that a modified version of it?' Felicia asked.

'No. That design could never have worked here. There was a mural and...' He shook his head. 'I worked on this with Hussain. He is from my homeland, and studied architecture with my father, but *his* hands are tied there too...' Kedah halted.

'In what way?'

He thought for a moment and realised there was no harm in telling her, and as they chatted they walked away from the car and towards the water's edge.

'There are so many regulations back home. No window can overlook the royal beach...no building can be as high as the palace...'

'I'm sure you could work your way around them.'

They had toyed with each other and, yes, occasionally they had flirted, and of course Kedah had wondered what it would be like to know Felicia in the bedroom.

Now with one sentence she had changed things.

It was as if she had a little jewelled sword in her hand and had sliced straight through the chains that kept anybody from entering his heart.

She was the very first person who had not immediately derided his vision for his homeland.

Here was someone who did not instantly reject nor dismiss his ideas.

Even Hussain, to whom he had entrusted his visions, constantly told Kedah that he dreamed too big for his home.

'It's complicated, Felicia.'

'Life *is*.'

'We should get back,' he said, and he took her elbow to guide her back towards the car.

'What time are we meeting the surveyor?'

'Two,' Kedah said, and his voice was suddenly brusque. 'Though I won't need you there. Go back to the hotel and use some of the facilities.'

'You're giving me the afternoon off?' Felicia frowned. 'Why?'

'I *can* be nice.'

'I never said you couldn't.' She gave him a little nudge.

It was just that—a playful nudge. But Felicia did not play like that and neither did Kedah.

It was a tease—a touch that would have gone unnoticed had they been more familiar.

Yet they were *not* familiar.

They just happened to ache to be.

And so instead of walking they stood there, on an empty man-made island. His driver was some distance away, endlessly on his phone, and as the hot wind whipped at one of her loose curls Kedah resisted tucking it behind her ear.

'Will you tell me something, Felicia?'

'Maybe.'

'Do you flirt with *all* your clients?'

'I don't flirt.'

'I disagree.'

He was rather too direct.

'While I accept,' Kedah continued, 'that you don't tip up your face or bat your lashes—in fact you don't invoke any of the more usual tactics—you *do* flirt. And I just wondered if it was the same with all your…*clients*?'

She heard the implication. 'You make me sound like a whore.'

'Please forgive me for any offence caused—absolutely none was meant. I am just curious as to what you are here for. I employed you as my PA and yet you don't seem to want that job.'

'I'm tired of the games, Kedah, and I'm tired

that even after eight weeks you still don't trust me with the truth.'

'Okay—here it is. I believe the Accession Council will meet soon, and that there will be turbulent times ahead as my suitability for the role of Crown Prince is called into question.'

'I know all that,' Felicia said. 'So where do I fit in?'

'I need someone who knows the business— someone who, when it all kicks off—'

'Kicks off?' she checked.

'I believe my brother will have the backing of the elders. More troubling for me is that I believe my father may support him also. If that is the case I shall be forced to take it to the people to decide. That would cause a lot of unrest and bad publicity...'

'You'd want me to convince your people that just because you've run a bit wild...?' She paused as Kedah smiled—a lightly mocking smile.

'Felicia,' he said. 'My people *love* me.'

She didn't get it. She could not see where she might fit in to all this. 'They love you regardless?'

'No.' He shook his head. 'I would never expect them to support me regardless. They love

me because of what I stand for, what I can do
for them.'

'Oh.'

Kedah did not want to tell anyone—unless
he was forced to—that the scandal that was
looming was not one of his making.

Correction.

Sometimes he *did* want to tell her.

Back in the restaurant, when Felicia had spoken of her father, he had wanted to share his
own truth. But that was an unfamiliar route for
Kedah and so still he'd held back.

He held back from revealing the full truth
now.

'I am spending time in Zazinia. You can deal
with the empire I have built and answer with
ease the many questions that will be hurled.'

'That's it?' Felicia frowned. 'That's all you
want me there for? To deal with the press? I
don't believe you.'

That *had* been it.

Kedah had wanted someone tough and strong
to take care of the press as he devoted his time
to his country. He knew how bad things were
likely to get if the elders and Mohammed called
his parentage into question.

Never had he considered revealing that to
another—especially not a lowly PA.

And he wasn't now.

Instead he was considering discussing it with Felicia—the woman who had held him entranced since she had stood outside his office eight weeks ago.

He was supposed to marry soon. He did not need her tearful and scorned. And yet with every minute that passed between them he felt as if they were falling slowly into bed, into sex, into want. She could deny it, yet he *felt* it. And if they were about to cave then he needed to know she could remain strong, that sex could be separated from the vital tasks ahead.

And possibly, Kedah pondered as she stared back at him, Felicia was the one person who would be able to do that.

It irked him that she considered him a *client*.

And it troubled him that she might have been involved with some of her clients in the past.

Then again, if he wanted the toughest of the tough perhaps it should not.

There was no polite way to ask.

'Your eyes were the shade of the sea at the restaurant. Now they are hooker green.'

Her breath tightened and she flashed him a look of fire.

'It's an actual shade,' he said. 'And you *are* flirting, Felicia. Your eyes invite me closer at times.'

'Perhaps I'm just responding in kind.'

'I want you,' he told her.

He just stated his case.

Her clothes felt as if they had disintegrated again. She felt as if she were standing there stark naked even though his eyes never left hers.

'I am thinking now that unless you go I shall cancel the surveyor and take you up to my suite…'

'And you presume that I'll join you? You just assume I want you too?'

Felicia tried—she really did. But had his driver got out and started clapping she'd have joined him. Because it was a joke that she didn't want Kedah. She was *so* turned on.

Click your fingers and I'll come turned on.

And he smiled that arrogant smile that told her he absolutely *knew* she would join him should he so choose.

'The thing is I need you working for me more than I need you between the sheets.' Right now that was debatable, but although Kedah regretted little, he knew that *this* he might. 'I don't want tears in the morning, and I want you to continue to work for me rather than moping about in Mustique, so I suggest that you go back to the hotel and have a think. I don't want you agreeing to something you might later regret.'

'You've got a nerve.'

'I know I have.'

'Kedah, I've booked for your date to be collected for you at ten tonight...'

'That gives you several hours to make up your mind. She can easily be cancelled.'

Oh, yes, if there was a scale of playboys then Kedah would definitely be at the extreme end.

In all her imaginings—and, yes, there had been plenty—they were talking one moment and then somehow had moved seamlessly to bed. Never had she thought she'd be so frankly propositioned. That Kedah would have her cancelling his date so he could slot *her* in.

Thankfully he'd just made it a whole lot easier to say no!

'I don't need several hours to make up my mind,' she answered. 'Enjoy your night.'

She turned her head as a car approached. It would seem that the surveyor was here.

'I'm going to enjoy my afternoon off.'

'Do.'

* * *

She didn't.

The lap pool was paid a visit, but it did not clear her head, and a lengthy massage, although divine, did little to relax her.

Dinner for one felt lonely that night.

But she made herself sit through it.

Ten p.m. came, and when it had safely passed she went up to his suite.

He was out.

Clearly Kedah waited for no one.

The maid was there, preparing the bed, and the butler helped her to pack up his things for their early-morning start.

She stared at the bed with a mixture of pride and regret.

Pride that she had not succumbed.

Regret that she would never know how it felt to be Kedah's lover.

She set his alarm for four and headed down to her own suite. As she opened the door, still cross—*so* cross with him for his suggestion— still he made her smile.

There were chocolates on her pillow.

Many, many chocolates on her pillow. All perfectly wrapped.

But more than that, as she walked into the

bathroom to strip, she was met with a rainbow of colour.

Kedah wasn't boring, and even towels could be sexy, Felicia thought as she showered and then chose from the selection.

There were deep crimsons and burnt oranges—but she bypassed them and reached for another towel...one possibly the shade of hooker green.

She should be offended, and yet Kedah had removed that. From the day she had met him she had rightly guessed that he saved his issues for outside the bedroom. If sex was reduced to a business arrangement then so be it for him.

Could *she* do it, though?

Could she simply submit for the bliss of knowing what it was like to be made love to by him?

Kedah seemed to think it was doable. But then he assumed that she was tough and that he was simply another client.

Oh, no, he wasn't.

He was slowly stealing her heart.

What if she never revealed that?

Felicia had been trained to hide her true feelings from a very young age. This could possibly serve as the ultimate test.

Wrapped in her towel, she walked to the bed and peeled open a chocolate. As she tasted it, dark, sweet and silky on her tongue, she saw a note.

Handwritten by him.

Think about it.

She couldn't *stop* thinking about it—no matter how she tried.

CHAPTER FOUR

WHERE WAS HE?

A pre-dawn Dubai sky offered no answers as Felicia peered out through the window of her hotel suite. There were yachts lit up on the marina. No doubt there were parties aplenty still happening, and if Kedah was running true to form he might well be down there amongst them.

His butler had just called her to say that there had been no response to his wake-up call.

'Can you go in and check?' Felicia had asked, but the butler had explained that because the 'Do Not Disturb' light was on he couldn't, even though it was doubtful Kedah was there.

Apparently the Sheikh had returned to the hotel after midnight, but had been seen heading out again around two a.m.

When Felicia tried his cell phone it was off.

He was *always* on time, Felicia told herself

as she headed into the bathroom and checked her appearance. She would have to change on the plane, as Kedah had told her the dress code was strict in Zazinia, but for now she was wearing a navy shift dress. Before heading out she would add to it a small short-sleeved bolero to cover her arms.

Felicia really needed her concealer this morning, after a night spent pondering their conversation, but she decided to do her make-up on the plane too.

Right now she was too busy ruing the hours she had spent considering getting further involved with Kedah if his reaction was simply to stay out all night.

Hell, yes, she was angry.

She had worked with him for eight weeks and the last four had been spent travelling.

Soon they would be back in London and a safer distance would be easier to maintain.

To think she might have succumbed at the last hurdle!

She wasn't just cross with Kedah, she was angry with herself as she marched out of her bathroom. She went to put up her hair, but simply didn't have the upper arm strength or the concentration this morning.

Another thing that could wait for the plane.

There was a knock on the door to her suite, and she opened it to the bellboy who had come to collect her luggage.

'Has Sheikh Kedah's luggage been taken down?' Felicia checked.

'Not yet,' the bellboy informed her. 'We cannot go in if the "Do Not Disturb" light is on.'

'Even if he's probably not there?'

'Even then.'

Felicia let out a tense breath as the door closed and she was again left alone with some choices to make.

She had access to his suite—of course she did. Last night she and the butler had packed his belongings there, leaving the necessaries out for the morning.

All Kedah had had to do was tumble into bed with the requisite blonde and then get up on time.

She headed out to the elevators, but instead of going down to the foyer, where they had arranged to meet, she used her security pass and pressed the button for the royal floor.

A rather worried butler greeted her.

'The "Do Not Disturb" light is still on. I really cannot go in.'

'Well, *I* can.'

The butler was slightly startled at her assertive tone, but she took out the swipe card for the room, gave the door several sharp knocks and then entered.

Please, she begged silently, *if he's in here then let him be alone.*

The suite was in darkness. There was the sound of running water and she wondered if he had fallen asleep in the sunken bath. The sound came from the pool, she realised as she saw the drapes gently billowing in the breeze and realised that the huge glass doors were open.

She walked silently over the thick carpet and out to the stunning alfresco area. It truly was an oasis. High in the sky, there was a colourful garden and a large pool that jutted out over the ocean.

It made her dizzy even to think of it, though Kedah told her he swam in it each day.

Felicia walked over. No, he was *not* practising the breaststroke.

She stepped back from the edge as the warm morning air dusted her cheeks and blew at her hair.

There weren't any signs of a wild party, though he must have been out here at some point for the doors to be open.

It really was beautiful, Felicia thought. So much so that for a moment she forget her mission to find the missing Sheikh and simply took in the stunning view.

The navy sky was fading and was now dressed in ribbons of silver and various shades of blue as the sun prepared to break into the horizon. Ahead, Felicia could see the island where they had stood yesterday and spoken.

She could stand and bristle with indignation, or she could wrap her arms around herself and try to hold on to the shiver within her that Kedah evoked.

He moved her.

Just that.

He took feelings and memories that were usually guarded and shook them. He jolted awake desires and emotions so that she was standing there feeling as if she was on the top of the world and convincing herself that she could handle it.

That a night or two would surely be worth it, just to have known that bliss.

And there was always the brochure. Yes, she would mope, but only for a week, and then she would circle Mustique and spend time there rehabilitating her heart.

No.

She could *not* sleep with him and then continue to work for him; she could *not* pretend it didn't matter when he discarded her and moved on to the next woman.

And there was no way she would be a filler between drinks.

She actually laughed at the nerve of him.

'Is everything all right, madam?'

Felicia turned and saw the butler, hovering in the doorway.

'Everything's fine.' She nodded. 'I'll just check to see if he's asleep.'

She headed back inside and with mounting trepidation walked towards the main bedroom in the suite. The double doors were closed and she glanced at the butler, who gave a worried shake of his head as she went to knock. He was certain that their most esteemed guest should not be disturbed.

'He might be unwell,' Felicia offered. She didn't think it for a moment, but it was the excuse she would give to Kedah if he called her out for disturbing him.

'Kedah!' Felicia knocked loudly. 'Kedah, the plane's scheduled to leave…'

When there was no response she opened the door.

Relief.

She wasn't disturbing an intimate moment.

He was not there, and yet she could see that

he had been—the bed was rumpled and unmade and there were several thick white towels dropped on the floor. And his visit had been a recent one, for the musky, woody scent of his cologne lingered.

Perhaps he had come back from the party and showered and changed before heading out again?

Bedded his date, showered and changed, Felicia thought with a gnawing unease as she closed the door.

She was tired of playing detective, tired of putting the pieces together on his depraved life.

Tired of it all, really.

Especially saying no.

'I'll just pack up the last of his things,' Felicia said to the butler as she turned off the alarm.

She headed to the wardrobe and took out the case she had left. There wasn't much to pack. Most of it had been done last night, and once the bellboy had come to collect his luggage she headed back down to the foyer.

His vehicle was waiting, the engine purring, and his driver was—as always—on the phone. Felicia was grateful that the doorman didn't attempt small talk. Instead he handed Felicia her preferred brew in a takeaway cup and she said her thanks and took a grateful sip.

Dawn was breaking and Dubai was now pretty in pink. And then, as transfixing as the sunrise, Kedah appeared, walking slowly as if there was no King or country awaiting his imminent arrival, no jet on the runway ready and primed to carry him there.

She would have loved to say, *Look what the cat dragged in*—but, as always, he was immaculate. In fact he looked as if he were just leaving for the night rather than arriving back at dawn. He was a sight for Felicia's sleep-deprived eyes.

'Good morning,' he greeted her.

'You're late,' Felicia responded.

'So?' His response was surly and brief, and he glanced down at the coffee she held in her hand and then back up to her eyes. 'May I?'

Felicia handed him her coffee and he drained it, but then pulled a face. 'Too sweet.'

'It didn't stop you, though.'

Actually, last night it had.

Last night his mind had been on Felicia—so much so that he'd dropped his pouting date back at her hotel and returned to his room. Sleep had proved elusive, and a shower had done nothing to temper the urge to call Felicia and summon her to his suite.

The trouble was, he had known she was the

one woman who might not take too kindly to
his summons, and so instead he had headed
onto the balcony and told himself to forget
about her—at least for now. There was his trip
home to get through first.

Zazinia had to be his priority—though he
wasn't looking forward to this visit in the least.
He knew there would be a confrontation with
his father, and that there would be a push towards him choosing a bride.

Last night he had hoped to take his mind off
his problems in the usual way, but he hadn't
been able to.

Now the reason that he hadn't smiled back
at him.

This morning her hair was worn down,
though it was more wavy and unkempt than
usual. She didn't wear a lot of make-up, but
she had on none today.

She belonged on his pillow.

'Are you ready?' she asked him.

'Am I?' he asked. 'Did you finish my pack-
ing?'

'Yes,' she said. 'I went into your suite with
the butler this morning. He didn't want to—
he was worried we might disturb something.'

'There was nothing to disturb last night,'

Kedah said. 'In fact there hasn't been anything to disturb for quite some time.'

'I don't believe you for a moment.'

'That's up to you. My theatre date bored me, as did my date last night. Did you get the chocolates?'

'You know I did.'

'Did you like the towels?' he asked. 'Oh, I apologise—I forgot there are things that bore you to discuss.'

She said nothing.

'Did you get my note?'

She nodded.

'And *did* you?' he asked.

And then he looked at the shadows under her eyes that were so much darker than before and the slight gritting of her jaw. The answer as to whether she had thought about it was clear.

'Of course you did.'

She wished she could go back to their first meeting, when she had been sure about never sleeping with him.

But she hadn't really been sure even then.

On sight she had wanted him, and that feeling remained.

'I'm going to freshen up,' Kedah said.

When he had left she stood there, as the

driver made small talk and worried about angering Kedah's father, the King.

She remembered the tingle at the base of her spine at the way he said her name.

She did not mix business with pleasure, but he blurred all the lines.

He wanted the tough woman who had stepped into his office—which she still was—and yet Felicia was also aware that she liked him more than she should for such a relationship to work.

He didn't need to know that.

More than anyone, Felicia knew how to hold onto her heart.

'How long did he say?' the driver asked now. 'Apparently they're furious at the palace that he's so late. The captain's trying to sort out a flight path to make up the time…'

'He shouldn't be too long,' Felicia replied. 'I'll just go and see.'

She should text him, really.

It would be far safer.

Instead, just a few moments later, she stood at the door of his hotel suite.

She had the access card—of course she did—but usually if he was in there she'd knock first.

This morning she didn't.

She stepped into the entrance hall and saw Kedah was emptying his safe.

'You forgot my diamond.'

'Sorry.'

'Attention to detail, Felicia,' he said, and wagged his finger in a small scold.

'I told you on the first day that I would not make a good PA.'

'You did.'

He closed the safe and pocketed the stone, but made no move to walk towards her.

'You need to hurry up.'

His eyes met hers. 'Says who?'

'Word from the palace is that the King is concerned you haven't left yet. The pilot is going to try to make up the time…' All this was said as he walked towards her, and her voice was breathless.

'Oh, well.' He shrugged.

And now he stood right in front of her, and Felicia looked at his mouth and wondered what the rest of her life would feel like should she never taste it.

'Did you think about it?'

'Yes.'

It was pointless to lie, and the fact that she stood there rather than stepped back, that she met his beautiful gaze, spoke of the decision she had come to.

'We have to continue to work together,' he warned her.

'I know that. So there are things we need to discuss…' Felicia attempted, because she *would* be laying a few ground rules.

'There's no time for that now,' that beautiful mouth said. 'We can speak on the plane.'

But that was a full twenty-six minutes away, at best. And she looked at the dark pink of his lips and then the black roughness of his jaw. It would be cruel to look back on this moment and regret walking away.

And so she did not turn to go.

Instead she stood as his hand moved to her shoulder and he peeled away the strap of her bag. He placed the bag on an occasional table, and that gesture alone told her of the thoroughness of the kiss to come.

She was shaking—not outwardly, but there was a low tremble that seemed to start at midthigh and inch with every heartbeat nearer to her throat.

'Kedah,' Felicia warned again, 'we have to speak.'

'First we taste.'

There was no time for this. Kedah knew that.

His father's mood would not be improved by his late arrival, and things were already tense.

And yet he too could not resist.

White-hot, Felicia turned him on. There had been a slow burn as he'd walked towards her. Now he was hard and ready, and he hadn't even tasted her mouth.

Now he did.

Their flesh, their tongues, finally met, and both were wet and wanting, and both moaned in mutual bliss as eight weeks of want found an outlet.

Their mouths moved slowly and appreciatively at first, relishing the heady taste that they made.

'That,' said Kedah, peeling his lips back just a little, 'was how I wanted to greet you on the first day.'

And there was something terribly freeing about it being a work deal, for she could be as provocative as all hell without being accused of being a tease.

'This,' she said, 'is how I wanted to greet *you*.'

She kissed him harder still, and Kedah loved it that she did not hold back from revealing her pleasure.

Her body was lithe, and it pressed into his

as their tongues met. Provocatively, he ran a hand down her spine until it came to rest on one heart-shaped buttock while the other hand went to the back of her head so that he could kiss her more thoroughly.

It was more of a kiss than she had ever known.

She had a brief wish that their clothes would evaporate, because she knew herself that in that space of time when he removed her clothes common sense would kick in.

And she knew Kedah and where a kiss would lead.

She pulled her face away, and her mouth was wet and swollen, her skin pink and inflamed from the roughness of his jaw.

He was hard against her, and her breasts were aching for his touch, for his mouth, for any contact he cared to bestow.

He kissed her again, but this time his fingers tightened in her hair, and it was the roughest, most thorough kissing of her life.

He held her hips and rubbed her against himself.

She peeled her mouth away and still he held her. He could feel her body trembling as she fought the writhing want within. Her eyes were green and her mouth was open, dragging in air, and he held her hair taut in his hand and fought not to tug it—hard. He fought not to pull back her head and lower his mouth again.

He stroked her where his hand cupped her bottom, and then he pulled her further in so she could feel every generous inch of his hard length against her stomach.

And it was too late to worry about the time, for her fingers had moved to the row of small buttons on his shirt and she'd exposed his muscular chest.

Kedah loved the way her hands were not shy—how, as her mouth still merged with his, she toyed with his flat nipples and then, bored with them, let her hand creep down to the soft snake of silken hair that had entranced her from that first glimpse.

From her bag on the table her phone bleeped with a text message, just as the head of his erection nudged her palm.

'That will be the driver, telling me to hurry you up.'

'Hurry me up, then.'

And he felt her smile, for her lips stretched beneath his as he took her hand and ran it the length of his long, hard shaft.

His other hand pressed at her head, and she knew—because this was the kind of man she was choosing to get involved with—that from the direction of the pressure Kedah exerted she should be dropping to her knees—oh, right about *now*.

But he was in for that shock. For she had needs of her own and it would never be all about *him*.

'Kedah,' she said, and removed her hand as she lifted her head. 'We really don't have time for foreplay.'

She watched his eyes flare as she stepped back from his embrace and reached for her bag.

'Foreplay?' he checked.

'It's when—'

'I *do* know what it is, thank you,' he snapped.

'Good.' She smirked. 'I've got news for you, Kedah. I didn't come up here just to satisfy your needs. I have terms and conditions of my own!'

And she was doing it.

Somehow, against this very powerful man, she was holding her own.

'We need to get a move on, Kedah. I'll see you down there.'

CHAPTER FIVE

SIX FOOT THREE of sulking Sheikh boarded the plane.

Kedah did *not* need the complication of Felicia.

But he had tasted her now.

And *she* did not need the arrogance of him.

She wanted him, though.

They sat on his private jet and her skin was prickling—so much so that she almost went through her bag for antihistamines, till she realised this was no allergic reaction. She was on fire for *him*.

The take-off was smooth and he glanced up as a flight attendant came over.

'Can I get you anything, Your Highness?'

'Shaii.' Kedah asked for tea, and it was served in a long crystal glass and cold, as he liked it. It was refreshing and sweet but not soothing.

He took out the diamond that he carried and

tapped it on the gleaming table. He saw Felicia glance over.

'That's a pretty elaborate worry bead.'

'I told you,' a surly Kedah replied. 'I never worry.'

The tapping resumed as he pulled up a file.

Not any old file.

He had been working on this for years, for it was Zazinia as he envisaged it.

Every plan he had submitted had been rejected, every vision he'd had for his home discounted, and they were all compiled in this one stunning display. He sat there watching as buildings rose before his eyes and bridges connected them. He had designed all the infrastructure—the roads and railways were splendidly linked—and yet none of it had been implemented. At every turn he had been thwarted. This was the reason Kedah was rarely home.

He closed the file and worked instead on a skyline that he *could* change. He started on some preliminary designs for his latest Dubai project.

He was considering linking the hotels—either with a monorail or possibly a tunnel. It would be a huge venture. Yet Felicia was right. Why link two hotels that were basically the same? Now, thanks to her, the gender was no longer clear, for he was thinking of a more recreational facility. One families or couples might choose to visit.

His plane was usually a second office, but she was invading his headspace. She was even influencing his hotel's design. So he closed the file. Hussain could work on it further, or tell him outright if he was dreaming too big, Kedah decided.

He opened his email and flicked over to Felicia the files he wanted her to tidy up. He added a message telling her that he wanted her to write a cover note for Hussain, but then, distracted, realised he'd sent the wrong file.

For the first time since leaving the hotel he spoke to her.

'Delete the last email I sent,' Kedah said. 'The information I want you to forward to Hussain is in the one I am sending now.'

Always he could separate work and pleasure.

Not today.

He looked over to her and saw that the dress she was wearing was modest, but it would not be suitable for his home.

'Felicia?'

'Yes?'

'Did I tell you about the dress code in Zazinia?'

'You did.' She nodded. 'I'll change closer to when we land.' She turned and rather pointedly looked out of the window rather than prolonging their conversation.

'I'm going for a rest,' he told her. Normally Kedah just stalked off and it was left to Felicia to guess where he'd gone.

She turned and their eyes met as he stood and headed to the bedroom. He halted when he got to the door.

'There are three more hours' flying time,' he said. 'Is that sufficient for you?'

He walked into the bedroom and Felicia went into her bag and took out a book. But the words all ran into each other and after a few minutes of pretending she put the book down.

There were moments in life from which you knew there would be no coming back.

If she entered his suite it would be one of those moments, she knew, for his kiss had offered her more than a glimpse of what it would be like to be with him.

He assumed she had slept with previous clients because she had let him assume that.

And she was lying to herself now, Felicia knew, by telling herself she could handle this.

Yet she had to.

He came with a warning, and he had stated the same.

This would end—and no doubt at a time of *his* choosing.

She sat for a moment and accepted that fact.

Desire won.

And yet she did have rules.

She wanted to be behind that door, wanted her time with him, and so she stood and headed to the bedroom.

She didn't knock. Instead she walked in. And there on the bed lay Kedah as she had never seen him before.

He had a sheet covering his lower half, but she knew that he was naked beneath the sheet. For now she just stood and stared at him and took in his beauty.

His chest was toned and there was a smattering of dark hair across it. His nipples were a deep shade of red and he was utterly exquisite. She followed the dark trail down, and through the sheet she could see the thick length of him against his thigh. The thought of him inside her was intensely thrilling.

'Undress,' he told her, and his voice had a rasp of impatience for she had kept him waiting again.

'Not yet,' she said, and then she stated her

case. 'Kedah, as long as we last, there's only me…'

He just stared.

'If you see someone else, don't expect me back in your bed.'

'I shan't.'

His response was surprising. She had expected debate, or for him to state that he would do as he pleased.

'I have no interest in others…' He didn't. He hadn't in a while. 'I do have to marry, though.'

'I know you do.'

'So how about a long fling before that…?'

It was what she wanted—more than she had expected—and yet a warning sounded in her head, because it was already more than sex for her, and a prolonged affair with Kedah could only hurt more in the end.

'A fidelity trial?' he said.

She wanted his kiss. She wanted him to stand and kiss her to oblivion as he undressed her with skilled ease. Yet he did not.

'Take off your shoes,' he told her, and she stood there for a few seconds before doing so. 'Now undo your buttons…'

'I do know how to undress myself,' she snapped. Her voice was tense, and her head felt as if she had stepped off a merry-go-round.

He was nothing like any lover she had known, and that secretly thrilled her.

'Undo the buttons,' he said, but with less patience this time.

Her hands were shaking as she undid the row of buttons at the side of her dress, and the tension in the air made her almost dizzy.

She recalled that tone now. It was the same one he had used on the day they had first met, when he had told her to sit back down and that he hadn't finished with her yet. The effect was the same, and yet multiplied a thousandfold.

'Take it off over your head.'

'It doesn't come off that way.'

And instead she peeled it down the arms and her dress slid to the floor. She stood there, cross with herself for doing as she was told, yet angrily awaiting further instruction.

'Nice bra,' Kedah said. 'Now, take it off.'

'You.'

He flashed her a look as he moved to stand and she took in a long breath. It was the kind of breath she might take in private, before making a difficult phone call. The kind of breath she might take before opening the door to a stranger.

Yet it was the right kind of breath to take before a lean, toned body rose from the bed and the sheet fell away, to reveal him aroused and hard and walking towards hers.

'Turn around,' he said.

She resisted, but only in the hope that he would touch her, for her skin was screaming for contact, yet contact he refused to give.

'Turn around,' he said again, and this time she did as she was told. 'Now, undo your bra...'

'You can do it.'

'Don't annoy me any more than you already have.'

'Why?'

His mouth came close to the back of her head and his low voice in her ear made her want to arch her neck, to turn to kiss him, but she stood staring ahead.

'For insinuating, back at the hotel, that I would have left you unsatisfied.'

She turned her head then, and found him smiling. And he smiled as only Kedah could. He smiled as he had when he'd walked into that restaurant and seen her sitting there waiting for him. He smiled as he did when he greeted her each morning.

Yet it was different today, for there was no mistaking the deep intimacy levelled at her. There was absolute seduction in his eyes, and Felicia knew that if all that was left was this—

if the plane fell from the sky right now—she was glad for this moment.

Game over. For it was Felicia who turned and smiled and wrapped her arms around his neck. They were back to deep kissing as he removed her bra—easily. His fingers stroked her breasts with feather-light strokes alternated with pinches that made her gasp in shocked pleasure.

Now, the solid nudge of his body was guiding her to the bed, and though she wanted to be there so badly still she wanted to stand for just a moment and fully savour the feel of him naked against her. He felt like silk beneath her fingers, and there was a wall of muscle that warned of pleasures to come. His mouth was firm and his tongue expert as his hands roamed her, strumming her rib cage or toying with her hip as he enjoyed the body he had been resisting for what felt like far too long.

She could feel the mattress pressing into the back of her thigh and fought to stay standing against him. Yet like a domino he toppled her onto the bed.

It was Kedah who remained standing, and she felt the scorch of his eyes as they roamed her flushed skin.

'Let's get rid of these,' he said.

He placed her feet on his thigh and she lifted

her bottom to allow him to peel off her knickers as if he was opening the most delicate gift. Down her thighs he slid them, with such a lack of haste that she let out a moan—an absolute whimper.

His shaft jerked in response to it as Kedah discovered that the sound of Felicia moaning was a sound he craved.

She was always so brittle, so contained, it was a pleasure to hear her unravel.

Past her knees came the knickers, and then he ripped them down the final stage. Now she was naked, and soon she'd be his.

He knelt between her legs and Felicia had never known such absolute scrutiny. It felt as if he were kissing her all over, yet only his eyes caressed her for now.

'Turn over,' he told her, and she rolled to her front.

She rested her head on her forearm and waited—for whatever he so chose. Anticipation thrummed as she heard his ragged breathing, and then he placed a wet kiss right at the base of her spine.

'Kedah…'

His tongue was hot and slow and it moved in long circles. Her free hand moved to touch herself at such bliss but he caught her wrist.

It was an attack of the senses. Because now he parted her thighs and slipped his long fingers into her as his mouth worked the length of her spine.

She lifted her hair, just so that he might have access to her skin, and did not know if it was the bruising kiss to her neck or the stretch of his fingers inside her that caused her to make a low choking noise.

'Please…' she said, not knowing how to say that she wanted—no, *needed* more and more of this.

But he removed the pleasure and rolled her onto her back. He opened her legs and moved so that he knelt between her knees. He wanted to take her there and then, and reached over the bedside for a condom, but the sight of her pink and glistening beckoned him for just a brief taste.

Felicia swore as he parted her lips and, instead of devouring her, licked her with just with the tip of his tongue. 'Don't…' she said, and her hands knotted into his hair as he teased her, scratched at her thighs with his jaw.

Kedah knew he was good, but he'd never enjoyed himself to this level. Hearing the panting in her voice and feeling the pressure of her thighs trapping him made him search deeper.

Her sweet, musky taste was like nectar. Hot, she writhed, and his tongue devoured.

He was too slow, she decided, for she was suddenly frantic.

The sounds he made were low, and his possessive growl reverberated through her.

Her hands left his head and went to her own, tense fingers tightening in her hair as he raised her bottom.

He was relentless.

He should stop now, she thought as she started to come.

Please stop, she thought. Because she had never come so fully to a man's mouth—in fact she couldn't remember feeling like this *ever*.

She wanted to push him away, and yet she wanted for this never to end.

He felt the pulsing and the tension rise within her. And for Kedah there was a giddy triumph at hearing Felicia in the throes of the pleasure that he had procured for her. She made no logical sense as she pleaded for less while her body urged for more. And then it faded, and he felt her relax and grow calm, but this wasn't even close to being over.

He wanted his own release, and so he took her slowly, just kneeling up and pulling her in.

He toyed at her entrance and Felicia pushed

herself up onto her elbows. She watched as he glanced over to the condoms scattered on the bed beside them, but they might as well have been in his office drawer back in London, for nothing must break the contact they made.

She told him that she was covered in ragged, breathless words. 'I'm on the pill…'

Both of them would usually have needed far more than that to continue. Felicia even let out a half-sob and a laugh at her own abandon. But both felt now that it was imperative not to lose the beauty of this moment.

They were on the edge of discovery, entering into uncharted water—and not just because of the lack of protection. It was the eye contact, the unbridled pleasure, and the care taken as he positioned her calves.

Kedah let out a moan as he slid into her oiled, tight warmth. His eyes came up to meet hers, but she was looking down at the blending of them.

'Felicia!'

He snapped her into eye contact with him, and she found there was nothing sexier than full-on looking into Kedah's eyes as he took her.

For a couple of moments that was exactly what he did. He moved to his whim along his thick length.

With anyone else she would have resisted, and yet he guided her so expertly and filled her so completely that all Felicia had to do was give in to the arm that held her up and lie back to receive the pleasure.

She felt the bliss of his weight and the reward of his kiss. His skin was immaculate as her hands slid down his loins and she knew that if she'd made a decision to do something rash then this was the right one.

He took her with force and passion and she returned the same—and almost a tussle ensued as they rolled so Felicia was on top.

'I want…' she said, but did not continue. She just wanted to come again, and there was such energy between them…such a mutual goal to give the other pleasure.

He had thought about what they might be like together and he had expected restraint, a tinge of regret too, and yet there was only fire and buried passion from Felicia.

'Slow down,' he said, and took her hips and jerked her down on his thick length over and over.

His hands moved up to her breasts and toyed with them, stretching her nipples as Felicia bit down on her lip. Then she leant forward to taste his salty skin as his hands roamed her buttocks.

He started thrusting upwards, and with that she had the pleasure of watching him release, and the sensation of the power of him within her.

She toppled forward, and as he came he slid her over and over down onto him, over the edge with him.

Their faces were next to each other and she could feel her hair was damp. Every part of her was more than warm, her skin was on fire, and she had never known anything like this feeling of silence and peace—this space they had walked into together.

He slipped her off him and she fell beside him, breathless, and looked him in the eye.

Then they smiled, because it had been better than they had hoped or dared to expect.

She wanted to touch and explore him, but they lay for just a moment, both thrumming in private bliss as they kissed each other down.

CHAPTER SIX

THEY LAY ENTWINED TOGETHER, and Kedah listened to the hum of the engines as the plane carried them to his home. Deeply sated, he found his mind was clearer.

Felicia's wasn't.

She lay with her head on his chest, listening to the steady thump of his heart as her hand toyed with the silky straight hair on his stomach that she had, right from the start, wanted to feel.

Now that she had, *still* she wanted.

'Can I ask you something?' Felicia spoke but, far too comfortable in his arms, did not raise her head.

'It depends what it is.'

Kedah was no open book.

'Do you want to be King?'

'Of course,' he answered as his hand stroked her bare arm. 'I was born to be King.'

'So why aren't you there all the time?'

'Because my plans to improve Zazinia are repeatedly turned down. I refuse to be an impotent Crown Prince…'

'I doubt there's any chance of that…' she said, and her hand crept down.

'I had a stand-off with my father and the old King some years ago,' Kedah told her. 'They had turned down every plan I had submitted and it was evident that they were never going to accept them. I asked for confirmation and they gave it to me—they did not welcome change. I love to design and so I chose to go it alone. That diamond I carry—it was from the sale of my first hotel. They loathe that I am self-made because it means that I am not beholden to them. I want, though, to make my land better for the people.'

'And now you can?'

'Perhaps.'

'The old King is dead,' Felicia pointed out.

'My father still chooses to listen to the elders and Mohammed.'

'I know you, Kedah—you could convince anyone of anything.' After all, she was in his bed. 'Your people love you.'

'I know they do.'

'What will happen when the Accession Council meet?'

'Mohammed shall state his case, and I shall state mine, and my father shall be asked to make a formal choice.'

'And if it isn't you, you'll take it to the people to vote?'

And it was then that she knew him. Or rather she knew for certain that there was far more to this than Kedah was admitting to.

She did not blush. She had been trained not to react from an early age. And Kedah was the same—he never revealed fear. And so the hand on her arm did not tighten, nor did his breathing change, but as she carried on speaking she heard his heart rate quicken.

'And who would the people chose?' she asked.

'I believe…me.'

'No problem, then.'

'None.'

His response was measured and calm. Had they been having this conversation standing and facing each other, she would not have known of the nerve she had just hit, but his heart beat like a jackhammer in his chest.

'So why are you busy making billions just in case?'

He did not answer, and she lay there listening to the rapid thud of his heart.

'Does Mohammed have something on you?'

'I told you,' Kedah answered evenly. 'I don't regret my past.'

'I know there's a scandal looming.' Felicia smiled. 'I can smell them a mile off.'

There was.

For the first time in his life he needed advice. The question as to how to approach his mother had been rolling around in his head like a ball bearing in a pinball machine. Ideas were bounced around and were rapidly dismissed, but over and over he returned to one small corner that said he should speak with *someone*.

Who?

And, though he kept flicking the thought away, always the ball rolled back and settled in a pocket marked 'Felicia.'

He trusted no one, and yet...

'Felicia?'

She was sleepy and warm in his arms, though her low murmur in answer to her name told him she was awake.

'If I were to tell you something, would it remain between us?'

'Of course.' She smiled again. 'Hit me with it—a pregnant prostitute?'

'Excuse me?' he said, and then smiled in the darkness as he realised she was still trying to guess what his secret was. 'Was that before or after I got married in Vegas?'

She pulled herself from his arms and onto her elbow and she looked at him as his smile faded. The truth was scary sometimes, and she felt its brief threat.

'What is it?'

He shook his head, and Felicia knew when to remain silent. Any guessing now would only irritate, so she lay back down and played with his chest instead as she thought how best to respond.

'If you decide to tell me it shan't go any further.'

'Thank you.'

The gift of time was the best he had known, and he was grateful for it. He was aware it would be all to easy to say what was on his mind in this post-coital haze only to regret it later.

Even that didn't make full sense to him, though, for he did not usually indulge in pillow talk.

There was a small buzzing sound. It would seem that their flying time was nearly over. He reached out and flicked on a light and for the first time Felicia took in their splendid surroundings. Apart from the hum of the engines there was no sign that they were on an aeroplane.

The bed was vast, and rumpled from their lovemaking, and there was no place in the world she would rather be.

'Can we be late?' she asked, and lifted her face for a kiss.

Kedah was tempted to lift the phone beside the bed and inform the captain there was a change of plan, and yet some things needed to be faced.

'Get dressed,' he told her, though it was said with regret. 'I'll have your clothes brought through.'

'Can you at least wait until I'm in the shower?'

He smiled at her modesty, but did as she asked and waited until she had gone through to the bathroom before calling for her overnight bag to be brought to his bedroom.

Felicia washed her hair and dried it, and then she came out.

Kedah lay on the bed with his hands behind his head, clearly deep in thought.

Another buzzer sounded, and now it was Kedah who rose from the bed and headed to the shower as Felicia put on the robe she had chosen to wear. It was a dusky pink with long sleeves and a high neckline. From neck to floor the gown was done up with a row of embroidered buttons, each one individually made. Felicia had bought it while they'd been on their travels and was glad to be able to wear it. Again she chose to wear no make-up.

Kedah soon reappeared, wearing just a towel around his hips. He wished she did not move him so. For the first time in his life he perhaps regretted sex.

She had never looked more beautiful.

Her robe was a light crushed velvet, and it was subtle, yet he had touched each curve that it gracefully concealed, and his fingers itched to undo each button and return her to his bed. Her hair was loose and the air was fragrant with the perfume she had worn on the day they'd met.

Today was not one for distraction, and Felicia was proving a huge one.

He was reeling from coming so close to telling her the secret he had kept for all these years, and—more troublesome for Kedah—he was still dangerously close to revealing it now.

'Why don't you go and have some breakfast?' he suggested. 'I'll join you soon.'

Felicia nodded, unsure as to the dynamics between them, but just as she turned to go he caught her and pulled her back into his arms.

'You know that nothing can happen at the palace?'

'Of course.'

'We will leave straight after dinner. You will be taken to the offices to work there.'

'Kedah,' Felicia said, 'I don't expect us to leave the plane holding hands.'

'I know…'

She stepped from his embrace and went out to the lounge, where she was served breakfast. She was too consumed by Kedah to be embarrassed by the staff, but she was a little worried that they might gossip.

When Kedah came out of the bedroom she was about to voice her concerns to him.

Then she saw him.

The man who would be King.

Always he was beautiful—he was exquisite now.

The robe he wore was silver, and over that was an embroidered coat. His *keffiyeh* was black, and a heavy silver rope fell to one side. She had never seen him carry a sword and it unnerved her—for this was not a Kedah she had ever seen before.

Not just exquisite…he was truly out of her reach.

He was regal, imposing, and it was hard to

imagine that less than an hour ago she had lain smiling in his arms.

An attendant served him strong coffee and he declined the sweet pastry she offered.

'They won't say anything?' Felicia checked, and he frowned. 'I mean, what happened won't get back to the palace?'

'Felicia, why do you think I use my own plane? You don't report to my father—none of my staff do. The only exception is Vadia.'

Kedah's success was not reliant on his title. But it was his hope for the future, and his heart belonged to the people he loved.

His words had come out perhaps more harshly than he'd intended—he had not meant to relegate her straight back to being staff—but he was having trouble with his worlds merging.

He had only ever brought Anu to his home, and there had never been anything between them. Anu was close to his mother's age and happily married.

Felicia would cause eyebrows to rise, and he wanted to spare her that shame.

Not that she knew that.

As they sat in silence Felicia looked out on Zazinia as the plane banked to the right and she got her first glimpse of his land from the sky. She understood a little more how thwarted

Kedah must feel. It was stunningly beautiful, and yet so ancient that it looked almost biblical.

And then she saw the palace.

It was easily the highest point in the land, set on a cliff along a stretch of white beach.

And it was huge.

As the plane lined up for its approach Felicia realised the palace had its own runway, with several private jets that bore the royal coat of arms on their tails.

The landing was a smooth one, and soon they prepared to disembark.

'Am I to call you Your Highness here?'

'We have already addressed that—you can still call me Kedah.'

'And when we get to the palace am I to—?'

'Enough questions, Felicia,' Kedah snapped.

It was a stern reminder that they had left the bedroom, and Felicia felt the sting of her cheeks at his reprimand.

They stepped from the plane, with Felicia walking a suitable distance behind him. Kedah was met by his personal aide, Vadia, whom Felicia had spoken to on several occasions.

There were no introductions for her, though.

The heat of the Zazinia air and the hot desert wind that whipped at her cheeks were not so hard for her to acclimatise to as her sudden relegation. An hour or so ago they had been in each other's arms, with Kedah almost revealing his darkest of secrets; now he didn't even glance over his shoulder as they stepped into the main entrance of the palace.

He indicated with a flick of his hand that she was to wait there.

A maid came over and she was informed in broken English that soon she would be taken to the offices in the royal wing.

And then Felicia stood, alone and ignored, as she heard a woman call out his name.

'Kedah!'

The woman who was walking towards him had to be his mother. She had the same winning smile as her son, and the robe she wore was a deep crimson. As Felicia glanced towards her she caught his mother's eyes and could see the question in her gaze.

Hurriedly she looked away.

Whatever was said was in Arabic as they embraced.

'Who is that?' Rina asked.

'That is my PA—Felicia.'

'Has Anu left?'

'No,' Kedah responded. 'But she wanted to pull back on the travel. Anu manages things in London now.'

'Well, your father and brother are looking forward to seeing you, Kedah. It has been far too long.'

Kedah doubted they *were* looking forward to seeing him, but they all tried to keep their troubles from his mother, and so he walked with her towards the main office.

Not once did he turn around.

Felicia felt less valuable than even his luggage, which was already being taken up to his suite. And it should not hurt quite so much, yet it did. To go from being his lover to less than nothing was not something she had prepared for. In all their time together he had never made her feel worthless.

He did now.

The guards opened the doors as Kedah and Rina approached, and inside Kedah kissed his father's cheek and shook his brother's hand.

Kumu—Mohammed's wife—was there, and she gave Kedah a small tap to the heart in greeting.

'Now we are all together,' Rina said, beaming, 'there is some good news that Mohammed and Kumu have been waiting to share.'

She clapped her hands and Kedah stood silent as his younger brother stepped forward.

'We have been gifted again,' Mohammed

announced. 'In November we are expecting a child.'

'That is wonderful news.' Omar beamed, though at the same time managed to freeze his eldest son with a glare.

Congratulations were offered, and Kedah gave his own. It would be another boy—of course it would. Mohammed did everything to perfection, and had already produced a potential heir and a spare.

All the right things were said, though, and Kedah enquired after his young nephews.

'I hear you are looking to build another hotel in Dubai?' his brother said.

'Another one?' Omar frowned.

'It is early days,' Kedah announced. 'I haven't yet shown the plans to Hussain.'

That silenced his father for a moment.

Hussain and Omar had studied together, and on occasion Hussain had told Kedah about the fine plans his father had once had for his country.

Those days were long gone now.

A maid came in and announced that the portrait artist was ready, but Omar was not letting Kedah off that lightly.

'He can wait,' the King said. 'Now that he is

finally here, I would like to speak with Kedah alone.'

'I don't mind staying,' Mohammed offered.

'That shan't be necessary,' Kedah said, and waited until he and his father were alone.

Omar cut straight to the chase.

'The elders are pushing for the royal lineage to move forward,' Omar said. 'Ours is a country that is divided, and there is unrest. Some want things to stay as they did under the rule of my father, and Mohammed is one of them—which is why the elders support him.'

'Your opinion is the one that matters,' Kedah pointed out.

'How can I support you when you are barely here?'

'You know why I stay away,' Kedah said. 'The people here need more infrastructure, healthcare, jobs—the list is endless. We have a country that could thrive, a tourism industry that could help people support their families. Instead they are poor while we continue to live in splendour. No, I cannot feast night after night in a palace when children go to bed hungry.'

'It is not so bad…' the King started, but then he saw Kedah's furious glare and hesitated.

It had been a long time since Kedah had lost

his temper on this subject and Omar did not want a repeat.

'Kedah…' He trod more carefully. 'There have long been calls for the Accession Council to meet,' Omar told him. 'But it is becoming more pressing now.'

'Then give me the power I seek. Give me permission to make changes to our land and I shall return. You *know* that I would make a better Crown Prince and ultimately King than Mohammed.'

'How do I know that when you are never here? Prove your devotion…'

'I don't need to prove it—my country has my heart.'

'Choose your bride, come home and settle down. That would satisfy the elders for now, and perhaps delay the calls for the Accession Council to meet…'

'I don't need to appease anyone. I know my people—they want *me* as Crown Prince. If you vote otherwise at the meeting then I shall take it to the people to cast their vote, as is my right.'

'Have you *any* idea of the unrest that would cause?' His father was breathing rapidly. 'Kedah, why can't you just choose a bride and toe the line…?'

'What *happened* to you?' Kedah asked. 'Hussain told me that when you studied together you had plans and dreams for our land... What happened to them?'

'The old King did not want change.'

'But *you* are King now. So why do you bow down to the elders?'

'They are wise.'

'Of course they are—but they are also staid. You are King. Your word is law and yet you choose not to use it.'

'It would be easier—'

'Easier?' Kedah interrupted. 'Since when did a king choose the easy option? Whatever hold the elders have on you, share it with me, and then together we can fight. But I shall not return to Zazinia just to sit idle and wait for you to pass.'

Kedah would not be pushed around by anyone. He knew his father was doing his best to protect his mother's reputation—he was quite sure that was why the King held back—but if only his father would voice the problem, together they could face the trouble.

Just so long as Kedah was indeed Omar's son.

There was a knock at the door and he knew there was only one person who would disturb an official meeting between the King and one of the Princes.

The door opened and the Queen stepped in, smiling widely.

'Rina,' the King scolded lightly, 'I am busy speaking with Kedah.'

'Well, the poor artist is waiting. He's so old that I am scared he will die if we keep him much longer.'

Omar laughed, and even Kedah smiled.

'Come, Kedah,' Rina said. 'I will walk with you.'

They walked through the palace and his mother stopped at a large floral arrangement and chose a bloom, which she placed in her hair, and then she selected a few more.

'It is so good to have both my sons home. Stay a while longer, Kedah.'

She was oblivious to the tension between him and Mohammed, and the terrible rumours had been kept from her. Kedah did not know how much longer they could remain so.

'I cannot stay. I have been away for a few weeks, and Felicia…'

He halted. Since when did he take into consideration the fact that his staff had not been home for a while?

And while Rina was oblivious to many things she was alert to others.

'Careful, Kedah.'

'Careful?' He frowned and stopped walking.

He almost wanted to confront her—to say that he was old enough now to understand an affair—but it was imperative, if he was to fight his brother, to know first that he was the King's son. But then he looked into her smiling chocolate-brown eyes that were flecked with gold like his and he couldn't do it.

There was a fragility to Rina—an air of impulsiveness and a little river of vulnerability that ran through her that sometimes darkened that winning smile.

If he confronted her now, Kedah would watch her fold and crumple. If he questioned her about what had happened all those years ago their relationship would never recover. That much he knew.

Yet if Mohammed called his lineage into question her shame would be held up for the elders and ultimately the people to discuss.

He was scared for his mother.

'Be careful with Felicia,' Rina said. 'Be careful with a young woman's heart.'

Kedah shook his head. His mother did not have to concern herself with his sex life, and especially not with Felicia's heart. This was a business arrangement, and if anyone could handle it, it was Felicia—she was the toughest person he knew.

'You don't have to worry about her.'

'But I do. You have never brought one of your lovers to the palace.'

They walked on and Kedah said nothing. But his mother was right. It was in part the reason he would not be staying longer. He wanted Felicia in his bed, and that could never happen here.

'You are choosing a bride soon,' his mother warned. 'It is not fair to her to be here.'

'Felicia is fine.'

Rina wasn't so sure. She had seen Felicia's angry glare as Kedah had made her walk behind him and ignored her.

And now there Felicia was, standing on a balcony, looking out at the view.

'Think about staying for a little while, Kedah,' Rina said, and kissed his cheek. 'I miss you.'

'I know.'

'Come home.'

He wanted to.

'I cannot sit idle for years like…' He halted.

'Like your father has?'

He nodded, and after a moment of sad thought Rina cupped his cheek.

'I do understand.'

Could he ask his mother for the truth? If he *was* his father's son then he could confront the rumours and douse them before the sun went down on this day.

If he wasn't…?

Kedah was ready to know.

'Mother…' He stood there and felt as if he had removed his sword and now held it over her head.

'Yes?'

Rina smiled. And he did not know how to ask her.

'Why don't you give Felicia these?' she suggested.

'You tell me to be careful and then you suggest that I give her flowers?'

'I often pick some flowers to sit on Vadia's desk while she works.'

Indeed Rina did.

'I need to get on,' he said to his mother.

No, he would not go to Felicia with flowers.

Felicia didn't turn when he came to join her— she was still smarting. She was a very modern woman, and while careerwise she would have been fine walking two steps behind him and being ignored, having just left his bed she could not accept it—though she was doing her best not to let it show.

'I want you to take some photos of this wing while I go and have my portrait finished...'

'Sure.'

They walked around the Crown Prince's wing as the staff prepared his office and brought in the artist to add the final touches to the painting.

'I think this area could be better used,' he mused. 'Perhaps as a pool or spa area?'

Felicia tried to keep her features expression-less, though she was aghast at the very thought. It was an ancient palace and absolutely beauti-ful. To think he would consider tearing up these walls and floors to transform them into some modern gym was appalling.

'You don't approve?'

'I think that it's far too beautiful to risk spoil-ing.'

'You've seen my work?' Kedah checked, and she nodded. 'So why do you think I would ruin it? I want to enhance what is already here. I want somewhere I can live rather than a mu-seum.'

They stopped by the portraits, and possibly

she could see what he meant. Cool grey eyes seemed to follow them, and they were a forbidding sight indeed.

'I'm meeting with Vadia in an hour,' Felicia said. 'We just spoke on the phone. She wants to take some time to go through your schedule. September is the King's birthday, yet that week you're booked to be in New York.'

'I have a friend's wedding.'

'Oh, and speaking of weddings… Vadia wants to go through potential dates for yours.'

She said it so calmly that Kedah honestly thought his mother was wrong and Felicia was fine with their arrangement.

'Tell Vadia that, given I haven't chosen my bride yet, it's a bit early to be discussing dates.'

'Sure.'

'I have a family dinner to attend after the portrait,' Kedah said. 'Your meal shall be served to you at your desk. Just call through with your order. We should fly out around midnight,' he told her. 'You'll be home by morning.'

But tomorrow was a day too late, Felicia thought.

If only this visit had been arranged for yesterday…if only she could have held out for a couple more days… Then she wouldn't be feeling as she did now.

She looked at the portraits of the men who had come before him. They were dressed in robes of black or white and the familiar chequered headwear. Kedah wore a gorgeous silken robe and an embroidered coat.

Somehow, even traditionally dressed, he made a statement.

'You're going to stand out amongst the others,' she said.

'I always do,' he answered, and looked at the portraits of his father and grandfather. The fact that he dressed differently had little to do with it. 'I don't look like any of them.'

He walked off and Felicia stood there, frowning—not at what he had said, more at *the way* he had said it.

She knew she was already in too deep, yet as she looked up at the portraits he dragged her in ever deeper.

She was beginning to understand.

Kedah stood for his portrait.

The artist was indeed ancient, and it was hard to believe that those shaky hands could produce something so beautiful.

'I have painted your grandfather, your father, and now you,' the old man said as he added the final touches. 'I hope to paint the next Crown Prince.'

'It might be Crown Princess,' Kedah answered. He was bored from standing so long, and ready for a little disagreement, but the old man just smiled at the provocation.

'That is something to stay alive just to see.'

Yes, Kedah thought, the people really were ready for change.

The painting had been done over many sessions and Kedah, who hated to be still for more than a moment, had found the entire process excruciating.

'Just turn your face a little to the left,' the old man said. 'And look out to the desert.' The sky was orange and he wanted it to light the gold flecks in Kedah's eyes.

And so Kedah sighed and stared out to the desert. No wonder the portraits were of men looking stern, Kedah thought as he dwelt on his problems and pondered again discussing things with Felicia.

A woman's view on things might help, and she might know better how to broach the subject with his mother.

And, given her own family and her job, if there was anyone who would not be shocked by an illicit affair it was Felicia.

But could he trust her?

Yes.

It was a revelation, for since the day he had discovered his mother and Abdal his childhood innocence had faded and trust had rapidly left his heart.

He had thought it gone for good, but now he looked back on his time with her and their conversations. He remembered sitting in the restaurant as she'd revealed the dark part of her heart, and then smiled as he recalled her forthright observations about his hotels.

And then he remembered her lying in his arms, and how close he had come to confiding in her.

Then he thought of her beauty today.

The sun was setting and the desert fired red in the distance as the old man put down his brush and his work was finally done.

'Would you care to see it, Your Highness?' he offered, but Kedah shook his head.

'I shall wait until it is framed,' Kedah told him.

He did not want to stare upon the truth.

CHAPTER SEVEN

THEIR DEPARTING FLIGHT from Zazinia was very different from their outward flight. Despite the pilot's best efforts to climb above it, turbulence carried them home.

Kedah tapped his diamond, cursing the missed opportunity with his mother, and Felicia looked out of the window to the seemingly black lake of desert below. She was still angry about being ignored and dining at her desk alone, while cross with herself for expecting it could be any other way.

As they bumped through the sky she decided to try to do some work and put on her headphones. She would look at the presentation that she had been asked to send to Hussain. But, without thinking, she opened the file in the first email that Kedah had sent her.

Realising it was the one he had sent in error—the one he had told her to delete—she was about to exit from it when she paused.

She had sat through a lot of presentations these past weeks. She had expected to see a proposal for the Dubai hotel and the walkway, and to label a few files, but instead she saw magic.

It was Zazinia, she quickly realised.

It was Kedah's vision of Zazinia.

With each passing frame the bare skyline was filled with graceful buildings, and each was a work of art in itself. Instead of gleaming silver or gold with mirrored windows, the buildings blended with the ancient surrounds. There were delicate artistic murals on the walls that faced the palace, and the city spread gently outwards rather than up. There were carefully thought out roads, railways and bridges to link communities, while the desert retained its remote beauty.

He had poured everything into this, Felicia knew.

It was a life's work in the making.

And she knew he had never meant her to see it.

She snapped off the presentation and then looked over. His eyes were waiting for hers to meet his. She pulled her earphones off, wondering if he somehow knew what she had just seen.

The truth proved to be just as disconcerting,

and it troubled her how deeply he could bore into her heart.

'I apologise for the way I treated you back at the palace.'

Despite being strapped in, she almost fell off her chair in surprise. The apology jolted her, even if her expression barely faltered.

'I have never brought a woman there. Colleagues, of course, but...' He gave a tense shake of his head. 'If there had been even a hint that we were involved then it could have made things awkward for you. I didn't handle it well.'

Please don't be nice, Felicia thought, because her feelings were so much easier to deal with when she was cross.

'Well, it's done now.' She shrugged. 'And I shan't be back there again.'

'I doubt there would be any reason...'

'No,' Felicia said. 'You misunderstand. I *shan't* be going back there again, Kedah. We all have our limits, and your treatment of me in Zazinia far exceeded mine. Anyway, there's no need for me to be there.'

'No.'

It had been too far out of her comfort zone. Had she only been working for him, she might not have liked it, but of course she would have accepted his treatment of her.

But they were lovers.

Oh, it was a business arrangement, perhaps, but still she could not flick a switch. She refused to go from being his lover to a servant who walked behind him, being ignored. His little hand-flick had incensed her.

An hour out of London the turbulence finally eased, and by then Felicia was dozing. Kedah went to his bedroom, but there wasn't time to shower so he just changed out of his traditional clothing into a suit.

He could have slept for an hour, maybe, but instead he sat on the bed with his head in his hands.

Despite his brave words, he did not know what his response would be should his father back Mohammed.

Should he risk his mother's past being exposed by taking it to a public vote? What if the title of Crown Prince wasn't rightly his?

Usually Kedah looked immaculate.

Not this morning.

London was beautiful, Felicia thought from the back of a luxurious car, and yet it wasn't the same as when she'd left. The last few weeks had been spent exclusively with Kedah, and nothing felt the same.

This wasn't a date. He didn't drop her home first. Kedah was both royal *and* her boss, so they pulled up outside his apartment and she got out and ensured all his luggage had been removed.

Here, they always said goodbye.

'I'm assuming that I've got the rest of the day off?'

'Of course.'

It had been a very long business trip, and new boundaries needed to be established now.

'I'll see you tomorrow at eight,' she said, and as she did so Big Ben chimed and they stood there. It was seven in the morning, which meant a separation of twenty-five hours.

'Come up,' Kedah said.

'I'm really tired.'

'I know you are.'

He could see the shadows under her eyes, and he was exhausted too. But the turbulence on the plane was nothing compared to now.

They were on the edge of being stupid.

Sleep-deprived, wanting, holding back…neither really knew.

She should run, Felicia thought. Jump in the car and go home.

Go to her mother's tonight for a timely reminder on what falling in love with a certain type of man could do.

But, truly, she didn't know how to play tough today—especially when Kedah spoke on.

'You said that if I decide to tell you it won't go any further. Does that still apply?'

And just when she knew she should walk away, he beckoned her in.

'You know it does.'

He took her hand as he signalled the driver to remove her cases from the car too.

She stood in the antique elevator beside him, and even then she knew she should get out.

But it wasn't curiosity that had led her back to him. It was desire.

Every minute available to them she wanted to claim.

She would heal later.

Felicia had been in his apartment a couple of times, though never with Kedah there. Usually she went there to speak with a maid, or went with his driver to collect his luggage.

Now, she was a little unsure of her role as she stepped into the magnificent abode.

The drapes were open, revealing beautiful private gardens, and she gazed out at them as the driver deposited their bags in the hallway.

Felicia knew she wasn't here as his PA, and yet she wasn't quite sure if it was her trouble-shooting skills that Kedah was seeking now.

'I'm going to shower,' he told her, and she nodded. 'Join me?'

She gave a tired laugh and carried on staring out of the window as Kedah headed off. His presumption should irk her, yet it didn't.

She wanted him, after all.

It was later that concerned her, not now.

Kedah walked into his large bathroom and removed his clothing. It should feel good to be home after all this time away, yet it never quite did.

Home was Zazinia.

He turned on the shower and the jets of water should have blasted him awake, but he was too tired for that. He stood soaping his body, still questioning the wisdom of telling the truth to another person.

But then he watched as Felicia, a little late, took up his offer to join him.

And for the first time it was good to be home.

'Wait,' he told her as she started to undress.

Kedah came out of the shower and she stood as he took care of the intricate buttons he had itched to undo so many hours ago.

This time he gave no orders. Instead he

simply did what he must to get her naked. He peeled off her robe and then helped her out of her underwear.

'You're shaking?' he said, because he could feel the tremble in her as she stepped out of her knickers.

'I think I officially have jet lag,' she said.

She didn't.

Well, she probably did. But in that walk from the lounge through his bedroom to the bathroom she had known she was entrenching herself deeper into his life.

He lifted her hair and kissed her neck softly, deeply, intimately, in a way that made her dizzy. And she wished he did not take quite such care, so that later she could fault him, but instead he took her, tired and aching, into the shower.

First he washed her hair, and those strong fingers worked her into a quiet frenzy. He soaped her body and he missed nothing—not a finger, nor that patch of skin behind her knees that she had become aware of on the very first day they met.

And she did nothing. She didn't even touch him. She just felt the arousal that swirled around them thicken and knew of his increasing pleasure as his breathing tripped on occasion.

She faced away from him and he splayed her hands against the glass. He kissed down her back and it was the first time since childhood that Felicia had cried. Not that he could see that she did, for the water took care of that, and not that he could hear that she did, for she sobbed also with desire.

'Turn around.'

They were the only words spoken, and when she did she was met with a wall of muscle. He held her and lifted her hair and kissed her, so the sound of water was but a distant thrum. It was so distant that it took her a moment to realise that he had turned the taps off. Taking her hand, he led her dripping wet to his bed.

They would pay for this later, Felicia was sure. They would wake up in soaked sheets, with her hair in chaos, but she cared nothing about that now.

She shivered—not just from the cool of the air on her wet skin, nor her building need, but from the darkness of the bedroom that shut out the morning sun, from the upending of her senses.

In his room, she was deeper into his life.

He pulled back the covers and she climbed in, and then he wrapped her not in linen but in the cocoon of his body. He was barely on his elbows, their skin was in full contact, and his weight was pleasurably heavy upon her.

Then he took her, and Kedah had never meant to take her like this. He drove in on a kiss and told her her name. He told her just who he needed to chase away the demons.

And she said stupid words—like *yes* and his name.

All her anger and fury at being ignored and having to walk behind him was not eliminated by his kiss—in fact it was intensified. As he took her, hard and fast, there was almost a fight to the death taking place. Delicious anger burned and cleansed.

He pounded her senses until she could take it no more, and she came but did not surrender, even while moaning his name and unfurling at her core.

He met her, matched her, he filled her deeply and she lay there beneath him, breathless.

And she was still angry.

Did he think this was a part of the service? Did he think she could just give herself to *anyone* like that?

Clearly he did, Felicia thought, for she assumed all his lovers were treated to such intimate bliss.

She could never have known she was the first in this bed.

He rolled from her.

He had spent a lifetime wishing he had never opened that door, wishing he had never seen what he had. Now he checked that Felicia wanted to come further into his world.

'Do you want to know?'

She glanced at the clock by the bed and it told her it was nine.

Her cases were there in the hall. She could easily dress now, make some casual comment and tell him it would keep and head for home.

Get out now, while she still had a chance.

It was already far too late for that.

Her tears in the shower had left her surprisingly clear-headed, and she knew now she could not leave him by simple choice.

'Yes.' She turned and nodded. 'I want to know.'

CHAPTER EIGHT

'THAT ARTICLE YOU read on the day of our first meeting,' Kedah said. 'Do you have it?'

'It was taken down from the internet.'

'Come off it, Felicia.'

He knew that she was savvy and would have taken a screenshot, and of course she confirmed it. 'I've got it on my phone.'

'Take a look.'

He got out of bed and it troubled Felicia how little it bothered her that he went into her bag and took out her phone, which he handed to her.

'Have another read of it while I go and make coffee.'

She moved over to the side of the bed that wasn't damp from the shower and read again about the very decadent Sheikh Kedah.

'What do you see?' He brought in some drinks and then climbed in beside her on the dry side of the bed.

'There's nothing I don't know. They're hinting that the Accession Council should meet...'

'Read on,' Kedah told her, and she frowned and read down.

'There's just a picture of Mohammed and your father.'

'And what does the caption say?'

"Like father, like son."

'There's a subtext there,' Kedah said. 'A warning that if I push for change then the truth might be revealed...'

Felicia frowned.

'The truth?'

'There is a rumour in Zazinia that I am not my father's son. It's not just that I look nothing like him—our visions are so different. Though the rumour persists, to date no one has dared voice it to my father or me. I believe soon they might. I need to be ready, and to quash it with the most withering riposte...'

She thought back to what he had said as they'd stood by those portraits—about looking nothing like any of them.

'I don't look like *my* father...' But Felicia knew there had to be more to it than just rumour, and so she asked the question no one dared. 'Is there a chance it might be true?'

'Yes,' Kedah told her, and he watched the

swallowing in her throat. 'I caught my mother cheating when I was a young child.'

'Does anyone else know?'

Kedah thought back and shook his head. 'I was on my own when I caught them.'

'Does your mother know what you saw?'

Kedah didn't answer.

'Tell me what happened.'

'You don't need the details. I made a decision a long time ago never to speak of it.'

She saw his eyes shutter and Felicia let out a tense, 'What happened?' Then she continued. 'Tell me what you saw. You hate it when I discredit your work—well, don't dismiss mine. I deal with this type of thing a lot. Well, maybe not with royalty, but I know I can help. Though you have to tell me it all.'

She knew he didn't believe there was any difference she could make but, to his credit—or perhaps to hers—he told her some more.

'I was young.'

'How young?'

'Just turning three.'

He was hesitant to say more, but then he looked at Felicia. Yes, Matteo had been right about her. She was tough and experienced—he himself had seen that. And now they were lovers. But, more than that, he trusted her.

'The office where you worked yesterday… just outside the one where my portrait was done…?' He offered the location and Felicia nodded as her mind's eye went there. 'I was hiding from the royal nanny. My grandfather and father had been away and I didn't want to go and welcome them back, so I ran off and hid under the desk. I could hear noises coming from inside the office, and at first I thought my mother was hurt. When I opened the door she was being held by Abdal.'

'Abdal?' Felicia checked, but then, aware of her own impatience, she shook her head—she would find out in time. 'Go on.'

'Abdal walked off and she told me she had been crying and that he had been comforting her. She told me not to tell the King or anyone else. I don't think she knows that I remember.'

'What about the nanny?' Felicia asked. 'The one you were hiding from?'

'She came in then, and apologised for losing sight of me.' Kedah thought back. 'She was awkward, though I don't think she would have seen…'

'She might have seen Abdal leaving.' It was good that Felicia had been to the palace and could picture it properly. That corridor was a long one, and if the nanny had seen Abdal leaving then it might have been clear he had been alone with the Queen.

While the King was away.

It was immaterial now, but possibly this helped Felicia understand how important it was to Kedah that no one guessed what was between them.

They were still in bed together, and Felicia had never worked like this before.

They were trying to unravel the past, to work out how best to deal with the future.

Now she sat up cross-legged, with the sheet around her, trying to imagine that the Queen she had met would risk it all for a brief fling.

'Why, if you were only almost three when you caught them, do you think it was a prolonged affair?'

'You don't take the Queen over a study desk unless you're very sure…'

He looked up, and he saw that Felicia smiled.

It felt odd to smile about something so dark, and yet it helped that she did and so he told her some more.

'My mother comes from a much more modern country. Abdal was an aide also from there. He came to Zazinia to help with the transition and to ensure my grandfather upheld his agreements.'

'Did he?'

'Minimally. There was a lot of hope for change when the marriage took place, but little transpired. If he wasn't dead I would cheerfully kill him...'

Felicia didn't doubt him. Kedah's voice was ominous.

'Abdal had been in Zazinia ever since the royal wedding,' he went on.

'How soon after you caught them did he leave?'

Kedah thought back. 'A few days afterwards.' Even at such a young age he had served his mother a warning that day, and it had been heeded. 'I look nothing like my brother or my grandfather. He must have been a risk-taker to do what he did. So am I—'

'Kedah,' Felicia interrupted, in a voice that was terribly practical. 'Let's assume you inherited your risk-taking behaviour from your mother.'

He gave a reluctant smile, because he had never thought of it like that.

'What about a DNA test?' she asked. 'You'd know once and for all.'

He liked it that she was practical, that she didn't judge his mother or wring her hands, just got straight to the pertinent facts and seemed to sense how vital it was that Kedah knew where he stood.

'I've already had my profile done,' Kedah admitted. 'Anonymously, of course. But you've seen how it is there. Can you imagine me creeping around trying to find a comb?'

'You can get it from other things,' Felicia said. 'One of my other clients…'

His jaw gritted. He loathed thinking of her other clients and their scandalous pasts—and he loathed, more than that, that she had ever been close to them. 'I don't need to hear about them.'

'Maybe you do. With one of them I got a sample from chewing gum.'

'He's a *king*,' Kedah said.

'I get that. I'm just saying…'

'Why don't I pull on some gloves and offer him a stick of chewing gum or snip off some hair? Do you think no one will notice?' He lay back and tucked his hand behind his head as he tried to think.

If there was a solution to be had, he would have come up with it by now.

'I'm thinking of asking her.'

'Oh, no!' Felicia shook her head. 'Kedah, even if she admits to the affair, she's never going to admit to *that*. Do you think your father knows about the rumours?'

'Possibly,' he said. 'But he still thinks my mother is perfection personified. He would defend her to the death. But I know that if he does then he could be made to look a fool. I need to know the truth.'

'Even if the result isn't the one you want?'

'I can handle the truth, Felicia.'

She believed him. 'But...?'

'I don't know that my mother could,' Kedah said. 'If even so much as the affair were exposed then my father would have no choice but to divorce her.'

'By the old rules?' Felicia said, and Kedah looked over to her. 'Does he love her?'

'Very much.' Kedah thought of how his father's face lit up whenever she came in the room. How he did all he could to shield her from the feud between her sons. 'I don't know how he'd be if the truth came out, though.'

He was done with talking about it.

'Come on,' he said. 'Sleep.'

And this time there was no thought of heading for her case, or making a feeble excuse that she needed to go home to water her plants.

Felicia slept.

CHAPTER NINE

FELICIA HAD NEVER known someone so able to separate the bedroom from work.

Kedah did it with ease.

And it helped.

At restaurants, her computer and her phone on the table served as a little wall between them. To remind her, as often as was necessary, that they were not lovers having lunch.

She was *working*.

Oh, but the nights!

In the evenings they ate at the best restaurants, without a computer between them, holding hands between courses and doing rude things under the table with their feet before returning home to his bed.

The bedroom was an entirely different thing. Her cases had long since been unpacked by his maids.

Her family and friends were very used to Felicia disappearing for weeks on end as she focused on her clients, so her absence was easily explained—even when she caught up with her mother for lunch.

'At least tell me who you're working for,' Susannah said.

'I can't just yet.' Felicia smiled and then looked at the time. 'I have to get back.'

Felicia *did* have to get back. Kedah had a two p.m. meeting with Hussain. But, knowing she needed supplies, after lunch Felicia decided to use lover's licence and dash back to her own flat.

Poor neglected flat, she thought as she grabbed some make-up wipes and tweezers from her bathroom cupboard. Two things that were sadly lacking at Kedah's.

Perhaps they should spend some time here…

And then she checked herself. It was easier that their time was spent at his apartment. She did not need constant reminders of him here when they were through.

And soon they would be.

Vadia's requests for a bridal selection date were almost daily now. The article that had been taken down from the internet was back up again, and there had been several more too.

Things were coming to a head, whether she wanted it or not.

Felicia opened up the cabinet and grabbed a fresh packet of contraceptive pills—the real reason she was there, for she was down to her last.

She went to grab some tampons too, but then remembered she'd already taken some to Kedah's last week.

She stilled as she realised she was down to her last pill and had nothing to show for it. Her tampons sat languishing in the glitzy mirrored cupboard in his bathroom.

Felicia stood for a very long moment and told herself it was the travel, it was exhaustion, it was being in love with a sexy sheikh who could never consider loving her back that had made her late.

And she *was* late.

Late with her period, late back from lunch.

And, because they kept things very separate, Kedah did not hold back from pointing this out.

'You're late.' He scowled.

'Indeed I am,' she responded.

'You haven't sent the file to Hussain…'

'No.' She sighed. She'd been too engrossed in that other file he'd mistakenly sent her to remember a small detail like that. 'I forgot.'

'Well, don't forget again,' he said, but then he halted.

He knew he was working her hard—both at work and in the bedroom.

Workwise… Well, he knew that time was running out, so he was trying to fit everything in.

And as for the other…

The same.

Still Felicia fascinated him. Still he wanted her over and over.

Usually his interest waned by the time the sun rose on a new day, but this fidelity trial was going exceptionally well.

Felicia did not wait for him to terminate the conversation. Every night she spent with him she felt as if she were handing over more and more of her heart, and she could not take it much longer.

She walked out and sat at her desk. She smiled at Anu, who brought some tea into her office and then left Felicia to work, but a few moments later Anu was back.

'Felicia…' She sounded concerned. 'That was Reception. Kedah's brother is here to see him, but he's in a meeting with Hussain and he told me that I am not to disturb him.'

'Well, he said nothing of the sort to *me*.'. Felicia smiled sweetly as she reached for the phone, which made Anu laugh.

Kedah was not impressed. 'I said that I wasn't to be disturbed.'

'Well, you might change your mind for this. Apparently Mohammed is down in Reception.'

Kedah looked over to Hussain. His first instinct was to tell Felicia to let Mohammed know he was in a meeting and that he would see him when he was ready.

But there was no point.

This was no idle visit, and Kedah had to show he had no reason to delay or hide.

'He can come up.'

He spoke to Hussain. 'I am going to have to cut our meeting short. It would seem Mohammed has flown in to speak with me. I hope you understand.'

'Of course.'

The men shook hands and suddenly, for Kedah, the design for a hotel in Dubai held little importance.

Hussain saw himself out of the office. He looked more serious than Felicia had ever seen him. Usually Hussain stopped and spoke, but today he just nodded to Anu, who also looked troubled.

Mohammed walked in, and when Anu did not move Felicia greeted the Prince and showed him through. 'Can I get you any refreshments?' she offered.

'No, thank you,' Kedah said. 'That shall be all.'

It was all supremely polite, but the air was so thick it was like closing the door on a tornado.

'Trouble is here,' Anu said once the door had closed.

'Not necessarily,' Felicia offered.

'I grew up knowing that this day would come.'

So had Kedah.

'This is a surprise.' Kedah's voice told his brother that it wasn't a particularly pleasant one.

'I only decided to come this morning,' Mohammed said as he took a seat. 'I sat in on a meeting about brides considered to be suitable as future Queen. It struck me as odd, given that I already have a wonderful bride, who would make an excellent queen, as well as two sons.'

'*I* am first in line,' Kedah answered smoothly. 'Why would you consider it odd?'

'Because I am the one sitting there discussing the future of our country and you are miles away, focusing on your own wealth.'

'As I have long said to our father, and to our grandfather before him, I am more than happy to devote my attention to Zazinia, and I shall do so when I am not thwarted at every turn. If I have to wait to be King to see my country flourish and thrive, then I shall do so—'

'I have been approached by Fatiq,' Mohammed broke in. Fatiq was a senior elder. 'I felt it only fair to warn you that there is a majority agreement amongst the elders that *I* would make a more suitable Crown Prince and King.'

'I could have told you that a decade ago.' Kedah shrugged. 'That is old news.'

'They feel that your interests are clearly removed from Zazinia…'

'Never.'

'And they suggest that it is time for you to step aside and make way for the most suitable heir.'

'Never,' Kedah said again.

'Some also say that I am the *rightful* heir.'

'Name them,' Kedah responded with a challenge.

Mohammed shook his head. 'I cannot do that. However, should an Accession Council meeting be called…'

'Why would that happen? Our father has

stated that once I choose my bride I will have his full support.'

'Kedah, we don't *want* it go to the Accession Council. You know as well as I do that there are things that should be left unsaid. You have the power to halt the elders.'

And Kedah saw his brother's game plan then. Mohammed wanted the threat of his mother's exposure to force Kedah aside.

He had chosen the wrong man, though, for Kedah would never be bullied.

'You really think I would step aside to appease the elders?'

'No, but I feel you would for the sake of our mother's integrity...'

Mohammed had intended to prompt his brother finally to back down. Instead Kedah picked up his phone and called the palace. He was through to the King in a matter of moments.

'I am calling a meeting of the Accession Council,' he said to his father, and he stared his brother in the eyes as he did so. 'This shall be dealt with once and for all. Do I have your support or do I not?'

'Kedah...' The King had known his youngest son had flown out and had been waiting for this call. 'There is no need to call for a meeting.

I have told you—return to Zazinia and choose your bride, appease the elders…'

Kedah had heard enough.

'The meeting will be held at sunset on Friday. You shall stand in support of your eldest son or not. If Mohammed is chosen it will not be left there. I shall take the decision to the people.'

He threw down the phone and looked to his brother. 'I mean it,' Kedah warned him.

'The elders say that if pushed they will demand a DNA test…'

He waited for Kedah to crumble, for the Crown Prince to pale, but his brother gave a black laugh.

'They embrace technology when it suits them.' He dismissed the threat with a flick of his wrist, though privately he fought to keep that hand steady. 'I am returning to Zazinia…'

'Even though you know what it might do to our mother?'

'Don't turn this onto me,' Kedah warned, and now he stood. 'Don't pretend for a minute that you are not behind this too. If and when I choose a bride—'

'You cannot!' Mohammed frowned, but backed off slightly as his brother approached. 'Why would you do that to her?'

'To whom?' Kedah frowned too.

'To your *wife*.' Mohammed had stopped even pretending he wasn't the one leading this coup. 'I was just saying yesterday to Kumu—*she* married a prince who might one day be King. Whereas *your* bride will marry the Crown Prince who might one day be a commoner. You are in no position to choose a wife.'

Kedah just gave another black laugh as he took his brother by the throat. He, too, had stopped pretending.

'If my mother's name is ever discredited I shall have you thrown in prison.'

'You don't seem to understand, Kedah. The power won't be yours.'

And Kedah's response…?

It had been banter when he had said it to Felicia, but there was no hint of that now, and he watched Mohammed pale as he delivered his threat. 'Then I shall deal with you outside of the law.'

CHAPTER TEN

FELICIA SAT IN her office as Kedah's other world intervened.

Or rather his real world.

This was all temporary. They had always had a use-by date and she had to remind herself of that.

Not any more, though, for now there was no hiding from the truth.

From her office she could see Mohammed striding out, one hand massaging his neck, and she guessed there had been a tussle.

Felicia honestly could not deal with it now. She had been going through her calendar and trying to work out when her last period had been. Her world was a blur since she'd been working for Kedah.

She *couldn't* be pregnant?

Surely!

'Hey.'

Felicia looked up and there he was. 'How did it go?' she asked.

'He stated his case.'

And, after weeks of wanting to know more, and a career based on revelation, suddenly Felicia didn't want to know what had been said. She did not want to hear that their time was running out.

'Shall we go and get dinner?' Kedah suggested.

'It's not even five.'

'Let's go back to my apartment, then. We need to talk.'

'I have a meeting with Vadia soon.'

'Well, cancel it,' he said. 'We need to talk. Things are coming to a head back home. My brother has spoken with the elders. They want *him* as Crown Prince.'

She said nothing.

'My father seems to think if I choose a bride then we can put things off...'

Very deliberately, Felicia did not flinch.

'I have called for a meeting of the Accession Council this Friday at sunset.' For once the arrogant Kedah was pale. 'I shall leave on Thursday.'

'For how long?'

'I doubt it will be dealt with quickly. If the

vote is in my favour I expect that things will get dirty, and the elders will do their best to question my lineage. I shall be busy there for the foreseeable future.'

'Where does that leave *me*?'

It was the neediest she had ever been, but thankfully Kedah took her at her selfish, career-focused best.

'Your contract is for a year. Whatever happens to me.'

It was like a slap on the cheek, but a necessary one, and it put her back in business mode.

'And if it goes in your favour?'

'Then it is time for me to step up.'

And, whatever way it went, Felicia knew things would never be the same.

'We need to sort out—' Kedah started, but she interrupted him.

'Not now.'

Felicia wanted to curl up on her sofa and hide from the building panic. She wanted a night spent with chocolate, convincing herself that she couldn't possibly be pregnant.

She had been right never to mix business with pleasure, because she was finding it impossible to think objectively now—and that was what he had hired her to do after all.

'I need to go home and think this through.'

'You can think it through with *me*.'

'No.'

She couldn't.

Because when she was with him feelings clouded the issue. A part of her didn't even *want* Kedah to be the rightful King, because if he was not that meant there might a chance for them.

Oh, surely not?

She had become Beth, Felicia realised, or one of the many others who had hoped against hope that things with Kedah might prove different for them. She had fallen head over heels, even with due warning, and had hoped he might somehow change.

One day she would laugh, she decided.

One night in the future she would sit with friends, sipping a cocktail, and make them laugh as she told them how, even as he'd spoken of his future bride, even as he'd told her not to worry about her contract, she had hoped—stupidly hoped—there was a chance for them.

'I'm going home.' Felicia stood. 'I'll think about it tonight…' And then she did it. She offered the lovely wide smile that she gave to all her clients. The one that told them she'd handle this, that they could leave it with her. 'I'll come up with something.'

And Kedah said nothing. He just stepped aside as she brushed past.

He hadn't been asking her to come up with a solution! Conversation and something rather more basic would have sufficed. He'd never needed anyone in his life, yet tonight he needed Felicia Hamilton.

And she had walked off.

She'd had no choice but to.

It had been walk away or break down and cry—something she had sworn never to do in front of someone else, especially Kedah.

And so she headed for home, turned the key in the door, and stepped into the flat that had once felt familiar but no longer did.

She felt upended now.

At the age of twenty-six Felicia had fallen in love.

Real love.

CHAPTER ELEVEN

KEDAH ARRIVED FOR work a little later than usual the next day, and stepped out of the elevator to the aroma of coffee.

It had been a long night.

As much as it galled him to admit it, Mohammed had made a very good point—how could he marry when one day his title might be held up for question?

Kedah was proud, and the selection of royal brides from whom he would choose all expected him to one day be King.

His problems had kept him awake for most of the night, and this morning, just as he had been leaving, Omar had rung to try to persuade Kedah to call off the meeting. But he had refused.

It would just delay the inevitable.

He headed towards his office and there was Anu at her desk, drinking coffee. 'Good morning,' he said, and it took him a moment to register that Felicia wasn't there. Her office door was closed and the light was off.

'Good morning.' Anu went to stand up. 'Would you like coffee?'

'Later,' he said, and waved her to sit back down. 'You look tired.'

'I couldn't sleep,' Anu admitted. 'My mother called late last night and said there are reports that the Accession Council are meeting.'

'On Friday.' Kedah nodded and thought of Felicia's response—*Where does that leave me?* 'Anu, whatever happens your job is safe. I shall be keeping all my hotels and—'

'I'm not worried about my job, Kedah,' Anu said. 'Well, a bit… But my mother was upset and my father is too. I worry for my country. Growing up, we all looked forward to the day you would be King…'

'And I shall be,' Kedah said, though he could see that Anu wasn't convinced.

She would have grown up on the rumours too.

'I would like to fly back to Zazinia tomorrow, some time midmorning,' he told Anu. 'Can you arrange that, please?'

Tomorrow was Thursday. He could possibly have left it another day, but he wanted some time in his country to prepare for the meeting. Perhaps he would go to the desert and draw on its wisdom. He was very aware that tonight would be his last in London for the foreseeable future.

'Can you ask Felicia to come and speak with me as soon as she gets in?'

'Felicia's not coming in today,' Anu said. 'She just called in sick.'

Oh, no, she didn't!

Kedah walked into his office and, closing the door behind him, immediately picked up his phone.

The first time she didn't answer, but he refused to speak to a machine and so immediately called again.

Felicia stared at her phone and something told her that if she didn't pick up then Kedah would soon be at her door.

'Hi.' Felicia did her best to keep her voice crisp, but she had woken in tears and they simply would not stop.

'Are you crying?' Kedah asked.

'Of course not. I've got a cold. I've already explained that to Anu.'

'It's summer,' he pointed out.

'I've got a summer cold.'

'You were fine yesterday...'

'Well. I'm not today. Look, I'm sorry it's not convenient, but I really can't work. I need to take the day off.'

'Felicia…' Kedah's impatience was rising. She had swanned off before five last night and now, when he properly needed her, she had called in sick—with a cold, of all things. 'I want you here within the hour,' he told her. 'I have a lot to sort out. You know that. I fly to Zazinia tomorrow.'

'I can't come into work,' she responded. She didn't need to be looking in a mirror to know that her face was red and that her eyes were swollen from crying. 'I have to take today off. I believe my contract allows for sick days with a medical certificate?'

Felicia ended the call and turned off her phone. Refusing to lie there worrying, she hauled herself out of bed and dressed. Grabbing her purse, she headed out.

Oh, she was doing her best to reassure herself that it was travel and exhaustion that accounted for her being late, as well as the uncertainty of being head over heels in love with the most insensitive man in the world.

A man who could hold you in his arms while discussing brides.

A man who had told her to her face that an

unplanned pregnancy wouldn't faze him and that the palace would 'handle' it.

Though for all he had stated it wouldn't be an issue, it might be a touch more scandal than he would want this close to a meeting of the Accession Council and the bridal selection.

Well, she didn't need Vadia to sort her out. Felicia would manage this herself!

She bought the necessary kit and, once home, did what the instructions said and waited, with mounting anxiety, trying to tell herself that she could *not* be pregnant.

Except just a moment later she found out that she was.

All the panic seemed to still inside her, and she waited for it to regroup and slam back. She waited for the tears she had sobbed this morning to return with renewed vigour, but nothing happened. She sat there, staring at the indicator, trying to comprehend the fact that she was going to be a mum.

It wasn't something she'd ever really considered before. A baby had never factored in her plans.

Her career had always come first and relationships had come last.

Till Kedah.

Only she wasn't thinking about Kedah and

scandals and the damage this might cause right now.

Instead she thought of herself and her own wants.

And she wanted her baby.

She wanted this little creation that had been made by them.

It was, for Felicia, a very instant love, for someone she knew she must protect.

And she had been told, though had never quite understood, that love was patient.

Could it be?

When she should be calling the doctor, or demanding Kedah's reaction, something told her that her baby would still be waiting on the other side.

There were other things that needed to be sorted now. It was time to focus on the job she had been hired to do.

Even though she had only known she was pregnant for an hour, right now Felicia needed to be a working mum.

Kedah's future might depend on it.

Yes, Felicia was *very* good at her job.

She went over and over their conversations and thought back to her time at the palace—it all came back to one thing.

Kedah needed to know, before he went into battle, whether or not he was the rightful Crown Prince.

Without that there could be no clear rebuttal, and if he *wasn't* his father's son…

Felicia sat in her little home study late into the afternoon. The shadows fell over her table and she was just about to put her desk lamp on when there was a knock at the door. She went down the hall, opened the door and signed for a box, which she took back to her study.

It was as if she had let in the sun, for now it streamed through the window, golden and warm. She smiled as she opened the box and took out a gorgeous basket. She looked at the contents.

There was a bottle of cognac and a glass, as well as a warmer. There was a dressing gown, silk handkerchiefs and organic honey. Felicia felt as though she was going to cry as she held lemons so perfect that they might have been chosen and hand-picked by angels.

There was everything you could possibly need if you did indeed have a cold and weren't in fact crying over Kedah.

What was it with him that he moved her so?

And not just her.

She thought of how he walked into a room

and the aura Felicia felt she could see, how heads turned when he passed.

It wasn't just his beauty.

There was more.

When he gave his attention it was completely, whether it was to her or to a waiter. Kedah had a way of giving full focus, and she had never witnessed it in another.

Kedah was his father's son. Felicia was sure.

She was as certain as she could be that he had been born to be King.

But how could she prove it?

There was a note too, handwritten by him.

And this was much better than choosing from a brochure or a huge bunch of flowers.

She could imagine the courier waiting as he penned it, and knew that whatever happened she would keep it for ever—because while he made her cry in private, always he made her smile.

Felicia,
Of course you don't need a medical cer-
tificate. I was just surprised that you were
sick and disappointed not to see you.
Things are about to get busy, but take the
time you need to get well and return when
you are ready.

*It would mean a lot if I could see you to-
morrow before I leave for Zazinia. If not,
I understand, and shall be in touch soon.
Kedah.*

Clearly he needed her on form to deal with
the press and believed that she really had a cold.

Yes, he could be arrogant at times, she
thought, but then he was so terribly kind.

And he must never know she had fallen in
love with him.

It had never been part of the deal.

CHAPTER TWELVE

FELICIA WOKE LONG before her alarm, and after showering she dressed for battle.

And it *would* be a battle to keep her true feelings from him.

But there was work to be done and finally, after a long night spent tossing and turning, she had a plan.

She went to her wardrobe and chose the white dress she had worn on the first day they had met.

It was her favourite lie.

It made her look sweet when she wasn't.

It made her appear a touch fragile when in fact she was very strong.

And she was strong enough to get through this.

She rubbed a little red lipstick into her nose and saw the redness of her eyes had gone down, so hopefully it looked as if she were at the end of a cold rather than in the throes of a broken heart.

Instead of arriving at work early she lingered over her breakfast, and then headed to a very exclusive department store and waited until its doors opened.

There she made a purchase, before going to his office where the doorman greeted her as she walked in.

'Can I help with your bags?' he offered.

'I'm fine, thank you,' she responded.

She would not let the bag and its contents out of her sight for even a moment.

It was far harder than facing the press—far harder than anything she had ever done—to walk out of the elevators with a smile and greet Anu, who looked as tearful and as anxious as Felicia felt on the inside.

'Is he in?' Felicia asked.

'He flies in a couple of hours.' Anu nodded. 'I just took a call from a reporter. He was asking for confirmation that he is flying today to Zazinia. I don't want to trouble Kedah with it, but I don't know what to say…'

'Just tell him that for security reasons you are not at liberty to discuss his movements,' Felicia answered, and then she looked at Anu's crestfallen face. 'Have some faith—Kedah will be fine.'

'You don't know that.'

'Of course I do.'

'You didn't grow up in Zazinia,' Anu said. 'The people there have always feared this. You don't know what is about to come…'

So Anu knew of the rumours, Felicia realised. Possibly the whole country did, and had been waiting for the black day when their Golden Prince was removed.

'When does he leave?'

'At midday.'

As Felicia headed towards Kedah's office Anu, the gatekeeper, stopped her. 'He said that he doesn't want to be disturbed.'

Felicia nodded, but would not be halted. 'I need to speak with him.'

She knocked on the door and when there was no response opened it. Kedah was on the phone, and he gestured for her to take a seat and then carried on speaking in Arabic for the best part of ten minutes before ending the call.

'Are you feeling better?' he checked.

'Much.' She nodded.

'Good—because the press have got hold of it already and my staff are starting to become concerned. Let them know that nothing has changed and—regarding the press—clarify, please, that it was I who called for a meeting of the Accession Council…' He stopped talking then and came around the desk. 'I didn't think you were coming in.' He went to take her in his arms. 'It's good to see you.'

Felicia pulled back. She could not take affection and also do what was required.

'Kedah, I've been thinking. Take me with you to Zazinia.'

'Felicia, I am going to be busy, and you know as well as I do that when I am there we can't do anything. Anyway, you said you'd never go back.'

'I know I did, but I'm not asking you to take me there for a romantic holiday. Kedah, if you knew for certain that you were your father's son, would it change things?'

'Of course.' He nodded. 'I am fighting blind at the moment, but…' he shook his head '…there is no way to find out unless I speak with my mother.'

'And we both know that no good can come from that.'

He didn't look convinced.

'Kedah, I've worked with people who've been caught red-handed and they'll all admit to once, but…' She shook her head. 'You need irrefutable proof—DNA testing.'

'I've told you—I couldn't get a sample without his knowing.' Kedah pressed his fingers to the bridge of his nose. 'Soon the elders will call for one.'

'Then find out *now*.'

'Ask him?'

'No.' Felicia shook her head. 'I doubt your father would want to know, unless forced. What if you asked him to come to your office?'

Felicia took a large box from the bag she had carried in and opened it. Along with a stunning crystal decanter and glasses there was a pair of white cotton gloves.

'I've got the buffering solution. I can prep the glass, and if he takes a drink from it I can fly straight back and have the test done. You said they already have your profile?'

Kedah nodded to that question, but then he shook his head. It could never work 'Felicia, you've seen how it is there. There is no way he would come into my office for a discussion, let alone stay long enough to have a drink. No, he would ask me to meet with him in his.'

'What if you had your office set up for a presentation?'

Kedah looked at her. 'What sort of presentation?'

'The one you've spent years working on— your hopes for Zazinia. Your vision for your country. All the plans you have made.'

All the plans that had been knocked back. 'I told you to delete that file.'

'Since when did I do as I was told?' Felicia shrugged. 'And I'm glad I watched it…'

'You watched it?'

'Of course I did.'

Of course she had, Kedah thought. This was the woman who had taken a screenshot of that article that had only briefly appeared online. He was a work project, a problem to solve, and for a while he had forgotten that.

'Aside from obtaining a DNA sample, I think it's something that your father ought to see. He needs to know what he's taking on—or turning his back on.'

Kedah had grown too used to the other side of Felicia—the softer side he sometimes glimpsed—not the very tough businesswoman she was.

And this, although private, *was* business.

The business of being royal.

'Show it to him,' Felicia said. 'We can set up for a presentation in your office and ask him to come and view it. It goes on for an hour…'

It could work, Kedah realised. By the time the Accession Council met he could know the truth.

'Whatever the result, I shall fight for my people.'

'Ah, but it will make it so much easier, Kedah, if you're able to laugh in Mohammed's face…'

'Assuming the result is the one I want.'

'And if it's not?'

'I can handle the truth, Felicia.'

Could he?

She thought of the baby within her and wondered for a brief moment if it might be better to tell him—but then, in the same instant, she changed her mind.

Kedah needed to find out who his father was before she told him that he would soon become one.

There was no question of them whiling away the flight in the bedroom.

Kedah had not only his presentation to his father to edit, but also his speech for the Accession Council to prepare.

Aside from that, Felicia didn't know if she could risk being close to him right now without confessing her own truths.

Not just the baby, but the fact that she loved him.

So she put herself firmly into Felicia mode.

Or rather the Felicia he had first met.

She only had one robe that complied with the dress code in Zazinia, so an hour from landing she went and changed into the dusky pink one.

Her hands were shaking as she did up the row of buttons and her breath was tight in her lungs. She feared that he might come in, for she was not sure she possessed the strength not to fold to his touch.

He did not come in.

Oh, he thought about it, but he didn't dare seek oblivion now. He knew he had to keep his mind on the game.

God, but he wanted her.

'Still working that worry bead?' she teased when she came out from getting changed and saw him tapping away.

'I told you—I never worry.'

'Liar.'

'I don't worry, Felicia. I come up with solutions. I've known for a long time that one day this would happen. While the outcome might not be favourable, I've prepared for every eventuality. I'm a self-made billionaire. I'll always get by.'

He flicked the diamond across the table to her and Felicia picked it up.

'It's exquisite.'

'When my designs for Zazinia were first knocked back I spoke with Hussain. He had studied architecture with my father, and when I told him the trouble I was having he said his struggles for change had been thwarted too, and he would not let history be repeated. He invited me to come in on a design with him in Dubai. It was my first hotel, and a stunning success. Back then I sold it. I had never had my own money. I cannot explain that…I was royal and rich, but to receive my first commission brought a freedom I had never imagined, and with the money I bought this. I know each time I look at it that, if need be, I can more than make my own way.'

'People will be hurt, Kedah, even if the result is what you want. If Mohammed discredits your mother…' Felicia had thought about that too. 'She will be okay. It would be awful for a while, but—'

'No,' Kedah interrupted. 'She would *not* be okay. She isn't strong in the way your mother is.'

Felicia looked up from the diamond she was examining. She had never heard her mother described as strong; in fact she had heard people suggest she was weak and a fool for standing by her father all those years.

'It must have taken strength of character to go through all she did,' Kedah said, and after a moment's thought Felicia nodded. 'My mother doesn't have that strength.'

It wasn't something that had ever been said outright, yet he had grown up knowing it to be true.

'I remember when my father went on that trip. His last words were, "Look after your mother."' Kedah hadn't even been three. 'My father always said it, and I always took it seriously. She is a wonderful woman, but she is emotionally fragile. All the arguments, all the politics—we do our best to keep them from her. She does so many good things for our country. She worries for the homeless and cries for them, pleads with my father to make better provision for them. She takes their hurts so personally…'

There was no easy answer.

'She'll be okay,' Felicia said again, and watched as Kedah gave a tense shrug.

Had she even listened to what he had just said? he wondered.

She had.

'Your mother *shall* be okay, Kedah, whatever happens. It sounds to me as if she has the King's love.'

Kedah nodded. 'She does.'

Rina, Felicia thought, was a lucky woman indeed.

Kedah went back and forth to his country often. Usually they were short visits, so that he didn't get embroiled in a row, but he was a regular visitor and so as he stepped out of the plane he knew what to expect.

Or he thought he did.

But this time, as Kedah stepped from the plane it was to the sound of cheering. From beyond the palace walls the people of Zazinia had gathered to cheer their Prince home.

They wanted Kedah to rule one day, and it was their way of letting the Accession Council know that he was the people's choice.

Kedah would make the better King.

'Kedah!' Rina embraced him, but she had a question to ask. 'Why now?'

'Because the elders have long wanted Mohammed and it is time to put this to rest once and for all.' He stepped back. 'I have some work to do. I shall be in my wing.'

'Kedah…' Omar came out to greet his son.

'I would like to speak with you,' Kedah told him.

'Of course,' the King agreed. 'I have much

to discuss with you also. Come through to my office.'

'I would prefer that we speak in mine,' Kedah responded but Omar shook his head.

'We shall meet in mine.'

'I have something I want you to see.' Kedah refused to be dissuaded. 'I will go and prepare for you now.'

He didn't even turn his head to address Felicia.

He just summoned her in a brusque tone and gave that annoying flick of his wrist.

He offered a small bow to his parents and walked off, with Felicia a suitable distance behind him.

Up the palace steps they went, past the statue where as a child Kedah had hidden, and then past the guards and down a long corridor. Felicia understood now why he wanted these offices destroyed, for events there had caused so much pain, and possibly were about to cause more—not just for Kedah, but for his family and the people.

He closed the heavy door behind them and dealt with the projector and computer as Felicia pulled on gloves and pulled out a decanter and glasses and filled them.

'If he asks for another drink don't top it up—

let him do it. You don't want anything from *you* on this glass.'

'He'll call for a maid to do it,' Kedah said. 'He is King.'

Felicia was confident that Omar would not be calling for a maid. After all, she had seen the presentation and had no doubt Omar would sit transfixed as he watched it, just as she had.

'Are you nervous?' she asked, and then went to correct herself. Of course he wasn't nervous—Kedah never was. Yet he surprised her.

'Yes.'

It was possibly the most honest he had ever been. In some ways more open than he had ever been, even in bed. She went straight over to him and as easily as that he accepted her in his arms.

Kedah took a long, steadying breath as she leant on his chest. Here, once the scene of such devastation, he found a moment of peace.

'I'm sure the result will be as you wish it to be.'

'No one has seen my work before...'

'Kedah?' She looked up to him. 'It might not count for much, but *I've* seen it and, for what it's worth, I thought it was amazing.'

He was about to say that he hadn't meant it like that—more that no one important had seen it—but then, as he stood there, holding her, it dawned on him that the presentation had been watched by someone *very* important to him.

'Did you watch it all the way through?'

'Yes.'

'And...?'

'The truth?' Felicia checked, and he nodded.

'I saw it first by mistake and I have watched it many times since. The designs are stunning, Kedah.'

'I thought you said my work was impersonal?' he teased, and Felicia looked up.

'Your vision for Zazinia isn't work.'

It was everything.

There was the sound of the guards standing to attention and, when he would have preferred to hold her for a moment longer, Kedah had no choice but to let her go.

Felicia's eyes were glassy and, rather than let him see, she busied herself, walking over to check the projector was set up correctly and that everything was in place.

And then the door opened and in came Omar the King.

'Thank you for coming,' Kedah said, and he stood proudly. He had possibly been preparing for this moment for most of his adult life. Not just the confrontation, but sharing his vision for Zazinia with his father. 'I have something I would like you to see.'

'Not without first hearing your choice.' Omar thrust a bundle of files onto Kedah's desk. 'This is a shortlist of suitable brides.'

Even though Omar spoke in Arabic, this was not something Kedah wanted to discuss with a certain person present. 'Felicia, could you excuse us, please?'

'Of course.'

Omar hadn't even noticed that a lowly assistant was present, but he simply stood until she had left and the door closed quietly behind her.

Kedah broke the silence.

'If I choose a bride, then I shall have your full support at the Accession Council tomorrow?' he checked, and then let out a mirthless laugh at his father's lack of response.

He knew for certain that his father was bluffing, for he saw a rare nervous swallow from him as he reached for the files as if to peruse them.

'I need to know that, once I'm married, I shall have your approval to make the necessary changes...'

'First things first,' Omar said.

'Isn't that what *your* father said to *you*?'

Kedah asked. 'Choose a bride, produce an heir, and *then* we can talk?'

Omar did not respond.

'Yet nothing got done, and all these years later still there is little progress in Zazinia…'

'I ensured an improved education system,' Omar interjected. 'I pushed for that.' Yet both men knew that he had pushed for little more. 'The King did not want change,' Omar said.

'What about *this* King?' Kedah asked, but again there was no response. 'Please,' Kedah said, 'have a seat.'

He dimmed the lights in the office and took a seat himself as the presentation commenced.

Kedah looked over to his father, but the King gave no comment—though he did, Kedah noted, take a sip of his drink. And, while that was supposed to be the reason they were there, suddenly his father's reaction to the presentation was more important to Kedah.

Felicia had been right. His father needed to see this.

And there it all played out.

Like golden snakes, roads wove across the screen and bridges did what they were designed to—bridged. Access was given to the remote west, where the poorest people fought to survive, and somehow it all connected.

Schools and hospitals appeared, and within the animation teachers, doctors and nurses walked. There were animated children too, playing in parks. Now, hotels rose, and there were pools. Restaurants and cafés appeared on bustling evening streets.

And the King sat in silence.

Kedah watched as his father took a drink, and another, yet made no comment. An hour later, when an animated sun had set on a very different Zazinia from the one they knew and the presentation had ended, it was Omar who stood and opened up the drapes.

Still he offered no comment. Omar just stared out to the golden desert beyond and it was Kedah who spoke.

'That is what you deny your people. All this is achievable and yet you do nothing…'

'No—'

'*Yes,*' Kedah refuted. 'Turn around and tell me that Mohammed would make the better Crown Prince.'

Omar did not.

'Turn around and tell me that you don't want a glittering future for our people.'

'That is enough, Kedah,' Omar said, but Kedah had not finished yet.

He picked up the files and held them out for

his father. 'As I said to you when I was eighteen, you shall not force me to take a bride. I will never be pushed into something that is not of my choice. If you want me gone then say so, but let us stop pretending that it has anything to do with my choosing a wife.'

Kedah tossed the files down on the desk in frustration as again his father said nothing. He simply walked out.

He had shown his father his best—the very best of his vision, all that he hoped to achieve— and his father had offered no comment.

Felicia was startled when the office door opened unexpectedly. She did not receive any greeting from the very angry King who stalked past.

She had been seated at the very desk where years ago Kedah had once hidden, and now she took the same steps that he had at three years old—though she opened the door with greater ease.

'How was it?'

Kedah shrugged. 'Hopeless.'

'He didn't have a drink?' Felicia checked, and then Kedah remembered the real reason for the meeting.

He looked over to his father's glass, which was empty.

'I meant that the presentation was hopeless. He's never going to change his mind.'

Felicia pulled on her gloves and popped the glass into a clear bag, and then another, then placed it in her purse. On the desk she saw that there were some photos of dark-haired and dark-eyed beauties. One of them, no doubt, would be his bride.

Kedah was too incensed by his father's lack of response to notice where her gaze fell. His mind was on other things. 'What am I fighting for?' Kedah asked, and for the briefest moment he wavered where he had always been resolute. 'Am I the only one who wants change?'

'Your people want it also,' Felicia said. 'I heard them cheering you, Kedah.'

She was right—it wasn't just his ego that insisted he could do things better than his brother. And after his father's pale reaction to the presentation it was as if she blew the wind back into his sails.

'I am going to speak again with Mohammed,' Kedah said.

'Do so,' Felicia agreed. 'I'm going to head back to London.'

She was meeting a courier at Heathrow, who would take the glass to a laboratory where the samples would be analysed.

'I'll call you as soon as I get the results.'

And this was it, she realised. It was the very last time she would be in Zazinia—for certainly she would not travel here as his PA once Kedah had chosen his bride.

'Don't leave now.'

Kedah stood and came around the desk. He felt her resistance when he took her in his arms.

His fingers went to her chin and he lifted her face to meet his gaze. He was going to kiss her, she realised. Right now, when she was doing all she could not to break down.

'I have to go.'

'Not yet.'

His mouth was fierce and claiming, and she tasted salt at the back of her throat as she squeezed her eyes closed and held on to the tears he must never see her shed.

'Not here,' she said.

'Yes, here.'

He did not want her gone.

He could not picture the future. He just wanted a moment of the oblivion that they created together. So he did what Abdal should have done all those years ago.

Felicia stood as he walked over and turned the lock on the door.

Kedah turned her on in a way no one else

ever had or ever would. He tossed his sword to the floor and was opening his robe as he walked back towards her.

His passion was so fierce and overpowering. His hands were at the buttons of her robe and he was holding back from tearing it open.

And she loathed herself for wanting him so badly.

Even with his future wife's photo on the desk she would do this. She *would*, Felicia decided as he lifted her onto the desk. Now, while she didn't know his wife's name, she would be taken for the last time.

His hands ruched up the skirt of her robe and lifted it over her thighs, and perhaps Kedah was aware that this was the last time because impatient fingers were tearing at the buttons.

She had to walk out of this office soon, so she tried to assist him. But the buttons gave way so that her legs and chest were exposed and he pulled down the cups of her bra. There was no time to take off her knickers. His erection moved the slip of fabric aside and he stabbed into her.

Felicia sobbed as he filled her.

Their mouths were frantic and bruising in their fast, urgent coupling.

He thrust hard, then pressed her so the desk

was hard against her back and her hair splayed out. Now he tore at her knickers, and the sight of them, of himself deep inside her, almost made him come. It was intense, it was fast, and as he scooped her up her legs wrapped around him and she bit his shoulder to fight the scream as her body beat with his.

And it could never be over—and yet it was.

He was lowering her down, and she rested her burning face against his chest and listened for the last time to his heart. She told herself that she would never succumb to this bliss again.

'Felicia…'

She peeled herself from him and started to do up her robe. She wanted to be away from Zazinia, in the safety of the plane and then back in London. There she could sort out her head.

'I'd better get going.'

'In a moment. But first…'

'Kedah, the plane is waiting—there's a courier at the other end. If there's to be any hope of getting the results back in time…'

'Can't you stop thinking about work?'

'You *are* work, Kedah.'

Felicia took a mirror from her bag and ran a comb through her hair, and she saw her own lips start to tremble as he spoke on.

'In that case, if all goes well, then I am going to be spending a lot more time here in Zazinia. I will need someone to help with my overseas investments, and there will be an opening for an executive assistant...'

And briefly she allowed herself to glimpse it—an amazing career, a stunning flat and a night with Kedah whenever time allowed. A part-time father...yet she would be his full-time mistress...

She snapped the compact mirror closed and managed to sneer as she faced him 'You mean an executive *whore*?'

'Felicia...'

'I have to go.'

She really did—because otherwise she would say yes to him. If she stayed for just a few moments longer she would accept his crumbs.

'I'm going to go.'

'Of course.' He nodded.

'I hope you get the result that you're hoping for.'

And they were through.

She had but one more smile left in her, and she gave it to him now as she held up her bag.

'My work here is done,' she said.

'No,' Kedah said. 'You will be back in the office tomorrow. I employed you to look out for my people. This was…' He hesitated. 'A personal favour. Thank you.'

He could not quite believe that she knew. That he had asked for and received her help.

'I trust you, Felicia.'

And she waited for him to warn her, to remind her that if she let him down then she would be dealt with 'outside the law', but there was no postscript.

'I hope it all goes well,' she said.

And maybe he shouldn't trust her, because right then she had lied—for there was a part of her that *didn't* want him to be Crown Prince.

No.

She wanted what was best for him.

'Hey, Kedah?' Felicia said. 'For what it's worth…' This was the hardest thing she had ever said, the least selfish words she had ever spoken, because she was very good at her job, and she could see another route even if the news for Kedah was not good. 'It's very hard to dissuade a loyal public.'

Kedah frowned.

'Your people know the rumours and yet they still cheered you home. Whatever the result, you can still fight.'

She walked out and she saw that Mohammed was deep in conversation with Kumu at the end of the long corridor. When he saw Felicia approaching Mohammed stalked off, leaving Kumu by the large statue at the top of the stairs.

'Are you leaving?' Kumu asked, for she had heard that Kedah's jet had been prepared to fly out and Mohammed had asked her to glean more information.

'Yes...' Felicia smiled politely, about to carry on down the stairs. But even if Kedah wouldn't let her help, it didn't mean she couldn't try. And so she paused and turned around. 'It's a relief, actually,' she said in a low voice, as if confiding a secret.

'A relief?' Kumu frowned, a little taken aback but curious.

'I always worry that I'll say the wrong thing,' Felicia admitted.

'The wrong thing?'

'You're very used to royalty...' Felicia sighed. 'It's just all so new to me. I keep worrying that I'm going to mess things up. I mean, King Omar has been perfectly kind, and he seems lovely—you just have to see how devoted he is to his wife to know that. Even so, I would *hate* to be the one to offend him.' She gave Kumu an eye roll. 'I mean, after all, he *is* the King.'

* * *

Kedah walked out of his office just in time to see the very end of a conversation between Kumu and Felicia, and almost instantly he doubted his thought process. Now Felicia was smiling and walking down the stairs, as confident as ever. Kumu, on the other hand, stood looking worried and clearly more than a little perplexed.

She hurried off, but Kedah's attention was no longer on Kumu. Instead he was looking again at Felicia.

Her slender frame packed a punch even from this distance. Confident, collected, she walked towards the grand entrance and nodded for the guards to open the doors. In her bag was the glass, the answer, but that wasn't all that was on Kedah's mind.

Yes, he would have to select a bride—and, given her response, that meant this was the end.

They were over—just as he had told her from the start that they would be.

'Felicia…'

The Queen called out to her as Felicia walked to the car.

'Your Majesty?'

'You're leaving already?'

'Yes, Kedah needs me to go back to London.'

The Queen frowned, for she had rather thought Kedah might need someone on his side here, for when the Accession Council met.

Felicia was driven the short distance to the private jet, which she boarded. It felt so odd to be there without him. Over the last few months they had flown together on many occasions.

The plane felt lonely without him.

Her *life* would from this point on.

'There's a slight delay getting clearance,' the steward informed her. 'It shouldn't be too long.'

But Felicia could no longer hold it in.

'I'll be in the bedroom. Call me when we're ready to take off.'

Felicia headed to the bedroom suite and lay on the bed and allowed the tears to come.

Oh, and they did come.

Except the slight delay wasn't in order to get clearance from Air Traffic Control—it was caused by a certain Crown Prince who did not like it that she had gone.

He was thinking of her on the long flight to London when, in truth, he would far rather she was here. For a moment he even considered the possibility of someone else taking the glass to have it tested.

But, no, that couldn't work. It would mean involving another person, and Kedah wanted it kept just between them.

She was crying too hard to hear her phone, but then there was a knock at the door.

'Kedah wishes to speak with you,' the steward informed her, and gestured to a phone by the bed.

Felicia furiously wiped away her tears and blew her nose before picking up.

'Hello?'

'Hey,' Kedah said.

'What do you want?'

Kedah had been about to talk dirty, to tell her to get back this minute, or maybe to be honest and tell her he wasn't ready to let her go. Then he heard her slightly thick voice and knew that unless Felicia had the most rapid-onset cold in medical history she was crying.

Which meant she'd been crying that other time. He knew that now.

It would seem that she did have a heart after all.

'How long will the results take?' he asked, and Felicia frowned.

Why would he ask when they'd already been through this numerous times?

'Overnight,' she answered. 'The results will

be couriered to your office, hopefully by lunch-time in the UK.' Which would be late afternoon in Zazinia—just a few hours before the Accession Council met.

A few hours before he was expected to choose his bride.

'Felicia?'

'I think we're about to take off,' she lied. 'Speak soon, Kedah.'

CHAPTER THIRTEEN

KEDAH WAS VERY used to women falling for him.

He *wasn't* used to them proudly walking away.

He looked at the slight chaos their lovemaking had created and righted the crystal decanter that had toppled over. Then his eyes took in the files and the photos of the women his father wanted him to choose from.

Felicia had seen them, he was certain.

Their lovemaking had been fierce and angry, and now possibly he understood a little more why.

Yet she had known all along that he was to marry and had seemed fine with it.

Possibly she wasn't so assured after all.

Even though he generally didn't use it, Kedah was tempted to summon the royal jet, so he could be in London, or nearly there, when she landed. He needed to speak with her—he wanted to know what her tears meant exactly.

He needed space, and so he walked along the pristine white beach. Suddenly everything had changed.

Always he had wanted to be King; he had spent his life knowing it could be taken away and protecting himself from that possibility. Now, when the coming days should have his full attention, when he should be devoting every thought to the potential battle ahead, he was staring up at the sky that carried her.

He *had* chosen wisely.

Kedah had protected all the people he loved and cared for in this. Tomorrow, when the press were crawling and the staff were afraid, he would ensure that the best of the best knew his business inside out.

He knew Felicia could face this crisis.

In these past months she had crept into his heart, and now she belonged there so absolutely that it had taken her leaving to expose the fact.

And her tears made him believe that she loved him too.

What to do?

Omar stood in his own office, looking out on Zazinia and thinking of the presentation his eldest son had just shown him. He saw Kedah walking along the beach alone. As always, he cut an impressive figure, but for once his son's stride was not purposeful, and instead of looking out to the land he so loved Omar saw Kedah pause and gaze out to the ocean and the sky.

The King did not turn his head when the door opened and Rina stepped into his office. Instead he focused on his eldest son. There was a pensive air to him, and the set of his shoulders showed he carried a weight that was a heavy one.

Kedah was the rightful Crown Prince. Omar knew that.

Yes, the road ahead might be easier if he followed the elders' wishes and stood behind his younger son, but it would be the wrong decision.

He turned his head a little as Rina came in and walked over to stand by his side. She stood quietly beside him, watching their son, who cut a proud and lonely figure as he walked.

'Felicia just left,' Rina said.

'Felicia?' Omar frowned, for he had no idea who his wife was referring to.

'Kedah says she is his PA, but I am certain there is more to it.'

'Nothing can come of it. There are many brides that would be far more suitable.'

Omar's response was instant, but then he felt his wife's hand on his shoulder.

'I am sure plenty say the same about me,' Rina said. 'There are many who don't consider *me* suitable.'

So rarely did they touch on that long-ago painful time.

'You are a wonderful queen.'

'*Now* I am,' Rina agreed.

Omar turned and looked again to his son, and he recalled himself striding into the office brandishing files on potential brides. He hoped Felicia had been unable to understand what he had said.

'Kedah showed me a presentation that he has been working on,' Omar said. 'It was very beautiful. In fact, it reminded me of my dreams for Zazinia.' He looked out to the city. 'He has a gift.'

'So do you.'

'Perhaps, but I could not express it properly to my father. Of course back then we did not have the technology to make such a presentation…'

'Nothing would have swayed your father,' Rina said. 'Remember how you tried?'

Omar nodded.

'And then you stopped trying.'

'I chose to focus on the things I *could* change,' Omar said. 'I wanted my bride to be happy. And you weren't.'

'But I am now,' she said. 'And I am much stronger for your love. I shall always have that.'

And then Rina was the bravest she had ever been.

'Come what may.'

Still, even now, they could not properly discuss her infidelity—and not just because of pride or shame, but also because walls might have ears and whispers might multiply.

'Speak to your eldest son, Omar. Now. Before it is too late. Offer him your full support.'

Rina stood after Omar had left and tears were streaming down her face. Oh, she knew how her husband and eldest son protected her, but she was a *good* queen and it was time for the people to come first.

And Rina had not lied.

She *was* stronger for her King's love.

Nothing could take that from her. Even if the law dictated that Omar must shame and divorce her, still she would have his love.

**

'Kedah?' Omar caught up with son. 'Can I walk with you?'

'Of course,' Kedah answered.

'Your presentation left me speechless. I had never considered using murals on the east-facing walls. It would be an incredible sight.'

'They could tell the tale of our history,' Kedah said. 'Of course scaffolding would be required to shield the beach during construction…'

'We are not at war now,' Omar said. 'Those rules were put in place at a time when the palace risked invasion. I pointed that out to my father many years ago…' He gave a low laugh. 'You are like a mirror image of me. When I see your visions it is like looking at my own designs…'

Kedah turned in brief surprise. 'We are nothing alike.'

'Not in looks,' Omar said. 'But we think the same.'

Kedah did not believe it. His father was staid and old-fashioned in his ways.

But Omar pressed on.

'You were right to challenge me in the office. When I studied architecture with Hussain we had such grand plans. My father said that once I had married he would listen to my thoughts. I returned from my honeymoon with so many plans and dreams. Your mother was already pregnant with you, and I can remember us walking along this very beach, talking of the schools and the hospitals that would soon be built. Your mother, being your mother, looked forward to the hotels and the shops. They were such exciting times. There was such an air of hope amongst the people. But even by the time you were born those dreams had died.'

'How?'

'My father preferred his own rules.'

For a moment they stopped walking.

Even though the old King was dead it was almost a forbidden conversation.

'He had always said that when I was married—when I was officially Crown Prince— then I could have input. And so I married. I chose a bride from a progressive country.'

'For that reason only?' Kedah checked.

'He was just delaying things, though. By the time you were born I knew he would never listen to what I had to say. It was a very difficult time…' Omar admitted. 'I was young and proud and I had promised your mother so many things—she had come from a modern country and I wanted the same. I wanted our people to prosper from our wealth too, but my hands were tied. I became very angry and bitter. I spent all my time trying to convince my father to listen to my ideas—travelling with him, pointing out how progressive other countries were. Your mother was in a foreign country with a new baby, but I had no time for either of you…'

They walked in silence as Omar remembered that difficult trip away, and coming home to a grim palace and a wife who had been utterly distraught.

And then had come her confession.

And as Omar remembered the past Kedah better understood his parents, for he could envisage how undermined his father would have felt. For a little while he pondered how he might feel, bringing Felicia here, to a land full of promises that did not come true.

'You have a good marriage now,' Kedah commented.

'We have worked hard to achieve that.' Omar nodded. 'I had been so caught up in my own ego that I forgot what it must be like for your mother…alone in a new country, with no one to speak of her problems with…'

Except Abdal.

'When did you realise you loved her?' Kedah

asked—not just because he was curious about his parents' marriage, but because it was a question from his own heart. Suddenly he could not bear to envisage a future without Felicia. Their conversations, their laughter, their occasional rows...he just could not see himself doing those things with anyone else. And yet she was flying further away from him with each moment that passed.

'When?' he asked again, for his father was lost in thought.

Omar was thinking back to the day Rina had confessed what had taken place and his reaction.

'The moment I realised I could lose her,' Omar answered. 'It was then I knew I was in love.'

Perhaps they were not so different after all.

'Your grandfather was not a fan of your mother. He seemed to think I would do better to take another bride.'

Nothing was said outright, but both knew the rumours were finally being addressed.

Kedah could see how things might have happened. Perhaps he understood his mother more. And yet he realised it was not *his* forgiveness that his mother needed.

It was the forgiveness of the man he looked to now.

'Not only did I not want to lose her, Kedah, I was scared for her also.'

Kedah looked at him, and it was then he knew that he was his father's son.

They had the same fears for a vibrant, impetuous woman.

Kedah had never admired his father more, for it took a strong king to be a loving one too—especially when wronged.

'How did you resolve things?' he asked, for he needed his father's wisdom.

'I accepted that my time would one day come and I went back to concentrating on my family. All that time I'd spent fruitlessly clashing with my father I had neglected your mother—and you...'

Here was a man who was far stronger than Kedah had given him credit for.

'You have the same visions I once did,' Omar said. 'But I am older now. I need support. And I do not want you to have to wait, as I did, to make changes. That is not good for the people. Your presentation has reminded me of my own fire. Together we could change things. But there is Mohammed and the elders to consider...'

'You are King.'

'Yes, but there is your mother…'

And Kedah thought of Felicia's words. His mother would be okay. After all, she had the King's love.

'Together,' Kedah said, 'we can protect her.'

So much was said without words.

'But there is a condition,' Kedah said to his father. 'I shall choose my own bride.'

'Perhaps we could wait until after the Accession Council meets?' Omar suggested, for he was quite sure who Kedah's choice would be—which would make for an even more difficult meeting.

But Kedah, now that his decision was made, could no longer wait.

He excused himself from his father and walked into the palace. As he did so he saw Mohammed walking into his office with Fatiq.

'Mohammed.' Kedah followed him in. 'We need to speak.' He didn't even look over to Fatiq as he addressed him. 'Please leave.'

'You can say what you have to in front of Fatiq,' Mohammed told him.

'Very well.'

The timbre of Kedah's voice was so ominous that Mohammed's hand moved to the hilt of his sword as his elder brother strode towards him.

'Know this. It is very hard to dissuade loyal people… If I am forced to I will take the decision to them and I know I will win.'

'Not if we call for—'

'I don't give a damn about some test that was invented ten minutes ago compared with the rich history of our land. I was born to be King, I was raised to be King. And if I have to I shall take it to the people. Tomorrow my father shall offer his full support for his eldest son, and I hope he shall also announce that I have chosen my bride—Felicia.'

There was a hiss of breath from Fatiq at his side, but instead of an angry response Mohammed gave a black smile.

'The elders would never accept her…'

'They will have no choice.' Omar came in then. 'I will offer my full support.' He glared at the feuding duo. 'Your mother is on her way.'

Rina arrived then, with Kumu.

'Kedah, your father tells me you have exciting news…'

'I *hope* to have exciting news.'

'But Felicia does not understand our ways… the people…' Kumu, who rarely spoke, did so now.

'Felicia understands *people*,' Kedah said. 'Full stop.'

'And our people would adore to see their Crown Prince happy.' Rina smiled. 'Just so long as you are married here.'

'I haven't asked her yet,' Kedah said. 'I think it's a bit early to be speaking of wedding plans.'

'It's never too early,' Rina said.

'And I happen to like a good English wedding,' Omar mused.

And then, just as Kedah was about to roll his eyes and excuse himself, his father took his wife's hand and spoke on.

'What is it they say in the English service? Speak now or for ever hold your peace?'

Omar was looking directly at Mohammed as he said it, and there was challenge in his tone.

Never had Kedah admired his father more.

His father.

Kedah no longer needed proof, for Omar stood proud and strong and he maintained his sovereignty.

'Do you have anything you would like to say, Mohammed?' Omar enquired.

His son blinked.

'Come on, Mohammed.' Kumu pulled at his arm. 'We should go and check on the children.'

Mohammed stood there. They all watched and waited, but it was Kedah who walked off.

He had rather more important things on his mind than waiting for his brother to speak…
Or for ever hold his peace.

CHAPTER FOURTEEN

THERE WAS NO thanking God that it was Friday.

Felicia had deposited the sample at midnight and now all she could do was wait.

Kedah had told her to go in to work as usual. The one thing she didn't have to worry about was money. Felicia had worked hard for many years and commanded an impressive wage. But work was still important to her and, like it or not, Kedah was her boss.

Yes, her boss.

Somehow she had turned into a real PA.

She had rescheduled her meeting with Vadia and knew they would be talking at ten. Before that she had to liaise with the manager at the Dubai hotel and arrange for some signatures from the surveyor.

Felicia chose a boxy little grey suit. She usually saved it for court appearances, but she could use a little power dressing today.

Felicia came out of the underground and

walked towards the office, but instead of seeing the doorman smiling at her, she saw he was obscured by the gathered press.

Felicia watched as poor Anu got out of her husband's car and shielded her face.

Finally, after three months, Felicia was being put to work. *This* was the reason she was here and the reason she had been hired, she realised as she stepped in and faced the cameras.

'The proposed hotel in Dubai—will it still go ahead?'

'How will this affect the European branch?'

'Is the Crown Prince stepping aside willingly or is he being forced to stand down?'

Questions were coming from every angle, and Felicia stood there as the microphones and cameras clamoured for a response and did what she did best.

She smiled.

Widely.

'Of course I'll take your questions,' she said, and proceeded to answer them in turn. 'I'm actually just about to speak with the surveyor. Absolutely the sister hotel will be going ahead.'

'Sister?'

'Yes, I believe the new complex is going to focus more on holidaymakers than the business traveller. Next?'

* * *

Kedah watched the live stream and knew he had been so right to hire her.

His employees could not be in better hands. She was taking the edge off the fear that would be sweeping through his empire today.

One by one she answered the questions and then, for Felicia, came the hardest of them all.

'Is it correct that his marriage will be announced later today?'

Kedah watched her closely for her response.

It was flawless.

'I'm more than happy to answer, where I can, your questions about the business side of things, but I would never comment on the Sheikh's personal life without his authority.'

'You *must* know...'

'I'm his PA.' Felicia smiled. 'Certainly he doesn't report to *me*.'

With question time over, she smiled at the relieved doorman, who held the door open for her, and took the elevator to the offices on the top floor.

Anu was crying as she walked in, and Felicia knew exactly why she had been hired.

Not for the press but for his staff.

Kedah had made provisions for them even on his darkest day.

'He'll be fine,' she assured Anu.

'You say that for the cameras,' Anu wept. 'But what if they choose Mohammed? Zazinia needs Kedah. We all want him to one day be King. Even when he was a little boy everyone adored him so much, but never more than now.'

And Felicia adored him too.

Which was why, when her heart was breaking, she kept on working. She fired back responses to emails from worried managers and investors the world over, she took phone calls and video calls, and she even managed to hold her composure when Vadia stuck a virtual knife through her heart.

'Whatever the outcome of the Accession Council meeting, there will be an announcement from the palace later tonight as to his chosen bride.'

It was a hellish Friday, made harder when a courier arrived and she had to sign for a plain package. She opened it, and inside there was a thick cream envelope. And, for all that today had been hard, now it tipped into agony.

She blew her nose and put on lip gloss before calling him. She forced her mouth into a smile as she waited for him to answer, because one of the assertiveness courses she had been to had told her it forced a happier and more confident tone.

No matter how fake.

'Hey,' Felicia said at the delicious sound of his voice. 'Your results just arrived.'

'What are you doing?' Kedah asked. 'How has it been?'

'Not too bad. A lot of press and a little bit of panic from some quarters, but it's dying down now.'

'Good.'

'When do the Accession Council meet?' Felicia asked, wondering why he didn't have her tearing the envelope open now.

'An hour or so,' he said, as if it hardly mattered. 'I want to ask you something. What did you say to Kumu on the stairs? She hasn't been quite the same since!'

Felicia let out a low chuckle. 'I just pointed out that, as nice as your father is, he's still King and he clearly loves his wife. I said that I'd *hate* to offend him.'

He laughed, and then he was serious. 'Are you going to open it?'

'Sure,' she said. 'I'm just going to put you down.'

She placed the phone on the desk and put

him on speaker, and then she took out a letter opener and sliced open the envelope.

Kedah listened carefully. There were no sniffles or heavy breathing. Felicia was indeed tough.

'Congratulations, Your Royal Highness.'

She smiled, and it was a genuine one.

No, she didn't want him to be King—but that was a selfish wish. She was also terribly pleased for him.

'Go get 'em,' she said.

'Hey, Felicia…?'

'I have to go, Kedah,' she said.

'You can talk for a moment.'

'No.' She smiled again. 'I really do have to go. Good luck!'

Absolutely she had to go. Because she was starting to break down.

He didn't need to know as he went into a fight for the throne that she loved him and would do so for ever. And neither did he need to be sideswiped by the news that she was pregnant.

In time she would tell him—somehow.

Yet she knew she was tough and could raise their child alone.

She thought of all the people who loved their Prince and needed change.

She just needed a moment to cry. And she put her head in her hands and sat at her desk to weep in a way she never had.

Oh, Felicia had cried before—of course she had—but she sobbed now.

There was no need to worry about Anu hearing, for Felicia's sobs were deep and quiet and racked her body. She wrapped her arms around herself, scared that if she let go she might fall apart.

She was so deep in grief that she didn't hear the door open.

'Felicia…'

His voice stilled her.

Kedah had been sure of her love, but as he'd watched her on the live stream and heard her speak on the phone moments before she had sounded so composed that for a moment his certainty had wavered.

She looked up, stood up, and there were so many questions.

'You should be there…' she said, and there was no way to hide her tears so she ran to him.

He held her tight in his arms and Kedah knew he had been right to return when he had. Sometimes you had to look after those you loved first.

'I'm not needed there. My father will go in and tell them who is the rightful Crown

Prince…' He held her closer. 'But I *am* needed here…'

He kissed her, and there were so many things that he wanted to say, but right now not one of them mattered.

It was a kiss so deep and so passionate that it should never have ended, and yet there were too many things she needed to know.

And Kedah too.

'Were you crying the morning I called you and you said that you had a cold?'

Felicia nodded.

'I have spoken with my father. I have told him that I have chosen my bride…'

And as she winced, as she braced herself to hear the chosen name, he pulled out a diamond that was familiar. He told her that soon it would be mounted on gold and worn on her finger.

'Every time I looked at this I knew I would be okay, and I want the same for you…'

The diamond had reassured him that come what may he would be taken care of, and in handing it over to Felicia he afforded her the same reassurance.

'Marry me?'

Never in her wildest dreams had she thought she might hear those words from Kedah.

Liar.

Had his driver been there he might have stood and applauded—and, yes, she might have joined in. For, yes, in her wildest dreams she *had* hoped that one day he would say those words, that there might somehow be hope for them.

'I didn't want you to be your father's son.' It was a terrible confession to make. 'I feel so guilty, because I've been hoping and wishing that you weren't because then there might be a chance for *us*...'

'I make my own chances, Felicia, and there is no need to feel guilty. I am glad that you wanted a chance for us.' He thought back to Mohammed's cruel words. 'It is wonderful that you love me whether or not I might one day be King.'

It would make her a princess, who would one day be Queen, and an extremely worrying thought occurred.

'Kedah, there's going to be the most terrible scandal...' Even if they married this week there would always be a question over the dates. 'I'm pregnant...'

She was starting to panic, for no spin doctor could fix this—no dates could be changed— and it would be she, Felicia, who brought discredit to his name.

Yet Kedah smiled. 'Really?'

'I took a test. They're going to know that we...'

'Felicia.' Kedah still smiled. 'If my people are going to be shocked that we have slept together, that I am not a virgin, then they don't know me at all.'

He made her laugh through her tears.

'But they *do* know me, and they care for me—just as they will care for you.'

'You're not cross?'

'Cross? I am stunned, I am thrilled and I am scared that you might not have told me.'

'I was trying to work out how.'

'Together we will sort out our problems,' he said. 'And right now I can't see that we have any. Can you?'

Felicia thought for a moment, but not long and hard.

Oh, there would surely be problems, but they would deal with them together.

She could cope with anything.

After all, she had Kedah's love.

EPILOGUE

SHE WOULD ALWAYS express her opinion.

Though occasionally, Felicia conceded, only to herself, she did get it wrong.

His work was stunning, and nowhere more so than here in the palace.

There were now no offices in the Crown Prince's wing. Kedah had indeed had them torn down. They had been replaced by walls of soft stone from the quarries, and a trickling noise lined them, coming from the soft fountains from a deep spring the diviner had found.

The sound soothed both Felicia and the baby she sat with this dawn. It felt as if she was sitting in a blissful sanctuary.

'You've got a big day today,' Felicia said to her daughter.

Yes, they had been gifted with a little girl.

She had been born eight months ago, and her public appearances since then had been brief.

She had been tiny enough to sleep through them, but she was bigger now—a bit more dramatic and clingy. Felicia was worried about how she would react to the crowds.

Kaina.

It meant both *female* and *leader*, and her name spoke of another of the changes that had been made.

She would one day be Queen of this magnificent land. But for now she was just a baby who really needed to sleep—except she had other ideas.

Kaina's long eyelashes were just closing when the gap in the half-open door widened, and Felicia watched as her daughter's little head turned.

'She was nearly asleep,' Felicia said as the baby smiled and wriggled and held out her arms.

'Go back to bed,' Kedah said as he took their daughter from her, for Felicia had been up for ages and he knew that she was worried about today.

'She's been fed,' Felicia said. 'She just won't settle.'

'Go back to bed,' he said again. 'I'll get her to sleep.'

He didn't suggest calling the royal nanny. Felicia was having none of that. And neither did their daughter sleep in a separate wing from her parents.

Times had finally changed, she thought as she climbed into their magnificent bed and closed her eyes.

And the landscape had changed also.

Kedah held his daughter and watched as the sun started to rise over Zazinia. A hotel had already been built and it was the most stunning building—his proudest work. No windows looked to the palace. Instead there was a beautiful mural that told some of the history of Zazinia. And close to the hotel in the modern city he was creating were the beginnings of a hospital, built with stone from the quarries of Zazinia but gleaming and modern inside. It was already functioning, but it would be a couple more years until it was complete.

'Today,' Kedah said, and he spoke in a low voice to his daughter, 'there are going to be a lot of people cheering and making noise...'

He didn't tell her that she was to behave and not cry. Of course Kaina was too young to understand, but there were other rules he had changed. Kaina would be herself, and go to school with her peers.

He looked down at his precious daughter, who was finally asleep, and walked out of the dark sanctuary and placed her in her crib.

There were no portraits on the wall as he walked back to his suite.

They were for the formal corridors now.

Here was home.

And home was a palace, and today the people would gather to see their beloved royals.

'You're going to be fine,' Kedah said to Felicia, who was very nervous.

Oh, she had faced angry press many times in her past, but facing these people was different. The men she had represented in the past had meant absolutely nothing to her.

This man did.

Her robe was that certain shade of green which brought out the best in her eyes, and Kedah had chosen white for today. He looked sultry and sexy, and the only thing marriage had done to tone him down was to direct all that passion to one woman.

'Felicia!'

Rina was chatting to Mohammed and Kumu as Felicia approached, but she was overtaken by a tiny little boy who had just found his feet.

'Abi...'

He called for his father and Felicia watched as Mohammed's austere face broke into a smile as his youngest son toddled over and Mohammed scooped him up.

For Mohammed was his father's son also.

When he had accepted that there was nothing he could do to change the lineage, instead of plotting bitterly he had chosen to focus on what he could do best. He had always loved his wife and children, and now he let it show.

And he had worked with Kedah to build a new Zazinia, and Kedah respected his brother's sage advice.

'I like it that the portraits are here by the main balcony...' Rina said. 'My husband hated standing for his. And look at Kedah!' Rina suddenly laughed. 'He looks nothing like the rest of them...'

Oblivious.

Rina had been coddled, shielded from the fact that everyone knew her secret—the terrible mistake she had made many years ago. To this day she thought only her husband knew about that week many years ago, when Omar had been away, and lost and lonely she had turned to the wrong man for comfort. But he had brought none.

'Really,' Rina said, with all the assuredness of someone who had *not* been having an affair around conception time, 'Kedah doesn't even look related. He takes after my side of the family, of course…'

And Felicia caught Kumu's eyes and both women shared a smile.

They loved Queen Rina. Yes, she was dramatic and flaky, but she was also the kindest woman—even if at times she ran a little wild.

Like her eldest son.

'We should go out now,' Omar said.

The King loathed these formal moments. His whole life had been spent being told to behave or to keep his family in check.

Today they all walked out to loud cheers.

Kaina was startled, and Felicia hushed her, but of course she started to cry.

'Give her to me,' Rina said. 'So you can wave. It is you they all want to see.'

No, it wasn't.

The crowd cheered as their lovely Queen took the little baby, and they cheered more loudly on seeing Omar looking so happy and relaxed.

And then they called out for Kedah.

He waved and he smiled. He was so proud of his lovely wife, and the people just adored him.

They loved the way he came down to the quarries and spoke with the workers, how when the hospital had opened he had stayed for hours to meet with the staff.

Kaina was really crying now, and refused to be held in Rina's arms. Kedah took his daughter and held her so she was sitting on his hip. And Kaina, safe in her daddy's arms, buried her face in his chest.

But then she peeked out.

To see all the people.

There were so many that she put her little hand over her eyes, so she didn't have to see them, and then she put her hand down and saw they were still there.

And they were laughing.

So she put her hand over her eyes again.

Oh, indeed she was her father's daughter.

She was playing peekaboo with the crowd, and from this day on she would hold them in the palm of her hand.

'You,' Kedah said to little Kaina as they headed inside, 'were amazing.'

The nanny came and took her. Kaina would go and play rather than sit through a long formal lunch.

There was an hour, though, before they had

to be seated, and Felicia wandered off to stand by the portraits.

The old artist was working on a portrait of little Kaina now.

All the portraits fascinated her, but one especially so.

She didn't turn as Kedah joined her. 'You *are* smiling.'

'No.'

They had argued about it often, but there amongst the stern faces of Crown Princes of old, she knew one stood out—and not just because of his attire. There was a certain Mona Lisa smile on Kedah's face, though he repeatedly denied it.

'Yes, you are,' Felicia insisted.

'I like your robe.' He did his best to change the subject. 'I love that shade of green.'

'I know you do.'

'We have forty minutes before we have to go through. Perhaps we should check on Kaina.'

'Kaina's fine.'

'We could make sure,' he said, and then he looked up at the portrait and conceded defeat. 'I was thinking of *you*,' he said in her ear, and Felicia resisted turning. 'And what had happened on the plane.'

She turned then, and looked into the eyes of the only man she had ever loved.

'Come on,' Kedah said.

There was love to be made.

* * * * *

If you enjoyed this story, check out these other great reads from Carol Marinelli:
RETURN OF THE UNTAMED BILLIONAIRE
BILLIONAIRE WITHOUT A PAST
THE COST OF THE FORBIDDEN
THE PRICE OF HIS REDEMPTION
Available now!

Also available in the
ONE NIGHT WITH CONSEQUENCES
series this month:
A RING FOR VINCENZO'S HEIR
by Jennie Lucas

LARGER-PRINT BOOKS!
GET 2 FREE LARGER-PRINT NOVELS PLUS
2 FREE GIFTS!

◆ HARLEQUIN®

Romance

From the Heart, For the Heart

LARGER-PRINT BOOKS!
GET 2 FREE LARGER-PRINT NOVELS PLUS
2 FREE GIFTS!

⟨H⟩ HARLEQUIN®

INTRIGUE
BREATHTAKING ROMANTIC SUSPENSE

YES! Please send me 2 FREE LARGER-PRINT Harlequin® Intrigue novels and my 2 FREE gifts (gifts are worth about $10). After receiving them, if I don't wish to receive any more books, I can return the shipping statement marked "cancel." If I don't cancel, I will receive 6 brand-new novels every month and be billed just $5.49 per book in the U.S. or $6.24 per book in Canada. That's a saving of at least 11% off the cover price! It's quite a bargain! Shipping and handling is just 50¢ per book in the U.S. and 75¢ per book in Canada.* I understand that accepting the 2 free books and gifts places me under no obligation to buy anything. I can always return a shipment and cancel at any time. Even if I never buy another book, the two free books and gifts are mine to keep forever.

199/399 HDN GHWN

Name	(PLEASE PRINT)

Address	Apt. #

City	State/Prov.	Zip/Postal Code

Signature (if under 18, a parent or guardian must sign)

Mail to the **Reader Service:**
IN U.S.A.: P.O. Box 1867, Buffalo, NY 14240-1867
IN CANADA: P.O. Box 609, Fort Erie, Ontario L2A 5X3

**Are you a subscriber to Harlequin® Intrigue books
and want to receive the larger-print edition?
Call 1-800-873-8635 today or visit www.ReaderService.com.**

* Terms and prices subject to change without notice. Prices do not include applicable taxes. Sales tax applicable in N.Y. Canadian residents will be charged applicable taxes. Offer not valid in Quebec. This offer is limited to one order per household. Not valid for current subscribers to Harlequin Intrigue Larger-Print books. All orders subject to credit approval. Credit or debit balances in a customer's account(s) may be offset by any other outstanding balance owed by or to the customer. Please allow 4 to 6 weeks for delivery. Offer available while quantities last.

Your Privacy—The Reader Service is committed to protecting your privacy. Our Privacy Policy is available online at www.ReaderService.com or upon request from the Reader Service.

We make a portion of our mailing list available to reputable third parties that offer products we believe may interest you. If you prefer that we not exchange your name with third parties, or if you wish to clarify or modify your communication preferences, please visit us at www.ReaderService.com/consumerschoice or write to us at Reader Service Preference Service, P.O. Box 9062, Buffalo, NY 14240-9062. Include your complete name and address.

WESTERN WP PROMISES

YES! Please send me **The Western Promises Collection** in Larger Print. This collection begins with 3 FREE books and 2 FREE gifts (gifts valued at approx. $14.00 retail) in the first shipment, along with the other first 4 books from the collection! If I do not cancel, I will receive 8 monthly shipments until I have the entire 51-book Western Promises collection. I will receive 2 or 3 FREE books in each shipment and I will pay just $4.99 US/ $5.89 CDN for each of the other four books in each shipment, plus $2.99 for shipping and handling per shipment. *If I decide to keep the entire collection, I'll have paid for only 32 books, because 19 books are FREE! I understand that accepting the 3 free books and gifts places me under no obligation to buy anything. I can always return a shipment and cancel at any time. My free books and gifts are mine to keep no matter what I decide.

272 HCN 3070 472 HCN 3070

Name   (PLEASE PRINT)

Address   Apt. #

City   State/Prov.   Zip/Postal Code

Signature (if under 18, a parent or guardian must sign)

Mail to the **Reader Service:**

IN U.S.A.: P.O. Box 1867, Buffalo, NY 14240-1867
IN CANADA: P.O. Box 609, Fort Erie, Ontario L2A 5X3

WPBPA16R